D1010550

Tor Books Edited by Kim Mohan

AMAZING® Stories: The Anthology
More AMAZING® Stories

EDITED BY

KIM MOHAN

TOR®

A Tom Doherty Associates Book
NEW YORK

This is a work of fiction. All the characters and events portrayed in this novel are either fictitious or are used fictitiously.

MORE *AMAZING*® STORIES

This book is printed on acid-free paper.

A Tor Book
Published by Tom Doherty Associates, Inc.
175 Fifth Avenue
New York, NY 10010

Tor Books on the World Wide Web:
http://www.tor.com

Tor® is a registered trademark of Tom Doherty Associates, Inc.
AMAZING® and the *AMAZING*® logo are registered trademarks of TSR, Inc.

Library of Congress Cataloging-in-Publication Data

More amazing stories / edited by Kim Mohan. — 1st ed.
      p.   cm.
   "A Tom Doherty Associates book."
   Short stories previously published in Amazing Stories.
   Includes bibliographical references (p.   ).
   ISBN 0-312-86473-6
   1. Science fiction, American.   I. Mohan, Kim.   II. Amazing stories.
PS648.S3A6   1998
813'.0876208—dc21   97-29861
                                                                   CIP

First Edition: February 1998

Printed in the United States of America

0 9 8 7 6 5 4 3 2 1

Copyright Acknowledgments

Contents

Contents

INTRODUCTION

. . . Where order in variety we see,
And where, though all things differ, all agree.
                    —Alexander Pope, *Windsor Forest,* 1713

I'm an eclectic reader, in and outside the genre of science fiction.
Without expressly trying to do so, I don't think I've ever read
two consecutive novels or short stories that were similar in subject matter, style, or flavor. There's an incredible amount of good
work out there to choose from, and you're cheating yourself of
the pleasure of variety if you don't take advantage of the opportunity presented by that diversity.

One of the most enjoyable aspects of my work as editor of
Amazing Stories has been the chance to encourage and promote
variety through what I decided to publish. I've always inter-
preted the title of the publication in the broadest and most lit-
eral way possible—all a piece of work has to do to qualify to be
published is to be an amazing story.

One of the simple tests I apply to evaluating a manuscript
submission is just a matter of recalling my thoughts right after
I finish reading. If one of those thoughts goes something like
"I've never read a story like that one before" (and I'm thinking
it in a *good* way), then I'm probably going to want to publish it.

Every story in this anthology passed that test, and every one
did so for a different reason. Some of these pieces made me

shake my head in wonder at the sheer craftsmanship their authors display—stories that are amazing because of the way they're told.

Some of them touched the right button inside me because their authors obviously weren't afraid to go where no short story had gone before; these are amazing stories because they explore subjects that didn't exist before the stories were written.

Some of them reached for my heart and found a place within it that no other story had ever touched. A story is amazing if it affects me in a way that's new and wonderful to me at the same time.

And some of them are just plain fun, with a twist or a spin or a quirk that's original and fits perfectly with what the story is trying to accomplish. There's humor aplenty in this book, some of it in pieces of writing that are not expressly meant to be funny, and in no case will you find an author going out of his or her way just to work in a joke. A story can be amazing because of how it handles humor, which is to my mind the most difficult kind of fiction to write (and to sell).

I've avoided mentioning any authors' names or story titles here because I want you to find out for yourself why each of these stories is amazing. Almost certainly your impressions of these works of fiction will differ from my own—you'll find some of them entertaining or enlightening or thought-provoking for reasons that are different from mine. I introduce them to you as a group, as a unit, because I think Alexander Pope got it exactly right: "Though all things differ, all agree."

The quality of "amazingness," in all its various manifestations, is the common thread woven through every issue of *Amazing Stories* since its beginning as a magazine more than seventy years ago—tying together stories written by past and present masters such as Robert Bloch, Ray Bradbury, Philip K. Dick, and Robert Silverberg, and extending to include future masters such as some of the people who contributed to this book.

This anthology is an acknowledgment and a celebration of the variety that makes science fiction the most vital and dynamic form of literature ever devised by men and women—and, at the same time, a homage to what *Amazing Stories* has stood for throughout its history. There is no power greater than imagination, and no better example of what imagination can accomplish, than the stories you are about to read.

— Kim Mohan
May 1, 1997

THE TIME OF HER LIFE

Nancy Springer

In shoes that pinched, with heels high enough to boost her career, she was hurrying back to her parked car one crowded lunch hour when she actually found some time, a year of it lying on the sidewalk and shining like a communion wafer made of orichalcum. She stopped, picked it up, and stood exalting it on the altar of her uplifted hands. Despite its size and import, it had no weight at all, but as she held it, the world looked different. With time on her hands, she could look around, and the chrysanthemums glowed like neon outside the dentist's office; along the curb sprouted a weed with glossy magenta leaves; in the window of the hobby shop across the street a "Copies 3¢" sign spread like a saffron butterfly. She could have looked all day.

But then she started to worry: to whom did this time belong? Somebody had lost it and was going to be very upset. Should she turn it in to the police?

No, she decided with instant selfish resolve and defiance, finders keepers. She needed time as badly as anybody. How long had it been since she had even had time to think? Quickly, before some passenger in one of the cars rushing by might look and notice, she slipped her resplendent find into the shadows of her purse.

Instantly she felt different; she was a person in possession of time. She stood smiling and contemplating: how was she going to spend it?

She turned off her pager. She no longer cared that she was late getting back to her office. With time on her side, riding in her handbag, she strode to her Volvo and headed toward the area's largest shopping mall, her heart pounding in delight and terror at her luck. She felt so fortunate, and therefore marked for a fall, that she became superstitiously afraid of being in an accident. She drove carefully, taking her time.

Like a phoenix on fire. Or a sailing ship. Outside the mall, she paused for a moment, gazing up at lambent clouds layered over the sun, rimmed with glory. *Oh! sun spokes, chariot wheels.* Aware of but not caring how absurd she appeared standing there in her business suit. *It's no wonder people used to believe in God. How long has it been since I looked at the sky?*

The clouds shifted like a signal. She went inside.

Though she had never been to this particular mall—nobody went to malls anymore; who had time?—nevertheless she found the store without difficulty. "Tempus Fugit Emporium," the large, elaborately gilded sign read. But the tall personage at the entrance was gruff. "No yuppies."

She opened her purse just a crack. Orichalcum glory beamed out between her fingers like chariot spokes.

"I see. Congratulations. Go on in."

The time store was lighted by only a single window of opportunity, but she stood bewildered by the dazzle of the displays themselves, packaging brighter than a phoenix on fire, gleaming like the golden scales of the carpe diem, shinier than a silver eely ebb tide under a moon one day past full. The angel behind the counter, exquisitely handsome in an Armani shirt, called, "May I help you?"

"I'm not sure. I'm a college graduate."

He smiled like morning in springtime. "Let me show you several of our more popular options." With wing tips that gleamed like Mylar, he pointed out items billowing above and behind him. "For working mothers with young children, we offer Flex

Time, Mommy Hours, Quality Time, and Time to Breathe. For those who are bored in their marriage and wish to begin an affair, there is the Stolen Moments of Romance package, paid for on the weekly installment plan. For aspiring novelists, we have Uninterrupted Creative Time. Or, a great many individuals come here seeking More Family Time."

She shook her head. "I'm a dink." Double income, no kids: did that make her tandem pairing less than a family? Was it not a good thing to be a couple? Yet she felt like one rubbery wheel on a cash axle. Her husband, a corporate lawyer, worked till seven every evening and networked on weekends while she, a city planning engineer, ran errands noon and night, yet never ran out of them. She felt flat. Tired.

She said, "I want the time of my life."

"Ah." The angel's voice softened and he swiveled his attenuated head, his ethereal face, to consider her more fully. "Did you not have it in college?"

"No. I studied. I got married."

"The time of *your* life—we must customize that for you. Personalize." His golden gaze remained intent on her. "Can you define it?"

"I . . . I want something to happen." she struggled to conceptualize her inchoate yearnings. "A . . . an adventure, an experience, a . . . some kind of encounter."

"Time travel has been discontinued," the angel said softly, mostly to himself, thinking, "since too many people were using it as a form of intergenerational incest."

"It wouldn't have to be time travel. Just . . . I just feel like I'm running out of time."

"For what?"

She gazed back at him. She didn't know.

"Might I interest you in our Timely Transformations, knife-free enhancement adding years of youth to your appearance?"

She shook her head. Appearance was not the problem. In

her life, all the appropriate appearances were firmly in place. "I'm not ready to commit to anything right now." She needed time to think.

"Of course. Look around. We have all the time in the world."

Leaving, still undecided, she discovered that night was falling with a silent thud. It was time to go home and prepare dinner for her husband. Usually he was unlovable after his eleven-hour workday. Usually she was tired from standing in line at the supermarket after a full day at her own job. Usually she was unable to provide the welcome-home he seemed to expect of her.

Tonight, though, she had time. Her heart rose like dayspring. Time was salvation. Time was going to change everything.

As she walked out of the mall, a gray van at the curb was delivering frail, silent people for a therapeutic outing. A thin young man in a wheelchair looked up at her. Plastic tubes ran up his nose from an oxygen tank in his lap. Dark sarcomas spotted one temple of his pale face. Blocking the sidewalk, he did not attempt to move but stared straight at her with the wincing defiance of the terminally ill.

"Hello," she said, smiling at him. She had time for him—there was no need to flinch away or hurry past. Moreover, he was achingly beautiful—or perhaps the whole world, even mortality, was beautiful to a person in possession of time? But the man in the wheelchair startled her heart with his beauty. His face was narrow and translucent, like the angel's. He did not speak.

All the way home her mind swirled with vague dreams that sometimes included his face. Once safely in the apartment, she pulled time from her purse and held it in her hands again. Its glow suffused her homecoming, letting her take a few minutes to change from her suit and career-boosting pumps to clothing she liked: brushed-cotton poet shirt, favorite jeans. She put a new white-linen cloth on the table, laid her find in the middle of it and, with an artistic flair rare for her, piled silk flowers around it in a wreath. Its light shone through the petals to cast a rose-window refulgence on the ceiling.

Dinner was going to have to be something out of the freezer. She loathed cooking when she was tired, and her husband always wanted a hot, cooked meal like Mama used to make—but when he saw what she had found, he would not mind having a microwave dinner again.

Time suffused the apartment with a rainbow-silver splendor that could not be missed or ignored. "What the hell is that?" Her husband demanded when he slammed in and slung down his briefcase.

Proud to be able to give him pleasure, she picked up the shining disc and handed it to him. He wobbled with astonishment and folded into a chair. "Where'd you get this?"

"Found it."

"What a babe!" With delight softening his face, with time's moonbright glow on him, he wasn't a bad-looking guy. Not at all.

"I figure we each get half," she said, turning to him, her heart lifting and opening like a rose. "So we can spend it together. Six months. Go somewhere."

His mouth closed into a flat line and he shook his head. "No, no, no." Annoyed at her stupidity. "What you do is, you cash this in. Time is money. You redeem this and you can take a year off work. Stay home, clean this dump, have time to keep ahead of the laundry and the cooking and all that stuff you're always complaining about."

Now her heart was a stone spearhead turning in her. Unable to respond, she gawked at him. She had spent the afternoon conversing with an angel. Who was this man?

"Have some sense," he grumbled.

She found her voice. "Why don't *you* take it and spend the year at home cleaning and cooking and doing laundry?"

"Are you nuts? I can't take time off, not if I ever want to get a promotion. I've got a career to think about." He laid the time that equaled money on the table. "For God's sake, get me a drink. What's for dinner?"

Having time changed everything. Having time to think. Time to see.

In time's limpid orichalcum light sat a man with the personality of a steel-belted radial tire. "You can eat my dust," she told him.

"Huh?"

"A year's not long enough to get away from you." She snatched up her prize and headed out the door.

No longer afraid of bad luck, she drove well above the speed limit all the way back to the mall. In the Tempus Fugit Emporium, she strode straight to the angel behind the counter. "Is it true that time wounds all heels?" she demanded.

"No. Just one of the dumb things Ann Landers says."

"Damn. Well, is it true that time heals all wounds?"

"Not necessarily."

She asked the questions without caring to hear the answers. Looking beyond the angel's folded wings and silky shoulders, staring out the window of opportunity, she could see the frail young man with oxygen tubes snaking up his nose. He sat in his wheelchair facing partially away from her. Waiting. For what?

"Did you ever wonder what a nick of time is?" she asked the angel.

"Actually, yes. The more modern expression is 'the psychological moment.' Are you—"

She was not listening. The man in the wheelchair had swiveled and rolled away. " 'Scuse me," she muttered, and she barged out.

Striding along in her Converse All Stars instead of pumps made her feel strong and young, but she hated her purse. She jammed her wallet into her jeans pocket and ditched her purse in a trash container. Heading down the mall after the man in the wheelchair, she broke into a jog. As her footfalls pursued him, he stopped, turned, and looked at her.

She did not want him peering up at her that way. She

crouched in front of him so that her eye level was below his. "Would it help if I bought you some time?" she asked.

He stared back at her without speaking. Come to think of it, she did not know for sure that he could talk. Maybe he was too beautiful to talk. His wide eyes were nearly golden, like the angel's.

"What have you got, AIDS?" she asked with feeling but no finesse. "Might they find a cure? Would it help if I bought you a year?"

He moved his lips twice before he managed to speak. "A year would be great," he whispered.

"Okay, that's what I'll do." She stood up, but he lifted his hand to stop her.

"Don't you need it yourself?" His voice rubbed in his throat.

"Me? Nah." She smiled. "I've got all the time in the world."

This was true.

Ten minutes later, the mall had spit her out into the dark parking lot and she was on her own. The angel, after ringing up her purchase, had given her a complimentary bumper sticker, and now she was plastering it onto the hind end of her Volvo, where no bumper sticker had gone before. Once she got that done, she would get into the car and just head toward the far end of the country. Go where the road took her, stop where she had a notion, eat, sleep, meet people. Already she was encountering someone important: herself. She had all the time she would ever have: the time of her life.

TIME FLIES LIKE AN ARROW, the bumper sticker read. FRUIT FLIES LIKE A BANANA.

Get it? the angel had asked as he handed it to her. She had just smiled and wished the ordinary-looking man getting up out of the wheelchair all the luck in the world. But now, rolling out of the parking lot and heading west on the Lincoln Highway, all of a sudden she got it, and she laughed like birds, like baying beagles, like temple bells, laughing so hard she pounded on her dashboard, smashing its clock with her fist.

SCIPIO

Daniel Hood

Looking back over his hundred-odd lifetimes, the slave called Scipio could not recall a single time when his honor had been so damaged. In the space of a year, he had been beaten in battle by a miserable coastal tribe, delivered bound hand and foot to the Dutch, and sold as a slave on the block in Nevis. He had been whipped by men he would not have deigned to kill with his own spear, men he would have handed over to the children of his kingdom for sport.

Worst, though, was the name they had fixed on him. Scipio Africanus, a joke the perverse Englishman who had bought him thought terribly funny, but that galled more than the dozens of lashings he had received.

Scipio had bought his memories with blood and fire, sacrificing the heads of enemies and scarring his own body so the shaman would reveal his past to him in the smoke. He had drunk up the wisdom of a hundred lives spent in war, and learned a thousand valuable lessons that had helped him become a king and a great warrior in his land. But the lesson he had learned first, the first vision to rise from the smoke of green leaves and burning blood and flesh, was his hatred of the Roman general Scipio Africanus, who had killed him in his first life.

Still, he bore the name with patience—another thing he had learned from his lives—taking it with the beatings and the degrading work in the cane fields, because he knew things would change.

Standing in the back of the cart, heavy chains burdening his legs and salt sweat stinging in the welts on his back, he reflected on how things would change, and glared his contempt and hatred at the broad, woolen-jacketed back of his English master.

The cart that jounced and swayed over the rutted track was taking him to Fair Point, the nightmare of every slave on Nevis Island. Fair Point was a sugar plantation like all the others on the island, but it was also a depository for refractory slaves, the basket in which the English planters put all their bad eggs. The mistress of Fair Point was said to have a way with wayward blacks; slaves around the island had but to hear her name mentioned and they quickly toed the line. It was said that she sowed her fields with the flesh and blood of slaves, and that the ghosts of those sent to her haunted the cane fields at night, trying to do penance for their failure to serve the English in life.

Scipio did not believe it. A hundred lives said that if you wanted to start a rebellion, you went to where the rebellious were, and Fair Point was just that.

Only the English, he thought, *would be so stupid as to put all the warriors and rebels in one place.* For he felt sure, as the cart plunged into a dell and darkness, the thick vegetation blocking out the sun, that that was who had ended up at Fair Point: the blacks with pride and honor, those who would not be slaves though their lives depended on it. And as a king and a great warrior, he knew he could lead them to a rebellion that would sweep the English from Nevis. He would create a black kingdom in this new world, and the English would water it with their blood.

The cart climbed out of the dell and back into the screaming sunlight. Scipio saw Belyer, his master, run a hand around his collar, collecting a thick film of sweat. He wanted to laugh, considering the irony of this fat, degenerate Englishman, his jug of rum at his side, pretending to be his master. By rights, their positions should be reversed—tall and proud, comfortable in the vicious heat of the Caribbean, he should have ruled the pale, fat English. And he would.

Belyer seemed to catch a hint of Scipio's hate: he shivered and looked back over his shoulder.

"Still standing, I see," he said, licking his lips nervously. "Just you wait, you black beast. Hades ain't in it at all—not at all. Kate Higgins'll have you on the ground begging for mercy, Scipio my boy. *Begging.*" With a sharp nod, the driver turned his attention back to the horse, to keep it from veering off into the fields of cane that lined the ruin of a road.

Scipio was torn between the two names. The mere mention of the latter—that of his oldest enemy, forced on him by his newest—made him grind his teeth with rage. But the woman's gave him pause. When he had first heard of Fair Point, he had imagined a man in command, and his plan for rebellion had involved a particularly vicious punishment for him. But Fair Point was the property of a woman, and while there were obvious punishments for women, he could not bring himself to use them. The reasons, when he thought about them, made him grind his teeth again.

When he met Scipio Africanus, he had been a woman, a mercenary spear in the army of Hannibal at Zama, the sort who would later be romanticized as an Amazon. As a woman, he had fought through the whole day of that bloody battle, the first he could remember, and as a woman, he had fallen into the hands of a Roman squad that presented him to their general as a trophy. In the cart on Nevis, blood oozed from his gums when he recalled the noble Roman crushing him down, raping him and then throwing him to the squad, which raped him to death.

He remembered Scipio's piercing gray eyes above him, remembered the caustic laugh when he was thrown to the waiting legionnaires, the joke.

"Remember, boys, I want salt sown into everything in Carthage."

The newly christened Scipio had never raped a woman, though rape was common in his land; nor had he ever raped a woman in any of the lives he could remember. He would have to honor Kate Higgins with a man's death.

Fair Point was on the far side of the island from his master's estate; the journey took most of the day. The tropic dusk was rushing to a close when the Englishman turned the weary horse into the gates. Scipio was surprised by the neatness of the grounds: the cobbled path, the clean-swept yard, the sparkling appearance of the low brick manor house. Even the slave huts looked well kept. No English planters he had ever heard of maintained their estates in such immaculate order. He frowned in the back of the cart.

"All right, you whoreson beast, get out." Belyer stood now below him, beckoning him to come down from the cart. Scipio fixed him with a glance, pausing for a moment just long enough, and then jumped suddenly and lightly down, the weight of his chains apparently nothing. The Englishman scuttled backward a few steps, then came forward angrily.

"You bastard," he grated. "You're going to regret you ever lived."

Scipio glared coldly at him until the white man lowered his eyes and started shouting for the overseer.

When the overseer—a thinner, healthier-looking white with calculating eyes—finally came, Scipio's master handed him over quickly.

"What's he done?" the overseer asked quietly.

"Tried to run three times," Belyer explained, already back up on the cart and turning it around in the yard. "He's a hard one— I'd watch it if I were you."

The overseer only laughed as Scipio's master urged his exhausted horse out of the yard.

When I am free, I will eat your soul, Scipio thought, following his former master's retreating back out the estate gates. And he could do it. He had learned more from the shaman than just the secrets of his pasts.

"You must be hard," the overseer said, sizing him up. "Belyer's no coward, and he's going to ride all the way home tonight rather than stay here one night with you. What's your name?"

"Scipio Africanus." He spat out the name, hating the sound.

"Not anymore," the overseer said simply. "The mistress'll not have it. Choose another."

For a long moment, Scipio goggled at him, unable to believe. He was being offered freedom already—freedom from the hated name.

"Hannibal," he finally replied, which drew a laugh from the other.

"As you like," the overseer said, smiling, "though the mistress isn't overfond of that name either, nor the man who once bore it. I've heard her say Hannibal's the most overrated of the Ancients. But it's your skin, isn't it?"

Without waiting for an answer, the overseer grabbed a link of Scipio's chain and pulled him to the slave quarters.

"Take a berth," he ordered, shoving Scipio into a pitch-black hut. "The mistress'll see you in the morning."

Left alone, Scipio felt his way around the edges of the hut, sinking down finally in a spot that allowed him to watch the yard through the doorless opening. Exhausted from his day standing in the cart, he began to doze almost immediately, and dreamed.

He saw Scipio again, the real Scipio, the Roman general, the man who had raped him in his first life. The man's features were indistinct, but his eyes were clear, sharp and gray like a hawk's. They haunted his brief dream, hanging over him in the sky as he relived the end of the hard day at Zama, once again under those eyes, enduring the pain and the humiliation.

Singing woke him only a few minutes later. In the yard, now lit by torches, he saw the overseer talking with a young woman, beautiful in the way of the English, slim and sprightly and blonde, with even, small features, but bronzed by the Nevis sun to a tawny gold. He quickly forgot his nightmare in contemplating the woman, whom he presumed to be Kate Higgins. She moved bewitchingly, swaying slightly as she spoke to the overseer. In the hut, Scipio's eyes grew round and hungry.

He would not rape her—never that—but he thought that when he was king of this island, he might try to win her. She would make a fine queen, and he did not believe that any woman so attractive could possibly prevent his rebellion.

Slaves began to file into the yard from the cane fields, slipping silently and humbly across the beaten earth to enter their huts, singing a sonorous melody. The woman nodded approvingly at the sound, and smiled once at the overseer before slipping into the manor house.

Scipio eyed the slaves that entered his hut, indistinguishable shadows in the dim light from the yard. This would be the making of his army, he knew, and he wished he could have seen their faces.

Light to see by would not have made a difference. Scipio learned that night, and confirmed it in the morning, that no slave at Fair Point would even consider rebellion. In the dark, he tried to speak to them, but beyond telling him to watch his step and mind the mistress, they would say no more. He tried to rouse them, called them cowards and dogs, saying they reminded him of boys who had not been weaned, but they only told him to be quiet in fearful voices, whispering that Mistress Kate would get him if he wasn't good.

He was amazed, and stopped speaking, unable to believe it. He had planned his way into Fair Point with the idea that he would find a willing army of rebels, but the ten men crammed into the hut with him were not even men at all. They had no spirit, no honor, a thing for which none of his lives had prepared him. Pondering this, he fell into exhausted sleep.

The next morning, none of them would look him in the eye. They scuffled around the hut, silently eating their rice in the misty dawn. One brought him a bowl but he waved it aside, though his stomach was growling with hunger. He did not want to associate with these wretches, these less-than-men. When they filed meekly out of the hut in answer to the overseer's call, he did not follow. If his lives had not taught him to expect men without spirit, they had taught him to plan. He remained stubbornly in the hut, thinking furiously. *Maybe,* he thought, *if they have no spirit now, I can show them spirit, and they will follow my example.*

Scipio was so caught up in his thoughts that he did not recognize his new name when the overseer called him.

"Hannibal! Hannibal! Get out here, you damned nigger!"

Only when the overseer appeared in the entrance of the hut did he remember his new christening and haul himself to his feet, dragging his chains with him.

"C'mon, beast," the overseer said darkly. "The mistress wants to see you."

Scipio pulled his chains with him out into the yard, where the other slaves were already dispersing into the cane fields. The door of the house opened and the woman he had seen the day before came out, even more beautiful in the soft light of dawn. He drank in the sight hungrily, and reveled in the way it restored his confidence. He found he could not fear a pretty woman, and even the scowl on her face as she crossed the yard did not bother him.

"Hannibal, you say?" She was speaking with the overseer, who trailed after her. "Well, we'll change that soon enough. I won't have any damned Hannibals in my gangs."

Scipio smiled to himself as she approached, wondering at the appearance of toughness in this slim, pretty witch. He drew himself up as she neared, proudly displaying his strong body. He thought that when he took this island—and even now he was sure he could; he had a hundred lives' worth of war and rebellion behind him—he wanted her as his queen.

Then he saw her eyes.

"This is Mistress Kate Higgins," the overseer was saying, but neither mistress nor slave heard him.

Their eyes had locked at the same time, and as Scipio recognized her sharp, gray eyes, she saw the impact on him. Kate Higgins spoke first.

"Hannibal, eh? What was your name before?"

The voice was not the same, of course, but he knew her eyes, and for the first time in this lifetime, he was afraid. He remembered the piercing gaze over his body, looking down into his face as he was raped, and the courage of a hundred lifetimes died beneath the shame and humiliation and pain of one. He could not stand those eyes; he dropped his gaze first.

"Scipio," he mumbled, staring at the ground to try to stop the world from whirling around him.

Kate Higgins laughed. "Jesus God, that must have hurt!" There was a long silence; the overseer, confused by the fact that his mistress apparently knew her new slave, took a step away. Then the woman reached out and grabbed Scipio's jaw. Scipio recognized the grip, though the hand was smaller than it had been a hundred lifetimes before; he recognized the gesture, forcing his head up so she could look in his eyes.

"Zama," she whispered in amazement, though she was clearly pleased. "It is so strange, isn't it? And here I have you again!"

He tried to muster his fading strength, but the sight of her eyes unnerved him. Tears gathered in his own and he tried to hide his face, but she held him where she could look at him.

"I don't know why you would choose the name Hannibal, though. He lost almost as much at Zama as you did." She laughed a musical, vicious laugh that finally sent the tears streaming down his cheeks. Still she held his head up, enjoying the sight of his weakness as she had when, a hundred lifetimes before, she had raped him in the person of the Roman general Scipio.

The moment stretched long and long, his tears flowing unstopped, running over her little hand and down her sleeve. Then the overseer, thoroughly ill at ease with the things they were saying, coughed and scuffed his boots in the dust of the yard.

"Of course, Joseph. We've things to do. But first," Kate Higgins said, letting go of Scipio's jaw so he could hang his head, "take Hannibal here and geld him."

He did not see the smile she threw at him, which was the same she used at Zama, but he did remember Belyer's words, and knew the man had been right.

Scipio was on the ground begging before it was over.

THE FLOOD

Linda Nagata

Mike lay awake in the night on a bed of damp leaves in the towering shelter of a eucalyptus grove, listening to the pounding surf. His young wife Holly slept on the ground beside him, clutching their thin blanket to her chin, her legs half-tangled with his. He rested his hand lightly on her rib cage, feeling her breathe.

Nights were the worst. At night he couldn't see the waters coming. So he listened to the surf, trying to measure the volume of the ocean by the sound. He'd seen the ocean rise as much as thirty meters in a night. Rising. Never receding.

Fear slipped like oil across his skin—cold, encompassing fear. Through his mind's eye he watched Holly drowning, her face pale and exhausted as she finally slipped beneath the relentless waters. Still, that sort of death was ancient and familiar.

God, God, God.

Sudden sweat coated his body despite the chill of the night. His stomach seemed to fold into a fist. This, he thought, would be a good time to recall some profound and comforting passage from the Bible. But he didn't know any. Religion had never been his thing.

Still, God was ever in his thoughts these days as he watched the world drown.

How could He let this happen?

Mike did not believe in the beneficence of God. He was not even sure he believed in the deity Himself. And alone among the survivors, he refused to accept that the end of the world might be a good thing.

Sometime before dawn the rising waters must have claimed a gentler shoreline, because the noise of the surf subsided. Mike slept then, waking only when the sun was well up. He cuddled against Holly on their bed of leaves, gazing downslope at the ocean. He could see it just beyond the grove of trees. Its surface was glassy in the crisp, still air of morning, the waters pale green over a pasture that had flooded in the night. Gentle swells rolled in from the deep to sweep upslope through the eucalyptus grove in flat, hissing crescents.

Mike watched them in a half-conscious state, pleasantly distanced from both his worrisome dreams and untenable reality, until a slight breeze rustled through the treetops, reminding him that he still needed to devise a sail for his newly finished boat.

Holly stirred sleepily. He bent over her, gently brushing aside her long dark hair to kiss her cheek, feeling yet again the sour clench of fear. He would not let her be taken. He could not. It would be better to drown. But better still to steal her away on his boat. Soon. Maybe even today.

She blinked and stretched, then smiled at him, a serene joy glowing in her dark eyes. "Mike. Do you feel it, Mike? It's very close now."

"We don't have any food left," he told her.

She shrugged, sitting up, her long tanned legs goose-bumped in the morning chill. "We don't need any food. Today will be the last day. I can feel it."

As if to emphasize her words, another wave slid up through the grove to swish against her feet, laying down a crescent of sand before subsiding. Mike found himself staring at the dread signature. In the weeks since the flood began, he'd watched the sand and waves take over roads, houses, forests, pastures, farms, as the ocean steadily rose, drowning the island that had always been their home. They'd retreated upslope as the waters advanced, but the highest point on the island had been only five hundred meters above sea level—

Mike squinted down at the new shoreline. Now, he guessed, the highest point might clear thirty meters. He frowned, trying to recall the exact geography of the island before the flood. Hadn't the meadow where he'd built his boat been *more* than thirty meters below the summit?

"The ark!" he yelped, leaping to his feet. "Holly . . ." He grabbed her hand and yanked her up. The roar of the night's surf resounded in his mind. His boat had been well above the waterline at nightfall, but now—

He ran through the grove, dragging Holly with him. He was afraid to leave her alone, afraid she would disappear like so many others had.

"Mike," she panted, bounding along in his rough wake. "It's all right, Mike. You don't need the boat. Everything will be all right."

But he couldn't believe her. He'd never been able to believe.

They splashed through a retreating wave, through rotten leaves half buried in sand. Their feet sank deep into the unstable mix. Tiny air bubbles erupted on the forming beach. Then they reached the edge of the grove and burst into the open.

Sunlight sparkled on green water. Children frolicked in the swell, riding the shore break at the edge of the insatiable ocean.

Finally letting go of Holly's hand, Mike scrambled up a scrub-covered ridge of ancient lava. By the time he reached the top, the cool air was tearing in and out of his lungs. He stood on the crest and looked down at his project.

Yesterday evening the boat had rested solidly on its platform, fifteen meters above the waterline and nearly completed, a tiny ark made of green eucalyptus wood. But the surf had seized it in the night, throwing it against the jagged lava of the ridge.

The shattered pieces bobbed and tumbled with the incoming waves.

Holly joined him, her breast heaving with exertion beneath the scanty coverage of her tank top. She glanced at the wreckage, hardly seeing it. "Come and swim, Mike," she pleaded. Her eyes were wide and soft. "The water's warm. The waves aren't big. It's a perfect day. A gift from God."

On the summit of the island a huge white wooden cross glowed in the morning light, a memory of earlier days.

Most of the people who'd lived on the island before the flood had already been taken away. There were only forty or fifty left, waiting patiently for their turn on the ropes.

Mike tore his gaze away from the shattered boat and rounded on Holly. "Wake up!" he shouted. "Wake up! You've been walking around in a daze for weeks. You and everyone else, while an act of genocide has been going on around you. We're dying, Holly. Family by family, your god is killing us."

Holly's gaze seemed suddenly weighted in concern. She raised her hand to brush Mike's wild hair away from his face, off his ears, as if by that simple measure she hoped to change a basic deficiency in his vision, in his hearing.

Mike knocked her hand away. "I'm not deaf and I'm not blind!" he shouted. "I can see what's going on — "

"But you can't feel it," she said softly.

"No. No, you're right. I can't feel it. I can't." His hands clenched into fists. He closed his eyes as anguish flooded his mind. "Why me, Holly? Why am I the only one who can't believe— "

A faraway rumble cut off his lament. The sound resembled the thunder of a distant jet, summoning a memory of childhood when he'd lain awake at night listening to the passage of an anomalous craft far overhead, imagining that what he heard was no commercial airliner on an unusual route; that instead, the nightfarer was a B-52, armed with nuclear missiles bound for a hardened target in Siberia. The overflight that presaged the end of the world.

His childhood fears had faded with the Cold War, had dulled with maturity. Now they were back, haunting him, as the end of the world loomed in unexpected reality.

He looked out across the ocean, to where he counted three twisting wires of brilliant golden light. They were thin, like cracks in the sky letting in the light of heaven. But vast, appearing to extend far beyond the luminous blue bowl of the sky, disappearing into some nebulous distance that seemed somehow utterly different from the sky Mike had known all his life. Light bleeding from some other place. Some other world. Hungry light that preyed on hope and faith.

The distant jet-roar faded to silence as the wires of light approached across the water. They swayed as they moved, not behaving at all like ordinary light, but instead, bending and floating like extremely low-density matter. Once again Mike felt himself astounded at their thinness. The first one swept across the shallows toward the children playing in the waves. At this distance it was easy to see that it was no thicker than the mooring lines once used to tie cruise ships to the docks.

The children had spotted the rope. Their joyous cries could be heard from the ridge as they scrambled and dove toward the light. Mike wanted to scream at them to stop, to run away. But they *believed.* . . .

A young girl just short of puberty reached the rope first. She grabbed it with her right hand and was immediately yanked off her feet. She rose skyward. At the same time, she seemed to shrink so that she was drawn *into* the column of light. Mike watched as she became a tiny silhouette within the golden glow, a dark figure receding at fabulous speed across a vast dimension that did not exist in this world. He watched until she became a black point on the visual horizon. And then he watched her disappear.

Other children followed her, six, then seven of them before

the rope left the now-empty water and swept ashore, zigzagging across the newly laid beach as it offered itself to the eager, waiting parents.

Mike fell to his knees, sickened. He bent over, holding his stomach. He wanted to puke. Holly crouched beside him. "It's all right, Mike," she said soothingly. "It's all right. God has come for us. You don't have to be afraid."

Her words made his hackles rise. Was a rope finally out to lure the two of them? After weeks of watching everyone they'd ever known disappear up the ropes, was this their time? His fingers clawed at the ground. Why couldn't he feel the grace the others felt? Why couldn't he *believe?*

A deep electric hum assaulted his ears. He felt his hair lift slightly, as if a field of static electricity had suddenly swept around him. Looking up, he saw a second golden rope racing in from the ocean toward the ridge. *"No!"* he shouted.

He dove at Holly, knocking her to the ground. He held her there with his weight, pinning her arms against her sides. "I won't let you go to it!" he screamed at her. "I won't let you go."

The rope was dancing, swaying up the jagged slope of the ridge. Holly's eyes filled with tears. A trace of blood wetted her lip. Her jaw trembled. "Please, Mike. Let me go. It's my time. It's our time. I don't know why you can't feel it. But I do know you love me. You have to trust me. You have to let me believe for you—"

He kissed her to stop the flow of words. His lips pressed against hers, his tongue probed her mouth, he tasted the sweet salt of her blood. It crossed the membranes of his mouth like a drug. Her love flowed into him, her trust, her faith. He felt a warm, golden glow fill him. He let go of her arms, to cradle her beautiful face in his hands. And then they were sitting up, spooning, her arms tight around the small of his back. And somehow after that, he found himself on his feet. She stood facing him, holding both his hands. A column of gold rose behind her. Her warm, dark eyes were locked on his. She nodded encouragement. Moving backward, she led him first one step, then another. Letting his left hand go, she half turned to seize the rope. *"Faith,"* she whispered.

Her body arched in sudden ecstasy as she was yanked up the rope. The gasp that escaped her lips was a knife that cut through Mike's consciousness. He stiffened as a dirty old awareness flooded his mind. "Holly, no!" he roared.

She was receding up the rope, her right side shrinking, darkening into a silhouette as she was swept into the narrow chasm of golden light, her left side yet in the flooded world. *"Holly!"*

He found that he still held her left hand. Now he seized it with both his hands and pulled. Her body continued to shrink, to recede into impossible distance. Her arm stretched in a long black ribbon. Then her hand turned palm up in his grip, and vanished. He found himself grasping at empty air.

A scream of utter rage ripped from his throat. Tears flooded his face.

The golden light hummed and shifted, awaiting him.

"Not me," he choked. "I won't go with you. Murderer! Murderer!" He turned and fled into the forest.

The island was empty, all the people finally gone.

Mike climbed the hill and sat at the base of the cross. Cool air washed over his face, while scudding clouds played with the sun's light. The remaining land mass was no more than a quarter-mile across now. Uninterrupted ocean surrounded him on all sides, the water appearing to rise up like a shallow bowl, with himself trapped in the bottom. How high would the waters rise? High enough to drown even continental mountains?

There is not that much water in the world!

Movement caught his eye. A sparkle of white against the cloud-shadowed sea. A bird, he realized. And as it drew nearer, he recognized the wandering albatross, gliding on its white wings just above the crest of the swell. A solitary creature.

He watched it in gratitude, and not a little wonder, realizing only then how much he'd missed the nonhuman life of the island. For the cats and dogs, birds, and cattle had disappeared with their masters. Even the fish had vanished from the ocean. He wondered if this bird could be as hungry as he.

It stayed with him, flying a restless circuit around the shrinking island as the floodwaters continued to rise. By noon, when hunger and thirst and utter isolation began to play upon his mind, it became the focus of his delirium. He found himself flying on long wings around and around the white wooden cross, as if he flew on the end of a chain. He wanted to turn tail to it. He wanted to glide across the open ocean into the blue promise of homogenous vistas: *just a little farther now, and you will find land, life.*

But the bird refused to leave.

The afternoon passed. Mike felt his skin burn in the intermittent sun. Thirst seemed to swell his tongue into a dry, dusty sponge. Hunger knotted his belly. He watched the waves roll in, from all sides now, higher and higher, until by late afternoon they met at the bottom of the cross.

He climbed the monument to escape the churning tumult of water that consumed the last bit of land. He hauled himself up on the crossbar, then hugged the post while the waters roiled below him, slowly, yet inevitably rising. Soon he would drown. Were there fish left in the water to eat him? Were there still microbes that might break down his flesh? Perhaps he would sink to the bottom and become covered with sediment and be converted to a fossil, the only evidence left of the original animal life of this world. For he sensed that the world was being cleansed, prepared for an entirely separate history to follow.

Tears filled his eyes as he looked out across the watery wasteland. He couldn't imagine worshiping any deity capable of creating this murderous scene.

All Gone.

The vast and empty ocean seemed to resound with that statement of finality.

All Gone.

When the last creatures were flushed out by the flood, the world would be clean, ready to be remade, renewed.

Mike held on. By evening, the ocean was nearly calm. The golden colors of sunset played across the uninterrupted horizon. He gazed at the sight, feeling the burnished hues enter his soul and warm him. Last day.

He was startled as the albatross swept past. It had been drawing nearer all day, perhaps emboldened by the retreat of the land. Now it floated by, scarcely an arm's length away, the wind abuzz in its feathers, a slight noise that seemed to grow in volume as the bird receded until the buzz became the ominous rumble of distant thunder, distant jets.

Mike looked up, to see a golden rope dancing on the horizon. A single rope. It was the first time he'd ever seen just one. His heart began to hammer as the old fury returned. He clung to the cross and screamed at the usurper, his voice rolling across the calm waters. *"Liar! Murderer!"*

A cold swell rose up to touch his dangling feet, bringing with it a sudden darkness. Fury flowed away, leaving behind the painful vacuum of despair. He bowed his head against the post and cried until the thunder faded and the hum of the rope filled his ears, until the deceiver's golden glow burned through his closed eyes.

He still didn't believe in the beneficence of God. He knew the flood was an act of genocide and the rope but a con game. Knew it by the anguish in his soul. But it didn't matter anymore. He was human, and he must follow his people, be it to hell or oblivion. He opened his eyes. The rope danced before him, an inexplicable golden cable let down at the end of the world. The albatross floated on a breeze, seemingly watching, waiting for his lead.

He grasped the rope in both hands, and was gone.

THE BUILDER

P h i l i p   K .   D i c k

"E. J. Elwood!" Liz said anxiously. "You aren't listening to anything we're saying. And you're not eating a bite. What in the world is the matter with you? Sometimes I just can't understand you."

For a long time there was no response. Ernest Elwood continued to stare past them, staring out the window at the semidarkness beyond, as if hearing something they did not hear. At last he sighed, drawing himself up in his chair, almost as if he were going to say something. But then his elbow knocked against his coffee cup and he turned instead to steady the cup, wiping spilled brown coffee from its side.

"Sorry," he murmured. "What were you saying?"

"Eat, dear," his wife said. She glanced at the two boys as she spoke to see if they had stopped eating also. "You know, I go to a great deal of trouble to fix your food." Bob, the older boy, was going right ahead, cutting his liver and bacon carefully into bits. But sure enough, little Toddy had put down his knife and fork as soon as E.J. had, and now he too was sitting silently, staring down at his plate.

"See?" Liz said. "You're not setting a very good example for the boys. Eat up your food. It's getting cold. You don't want to eat cold liver, do you? There's nothing worse than liver when it gets cold and the fat all over the bacon hardens. It's harder to digest cold fat than anything else in the world. Especially lamb fat.

They say a lot of people can't eat lamb fat at all. Dear, please eat."

Elwood nodded. He lifted his fork and spooned up some peas and potatoes, carrying them to his mouth. Little Toddy did the same, gravely and seriously, a small edition of his father.

"Say," Bob said. "We had an atomic bomb drill at school today. We lay under the desks."

"Is that right?" Liz said.

"But Mr. Pearson, our science teacher, says that if they drop a bomb on us, the whole town'll be demolished, so I can't see what good getting under the desk will do. I think they ought to realize what advances science has made. There are bombs now that'll destroy miles, leaving nothing standing."

"You sure know a lot," Toddy muttered.

"Oh, shut up."

"Boys," Liz said.

"It's true," Bob said earnestly. "A fellow I know is in the Marine Corps Reserve and he says they have new weapons that will destroy wheat crops and poison water supplies. It's some kind of crystals."

"Heavens," Liz said.

"They didn't have things like that in the last war. Atomic development came almost at the end without there really being an opportunity to make use of it on a full scale." Bob turned to his father. "Dad, isn't that true? I'll bet when you were in the Army, you didn't have any of the fully atomic—"

Elwood threw down his fork. He pushed his chair back and stood. Liz stared up in astonishment at him, her cup half raised. Bob's mouth hung open, his sentence unfinished. Little Toddy said nothing.

"Dear, what's the matter?" Liz asked.

"I'll see you later."

They gazed after him in amazement as he walked away from the table, out of the dining room. They heard him go into the kitchen and pull open the back door. A moment later, the back door slammed behind him.

"He went out in the backyard," Bob said. "Mom, was he always like this? Why does he act so funny? It isn't some kind of war psychosis he got in the Philippines, is it? In the First World War, they called it shell shock, but now they know it's a form of war psychosis. Is it something like that?"

"Eat your food," Liz said, red spots of anger burning in her cheeks. She shook her head. "Darn that man. I just can't imagine . . ."

The boys ate their food.

It was dark out in the backyard. The sun had set and the air was cool and thin, filled with dancing specks of night insects. In the next yard, Joe Hunt was working, raking leaves from under his cherry tree. He nodded to Elwood.

Elwood walked slowly down the path, across the yard toward the garage. He stopped, his hands in his pockets. By the garage, something immense and white loomed up, a vast pale shape in the evening gloom. As he stood gazing at it, a kind of warmth began to glow inside him. It was a strange warmth, something like pride, a little pleasure mixed in, and . . . and excitement. Looking at the boat always made him excited. Even when he was first starting on it, he had felt the sudden race of his heart, the shaking of his hands, sweat on his face.

His boat. He grinned, walking closer. He reached up and thumped the solid side. What a fine boat it was, and coming along damn well. Almost done. A lot of work had gone into that, a lot of work and time. Afternoons off from the job, Sundays, and even sometimes early in the morning before work.

That was best, early in the morning, with the bright sun shining down and the air good-smelling and fresh, and everything wet and sparkling. He liked that time best of all, and there was no one else up to bother him and ask him questions. He thumped the solid side again. A lot of work and material, all right. Lumber and nails, sawing and hammering and bending.

Of course, Toddy had helped him. He certainly couldn't have done it alone; no doubt of that. If Toddy hadn't drawn the lines on the boards and—

"Hey," Joe Hunt said.

Elwood started, turning. Joe was leaning on the fence, looking at him. "Sorry," Elwood said. "What did you say?"

"Your mind was a million miles away," Hunt said. He took a puff on his cigar. "Nice night."

"Yes."

"That's some boat you got there, Elwood."

"Thanks," Elwood murmured. He walked away from it, back toward the house. "Good night, Joe."

"How long is it you been working on that boat?" Hunt reflected. "Seems like about a year in all, doesn't it? About twelve months. You sure put a lot of time and effort into it. Seems like every time I see you, you're carting lumber back here and sawing and hammering away."

Elwood nodded, moving toward the back door.

"You even got your kids working. At least, the little tyke. Yes, it's quite a boat." Hunt paused. "You sure must be going to go quite a way with it, by the size of it. Now exactly where was it you told me you're going? I forget."

There was silence.

"I can't hear you, Elwood," Hunt said. "Speak up. A boat that big, you must be—"

"Lay off."

Hunt laughed easily. "What's the matter, Elwood? I'm just having a little harmless fun, pulling your leg. But seriously, where are you going with that? You going to drag it down to the beach and float it? I know a guy has a little sailboat he fits onto a trailer cart, hooks it up to his car. He drives down to the yacht harbor every week or so. But my God, you can't get that big thing onto a trailer. You know, I heard about a guy built a boat in his cellar. Well, he got done and you know what he discovered? He discovered that the boat was so big that when he tried to get it out the door—"

Liz Elwood came to the back door, snapping on the kitchen light and pushing the door open. She stepped out onto the grass, her arms folded.

"Good evening, Mrs. Elwood," Hunt said, touching his hat. "Sure a nice night."

"Good evening." Liz turned to E.J. "For heaven's sake, are you going to come in?" Her voice was low and hard.

"Sure." Elwood reached out listlessly for the door. "I'm coming in. Good night, Joe."

"Good night," Hunt said. He watched the two of them go inside. The door closed, the light went off. Hunt shook his head. "Funny guy," he murmured. "Getting funnier all the time. Like he's in a different world. Him and his boat!"

He went indoors.

"**S**he was just eighteen," Jack Fredericks said, "but she sure knew what it was all about."

"Those southern girls are that way," Charlie said, "It's the climate. They ripen faster. It's like fruit, nice, soft, ripe, slightly damp fruit."

"There's a passage in Hemingway like that," Ann Pike said. "I can't remember what it's from. He compares a—"

"But the way they talk," Charlie said. "Who can stand the way those southern girls talk?"

"What's the matter with the way they talk?" Jack demanded. "They talk different, but you get used to it."

"Why can't they talk right?"

"What do you mean?"

"They talk like . . . colored people."

"It's because they all come from the same region," Ann said.

"Are you saying this girl was colored?" Jack asked.

"No, of course not. Finish your pie." Charlie looked at his

wristwatch. "Almost one. We have to be getting on back to the office."

"I'm not finished eating," Jack said. "Hold on!"

"You know, there're a lot of colored people moving into my area," Ann said. "There's a real-estate sign up on a house about a block from me. 'All Races Welcomed.' I almost fell over dead when I saw it."

"What did you do?"

"I didn't do anything. What can you do?"

"You know, if you work for the government, they can put a colored man or a Chinese next to you," Jack said, "and you can't do anything about it."

"Except quit."

"It interferes with your right to work," Charlie said. "How can you work like that? Answer me."

"There's too many pinks in the government," Jack said. "That's how they got that, about hiring people for government jobs without looking to see what race they belong to. During WPA days, when Harry Hopkins was in."

"You know where Harry Hopkins was born?" Ann said. "He was born in Russia."

"That was Sidney Hillman," Jack said.

"It's all the same," Charlie said. "They all ought to be sent back there."

Ann looked curiously at Ernest Elwood. He was sitting quietly, reading his newspaper, not saying anything. The cafeteria was alive with movement and noise. Everyone was eating and talking, coming and going, back and forth.

"E. J., are you all right?" Ann asked.

"Yes."

"He's reading about the White Sox," Charlie said. "He has that intent look. Say, you know, I took my kids to the game the other night, and—"

"Come on," Jack said. "We have to get back."

They all rose. Elwood folded his newspaper silently, put it in his pocket.

"Say, you're not talking much," Charlie said to him as they went up the aisle.

Elwood glanced up. "Sorry."

"I've been meaning to ask you something. Do you want to come over Saturday night for a little game? You haven't played with us for a hell of a long time."

"Don't ask him," Jack said, paying for his meal at the cash register. "He always wants to play queer games like deuces wild, baseball, spit in the ocean—"

"Straight poker for me," Charlie said. "Come on, Elwood. The more the better. Have a couple of beers, chew the fat, get away from the wife, eh?" He grinned.

"One of these days we're going to have a good old stag party," Jack said, pocketing his change. "You know the kind I mean? We get some gals together, have a little show . . ." He made a motion with his hand.

Elwood moved off. "Maybe. I'll think it over." He paid for his lunch. Then he went outside, out onto the bright sidewalk. The others were still inside, waiting for Ann. She had gone into the powder room.

Suddenly Elwood turned and walked hurriedly down the sidewalk, away from the cafeteria. He rounded the corner quickly and found himself on Cedar Street, in front of a television store. Shoppers and clerks out on their lunch hour pushed and crowded past him, laughing and talking, bits of their conversation rising and falling around him like waves of the sea. He stepped into the doorway of the television shop and stood, his hands in his pockets, like a man hiding from the rain.

What was the matter with him? Maybe he should go see a doctor. The sounds, the people, everything bothered him. Noise and motion everywhere. He wasn't sleeping enough at night. Maybe it was something in his diet. And he was working so damn hard out in the yard. By the time he went to bed at night, he was exhausted. Elwood rubbed his forehead. People and sounds, talking, streaming past him, endless shapes moving in the streets and stores.

In the window of the television shop, a big television set blinked and winked a soundless program, the images leaping merrily. Elwood watched passively. A woman in tights was doing acrobatics, first a series of splits, then cartwheels and spins. She walked on her hands for a moment, her legs waving above her, smiling at the audience. Then she disappeared and a brightly dressed man came on, leading a dog.

Elwood looked at his watch. Five minutes to one. He had five minutes to get back to the office. He went back onto the sidewalk and looked around the corner. Ann and Charlie and Jack were no place to be seen. They had gone on. Elwood walked slowly along, past the stores, his hands in his pockets. He stopped for a moment in front of the ten-cent store, watching the milling women pushing and shoving around the imitation-jewelry counters, touching things, picking them up, examining them. Before the window of a drugstore, he stared at an ad for athlete's foot, some kind of a powder being sprinkled between two cracked and blistered toes. He crossed the street.

On the other side, he paused to look at a display of women's clothing: skirts and blouses and wool sweaters. In a color photograph, a handsomely dressed girl was removing her blouse to show the world her elegant bra. Elwood went on. The next window was suitcases, luggage and trunks.

Luggage. He stopped, frowning. Something wandered through his mind, some loose, vague thought, too nebulous to catch. He felt, suddenly, a deep inner urgency. He examined his watch. Ten past one. He was late. He hurried to the corner and stood waiting impatiently for the light to change. A handful of men and women pressed past him, moving out to the curb to catch an oncoming bus. Elwood watched the bus. It halted, its doors open-

ing. The people pushed onto it. Suddenly Elwood joined them,
climbing up the steps of the bus. The doors closed behind him
as he fished out change from his pocket.

A moment later, he took his seat, next to an immense old
woman with a child on her lap. Elwood sat quietly, his hands
folded, staring ahead and waiting, as the bus moved off down
the street, heading toward the residential district.

When he got home, there was no one there. The house was
dark and cool. He went to the bedroom and took his old clothes
from the closet. He was just going out into the backyard when
Liz appeared in the driveway, her arms loaded with groceries.

"E.J.!" she said. "What's the matter? Why are you home?"

"I don't know. I took some leave. It's all right."

Liz rested her packages on the fence. "For heaven's sake," she
said irritably. "You frightened me." She stared at him intently.
"You took *leave?*"

"Yes."

"How much does that make, this year? How much leave have
you taken in all?"

"I don't know."

"You don't know? Well, is there any left?"

"Left for what?"

Liz stared at him. Then she picked up her packages and went
inside the house, the back door banging after her. Elwood
frowned. What was the matter? He went on into the garage and
began to drag lumber and tools out onto the lawn, beside the
boat.

He gazed up at it. It was square, big and square, like some
enormous solid packing crate. Lord, but it was solid. He had put
endless beams into it. There was a covered cabin with a big window, the roof tarred over. Quite a boat.

He began to work. Presently Liz came out of the house. She
crossed the yard silently, so that he did not notice her until he
came to get some large nails.

"Well?" Liz said.

Elwood stopped for a moment. "What is it?"

Liz folded her arms.

Elwood became impatient. "What is it? Why are you looking at me?"

"Did you really take more leave? I can't believe it. You really came home again to work on . . . on that?"

Elwood turned away.

"Wait." She came up beside him. "Don't walk off from me. Stand still."

"Be quiet. Don't shout."

"I'm not shouting. I want to talk to you. I want to ask you something. May I? May I ask you something? You don't mind talking to me?"

Elwood nodded.

"*Why?*" Liz asked, her voice low and intense. "Why? Will you tell me that? Why?"

"Why what?"

"That. That . . . that thing. What is it for? Why are you here in the yard in the middle of the day? For a whole year it's been like this. At the table last night, all of a sudden you got up and walked out. Why? What's it all for?"

"It's almost done," Elwood murmured. "A few more licks here and there and it'll be—"

"And then what?" Liz came around in front of him, standing in his path. "And then what? What are you going to do with it? Sell it? Float it? All the neighbors are laughing at you. Everybody in the block knows"—her voice broke suddenly—"knows about you, and this. The kids at school make fun of Bob and Toddy. They tell them their father is . . . that he's . . ."

"That he's crazy?"

"Please, E.J. Tell me what it's for. Will you do that? Maybe I can understand. You never told me. Wouldn't it help? Can't you even do that?"

"I can't," Elwood said.

"You can't? Why not?"

"Because I don't know," Elwood said. "I don't know what it's for. Maybe it isn't for anything."

"But if it isn't for anything, why do you work on it?"

"I don't know. I like to work on it. Maybe it's like whittling." He waved his hand impatiently. "I've always had a workshop of some kind. When I was a kid, I used to build model airplanes. I have tools. I've always had tools."

"But why do you come home in the middle of the day?"

"I get restless."

"Why?"

"I . . . I hear people talking, and it makes me uneasy. I want to get away from them. There's something about it all, about them. Their ways. Maybe I have claustrophobia."

"Shall I call Doctor Evans and make an appointment?"

"No. No, I'm all right. Please, Liz, get out of the way so I can work. I want to finish."

"And you don't even know what it's for." She shook her head. "So all this time you've been working without knowing why. Like some animal that goes out at night and fights, like a cat on the back fence. You leave your work and us to—"

"Get out of the way."

"Listen to me. You put down that hammer and come inside. You're getting your suit on and going right back to the office. Do you hear? If you don't, I'm never going to let you inside the house again. You can break down the door if you want, with your hammer. But it'll be locked for you from now on if you don't forget that boat and go back to work."

There was silence.

"Get out of the way," Elwood said. "I have to finish."

Liz stared at him. "You're going on?" The man pushed by her. "You're going to go ahead? There's something wrong with you. Something wrong with your mind. You're—"

"Stop," Elwood said, looking past her. Liz turned.

Toddy was standing silently in the driveway, his lunch pail

under his arm. His small face was grave and solemn. He did not say anything to them.

"Tod!" Liz said. "Is it that late already?"

Toddy came across the grass to his father. "Hello, boy," Elwood said. "How was school?"

"Fine."

"I'm going in the house," Liz said. "I meant it, E.J. Remember that I meant it."

She went up the walk. The back door slammed behind her.

Elwood sighed. He sat down on the ladder leading up the side of the boat and put his hammer down. He lit a cigarette and smoked silently. Toddy was waited without speaking.

"Well, boy?" Elwood said at last. "What do you say?"

"What do you want done, Dad?"

"Done?" Elwood smiled. "Well, there's not too much left. A few things here and there. We'll be through soon. You might look around for boards we didn't nail down on the deck." He rubbed his jaw. "Almost done. We've been working a long time. You could paint, if you want. I want to get the cabin painted. Red, I think. How would red be?"

"Green."

"Green? All right. There's some green porch paint in the garage. Do you want to start stirring it up?"

"Sure," Toddy said. He headed toward the garage.

Elwood watched him go. "Toddy . . ."

The boy turned. "Yes?"

"Toddy, wait." Elwood went slowly toward him. "I want to ask you something."

"What is it, Dad?"

"You . . . you don't mind helping me, do you? You don't mind working on the boat?"

Toddy looked up gravely into his father's face. He said nothing. For a long time the two of them gazed at each other.

"Okay!" Elwood said suddenly. "You run along and get the paint started."

Bob came swinging along the driveway with two of the kids from the junior high school. "Hi, Dad," Bob called, grinning. "Say, how's it coming?"

"Fine," Elwood said.

"Look," Bob said to his pals, pointing to the boat. "You see that? You know what that is?"

"What is it?" one of them asked.

Bob opened the kitchen door. "That's an atomic-powered sub." He grinned, and the two boys grinned back. "It's full of Uranium-235. Dad's going all the way to Russia with it. When he gets through, there won't be a thing left of Moscow."

The boys went inside, the door slamming behind them.

Elwood stood looking up at the boat. In the next yard, Mrs. Hunt stopped for a moment with taking down her washing, looking at him and the big square hull rising above him.

"Is it really atomic-powered, Mr. Elwood?" she asked.

"No."

"What makes it run, then? I don't see any sails. What kind of motor is in it? Steam?"

Elwood bit his lip. Strangely, he had never thought of that part. There was no motor in it, no motor at all. There were no sails, no boiler. He had put no engine into it, no turbines, no fuel. Nothing. It was a wood hull, an immense box, and that was all. He had never thought of what would make it go, never in all the time he and Toddy had worked on it.

Suddenly a torrent of despair descended over him. There was no engine, nothing. It was not a boat, it was only a great mass of wood and tar and nails. It would never go, never leave the yard. Liz was right: he was like some animal going out into the yard at night, to fight and kill in the darkness, to struggle dimly, without sight or understanding, equally blind, equally pathetic.

What had he built it for? He did not know. Where was it going? He did not know that either. What would make it run? How would he get it out of the yard? What was it all for, to build without understanding, darkly, like a creature in the night?

Toddy came from the garage, stirring a quart can of paint. He nodded to his father and set the can down by the ladder. Then he went back to get the brush.

Toddy had worked alongside him the whole time. Why had *he* worked? Did he know? Did the boy know what the boat was for, why they were building? Toddy had never asked. The boy had never asked because he trusted his father to know.

But he did not know. He, the father, he did not know either, and soon it would be done, finished, ready. And then what? Soon Toddy would lay down his paint brush, cover the last can of paint, put away the nails, the scraps of wood, hang the saw and hammer up in the garage again. And *then* he would ask, ask the question he had never asked before but that must come finally.

And he could not answer him.

Elwood stood, staring up at it, the great hulk they had built, struggling to understand. Why had he worked? What was it all for? When would he know? Would he *ever* know? For an endless time, he stood there, staring up.

It was not until the first great black drops of rain began to splash about him that he understood.

Quantity *and* Quality: The Short Fiction of Philip K. Dick

Robert Silverberg

It was the late spring of 1953, and I was eighteen years old and finishing my freshman year of college, and despite a heavy academic load, I was writing a short story just about every other week in the hope that if I only wrote *enough* of the things, one of them eventually would be bought and published by a science-fiction magazine. My real ambition, which, to the amazement of most of my friends and relatives I actually would achieve in another few years, was to sell a *lot* of stories, to see them published in every magazine of the era (*Amazing Stories, Fantastic, Astounding, Galaxy, Fantasy & Science Fiction, If, Future,* and all the rest), and to be widely admired for my cleverness and productivity. But as of the late spring of 1953, I had nothing to show for these fantasies except a thick sheaf of rejection slips, and I would have been deliriously happy if just one, *one* of all my many stories, could win editorial acceptance somewhere.

Meanwhile, a couple of guys six or seven years older than I was were already living the very fantasy that was at the center of my feverish dreams. Coming out of nowhere, they suddenly were appearing on the contents pages of just about every science-fiction magazine, from the classiest to the pulpiest, turning out an astonishing stream of bright, lively, original short stories at a rate of one every two weeks or so. I admired and envied both of them inordinately. One of them was Robert Sheckley and the other was Philip K. Dick. I know how prolific they were, because I kept a little list of all their stories by way of reminding myself of what it was possible to accomplish if only you were quick-witted enough and hard-working enough and talented enough. Sheckley had six stories published in 1952—his first year—and followed them with twelve more in the first half of 1953. Dick announced himself with four in 1952 and published *seventeen* in the first six months of 1953, seven of them in June alone, on his way to a total of thirty that year.

I was paying attention to their feats. Boy, was I ever paying attention.

Sheckley and the even more prolific Dick were of special interest to me because my own ambitions revolved about quantity as well as quality. I wanted to be a good science-fiction writer, yes, but also I sensed in myself some peculiar quality of discipline or energy or simple manic fervor for writing that would permit me to be more than usually productive. Henry Kuttner, that great and now largely forgotten sf writer of the 1940s, was one of my idols, in part because he was so prolific that he found it necessary to use fifteen or twenty pseudonyms to conceal the full volume of his output. (And the quality of Kuttner's work did not seem to be impaired by the speed with which he turned it out.) Dick and Sheckley were Kuttneresque figures to me, versatile and inexhaustible. Their stories, too, seemed to me to show the influence of Kuttner's approach to writing fiction, which was another reason for my admiration. Kuttner's approach struck me as a very fine approach indeed, and anyone who employed Kuttner as a model was likely to find a sympathetic reader in me.

The dark side of being a swift and efficient writer who can write and sell a short story every week or two is that that very productivity engenders the suspicion that the work of such a writer is glib or superficial, whereas the work of a writer who labors interminably to produce a sparse and slender *oeuvre* often is regarded as profound, mainly because of its rarity. This is as true outside the science-fiction world as within it, and many a prolific writer (Charles Dickens, William Shakespeare, John Updike, Joyce Carol Oates, Irwin Shaw) has had to struggle against that subtle unwillingness to accept the fact that some writers can perform consistently well at a fast pace of production.

I was, naturally, fascinated and thrilled by Dick's astonishing everywhere-at-once debut as a science-fiction writer. When an editorial blurb such as this accompanied one of his stories ("The Preserving Machine," in the June 1953 *Fantasy & Science Fiction,* edited by Dick's friend and mentor, Anthony Boucher), it was only too easy for me to drift into a pleasant adolescent daydream in which my name replaced Dick's as the subject of the encomium:

> In November of 1951, Philip Dick sold his first story (to *F&SF,* we may add proudly), and within a very few months thereafter he had established himself as one of the most prolific new professionals in the field. By now he has appeared in almost every science-fiction publication—and what's most surprising, in each case with stories exactly suited to the editorial tastes and needs of that particular publication: the editors of *Whizzing Star Patrol* and of the *Quaint Quality Quarterly* are in complete agreement upon Mr. Dick as a singular satisfactory contributor. Joining with them, we consider this latest Dick precisely our kind of story: gently witty, observant and pointed, with a striking new idea attractively blending science and fantasy.

But the sheer volume of Dick's early short fiction operated against him, too. Certainly there is a condescending tone to this 1956 review by the critic Damon Knight of Dick's first novel, *Solar Lottery:*

Philip K. Dick is that short story writer who for the past
five years or so has kept popping up all over with a sort of
unobtrusive and chameleonlike competence. . . . Entering
and leaving as he does by so many doors at once, Dick creates a blurred impression of pleasant, small literary gifts,
coupled with a nearsighted canniness about the market—
he writes the trivial, short, bland sort of story that amuses
without exciting, is instantly saleable and instantly forget-
table.

The surprise of a book like *Solar Lottery* from such an
author is more than considerable.

Solar Lottery, as Knight goes on to demonstrate, was in fact a superb novel, so vividly told and inventively constructed that
Knight was flabbergasted to find that the author of all those
"trivial" stories had been capable of writing it: "Dick states his
premises, shows you enough of his crowded, complex world to
give you your bearings—and then puts away his maps and
charts for good. You are in the world of the bottle and the Quiz-
master, the Hills and the legal assassins, and you see the living
surface of it, not the bones. . . .

"Then there's the plottiness . . . each new development not
merely startling—anybody can startle—but startling *and logi-
cally necessary.* This is architectural plotting, a rare and inhu-
manly difficult thing; and who in blazes ever expected Dick to
turn up as one of the few masters of it?"

Who in blazes, indeed? Certainly not Damon Knight, who at
least in 1956 was mysteriously unable to see the promise in-
herent in Dick's sparkling early stories or to recognize the technical storytelling skill that permitted Dick to turn those stories
out with such speed. But within a couple of years, years in
which the seemingly indefatigable Dick published novels with
the same relentless rapidity as he had offered short stories—two
books in 1957, three in 1958—even Knight found it necessary

to concede that "at his intermittent best, Dick is still one of the most vital and honest working science-fiction writers." Phil Dick would, of course, go on to produce a whole bookshelf of extraordinary novels—*The Man in the High Castle, Do Androids Dream of Electric Sheep, Ubik, The Three Stigmata of Palmer Eldritch, Martian Time-Slip,* and ever so many more—and by the time of his premature death in 1982 would be considered one of the great modern masters of the genre.

But let's keep the focus on those early stories, the ones that seemed to be winning Dick at the outset of his career a reputation for little more than facility and excessive willingness to please editors, rather than examining yet again the famous works of his later years.

Were they all as "trivial" and "bland" as Knight, taking his first critical look at Dick's work forty years ago, believed?

Consider "Impostor," one of the seven Dick stories of June 1953. (It appeared in John W. Campbell's *Astounding Science Fiction,* the most highly regarded of the old science-fiction magazines.) Spence Olham is the protagonist: a high-ranking weapons-research expert in an era not too far in the future when Earth is under attack by invaders from Alpha Centauri. Olham, wearily working to design some sort of device that will allow beleaguered Earth to strike back at the so-far invincible outworlders, finds himself suddenly arrested by a security official who accuses him of being an alien spy. The official tells the bewildered Olham that the invaders have infiltrated Earth's defensive bubble with a humanoid robot whose task it is to destroy a particular human being and take his place. "Inside the robot," Olham is told, "was a U-bomb. Our agent did not know how the bomb was to be detonated, but he conjectured that it might be by a particular spoken phrase, a certain group of words. The robot would live the life of the person he killed, entering into his usual activities, his job, his social life. He had been constructed to resemble that person. No one would know the difference. . . . The person whom the robot was to impersonate was Spence Olham."

Olham is informed that he will be taken off to an isolation camp on the Moon, where he will be disassembled so that the bomb within him can be rendered harmless.

It's quite clear to Olham—who just a little while before has been discussing vacation plans with his wife—that some terrible mistake has been made. He knows that he isn't an alien humanoid robot; and we know it too, because Olham is the highly sympathetic and quite recognizably human character through whose viewpoint all this is being told. En route to the Moon, he envisions the terrible fate in store for him: "There were men in the building, the demolition team, waiting to tear him to bits. They would rip him open, pull off his arms and legs, break him apart. When they found no bomb, they would be surprised; they would know, but it would be too late."

Desperate, the terrified Olham escapes from his captors when they reach the Moon by pretending to be the very robot they suspect him of being and bluffing the security men into believing that the bomb within him is about to go off. They flee in panic, and he returns to Earth alone aboard the ship in which they had brought him to the Moon. Olham contacts his wife and urges her to locate the staff doctor of his weapons project, who will be able to conduct tests proving that he is human. Tense chase scenes follow as security officers pursue Olham into a forest near his home, where he has gone hoping to find the actual alien robot aboard its crashed spaceship. The security men close in just as—to his great relief and ours—he finds the wrecked ship. The robot, badly burned, is on board. Olham has managed to demonstrate in the nick of time that he is an authentic human being.

The security officers, apologetic now, are still congratulating Olham on his miraculous last-minute escape from peril when one of them, taking a close look at the charred robot, sees a bloody knife sticking out of its chest. What they had taken to be a robot is in fact the murdered body of the real Spence Olham. And then—Dick's stunningly economical final few lines:

> "This killed him," Nelson whispered. "My friend was killed with this." He looked at Olham. "You killed him with this and left him beside the ship."
>
> Olham was trembling. His teeth chattered. He looked from the knife to the body. "This can't be Olham," he said. His mind spun, everything was whirling. "Was I wrong?"
>
> He gaped.
>
> "But if that's Olham, then I must be—"
>
> He did not complete the sentence, only the first phrase. The blast was visible all the way to Alpha Centauri.

Dick's setup is marvelously elegant. Not only does the pitifully misunderstood protagonist turn out to be the alien robot after all, but the very words of stunned acknowledgment of the fact that he utters are, in fact, the previously coded signal that will detonate the bomb within him. In "Impostor" we see not only the first statement of the overriding obsessional theme that would make Dick famous—*How can we trust our perceptions of reality?*—but also his enormous skill, here at virtually the beginning of his career, at putting a story together.

This early mastery did not go unrecognized even then, despite the uneasiness Dick's prolificity caused in those first years in critics like Damon Knight. Dick's "Impostor" of 1953 has turned up in a dozen or more anthologies over the years, beginning with Groff Conklin's *Science Fiction Terror Tales* in 1955, Edmund Crispin's *Best SF 2* the following year, and, among many others, a book called *The Metal Smile,* published in 1968 and edited by—yes—Damon Knight.

Among those who applauded Dick's work right at the outset and learned quickly to search the magazines for more of it was, as I have already said, the young Robert Silverberg. Like any number of would-be writers before me, I was then in the stage of ferociously studying How It Is Done, and the spectacular debut of Philip K. Dick (and also that of Robert Sheckley) in 1952–53 had caused me to give those two writers particular attention. Compare Ray Bradbury's remarks, written in 1948, about one of his own special literary heroes, Theodore Sturgeon: "Perhaps the best way I can tell you what I think of a Theodore Sturgeon story is to explain with what diligent interest, in the year 1940, I split every Sturgeon tale down the middle and fetched out its innards to see what made it function. At that time I had not sold one story, I was twenty, I was feverish for the vast secrets of successful writers." What Bradbury was doing to Sturgeon's stories in 1940, I was doing to those of Dick and Sheckley thirteen years later. Sturgeon, by then, was too supreme a master for me to hope to equal, but there was some reason to think that I could, with enough study and practice, reach the level of accomplishment that these two bright new writers had managed to attain, and I studied each new story of Dick's and Sheckley's with infinite care.

Dick had caught my eye right away, before anyone knew how prolific he was going to be, with his very first story: "Beyond Lies the Wub," in the July 1952 issue of *Planet Stories*. That magazine was the pulpiest of all the science-fiction pulps, famous in its time (and cherished now by the cognoscenti) because of the utter wildness and woolliness of the action-adventure, space-opera stuff that it published. (Writers of the caliber of Sturgeon, Bradbury, Leigh Brackett, Isaac Asimov, and Poul Anderson loved to write for it. I wish it had lasted long enough for me to have had a chance.) Dick's "Beyond Lies the Wub" is the story of a spacegoing transport ship, one of whose crewmen has somehow acquired a huge piglike Martian beast called a wub. Food starts to run short aboard the ship and the captain announces plans to have the wub butchered and served. But as he is telling the ship's cook to figure out how best to prepare it, the wub unexpectedly speaks up:

"I think we should have a talk," it says. "I'd like to discuss this with you, Captain, if I might. I can see that you and I do not agree on some basic issues."

The unexpected tone of wacky solemnity—in the pages of a magazine where aliens customarily were hideous fanged killers with beady eyes and glittering scales—told me instantly that I had found something unusual.

The captain feels that he has found something unusual, too. He beckons the wub into his office and they discuss the situation. The wub is telepathic and highly intelligent. "We are a very old race," it tells him. "Very old and very ponderous. It is difficult for us to move around. You can appreciate that anything so slow and heavy would be at the mercy of more agile forms of life." The wub explains that it lives by eating plants, mostly. "We're very catholic. Tolerant, eclectic, catholic. We live and let live. That's how we've gotten along." It is aware that the captain wants to have it cooked, and it can quite understand his desire to do so. "You spoke of dining on me. The taste, I am told, is good. A little fatty, but tender. But how can any lasting contact be established between your people and mine if you resort to such barbaric attitudes? Eat me? Rather, you should discuss questions with me, philosophy, the arts—"

This, in *Planet Stories*?

The debate goes on. The captain points out that the ship's food supplies are unfortunately quite low and the wub's meat is needed. The wub is sympathetic but unwilling; it suggests that everyone on board draw straws to see who is to be eaten. Which is not what the captain cares to do. Some philosophical discussion between the wub and the crewman who is its actual owner follows: "So you see," the wub says, "we have a common myth. Your mind contains many familiar myth symbols. Ishtar—Odysseus—" The conversation is interrupted by the captain, who still has his mind on food; in the end, the outcome is unhappy for the wub, but Dick has a diabolical little sting at the end of his tale that implies that the unfortunate alien has had the last word after all.

A few months later came "Roog," in *Fantasy & Science Fiction*—the first story Dick had ever sold, though several others had reached print ahead of it. There were aliens in this one, too—roaming through a suburban neighborhood. The dogs spot them first:

> "Roog!" the dog said. He rested his paws on the top of the fence and looked around him.
>
> The Roog came running into the yard.
>
> It was early morning, and the sun had not really come up yet. The air was cold and gray, and the walls of the house were damp with moisture. The dog opened his jaw a little as he watched, his big black paws clutching the wood of the fence.
>
> The Roog stood by the open gate, looking into the yard. He was a small Roog, thin and white, on wobbly legs. The Roog blinked at the dog, and the dog showed his teeth.
>
> "Roog!" he said again.

Unfortunately, the dogs are the only ones who can see the Roogs. And though they shout "Roog! Roog!" in increasing alarm, the dull-witted humans all about them simply wonder why the dogs are barking so much. So the invasion proceeds.

A singular mind was at work in these little stories. And the stories never struck me as bland or trivial in the least. Quickly I learned to look forward to each new story by Philip K. Dick.

And, as we all came to see, there would be plenty of them. Why was Dick so prolific? In part, it was the sheer exuberance of his magnificent imagination that brought all those stories forth in such a great rush. He had read science fiction since he was a boy—a lonely, insecure, ill-adjusted boy—and his head teemed with the marvels that A.E. van Vogt, Henry Kuttner,

Robert A. Heinlein, and the rest of the great writers of the so-called Golden Age of Science Fiction had put there. Now his own variations on their themes came flooding freely out. Once he had sold "Roog" to Anthony Boucher—for a munificent $75, close to the top rate for science fiction in those days—Dick devoted himself with furious energy to writing. "I began to mail off stories to other sf magazines," he recalled in 1968, "and lo and behold, *Planet Stories* bought a short story of mine. In a blaze of Faustian-like fury, I abruptly quit my job at the record shop, forgot my career in records, and began to write all the time. (How I did it, I don't yet know; I worked until four each morning.) Within the month after quitting my job, I made a sale to *Astounding* (now called *Analog*) and another to *Galaxy*. They paid very well, and I knew that I would never give up trying to build my life around a science-fiction career."

But of course those magazines *didn't* pay very well, except perhaps by the standards of the record-store clerk that Phil Dick had been when his writing career took off in 1953. The best that any writer could hope for from a science-fiction magazine back then was the three cents a word that the top magazines paid. Three cents a word for a story like "Impostor" is $180. Not bad, maybe, for a story written in two or three days, at a time when Dick could rent a small two-story house in Berkeley, California, for just $27.50 a month. But what about the stories that trailed off into incompletion, or the ones that no editor wanted to buy, or the ones that had to be sold to the bottom-rung magazines at *half* a cent a word, payable on publication six months or a year after acceptance? It was, actually, a life of poverty that Dick had chosen for himself, a life of cheap, ramshackle rented houses and ground horsemeat for dinner. Things grew better for him later on, but never very *much* better. The irony of Phil Dick's career is that the big movie sales, the international fame that came to him when *Blade Runner* and *Total Recall* were filmed from his work, the reissues of his novels in a dozen countries, the flood of income from a myriad sources, all happened after his death at the age of fifty-four, fourteen years ago.

And so he wrote all those short stories for love and for money, a great deal of love and not very much money. Then, exhausted by the need to come up with a brilliant story idea every few days, year in and year out, he turned to writing novels—for a thousand dollars each in those days. It was a tough life. It wore him down and, I think, eventually it killed him.

The story that is reprinted in this anthology is one of a number that he sold to *Amazing Stories* during that early period of dazzling short-story production. *Amazing,* in 1953, had come out of a long period of dreary decline, transforming itself from a shabby pulp magazine to an elegant little slick publication with handsome cover paintings and color illustrations inside, then unheard of in a fiction magazine. The old pulp *Amazing* had largely been staff-written by hacks; the new slick one featured material by the best science-fiction writers of the time: Robert Heinlein, Theodore Sturgeon, Ray Bradbury, Arthur C. Clarke, Henry Kuttner, Walter M. Miller, Jr. It was in the fourth of these slick *Amazings* that the name of Philip K. Dick appeared on the contents page, just below those of Kuttner and Miller, with a deft little piece called "The Commuter," and two issues later, he was back again, with "The Builder," included in this collection.

How I stared at those beautiful issues of *Amazing Stories* forty-odd years ago and dreamed of being published in one myself someday! How I longed to follow the route of Philip K. Dick, seven years my senior, and find my own stories listed there along with those of his and Sheckley's and Kuttner's! With mounting pleasure—and, I admit it freely, no little envy—I watched the career of Philip K. Dick unfold from story to story and then blossom out into the novels that would win him his real fame; and later, much later, when my own career had begun in a way rather like Dick's, I came to meet him and to get to know him and to count him among my friends. Our lives diverged eventually—his became increasingly dark and troubled, plagued by messy personal entanglements, money troubles, and steadily worsening health—and toward the end, I felt little envy for him indeed, though my admiration for his work remained undimmed. He seems to me today one of the greatest of all science-fiction writers, both in the short-story form and as a novelist. His artistic influence is readily visible in the themes and approaches of many of today's most celebrated sf writers, especially in book form. I think his superb short fiction is no longer as well known as it deserves to be, and I direct your attention to it wherever you can find it—starting right here with the book in your hands.

THE PERSISTENCE OF MEMORY

John Morressy

The Gramper didn't mumble and groan the way the others in Last Lodge always did. He kept on talking every minute he was awake. His voice was weak now, but it didn't stop.

Pacer had once heard his father say that the old man wouldn't be quiet until he was stone dead, and maybe not even then. One of the clan chiefs overheard and said that Pa had better watch out for that kind of talk or he'd bring bad things down on the family. Pa made like he didn't care, but Pacer never heard him say anything like that again.

The Gramper wasn't asking questions, the way everyone said he did in the old days, and he wasn't telling clan law, or tradition. Now he was telling true past, nothing else, the same things over and over to each watcher, and warning that they mustn't be forgotten, not one thing. It all had to be remembered and passed down to the next generation and the next for as long as the clans survived: that's what The Gramper said.

He wasn't rambling either, or mixing things up. The Gramper was still the best of the telling men. Some of them got story and law and tradition all tangled up when they were old, and even added crazy ideas of their own, but The Gramper still told it all just the way he always had.

Tonight was Pacer's time to watch again. The Gramper

wanted him there specially. The boy wanted to be out in the forest seeing to his traps and snares, or with Callie Blue, but he had to take his turn at watching, and extra turns because he was picked. That was the law of family and clan, and could not be avoided.

He entered Last Lodge at sunset. The Gramper was sleeping when Pacer arrived to spell his father, but when father and son spoke at the entrance, the old man stirred and made a noise like clearing his throat, and then was quiet again.

"Good hunting today?" the father asked.

"Got two rabbits. There's a stew cooking." Pacer had caught three, but one had gone to Callie Blue. He always caught something just for her. They were promised. They were going to set up together as soon as they were old enough to declare.

"Good boy. You stay awake now, and listen good to what The Gramper says. You're the one's got to do the remembering when he's gone."

Pacer nodded without speaking, hoping that if he kept quiet, the old man would not awaken for a long time. Everybody talked as though he was lucky to be the one picked by The Gramper. They all said it was a good thing to be a telling man, and be respected everywhere. Pacer had his doubts. He didn't really want to spend his life passing down a lot of laws he couldn't half understand and stories he didn't like much even when he could make sense of them. He would rather set up with Callie Blue and make a family of his own, and hunt along with the clan, like his father and the other men. But he had been picked, and that was final. And maybe it would be all right. What White Dog had said could make everything a lot better.

His father left. Pacer took his place by the wall as quietly as he could, hoping not to wake The Gramper, but the old man raised his head, peering through the gloom to where the boy sat. He could hardly see, even in the light.

"Who's there? Who's with me?" he asked.

"It's Pacer."

"Good. You're the only one ought to be here. The rest don't care. Once I'm gone, you're the one has to remember it all and pass it on."

"I know, Gramper."

"You don't know anything!" the old man snapped, his voice cracking in sudden anger. He stared up into the darkness. "Nobody does and nobody wants to! They don't want to hear. Prop up my head, so's I can look at you when I talk." He was silent while Pacer lifted up his head and pushed the soft pillow into place; then he spoke more softly, his voice friendly now and confiding. "You know how to listen and remember. You had clan law and traditions perfect in your memory before you was ten years old. But true past is even more important. The others don't understand how important it is. They don't care. They try to make like they're listening, and as soon as I'm done talking to them, they forget it all. But the memory has to be kept alive. Someone has to tell how high up we was once, and how we was brought down." He paused, breathing deeply; then, his voice intense, he said, "Don't you never forget that. We was beat, Pacer, no matter what anybody says. We was beat, and it humbled us. Broke our spirits. It wasn't always like it is now. We didn't live like this before the Ships. We was a proud people once. Too proud, that was our weakness, we was so proud that we thought nothing could ever beat us. But the Ships came."

"I know, Gramper. 'The Ships came and they just took over,' " Pacer said, sighing over the familiar words. The old man was wide awake now. He would go on all night.

"None of them want to listen. Just because they're gone, they tell themselves it's all over, and it can never happen again. But they could come back. Or others might come. Worse ones, maybe."

"We'll be ready for them, Gramper."

"Don't talk like an idiot!" the old man snapped, glowering at the boy. "We thought we could lick anybody, and they come out of nowhere and we was helpless as a lot of babies! Don't you remember anything I tell you?"

"Course I do, Gramper. But folks say—"

"Folks is dumb as dirt. They talk like they know, but they don't know. Never been nowhere, never seen nothing. Shut up now, and listen to what I tell you. I don't know everything that happened, nobody does or ever did, and I don't know why it happened the way it did, and when. But I know all there is to be known, and you've got to learn it before I go. I thought there'd be more time, but I was wrong. So you listen to me, and listen good. I might not be here to tell you tomorrow."

"We'll take care of you, Gramper."

"I'm dying, and I know it. Ain't nothing you can do for me but listen."

"Yes, Gramper," said Pacer. He stretched out his long legs and settled back against the wall of the lodge, trying to find a soft place in the wattling so he could sleep while the old man went on with his stories. He had heard so many, could repeat them word for word, and he did not care. True or not, it was the past, it was over with and did not matter, whatever The Gramper might think. The Ships were gone. Everything was different now.

"It was all done so fast. You got to make them understand that, Pacer. It wasn't like no clan battle. No threats or warnings, they just all at once was here. Everywhere in the world, people looked up at the skies, and there was the Ships, big silver things, hundreds of them. Thousands. Just floating there, way up, bigger than mountains. And quiet. They didn't do nothing nor say nothing. Wasn't no war, no struggle, just the dying.

"Nobody had a chance to fight back, whatever they tell you now. We had powerful weapons in those times, but nobody got to use them. Maybe we could have hurt them with our weapons, and maybe we couldn't, but we never got a chance to do nothing at all. The Ships didn't even care enough about us to fight us. As if we wasn't even worth it. They didn't leave us nothing to remember but our shame. A man can keep his pride if he goes down fighting, but they wouldn't allow us that. They didn't send nobody down to fight us. Didn't even kill anybody, not outright. Didn't have to. They just stopped the machines, took away the power and stopped them dead, and we was helpless. Couldn't fight, couldn't see what we was doing. Couldn't even ask each other what was happening. That's how they beat us, Pacer. They made us helpless. They shamed us."

Pacer grunted to acknowledge attention. It was hard to understand this part of The Gramper's stories, and harder to believe it. He could picture the other things the old man told him, the stories about the cities and all, and the machines that were so much smarter and stronger and faster than people, and the ships floating up there like clouds, but the power inside the machines was like something in Blind Dan's stories about the Wood Spirit and the Hand in the Lake, only stronger. It was some kind of power that was everywhere, making the whole world run. Like God, only not God.

Nobody could see the power. Nobody understood it anymore, but The Gramper said everybody knew all about it and used it in the old times. It took them traveling faster than anyone could run and made the sun shine all night long. People used to stick machines into the walls of their lodges, The Gramper said, and the power would make the machines come to life and do all their work for them, even move and talk for them. That power was still out there someplace, the old man said, and if we could only figure out how to bring it back to life, we could make the world like it was before the Ships, with machines doing all the work and all the thinking, everybody strong and well fed, warm in winter and cool in summer, and no hunting unless you felt like it. The first time The Gramper told him about the power, Pacer kept sticking his fingers into the walls of the family lodge, trying to get that power into him, until his father swatted him.

Pacer had seen windmills and waterwheels, and the way they did more work than people could do, and did it faster. But the power in the old machines was not like wind or water. You couldn't see it, or feel it against your hands or your skin. It could kill you if it took a mind to, but as long as you used it with respect and paid fair wages, it would be your friend. The Gramper said that it was sort of like lightning, only tamed down. That was a hard thought. Lightning was not something that anyone could tame and keep in a house. Just last month, the lightning had killed a whole lodge full of Bend of River people.

"We don't know how they done it, or why. We don't know nothing about the Ships, or who was in them, or what they wanted from us. They was up there all that time, and nobody ever found out nothing. All the time they was there, they never sent one message down. Not one word. They never come down here, and nobody who was took up to them ever come back to tell about them. All we know is that the Ships come here and stayed for a couple hundred years, and then they was gone. And nothing was the same. A man in Three Hills clan told me . . ."

Pacer thought about the power hiding in the air all around him, still strong and dangerous. He wanted to make sense of the things The Gramper had told him, and he tried, but he got confused, and his thoughts wandered, and several times he nodded off. Then The Gramper started talking about the cities, and Pacer snapped awake. The stories about the cities were the best.

". . . and terrible things happened. Nobody knows all the things that happened in the cities in those first days, and there's no way of finding out now, but we know they was awful. You could tell that just from looking at what was left. Used to be light everywhere in the time of the cities, all through the night, and the light went out all at once and everybody was in the dark. They wasn't like us, didn't know how to keep to a trail in the dark. Couldn't even call out to each other, because the machines did all their talking for them. They went crazy, killing each other and setting fire to everything just to get some light. They had lodges in those times that reached higher than Watcher's Rock, up at Bend of River, and people went so crazy with the fear that they jumped off the tops of them and smashed themselves to death. I been to the cities, Pacer. Seen what was left."

"I know, Gramper. You seen some awful things, too."

That much was true. When he was younger, and his name, too, was Pacer, The Gramper had gone on long trips to places no one else dared to go anymore, looking to find out how things were in the old times. Everybody else kept close to home, where they knew the dangers, but The Gramper wasn't afraid. He was called in a dream, and given a mission, so he knew he'd be safe. He wasn't to be just a telling man, remembering clan laws and traditions and stories. Somebody had to learn the true past, the time of the Ships and before, and remember, and pass it on down, a voice kept saying to him, and he was chosen.

The Gramper had sometimes been away for years, exploring the old ruins and empty places, and visiting other clans to collect their knowledge about the time before the Ships. He was made welcome most of the time, but there were some clans that didn't like strangers. More than once he had to run for his life. He had a long scar down his back and two fingers missing from his left hand, mementos of those flights.

Mostly, though, people talked to him. They were curious about the true past, too, and told him what they had heard from their forefathers. They were glad to hear whatever he could add. Some of what they told him made no sense, or was clearly made up, but The Gramper believed that everything had to be saved, even the lies. People would sort things out in time. He listened to everyone and kept their stories in his memory, so he could pass it all on to his family and their descendants.

"Awful things, Pacer. The world was full of people in those days, more people than we can imagine. They didn't know what it was to be afraid, or hungry, or wore out with hunting and planting. And when the Ships came, they died, most of them, and died bad, real bad. A lot of them died all crammed together in tunnels down in the dark. I saw the bones, all jumbled and heaped up. There was piles of bones out in the open, too, and in the lodges. I climbed up in the tallest lodges, all the way to the top sometimes. Bones everywhere."

"You must have found a lot of stuff."

"Wasn't much left to find. I was born more than a hundred years after the Ships come, you know, and by the time I got to places, the looters had picked them clean. Only stuff left was all rusty or busted up or too heavy to move. And dry bones everywhere."

Pacer liked the stories about the cities. He could picture himself wandering along among the boneheaps. The Gramper had found nothing, but Pacer imagined treasure hidden everywhere, and nobody guarding it. He might even find one of the old machines with some of the power still in it, sleeping, and bring it back here to work for the family.

"Looters took bones, too, didn't they?"

"Somebody did. I met only one clan that took bones from the cities, and it was a bad bunch. Animals was probably the ones took most of them. I always believed the Ships took some, too, but I don't know why they did. Maybe they just wanted to see what we look like inside, and bones was easier to take than people. They took people, too, sometimes. Never saw that, but lots of people told me, so I know they did. I know for sure the Ships sent looters down, because I saw one once."

"That must have been real scary, Gramper, seeing that looter."

The Gramper began to speak, but succumbed to a coughing fit. Pacer held the water jug to his lips, and the old man drank a few sips, then waved it aside. He was silent for a time, breathing slowly and loudly; then he said, "I guess that was the scariest thing ever happened to me, Pacer. It looked like a big beetle. Walked on six legs and moved real slow, turning things over and poking into places, like it was looking for something. It had a big claw that come out of its back and moved all around and up and down, and it could pick up stuff that twenty men couldn't lift. I thought maybe it was after me, wanted to take me up to the Ships, where nobody ever come back. I froze and stayed froze until it was gone. But it just picked up some stuff and tucked it inside."

"And you was watching it all the time," Pacer said. This story always frightened him. It was hard to imagine this old stick of a man being so brave once, and having such an adventure, but he could picture himself in that predicament and feel the fear.

"All the time, and it never caught sight of me. That's why I think it was just a machine. Had to be something smarter running it, somebody up in the Ships."

"What did it look like, Gramper?" Pacer had heard the description a score of times, knew it by heart, but it was exciting to hear every time.

"Like I said, it was kind of like a beetle, only bigger than the family lodge. Must have been eight men long and maybe three men high, and all iron and glass, only it was smooth iron, shiny, no rust on it anyplace, and supple as a snake. Like skin, almost, but I heard something fall on it, and it wasn't no skin. Rang like iron. That thing moved fast, too, when it wanted. Skittered along faster than any animal I ever seen run. And when it was all done doing whatever it come down to do, it just lifted up off the ground and flew."

"I wish I'd seen that."

"I wish you had, too. I wish a lot of people had, so's they'd believe me, and remember what I tell them when I'm gone. I only met three people who seen one of the machines, and only one of them seen it fly."

"I'll remember, Gramper."

"That's not enough, boy. You got to make them believe you!" The Gramper cried. "The Ships haven't been gone more than twenty years, and already people have forgot what it was like to look up and see them there every morning. There's too many people never knew what it was like. You got to make yourself feel it so's you can pass the feeling on."

Taken aback by the old man's sudden outburst, Pacer repeated, "I'll do it. Honest I will."

His anger drained, the old man said, "I believe you, Pacer. You're a good boy. You'll keep the truth alive. Let me tell you something I was told by the Bitter Lake people. It's real important. There was a place in the city . . ."

Pacer leaned back and let the old man drone on with a story he had heard a dozen times. He was thinking of the beetle from the Ships, big and strong and able to fly.

People used to be able to fly, too. That's what The Gramper said. Big iron things like birds took whole families in their bellies and carried them wherever they wanted to go. It was long ago, in the time before the Ships. The Gramper had heard about them from an old, old man who said that his father's father's father had once been up in one of those things.

Much as he wanted to believe, Pacer found it incredible that people could ever fly. But those beetles could. If only he could find one of them, and go traveling everywhere faster than anyone could run, and have a claw that came out of his back and took up all the things he found. That would be a lot better than passing on stories, the way The Gramper and the family wanted him to do.

" . . . Like a big egg, only iron. Hard as iron, and shiny, and it was lying right out in the open where anybody could see it. And the next day they found another one, just exactly like the first, and then three more. And I heard that other clans found them, too. And then, a little while later, the Ships left. That was twenty winters back. Your father was a boy then, just like you are now."

"And them eggs never hatched, did they?" Pacer asked, although he knew this story well.

"Never. And after a while there was a lot of arguing about what to do. Some people said bury them, and other people said no, let's bust them open and see what's inside, because they can't be eggs, they got to be some kind of payment, or gift, and we're meant to open them. But what if they're full of poison, or maybe something worse, other people said. That scared off most everyone. There were a few who went right ahead and tried to bust them open, but they couldn't make a dent no matter how hard they tried. So everybody kept talking and arguing and the eggs are still sitting there, just like the day they was left. I seen three of them with my own eyes two summers back. Was going out to see another one when I was took weak. You'll be the one sees it now."

"And you touched them, didn't you?"

The Gramper, remembering, did not reply for a long time. At last he said, "I was with the Long Wall people then. Real brave people, they was. When they heard everything I had to tell, six of their hunters took me out to see the eggs. I had to show that I wasn't just a telling man, that I could be as brave as any hunter, so I went right up to one and laid my hands on it." He extended his palms, as if they were proof of his words. "Nice and cool it was, nice and smooth. Never felt anything so smooth. Then the others laid their hands on, and nothing happened to us, so we rolled that egg a little ways, and we felt all over it, looking for a crack, or a door, or something like that, but we couldn't find any. So I suppose they're still out there, and I bet they don't look a bit different from the day they was found."

"What do you think they are, Gramper?"

"I don't know. I been thinking and thinking about them ever since I saw the first one, and I just don't know. Could be we'll never know. Some people say we ought to worship them, but that don't make sense. Without we know something about who put them there, and why, we can't know what they are, and we don't know nothing about the Ships except that they come here and beat us and went. Sometimes, though, I wonder if maybe the eggs are nothing but trash. Just some junk the Ships didn't want to bother taking with them wherever they was going."

"I heard a man say they was payment."

"That man don't know what he's talking about, Pacer. He's a fool, like the ones who say we ought to pray to them. The Ships didn't care enough about us to leave payment, or a gift, or anything like that. They didn't care about us at all. We was like ants to them. Did you ever hear of a man leaving payment because he stepped on an anthill?"

The Gramper's voice dropped. He said something about young fools who make up stories about things they don't know, and then he was quiet. Pacer leaned back and thought of the story told last night by White Dog. It was different from anything The Gramper told, but Pacer liked hearing it. It made him feel a lot better than any of The Gramper's stories. His friends liked White Dog's stories, too, and the way he told them, with the rattledrum and the different voices. Old Crooked Hand and some of the other elders said they'd bring trouble, but the young folk liked them.

The old man coughed, a soft, dry cough. "I can't talk no more, Pacer. Let me hear you tell all this back to me."

"You know I'll remember it, Gramper. You don't have to hear me tell it all the way through."

"Yes, I do. You got to have all the stories right. You'll work out your own way of telling, but you got to know what you're telling. Got to make people listen and believe what you tell them. If you don't keep telling the stories over and over, you'll forget some of them."

Pacer wanted to say that a little forgetting didn't matter, but he knew that The Gramper would only get angry. Things were important just because they happened; that was The Gramper's belief. Pacer had to remember everything because The Gramper had chosen him to be telling man and the clan expected him to do it.

He sighed and began to recite from the beginning, that day when the Ships appeared overhead everywhere on Earth, and the power that had kept Earth strong and made the people of this world unconquerable was gone in an instant. He told of the darkness, the death, and the terror in the cities, and the flight to the open places, where the families and clans started over. He was tired, and sometimes he put a detail where it didn't belong, or got a name wrong, and The Gramper corrected him. But after a time the interruptions stopped. Pacer went on, talking softer, until the old man's regular slow breathing showed that he was asleep, and then he stopped and went to sleep himself.

Pacer's sister relieved him at sunset, shaking him awake gently. The Gramper was sleeping, and did not move.

"Has he been sleeping long?" she asked.

"Pretty long. He talked a lot at first."

"He wants you to learn his stories, Pacer. That's your obligation."

"I know them," the boy said, rising and stretching.

He mumbled a good-bye and left Last Lodge. He went to the family lodge. No one was there but his mother and two of the babies. He took a bowl of stew and then he slept for a time, but he was up just after moonrise.

White Dog was still in the settlement, and was telling tonight. He didn't come by often, and had never stayed more than three days, but with The Gramper in Last lodge, near the end of his time, White Dog was staying on longer, and Pacer figured he knew the reason.

White Dog had a bent leg, from a fall a couple years back. It bothered him bad, and he needed someone to hunt for him and cook his food and carry his pack. He had a woman, Longshadow, who took good care of him, but she couldn't tell stories the way he could. She had a bad cough, too. Pacer had seen her cough so bad she couldn't talk, and when the coughing passed, she had little specks of blood on her lips.

Couple nights back, when they stayed with the family, Pacer had told some of The Gramper's stories, and White Dog had said that Pacer was going to be a fine telling man. His father and mother didn't say anything then, but Pacer heard them all talking later, when they thought he was asleep.

Tonight White Dog was sitting by the fire in front of Chief's Lodge, Longshadow at his side. His dogs, cold-eyed like wolves, lay on their bellies on either side of them, paws straight out to front, heads high. He sat cross-legged, with plenty of room around him. Nobody wanted to sit close to those dogs. His little rattledrum was strapped to one hand. He shook it every now and then, or tapped it with his fingertips. He was already in the middle of his story about the departure.

Pacer looked around for Callie Blue, but she wasn't there. He would have liked to sit by White Dog, but he knew that you don't interrupt a telling man. He squatted by one of his friends.

". . . waited, and waited, and waited," White Dog said, in a slow voice that made everyone feel they were waiting, too. "Grandfathers and fathers and sons, and back before the grandfathers and down after the grandsons, all the way back to the day the Ships came and right down to the day they ran off. Everybody watched and waited, just saving up their anger. And all that time the Ships was floating up there, all quiet, thinking that they had us beat.

" 'These people ain't going to fight us,' the Ships said. 'They going to lie down and die, or run away and hide in holes and let us stay here and take what we like and hope we don't get mad and give them a good licking. These people afraid of us, that's what.' And up there in the sky they'd laugh and make jokes about us among themselves. But they didn't know the people. They didn't know what we was doing. We wasn't scared of them, we was waiting. All the anger was there, like hot coals under ashes. We was biding our time, that's what we was doing."

Pacer turned to his friend, and they exchanged eager grins. This was the kind of story they liked to hear.

"So one day, while the Ships was all contented, and laughing and joking up there, and telling themselves they had us beat good, the people raised their voices, all of them together in a shout that went clear up to the Ships and all the way through every one of them, end to end, and we told them, 'It's time you got going, you hear? We been patient with you and let you stay for a time, but now we're mad, and if you don't get out of our sky, we're going to pull you down here and shake you out of them ships of yours and kick you all the way back to where you come from.' "

A murmur of approval and contentment ran through his little audience. A couple of men shouted encouragement. White Dog looked around, nodding.

" 'Going to kick you all the way back to where you come from,' " he repeated, louder, " 'and when we get there, going to burn your lodges and break your weapons and take your stores. We're an angry people. But we're a forgiving people, too. So we're giving you a chance. Go home right now, and we'll let you leave without a beating.' And they heard us. And they started shaking," said White Dog with a slow, steady shake of his rattledrum, while Longshadow began on her big drum a beat that grew gradually louder and faster, "and before we had to shout a second time, they was gone! Clean gone, every one of them! They didn't leave nothing behind but sky."

A lot of the listeners cheered and called out. White Dog sat quiet until they were all finished; then he said, gentle and friendly, "That's the way we are. We're a good people, a peaceful people, and we treat strangers decent if they act like good clanfolk should. Somebody visits us, we feed them our best meat, and give them our best shelter, and share our dances and songs and stories. Sometimes a visitor marries into the clan, and we treat that man or woman just like they was born kin to us. But if somebody thinks this means we're weak, or afraid of strangers, and busts in and takes the warm corner of our lodge and our best bowl and tries to walk big, we teach them how to behave themselves. We give everybody a chance to act right, but if they don't, we rear up and make them run."

There was more cheering, and it lasted longer. "And those Ships, they probably think that leaving us a bunch of big fool eggs is going to make us think they only wanted to pay us a visit, and be our friends. Well, we know better. We didn't want their gifts. We didn't want nothing from them but that they get going, and that's what we made them do. We made them turn tail and run. And they ain't never coming back."

People were laughing and cheering, calling out encouragement and praise. Pacer poked his friend in the arm, and his friend poked him back, and they started wrestling, and another friend joined in, all of them laughing.

When the crowd had settled down, White Dog looked them over, his eyes going from face to face until he fixed on Pacer. He called out, "Hey, Pacer! Pacer, my telling man, come over here and sit by me." Pacer blinked, astonished to hear himself summoned. He stood and looked awkwardly around him, blinking, a bit nervous but proud of the attention. His friends looked at him, every bit as surprised as he was and envious of this sudden glory. "Come on now, Pacer, hurry up over here. I got work for you," White Dog said, and several in the crowd called out encouragement.

With all the dignity he could muster, Pacer walked to White Dog's side. The man shifted over to make room, and Pacer squeezed in between him and the larger of his dogs. He was a little nervous, but he laid his hand on the dog's snow-white back, and the dog turned its head and lolled out its tongue as if it would have given Pacer's hand a friendly lick if it could. Longshadow smiled at him, and White Dog laughed and clapped him on the back. "They're your friends, Pacer. They know a telling man. Now I want you to show that you're a real telling man. You tell us about the time The Gramper went into the city and saw that big beetle thing and chased it right back to the Ships. Go on, now. Everybody's just bursting to hear that."

That wasn't the way the story went. The Gramper would have been wild angry just to hear someone suggest telling it different from his way. But Pacer felt in his bones that that's the way the story should have gone. He couldn't tell it The Gramper's way, not now.

White Dog's story made him feel so good after all The Gramper's talk of losing and fear and being humbled, and he wanted to keep that feeling, and spread it to the others. The Gramper said his way was true, but that wasn't what really mattered. White Dog's way was better. Even if The Gramper's way was true, Pacer didn't want to tell that kind of story, and nobody wanted to listen. Nobody wanted to hear about losing, and being brought down and made small and weak.

People wanted White Dog's stories. He told the kind of history they wanted to hear. Pacer knew he was obliged to do the same.

STILETTO

Martin E. Cirulis

The way I figure, everybody in the world has somebody who's got their number, down to about thirty decimal places. Somebody who could get under your skin even if you'd been dead for six months. Now, if you're lucky, you've got the number of the person who has yours, and the two of you live like horny little bunnies for the rest of your happy little lives. And if you're even luckier, you never meet the person you'd die for. But if you're unlucky, it turns out to be your brother's wife or someone equally inconvenient. And if you're real unlucky, like your parents ran over a gypsy on the way to the hospital, then the person with your number is somebody like Stella.

I'm pretty sure my old man must have run over a whole family of gypsies.

Sometimes I find myself staring into the eyes of the working girls that come around. Not the skanky little girls with their dirty nails and fake frightened glances, but the older ones. The hard ones. The ones always trying to cut an angle, always trying to get more for their flesh than a few bucks and a coating of some loser's sweat. I keep hoping to find another blade there, another Stella. But one I can control this time, one that can burn me but only as much as I want. As much as I need.

I know how they must be. How they give it up with just enough struggle to let you know they're pretending. The iron hand inside the velvet glove. I see the guys they drag around, not the paying customers but the fools who must have them. Some poor slob who'll give everything to feel that kind of edge against his skin. Out of respect, I give them a couple of drinks on the house and tell them I know how they feel. They smirk at a bartender's litany at first, but then they look at my face and see the envy and they know I am a brother. They tell me the tale of fire and ice and I make up a version of my own, changing things to protect the guilty, and we drink some more, nodding sadly and ending with much bitter bravado and insincere back-slapping. But I never see them around again, and I know why. Women of the knife are rare, far more scarce than those who would possess them. There can be no competition that wouldn't end, eventually, with killing.

But they shouldn't worry. My thoughts of finding another Stella are just closing-time fantasies. Lusts to remind myself that I am still alive inside this contentment. Because no matter how much I might search for that cold fire behind their eyes, I know they aren't going to be as good as Stella. They can't be. No matter how hungry, how hard, how beautiful, they are still human. And Stella isn't. Not since the last time.

The crowd wasn't unusual for the Lucky Lady on a Saturday night. Sure, there was a little tension between a couple of WhiPs and a table of JapHanese sailors off the cruiser that had been loitering in English Bay all week, but nothing a couple of stern looks from the Bob Twins couldn't handle. Some places in town let boys like that work out their little political differences on the floor and then fleece the losers, but not me. The EastRim and the Washington Protectorate might be in the middle of an undeclared war, but Vancouver was still a free city, and that went more than double for my bar. I valued the furniture more than extra cash; hell, most of it's real wood. None of that mold-formed bugshit cellulose for my place.

J.J. and I were in the middle of our monthly game of Alaskan Gambit, the table transformed by a shifting, holographic collage of map and terrain. We were at my table, in the back room, the baffles set at maximum so that the chaos of the bar was nothing more than a blurry hum. Shifting sonic fields blended the air so that the doorway resembled an old television with bad reception.

That night's game had been nasty; the sim had already gone six weeks longer than the real war, and we were both showing the pressure. My routine was to review inventory lists on my wrist rollup between turns, while Jay's was to rhythmically engage and disengage the drive on her rusting servopod. The clank-whir of the overgrown wheelchair always blew my concentration, but I could never force her to admit that's why she did it. Her motions had left permanent grooves in the old hardwood floor over the years. Her stamp. Marking her as much a fixture of this place as the secondhand hockey trophies along the walls or the Raven totem behind the bar.

The sides of her egg-shaped pod were scarred by innumerable welds and additions, everything from grabbers to obstacle jets. J.J. never could never leave well enough alone. She could have afforded a new life-support chair, and if she couldn't have, I would have bought one and forced her to take it, but she preferred the Air Force clunker she had woken up in the evac with.

We had met in a Prince George hospital during the Arctic Secession. I was there courtesy of some renegade Yukon commander's clever idea to louse up NORAD supply lines by gassing command centers. I was slow getting into my gear, but I got off lucky; my fiber-lungs only act up when it's cold and wet. Luckier than J.J. had been when an Alaskan smart missile tore the bottom out of her attack fighter and shredded most of her body from the waist down.

After the war, we both settled down in Vancouver, just before Canada gave the city up instead of having it taken away in another war the overburdened country couldn't afford. I was a supply sergeant in my time, and some of my more lucrative "arrangements" paid for the Lady, while J.J.'s pension and tech-work kept her off the streets. We both had every reason to forget the past, yet here we sat, every second Saturday of the month, replaying the war that had stolen our future. Anyone who says humans make sense is either a idiot or an asshole.

It was in the midst of all this twisted nostalgia that I heard the distortion hum of someone slipping through the baffles. I was all ready to give that someone royal shit for disturbing me while I was busy getting my ass wiped all over the Pole, but then I saw who it was and I suddenly had trouble drawing my next breath. It was like being kicked in the chest, minus the footprint.

Stella was back.

"Michael." She purred my name like a steel cat as the smoky light was sucked into her widening black pupils. "Still playing games, I see."

"Hiya, Stella." A blaze of eloquence.

She frowned at the use of her real name, as if she had bitten into something rotten. I used the respite to gain my feet, the small difference in our heights being one of the few advantages I had left over her. The electronic war and J.J. slipped behind me, forgotten.

"You look okay, Michael. Everything still work?"

"No complaints. You're not doing too bad yourself."

That was the biggest understatement since the Russian States said they needed to borrow a little money. Her hair was red again, threads of a dying sun that glinted on her bare caramel shoulders. Both sides were held back in copper combs to accent ears that came to almost elfin points. She hadn't changed her eyes; they were still almond-shaped, clear topaz, feral. The effect was somewhere beyond exotic. Just for a moment I thought I saw genuine affection in that surgically perfect face, but before I could be sure, it was gone like a reflection splashed out of a puddle. In its place was a perfect mask of vulnerability and desire that I didn't have the strength to disbelieve. I never had.

She was wearing a long, gray shawl and pants, folds opening on soft skin and clinging to curves. She had nothing on under the wrap but an old leather vest I had given her years ago, which accented more than it covered. Though I had intended to hold my ground, I felt myself drifting toward her, feeling very much like a black widow on its wedding night.

Probably I'd still be there, staring like a fool, if it hadn't been for J.J.'s frustrated cough and the less-than-gentle nudge as her pod whined its way between me and Stella.

The war in progress came crashing back into my mind. "Ah, shit, Jay! I'm sorry. I forgot—"

"Hey, Chief, no fucking kidding. You got me confused with the toaster again. I ain't got all night to sit around." I winced. J.J. doesn't get pissed very often.

I glanced back to the table, but the display had evaporated.

"Don't worry, I saved it when I saw the tits on her." She looked up at Stella with studied indifference.

Not knowing what else to do, I introduced them. "Uhh, Jay? This is Stiletto. Stiletto, J.J."

Jay's expression didn't change.

"Any friend of Michael's . . ." Stella extended her hand, red enameled nails flashing through the haze; but Jay had already turned away to mark me with her gaze.

"I'm gone. I have to rig up that jammer for the Dekkard brothers. Later." Her pod groaned into motion and parted the baffle.

"We'll pick it up Saturday?" I called out over the babble.

Anything she might have said was guillotined by the baffle re-forming behind her pod, leaving me feeling like a complete bastard.

"My, my," murmured Stella behind me. "I didn't know you had picked up a mech-fetish since last time I saw you." She left a pause. "Isn't that pod a little bulky in bed?"

"Some of us don't sleep with every friend we have."

She cocked her head, as if having trouble with the concept, and then perched herself atop the table that had so recently held scarred tundra. "You getting prudish on me, old man?"

"So what do you want this time, Stella?"

"Is that any way to treat an old friend? One who's come all this way just to see you?" She didn't even try to sound sincere.

"What have you stolen now?"

"I like to think of it as a gift," she said with a laugh. Her face was still beautiful, but it wasn't the beauty that had first drawn me in. That girl lost in the rain when I first met her was gone, refashioned into the kind of perfection only science could effect. But even that perfection seemed etched; the role she had played for so many years was finally beginning to set in her soul.

My body started to fall for her lies. Memories of sweat, cries, and torn sheets burned through my mind. But then her expression turned cold and calculating—it was only for a moment, invisible if I had blinked, but I hadn't. The spell was broken. The mental equivalent of a cold shower.

I pushed her away, hard, but instead of getting angry, she changed her act; her voice took on a nostalgic, faltering tone. From some musty closet in her mind, she produced the streeter girl she had been long ago. Her smile slipped away into uncertainty and her eyes went to her boots. "You're still mad about what happened to Paco and—"

"Warren!" I shouted. "His bloody name was Warren."

"I knew that," she whispered, turning away as if suddenly fascinated by my desk. "It wasn't my fault. We couldn't get out of Singapore. The fighting started. And then . . . then the goons found us. I barely made it out." She popped the hidden latch on my desk and slid open the guts on my Frame.

For a moment I watched her run her hand over the inset data-spheres. Red nails clicked softly against translucent pearls. "And they didn't."

"No. No, they didn't."

"But somehow that warsuit turned up in China and you turn up here, looking a lot richer than you did two years ago. Isn't that fucking convenient?"

The clicking got louder, as if she were trying to crack each egg-sized polymer crystal. "What was I supposed to do? I knew where we had ditched it, and there was no way I could get the suit back here. I had a friend in the Forbidden City, and she got me out. It wasn't my fault. Shit, Michael. They were unprofessional."

"I knew them! I set you up with them." And then the little sack of guilt I had been carrying around with me for the last couple of years spilled. "I helped you set them up."

"Nobody set anybody up. The job just went sour. It wasn't my fault, and you don't have to feel guilty. They knew what they were getting into. Things just go bad sometimes." She still didn't look up.

She was right; I didn't have any evidence except my suspicions. Yeah, I thought, things go bad, but somehow never for you. I sighed and ran my hands through my retreating hair. Stella began prying a sphere from its cradle with a tip of a nail. "Not that one," I said automatically. "Haven't backed it up in a while. The one in the upper left is crashed."

She flicked out the one I indicated and held it up to the light panels. Pale arcs of refracted light flitted across her face and she smiled. With a fluid movement that was hard to follow, she lowered her arm, and the defective data-sphere disappeared into the folds of her clothing. She looked back at me, pleased and untroubled. There was no point in trying to pin her down, no reason not to find out what she was here for.

"You still haven't told me about your 'gift.' "

Those topaz eyes filled with a light I hadn't seen since her first job. "It's a big one this time, Michael. They'll be talking about it into the next century! And I need the best Arranger on the coast to turn it for me."

For a second I started to get infected by her excitement, and then I realized what she must be talking about. My spine tried to curl up and hide in my skull. "This wouldn't happen to have anything to do with the brewup down at the SeaTac Arcology last month, would it?" I was whispering now, like the WhiPs out in the bar could somehow hear through the baffle's curtain of white noise.

And I'll be damned if she wasn't fool enough to be pleased that the news of her grab was common knowledge. She grinned. "Straight from the NanoLab, to be exact."

Sometimes terror can beat out lust. Too bad it wouldn't last.

"I'm outta the biz." I hoped that I sounded convincing. "I guess you didn't hear, eh? Well, I'm sure you'll find somebody else to set up a deal for you. Let me know how it turns out." I was babbling now, backing slowly out of her reach like she was tottering forward with one of the gray plagues. "Better yet, you forget you know me, and I'll find you some—"

"MICHAEL!"

Her shout was so sharp, the rest of the bar probably heard it; baffles weren't designed to stand up to that kind of sonic attack. "What the hell is wrong with you?" she hissed.

"Wrong with *me*? What the hell's wrong with you? You been on the fucking B-net lately, girl? You've thrown both sides of the rim into a frag party, and you sit here all pleased with yourself. City council's given the WhiPs *and* the Japs full sanction on this thing. I don't know what you've gotten your hands on, but the coast is crawling with goons who're gonna burn first and ask questions later."

She only laughed at me. "I can't believe it. You're scared!"

"Damn right I'm scared. And if you remembered any of the shit I taught you, we wouldn't be having this conversation. The first law, baby: 'Never score anything too hot to fence.' "

"Nothing's too hot for you."

"Save that sludge for the streets, girl. Anybody who got their hands on me would keep me sucking wind just long enough to do a cerebral dump, and then they'd be after you."

She got that hungry look again. "No, they won't. Your rep's too established. Anybody who burns you won't get shit from the street for the next twenty years. We can pull this off. Just listen to me."

And, to my eternal regret, I did.

"It'll be easy, relatively. You just set up an auction between the JapHan and the Washington Protectorate. Their goons will cancel each other out and if the WimPs want it back bad enough, they'll pay for it. If they want to screw around, it'll be with each other, and we slip out the back. With gigabucks."

"Gigabucks? What the fuck do you have?"

"Just do it, Michael?"

"A straight auction? No frills?"

"No frills. And with a pro like you setting it up, nothing can go bad. We can retire to one of the Arctic Domes after this. Or buy our own water tower in old L.A., spend our days diving in the shopping centers; have the medical to lie around in the sun. Together."

Our faces were close together now as we whispered like conspirators from some ancient monochrome flat. Every word caused her lips to brush against mine. She reached around behind me with one cool hand and began to knead the tension from my neck. Quick fingers found wary muscles and coaxed flexibility from them.

"One wrong move and we're so much spare parts." My voice was choked, stupid. I breathed her in, wanting more and starting not to care how I got it. She smelled of sex, and expensive gin, and a girl's shampoo. Her hand worked deep along my shoulders. Stifling a groan, I shrugged her off. I didn't need to be groaning. Didn't need to be reminded what her touch could do.

"I know I've let you down before," she whispered into my ear. "But you know it's you I come back to. No matter what's happened. No matter who I've known. It's always been you I've trusted. Always you I end up with."

I turned away, looking for room to pace, to retreat and regroup, but I found myself up against the baffles. My office, which had seemed more than roomy enough for a big desk and two old war-crips, was now hot and crowded. Nowhere for a hungry man to run from his ghosts.

"Look," I said, straining to sound credible. "All I can tell you is that I'll think about it."

"Think about it?" She didn't sound too concerned.

A leering, distorted face appeared in the doorway, everything except the closest inch blurred into a phantom backdrop. "Yeah, I'll think about it." A flipped finger appeared briefly beside the face before both rippled away, the drinker fading to join the other shadow patrons. "Right now, I've got a bar to run."

"Come in with me, and you won't need the bar."

In spite of what I did or didn't need, I found myself turning back to her. My neck was still hot where she had worked me. We both knew I needed to feel her again. A few shuffled steps took me there.

She smiled and tilted her head to one side, hair slipping aside to reveal that long curve of vulnerable neck. Her eyes were half-closed, dreamy. "It'll be so easy for us. For you. For us."

"Nothing's easy," I muttered.

She was still sitting on the desktop, and her legs slid out to wrap around my waist, pulling me tight, her chest pressed against mine, allowing me to believe I was exciting her. "You can do it, I know you can."

"I don't know . . ."

"Michael, please. I need you." I silenced her mouth with mine, wanting to end it on that truth. To fall and take her before she had to resort to her last bullet. Before she tried to tell me that she loved me. Deep down I knew what Paco and Warren had been arguing over, but the blood roared away from my brain, and there were no coherent thoughts for a long time.

Nobody in the Biz should let themselves get sucked in by the old skin game. I knew that; I wasn't sucked in. I'm a professional. I knew exactly what she was doing and why. This sort of thing had been tried on me before. Someone trying to curve the edges of a deal, either for themselves or friends, with easily accessible body parts. I've always let that kind of people slide right off me—every one except Stella.

Not to say I was reminding myself of any of this while watching Stella writhe on top of me, saying all the things you never believe in the light of day. She was dragging me over that cliff for the third time that night.

Her body rocked in time with my growing shudders as she ran her hands across her breasts, stopping only for a moment to roll the tiny pink nipples between thumb and forefinger, and then down to where our bodies joined, making love to both herself and me in equal measure. I didn't mind; I'm not the greedy type. Her lazy half-smile curled at the edges as her legs began to twitch against my hips.

I could see the sweat glistening on her every edge in the half-light; city glow returned from clouds and leaked through ratty curtains. I could smell her underneath the perfume. Not the haze of pharmicones and subliminals but the real woman: sweat, cum, the air gasped from deep in her lungs, her soul breath, burnt iron and honey. What she gave only to me. This was real. I found the strength to thrust upward, forcing myself into her, forcing out more of her essence so I could inhale it all, leaving nothing for those who would follow me. She gasped at my surge, but the smile never faltered; she only opened her eyes to look down on me from so far away.

It was the perfect image to burn into my mental scrapbook, perfect except for the dull blue glow where her eyes should have been, the glow of virt-lenses working overtime. Now, I may not be some trid-stud out of Rome, but I like to think I'm skilled enough to keep my partner from being someplace else. My fragile male ego began to wail.

Stella must have noticed the lurch in my rhythms.

"Don't worry, Michael, I'm still here," she whispered as she did something with her muscles that made me groan. "I'm just connecting to a remote. I wanted to introduce you to my new friends."

I came pretty damn close to jumping out of bed right then. Call me old-fashioned, but I've never been comfortable with sex as a team sport. But then I realized it wasn't just my badly poetic imagination giving Stella a light of her own. She was actually glowing, or at least something around her was glowing.

Stella laughed like a child, and the glow intensified, forming a flaring cloud around us. The glow congealed into thousands of tiny whorls of light that began to orbit Stella, making her the center of a perfect miniature galaxy.

"Do you like them?" she asked between deep breaths.

I reached out hesitantly, not knowing what to expect. Heat, an electrical shock maybe, but there was nothing, only light, like the ghosts of plankton moving through the air. No, not nothing. An absence of nothing. Not the sense of touch but an awareness of it, as if every molecule of the air had come alive at Stella's command. Not a hair on my hand twitched, yet somehow I could feel movement. Worlds of it. It should have been beautiful, but somehow I was terrified. The dagger tattoo below her left ear pulsed with a bloody glow.

"What are they?"

"My new friends. All ready to do anything I tell them. I'm still learning what they can do. Did you know that rubbing air together makes it light up?" she asked with a giggle.

"The nanobots," I whispered. The lights didn't so much move around us as become us. Our bodies were infused with the glow, and the glow connected us as much as the physical contact of our bodies. More so. I could feel her now, not the crude touch of skin on skin but her entire body. My nerves fired in sympathy with hers. I was in her, she in me. One body joined at the spasming waist. The 'bots weren't just around us, they were in us. I screamed in terror; it came out a hungry cry for more. She laughed.

Her face twisted with rapture, her coolly glowing eyes giving her the image of a crazed goddess. "Yesssss. They're mine!" Her back arched as the orgasm took us, and the motes of light flared and disappeared.

"Mine," she groaned.

The connection suddenly broke, and we were two mortals again.

"So this is it?"

"That's it, lover. And it's going to make us rich beyond your wildest dreams."

I looked away from the table to where she lay sprawled across my bed, taking in every ounce of rare sunlight that slid through the small window. "Just my dreams?"

Stella laughed and arched her back, the sallow light giving her stomach and breasts a bronze sheen, like the daughter of some silent movie robot.

I went back to looking at the gear she had stolen, considering what I had instead of what I wanted. And what I was going to do with it. It all looked pretty mundane: a couple of silver cylinders the length of your forearm, a standard-looking BBcon, and a set of virtual lenses. It all looked top-of-the-line and expensive, but nothing to put the coast into an uproar. I handled the cylinders gingerly. One was still sealed with the faint sheen of a steelmem layer. The other had a small rollup in the side, but the arcane readouts made no sense to me.

I pointed the compromised cylinder at Stella and fought the ridiculous urge to shake it. "They all back in here?"

"They should be." She looked away from me, uninterested, and scanned the walls of my room. They were bare except for a couple of old pictures of us and a trid-plaque of a lunarscape, from back before they abandoned the colony.

"What do you mean, 'should be'? What the hell did you have to open this thing for, anyway? You know it's going to make the new owner edgy, maybe edgy enough to strip every neuron I've got just to be sure nothing's been copied."

"Relax, Michael. Stop treating me like fresh meat."

"Then maybe you should stop acting like it."

Her voice went ice cold. "It's been fifteen years, old man. Maybe you should stop lording it over my head."

"So you don't need my advice anymore? I'm just another rube to be fucked, flamed, and forgotten like everyone else? I didn't teach you a trade, I created a bloody monster."

We locked eyes for a moment. I had shocked both of us by not backing down immediately. Her mouth twisted into something ugly, and she started to speak again, probably something crueler and more cutting than anything I could counter, but then she stopped. Maybe she felt bad that her casual indifference was gutting me so badly, or maybe she just sensed I was finally getting close to my limit and the deal was in jeopardy. Whatever the reason, she reined in and smiled apologetically.

"You're the one I keep coming back to."

"Because you need me, because you love me?"

"You know which."

Before I could decide what it was I knew, there was a loud knock on the door.

"Leonard, boss. You want some lunch?"

I'd been so angry with Stella, I hadn't heard him come up the stairs. I flung a sheet over the table and slid the cylinder underneath it. Leonard couldn't get killed for what he didn't know, or so I hoped. I nodded to Stella to slip under the sheets, but she only smiled and draped one hand between her thighs, taking her revenge in watching me squirm.

"Come on in, Lenny."

The old oak door creaked open and Lenny's lanky frame came through backwards, carrying a tray piled high with fish, chips, and sandwiches. He turned around and set it down on a chair with a small flourish. He never batted an eyelash at Stella.

I snagged a piece of batter-covered fish and gulped it down. I'd swear it was completely digested by the time it hit my stomach. "What are you doing in this early, man?" I asked around a mouthful of fries.

"By the time the place emptied out and I cleaned up behind the bar, it was almost four. I decided to sleep on the couch in your office." He was smiling in a self-satisfied way, obviously counting up the perks he could guilt off of me for disappearing last night. Hell, he may have slept on the couch, but he was looking less rumpled than I was. White shirt, real denim jeans, and barely a wrinkle.

"My, how dedicated," observed Stella. She craned her neck to get a better look at the tray and the single napkin-wrapped fork half buried by the food. "No plate for me, Leonard?"

Lenny turned to her with cool indifference, his smile gone. "I had assumed mademoiselle would be gone by the light of day. But if you wish a plate, the bar is empty; there is no one else to witness your tribute to Godiva." Only the Quebecois can tell you to fuck right off so elegantly.

"That's no fun, then," she sighed. "I guess I'll just nibble off Michael's plate."

"As mademoiselle wishes." Lenny turned to leave. "I'll be restocking from the vats all afternoon, boss. Call down if you need anything."

"Remind me to give you a raise, pal."

"I already gave myself one last week," he replied dryly as the door closed behind him.

Stella stared after him for a few moments. "Is he gay?" she finally asked, absently holding out one hand toward me.

I tossed her a sandwich, which she caught without looking.

"He never made a pass at me," I told her with some satisfaction.

We were too busy eating to talk much for the next few minutes. Stella finally got it into her head to get dressed, while I went back to examining the gear that at least a thousand other people would kill to get their hands on. It gave me no small pleasure to be one up on so many big-time players, but it scared the shit out of me too. No matter how hard I tried, I couldn't shake the feeling that nothing good would come of this. I decided to give sanity one last chance.

"I think it might be wiser to unload this on another operator. Take a meg or so and still be alive to enjoy it."

Stella finished pulling on her boots and started searching through my closet for the coat she had left last time. She knew I wouldn't have thrown it out. "And let someone else get the real money?" she said, each word marking the death of her patience.

"And get killed? Yeah."

"We've gone over this already, old man. What are you, holding out for another fuck?"

"Don't flatter yourself."

She spun on me with an angry smile. "I will. And you are going to set up the deal."

I tried to laugh. "Oh, really. What makes you think so, girl? I'm not that hung up on the big bucks. Or that hard up either."

Stella stalked toward me and ran one hand down across my chest, her nails biting even through my shirt. She kissed me hard and deep, and I clutched at her in spite of the rage I was feeling. Her back bent, letting me press on her. Letting my blood get the feel of overpowering her. And then she broke away and slid toward the window and the rusting fire escape.

"Fuck you," I croaked.

"As much as you can handle, old man," she laughed, opening the window and slipping through. "Stop bitching and just set up the deal. You know you want it as much as I do. I'll check in later." She blew me another kiss and disappeared.

I set up the deal.

All things considered, it slid into place easier than I could have hoped. I spent the better part of two days deep in the wilds of the B-net, skimming the whole sit, quizzing a few old corporate connections, and finally establishing discreet contact with the interested parties. The Blacknet is the natural underbelly to the corporate and civil data-nets that keep society running with a minimum of actual face-to-face contact. In a world where nothing can stay hidden for very long, there has to be an info-space evolved that didn't officially exist, in order to conduct the business that never officially happened. Too useful to the countries and corps to shut down and far too intricate to manipulate, the B-net has its place beside the street corner and the barstool as the office for the folks who live in the cracks of our always fracturing society.

I set up the initial bidding, all the while hopping from node to node a dozen times a second to keep any hotshot from running a track-n-stab, and let the world beat a path to my door. It was enough to turn a boy's head; even the fucking Euro-weenies wanted in. I was sure they would be too wrapped up in "re-educating" North Africa to pay any attention to us grubby colonials. Goes to show you, even an old man like me can still be surprised by the drawing power of greed.

Luckily, I was dead-on about the big players; I only had to dick with the numbers a bit to make sure it came down to my favorite boys in this race. The Protectorate and the Rim. Neck and neck. The Japs with a little more money, the Wimps with a little more muscle. They shouldn't have bothered being pushy; I knew better. You can bounce all the checks you want in the next city over, but you never shit in your neighbor's backyard. SeaTac would get their tiny little toys back, the JapHan would down some sake to a missed opportunity, maybe even pull their cruiser out of the bay, but they'd get over it. I found that for all their infighting, the big boys are most comfortable when the fur finally settles over the comfy status quo.

Stella knew the drill as well as I did. While I tidied things up, she kept to the streets, making sure there was nothing nasty trying to climb up our asses the old-fashioned way, muscles in-

stead of microcircuits. In this world, there're only two ways behind a person's back: the nets and the streets. I covered the first,
and she had mastered the second a long time ago. We were a hell
of a team, and things slid into place without a fuckup.

With everything loaded and running, I filed the deal's parameters with the council, cutting them in for a hefty piece and in
return, receiving a fair amount of city protection. Not that it
would make me any less dead if one of our lovely contestants
decided to screw me, but at least their side would be barred
from the city state for a suitable length of time. Or suitable
amount of money, I guess. Hopefully, it would be that extra little pain in the ass that would keep all the players' hands on the
table.

Now all that was left was the last-minute checking that did
more to calm my nerves than anything else. Trusting that this
wouldn't be the one time in my life to get mugged, I snogged
over to J.J.'s workshop, an old mechanic's garage at the bottom
of Main, near the water. The street side of her place was a maze
of rusting plates of scrapped ship's hull, leaning against one another like a fifty-ton house of cards. Intimidating even if you
knew the way through. I slipped around to the alley entrance
with one of the precious cylinders under my arm. I was here to
let her play sorcerer's apprentice with it. The canister was already
open, and I wanted to know exactly what I was trading in. And
I wanted to hear it from someone I could trust.

By the time Jay came out from under the hood, I was nurs-
ing my third beer and on my second count of all the gadgets and
tools strewn across the low workbench that ran the length of the
opposite wall. Her hair was matted under the shimmering fibers
of the Squid netting and her eyes were wide, unfocused. I had
seen her doing tight work in the hood environment before, her
body and pod merged with the analytical contraption. It looked
like a bad date between an ancient hairdresser's dryer and an ob-
solete CAT scanner, and it took rigid concentration to control

the filaments and micromanipulators by direct link. She didn't have that familiar haggard look now; it was more like part of her was still back in the land of virt, lost in the world of vast plains and jagged canyons revealed by the tunneling of electrons and reproduced in the imaging helmet.

"You okay, kid?"

She shook her head, and I couldn't tell if she was getting closer or farther away.

"Jay!" I hadn't meant to yell, but I was a little tense. How the hell did I know that fancy hairnet hadn't backfired and fused a few neurons?

She shook her head again and finally focused on me, annoyed: caught napping at the opera. "What? What the hell are you yelling about, Sporto?" She backed her pod out of the analyzer and spun it toward me. The scarred metal stopped less than a centimeter from my shins.

Yeah, she was back.

"Sorry. You were under a long time." I took another beer out of the box and tossed it to her.

J.J. caught the suds clumsily in hands made cartoonish by thick, black control gloves. She looked dumbly at the bag for a moment, as if trying to figure out what was wrong with her hands, and then she dropped the beer in her lap. With a snarl, she tore the gloves off and tossed them across the room, where they scattered numerous lesser citizens of her toolbench.

"I was starting to worry about you," I offered.

She gave a derisive snort and picked the beer up from her lap. "I doubt it."

I ignored the shot. "So, what's the dump on the bugs?"

"The dump?" She took a long pull from the reseal bag. "I think you should take this cylinder over to the university . . ."

"And?"

". . . and drop it in their fusion torch."

My spit-take was one for the books. "Are you fucking nuts?"

"I'm dead serious, and if you don't want to be just plain dead, you'll do what I say."

"Why the hell for?"

" 'Cause you have no fucking idea what you're dealing with, Chief."

"I'm no tech-stooge, but I read the odd journal. It's just another big, expensive breakthrough."

She sighed. "It's more than that. It's the next generation. Have you ever heard of a Flying Loom?"

"Flying what?"

"A cloth-making gadget. Big in Industrial Revolution England. It made a lot of folks incredibly rich. It also kept a lot more folks incredibly poor."

"Great, kid, but I know I've got some history spheres in a drawer somewhere. When I'm not quite so busy, I'll look this shit up and we can bull over it. But right now, I gotta know why this should make me throw away the biggest score ever."

She swore and slapped the sweat away from her forehead. "Seems like all they want left in the world are techs and soldiers. And that cylinder is going to make it easier. With a world full of those bugs controlled by the privileged few, nothing anybody can do will make any difference anymore."

"Huh?"

From somewhere in the depths of her pod, she produced a BBcon. She held the black box in the palm of her hand and thrust it toward me. "With a simple controller like this, some kind of virt environment and the nanobots in that cylinder, anybody can make anything, one fucking atom at a time. And the little bastards will duplicate themselves until there's enough of them to do the job as fast you wanted."

This was getting a little thick for me, and I struggled to get an angle on it. "So, we grow a lot of stuff already."

She threw the BBcon. I ducked it, barely.

"Yeah, we grow shit! Like furniture and car bodies. Not fucking Rembrandts identical to the last molecule! We grow shit in fucking vats, between fucking suspension matrices, with god-damned amoebae shit! Not out of thin fucking air!"

I thought about Stella with the air on fire around her, her nerves connecting with mine. My stomach started to churn, but I was in too deep to start going with J.J.'s logic. "The WhiPs are just paying to make sure the Rim doesn't get their hands on it. They've probably got all the bugbots they need by now."

She gave a sour laugh. " 'Fraid not, Chief. I did some real digging. Raided a few serious Frames. Seems your little girl was real thorough this time. Not only did she slag the lab on her way out, but she used her pet tech's access to lay a real subtle virus into the SeaTac Frame, ate all the nanobot data from there and every system they touched. Got all the backed data before they caught on. Guess she wanted to push the price as high as it could go. You teach her that? Wonder why she didn't tell you that she was selling the only copy."

I just sucked the damp air through my teeth and winced until I could find an answer. "Probably because it's not. The Tech should be able—"

She stopped me with another laugh. "You'd think, but no! Wrong again. Seems SeaTac was more than a little peeved and neural-dumped the poor boy right off the mark. An example to the rest of the techies, I guess. They pour the boy's brain into the Frame with everything they think they'll need to build the bots and . . ."

"SHIIIIiiiiiit . . . and the worm in SeaTac's Frame promptly eats every pattern that has to do with the 'bots." I groaned as my head began to ache with the quantum leap in tension.

"You got it, groundpounder."

"I should have doubled the price. Why didn't she bloody tell me?"

Jay looked disappointed. "That's it? That's all you can say?"

"What!? I'm just talking business. Bigger business than I thought, but still business. What the hell are you talking about?"

"All I'm saying is maybe we don't need to make the corps that much more omnipotent than they already are. I'm talking about making a difference in this shitty world."

"Not my cause, kid." I never figured her for the windmill type. "Hey, I'm just a commodities trader. If you wanted moral guidance, you should have gotten the Utah Territories to bid higher."

She looked away from me and down the rest of her beer. "It's that easy for you, eh?"

"What the hell's up your yoni tonight?"

J.J. kept looking at the walls, as if checking on all the cables and power taps that hung around her like arteries in some gigantic artificial heart. "This isn't your kind of deal. Way too big. Too flashy. You should've shunted it to one of your SoCal buddies." The drive on her pod began to clank like two skeletons fucking on a tin roof.

"Look, I'm tense enough about this deal, I don't need you running me down."

"I'm just being honest. Somebody has to try to balance out your little pumptoy."

"Honesty," I snorted. "Right. You want it to have something to do with her, but it doesn't." I think we were both surprised I could choke that one out with a straight face.

"Shit. We both know if I'd come to you with a bomb like this, you would've hustled me off on some other sucker."

She was right. I did the only thing one can do when faced wth an ugly truth. I denied it and got angry. "That squid interface has fried whatever brain you've got left."

"You'd think the older a man got, the farther apart his brains and balls would get." Jay was glaring at me now angrier than I had ever seen her. "I'm just sick," she spat. "Sick of watching you make a fool of yourself."

"Since when is my sex life your biz?"

"She's using you, you dumb old shit."

"Fuck off. Stella loves me." I sounded like I believed that, but I couldn't look Jay in the eye when I said it. Suddenly it was very important to study the ancient oil stains in the chipped concrete.

"You're so strippin' blind. She hates you. Figure it out, Sporto. She rewrites her history a dozen times a day. You've said it yourself. Whatever tale that fits the moment. She freed herself of everything from her shitty little past except you. As long as you're still alive, she can never forget what she was."

"You don't know what the fuck you're talking about. We're retiring together when this is all over. She wants us to take the money and run away. Maybe we'll even get hitched." Who knew where the hell that last bit had come from, but it worked. Jay looked like I had bounced a brick off her forehead. "Doesn't sound like she hates me too much, eh?" That's me, never too subtle to butcher a point.

J.J. just stared at me, long enough for me to imagine an atlas full of places I'd rather be. "So that's it?" she asked quietly, suddenly calm and distant.

Nothing makes you feel more like shit than winning an argument with a friend. "Yeah, that's it."

"You make a killing and just leave in a blink. No second thoughts, no regrets."

Another long silence. I pulled the rollup from my wristcomp, trying to decide which inventory to call up. Jay saved me the choice.

"You are such an asshole, Michael."

With a sudden lurch, she spun toward her worktable, reaching out and tugging my cylinder free of the scanning rig. She tossed it to me. "Everything checks out. The little shits are all here. You've got everything you could want in there."

I scrambled to catch the precious tube. "Hey! Careful with th—"

"Now get out."

I was about to complain about the rough treatment, but the

look on her face when she turned to me killed any hopes of conversation. Or even argument.

I turned to leave, but I stopped at the door. For a moment I thought I could feel her eyes boring into me, but when I looked back, she was poring over some new piece of equipment.

"Look," I began awkwardly. "I'm sorry if I—"

"Make sure the back door is locked when you leave." She didn't look up.

". . . Right."

"And an extra twenty for the beer."

I turned and closed the door behind me, hawking up some of the condensation from my lungs as I stepped around the bigger puddles in the back hall. Even before I opened the storm door out onto the alley, I could hear the pounding rain. It was going to be a shitty walk back.

The passage of forty-eight hours found me standing high on the muddy hill of Liztown. I had played here as a kid, back when it had been a city park. Back then we told each other the reclaimed quarry was an ancient volcano, and we picked through the gardens looking for dinosaur bones. Now I heard the streeter kids telling each other it was an old tac-nuke crater as they scrabbled around the bare rocks hunting rats. Like in every other city I'd ever seen, Vancouver's streeters had taken over every bare patch of ground within fifty klicks of the city center. Years ago, the long slopes that fell away from the quarry crater were covered in trees and tended lawns; now all that grew were cardboard and sheet-metal hovels, none of them over a meter and a half high. Sometimes I liked to pretend it was the war that did this, the refugees, the stray bombs, but no. The war had only given us an excuse to stop pretending.

From the top of this hill I could see a long way, even at this time of year, and it would take a long time for anybody to reach me through the maze. It was my favorite meeting place. I just hoped the laser sniffer J.J. had patched into my coat still worked after all these years. Of course, an old-fashioned type with a scope would punch a hole through me without any warning at all. Gods protect me from traditionalists.

Things were almost as quiet as I could have hoped. There was a black smudge out toward Granville Island, but no bleat of aging sirens. Some poor sap had forgotten to pay for his fire protection again. Things would pick up as soon as the fire spread to somebody who could afford the going rate. This town had slipped into the role of an all-cash/no-credit whore like a natural. Maybe underneath the thin coating of civil services and government programs all cities were like this, the true essence of urban existence. Survival of the fittest, and screw the rest. Vancouver had just lost the ability to shore up the facades of civilization.

At least she was still alive, a city without a country, selling her wares for those who could afford them and taking care only of those who paid their way in full. The shaggy, defoliated mountains, tops hidden beyond cement-gray clouds, seemed weary and brittle that afternoon, as if even they were getting tired of this high-wire act, of being pulled apart by jealous lovers. But Vancouver still sheltered us all. The warring states got their precious arms and goods shipped south, and the JapHan conglomerates had their beachhead. And here I was about to use her body again and then slip away before dawn. I just hoped nothing I did would hurt her. At least, not too badly.

I brought up my binoc and scanned the harbor. A carrier had joined the JapHan cruiser. A tap, and its rusty hull zoomed into sharp relief. I thought it might be the *Myoko,* or maybe that other one, the old tub they had bought off the Russians. With Kiev gone, I guess they had no need for a ship bearing the name. Whatever this ship's original ownership, she was now an extension of EastRim policy, and I tried not to get nervous at the two remora shapes of gunships sitting on her deck, their X-wings rotating slowly at standby, reflecting the gray sunlight like a dull pulse.

Gunships on standby, and the city filled with Whip soldiers on leave. It could have been a coincidence. And a herd of black rhinos could be discovered living peacefully in my butt. I zoomed back out and starting roaming the nearby streets, looking for portents among the blank faces of squat, sagging apartment buildings, most of them with boarded windows hiding overcrowded rooms. I was so paranoid, so desperate for some sign of support, that for a moment I thought I spotted J.J.'s pod, but a passing dronetruck blocked my view, and by the time it had passed, whatever I'd seen was gone.

A shrill set of whistles brought me back fast. Down below, through the oily fog from dozens of cookfires, I could make out the arrival of my benefactors. From the south side of the shantytown, two crammed Prowlers arrived, their six bloated tires nearly crushing a set of chipboard dwellings. Four WhiPs piled out of the first ATV, looking casually threatening. When a few seconds passed without any obvious reaction from the natives, a single soldier with a suitcase stepped from the second Prowler.

At the same time, from the north, a black linehound broke contact with the center strip and pulled up to the ridge of trash that served as a curb. The passenger door slid up and somebody eased out. It was difficult to tell much about the JapHan representative at a distance. It was like watching a shadow poured into a suit.

Now was the time for the second reason why I liked to do business here: I have lots of friends on the streets, some on their way up, some on their way down, but all of them tight. I whistled, and some of the streeters wandering Liztown became a little less random, closing ranks somewhat and hampering the movements of the Suit and the Soldier, forcing them to step over smoldering ashes and outstretched hands. I wanted to know how jumpy my little shoppers were. They weren't. Both reps were as professional as all hell, and the old crowd dodge didn't ruffle them a bit. They made their way quickly and efficiently up the trail of mud and broken asphalt.

In less than a couple minutes, the two bidders were standing in front of the small clearing that had suddenly appeared around me. This had been a cement observation deck in the old days; I gave them the outside edge, their backs to the city. The WhiP was some kind of Nordic genejob with those precise, sharp movements that only a nerve extension can give you. I guess the Protectorate had promised him a new heart to replace the one that was bound to blow before he reached thirty-five. I had no doubts this soldier could draw the weapon under his coat and blow me to fragments before I could complete a belch.

The JapHan was only slightly smaller, lithe and androgynous. I hear a lot of agents go this route; harder to get a handle on them this way. I don't think I ever wanted to love a job that much. I had him/her pegged for Navy Intel, probably packing enough psychware to tell how Oedipal I am by the way my eyes blink. Since these two were so obviously suited for this kind of thing, far more than a skinny old man like myself, I thought I'd let them start things off.

I didn't have to wait long.

"You have our property," growled the WhiP. So much for a subtle negotiating round. "I'm here to make sure it goes to its rightful owner."

"Please forgive me, but I think any claims of previous ownership are irrelevant." The Suit spoke in a dead neutral tone that didn't sound affected. It must have been one of the best if the JapHan government was willing to fork over for larynx surgery just to fit sound to fashion. "This gentlemen is not here to judge right of ownership, he simply has an item to sell and we are here to bid upon it. A simple business transaction, not a court of law."

I smiled. "Right. Now, if you have my finder's fee . . ."

Andro gazed at me with pathological rigor. "May we see the items, if you please." Even a neutral tone can tell you it would be bad to argue. I lifted the briefcase at my feet and held it out to them. It's not like there were many variables for me at this point; if they had agreed earlier to cut out the middleman and deal with each other, there was nothing I could do about it but fall over, bleeding. I muttered a brief prayer to the spite of nations and hoped Stella was right about my kevlar rep.

Things had gone quiet around us. The grubby kids had started to disappear with the first set of whistles, and now there wasn't even a scrawny dog to be seen. Nothing disturbed us except the occasional blast of wind. Nothing seemed to be moving except the clouds that rolled up against the North Shore mountains.

Nordic stepped forward and took the case, carefully studying it for traps. He turned his back on Andro, but by the time he unlatched the case and opened it, the JapHan officer had found the precise angle he needed to see the actions of his competitor. The two of them were sort of cute together when you thought about it. Do all warring countries reduce to rival siblings at the individual level?

The WhiP withdrew one of the small gray cylinders, examining and paying special attention to the etched Protectorate eagle at the top. He ran his fingertips back and forth across the engraving, and seemingly satisfied, he turned and grudgingly handed the cylinder over to Andro, who proceeded to slide it into a groove in the top of his wristcomp. Andro typed furiously for a little over a minute before nodding and replacing the item in its case.

He/she looked up; I've seen more lifelike cadavers. "The original seals have been breached."

Okay, so I knew this would come up, and I'd rehearsed a thousand times in my head, but it still didn't stop my sphincter from tightening into a singularity or remove the image of Stella's pale throat between my hands. "Of course," I grumbled in my best insulted pro tone. "You didn't expect me to effect a transaction without being assured of the quality of the goods. I represent both my client and you, and I have to make sure there are no attempts at fraud. You understand, of course."

Andro only raised his/her eyebrows a tiny notch in the face of my bullshit storm, but the WhiP settled things with a growl.

"They're all there. No duplications." How the hell he knew when even I didn't is something I never have figured out. The goon must have had one hell of a sensitive touch.

This seemed to be enough for Andro, and he/she nodded. "Then it is time to tender our bids."

Each of my lovely contestants held out data-spheres for me to check. Nordic's buckball was silvery gray, while the JapHan had decided to be aesthetically clever and deliver a bright red one. Taking a breath and trying to force down the dancing devil of greed, I reached out and snatched the fiscal-spheres from them, though it took me a moment to pry Nordic's out of his meat-cleaver hand. Since he looked like the one here most likely to just say, "Fuck it," and waste me on the spot, I mated the Protectorate sphere to my wristcomp first.

Sometimes even a professional has to choke back a smile. The sphere was nulled, no ID flag; it would pay out to anybody who accessed their accounts through it, and man, would it ever pay. I'd never seen a number that big outside of a deficit report from back when there was a United States. And the JapHan bid was a third more on top of that. Ah, to live in a perfect world and keep both, or even the bigger one.

With more effort than it would have taken to give up my firstborn, I handed the red BB back to the JapHan official. "Please tell your superiors that while your offer was more than generous, the Washington Protectorate was even more so. I'm sorry."

Andro actually frowned but said nothing, just turned away with perfect precision and slipped down the hill, dodging hovels and streeters like a figure skater. The WhiP bruiser gave me his best you-know-what's-good-for-you grin, hid the briefcase under his armpit, and bulldozed back to his ATV. I went to the edge of the hill and watched both parties withdraw from the arena while I worked on my breathing, the precious little buckball clenched in my fist.

And that was it. My last and biggest deal done, not with a bang but a sigh of satisfaction. No fanfares, no gunplay, no roar of the crowds. Just a happy idiot, sweating palms, and a datasphere worth more than I had made all together in my entire life up to this day.

Now all I had to do was gather up Stella, get the fuck out of town, and live happily ever after under a dome in NovaSibirsk or surfing the ruins of Hollywood.

The weather had closed in again by the time I made it back to the empty Lucky Lady; Lenny wouldn't be in for another hour or so. I wasted no time in dumping that hot little datball into the Blacknet, where it skittered off into all the laundering services I had arranged. That huge lump sum would be divided, subdivided, invested, divested, and deposited into thousands of dummy accounts before finally finding its way into twin portfolios in the Orbital Bank of Singapore.

It would take a couple of months to materialize and we'd probably lose about half of it in "handling fees," but at least this way we'd probably live long enough to spend some of it. A customer is far more tempted to track you down and try to retrieve his money if he gets a flag showing a billion or so showing up in your account with your home address on it first thing Monday morning.

That done, I went behind the bar and poured myself a celebratory vodka. I was enjoying the glow of frozen warmth in my throat when my wristcomp started humming through the bones of my forearm. I put down the drink with a sigh and keyed up the sender.

The message was short, to the point, and terrifying:

MICHAEL, GO TO GROUND. YOU KNOW WHERE.— Stiletto

I knew it had all been too sweet to be true. Now that the dream was up, I could wake up anytime. But no such luck.

I was still calm enough to try to convince myself that the distant rumblings I started to hear were nothing more than some of those winter thunderheads we'd been getting the last few years. But when the building shuddered from what could only have been a low pass from an X-wing chopper, it was time to go. Fast.

I had just turned to look under the back shelves for my old pack when a blast of wet wind slapped me across the back of my neck. I looked up into the mirror, hoping beyond prayer to see Lenny in a little early, or even better, Stella there, waiting for me to get us a ride down to the docks. But no, there could really be no doubt. I raised my hands slightly, to show that they were empty, and turned around slowly.

"Welcome to The Lucky Lady, folks," I called jauntily. "We're not really open yet, but what can I get you?" I was proud of myself; my voice didn't squeak.

"Michael Crow. You will come with us, please." Andro was back, and he/she had brought along a set of quints that could have been Nordic's Filipino brothers. They filled the double doorway and spread to block out the fake stained English windows. All had weapons visible.

Right now, all that was separating me from a short and unpleasant future was about ten meters of beer-stained hardwood and a dozen wobbly tables. I had to stall and find out what the hell had happened. "Of course," I replied sweetly, as Andro had made a request. "Do you mind telling me what this is about? I'm sorry, but I don't think I have any other goods your country would be interested in."

"Seventy-two minutes ago you completed a transaction with a representative of the Washington Protectorate."

"Yes." If she was stating the obvious, then this was all going down on the record somewhere, which meant I was completely fucked.

"Twenty-four minutes ago we received data through channels indicating the wreck of the vehicle containing the Protectorate representative and his driver. Both were dead from massive cerebral hemorrhaging. All the trade items were missing from the two containers."

"What?!" The news had the intended effect; my composure blew for a precious second. I'm sure my vital signs were playing across the insides of Andro's contact lenses. "I have no idea what you are talking about," I stated more calmly, at least hoping for some kind of discussion. Praying that there was some other way out of this, I slid my foot beneath the bar and tapped around for a few eternal moments before I finally flipped up the tiny floor panel and toed the recessed switch. "How could I have anything to do with some sort of traffic accident?"

Andro ignored me and cocked his/her head to one side, listening to the orders of distant superiors who must be monitoring this whole debacle. "The city council has revoked your Trader status. You are a non-citizen. You will come with us to the *Myoko*. No head trauma, there will be a neural dump." I swear those five giants had to duck the pine beams as they spread out to form a skirmish line. They came through the tables and chairs like icebreakers.

"Surely I can pour you a beer before you suck out my fucking brain." I reached out and grabbed the center tap.

Andro tried to scream a warning, but it was too late. With all my strength I yanked the tap down, breaking it off in my hand. I dove to the floor as the air exploded with a flash, a bang, and a hail of wooden fragments that used to be the front of my expensive carved bar. There could have been a scream, maybe a few shots in the bright eyeblink, I couldn't be sure: I was busy being struck blind and deaf.

Lying there on the floor waiting for my errant senses to return, I began to feel a burning in my side, but even as I acknowledged the pain, it began to fade. If all I was going to get out of this was a big splinter, I was happy. After lying very still for a number of very long seconds, and hearing nothing but a wet gurgle from the other side of the bar, I peeked over at the carnage.

In my business you hope this sort of thing will never happen, but you'd be a fool not to be prepared. The row of scattershells embedded behind the outside rim of the bar had worked like a shaman's charm. The rigged spigot had triggered the charges, and my attackers had run into a waist-high storm of Teflon-coated fragments doing twice the speed of sound. It wasn't a pretty sight, but then neither would I have been after the JapHan Navy got through with me. A chunk of something once human twitched a bit, then went still.

I noticed the blood dripping from my side and was surprised to realize that I could barely feel the wound. I was assuming shock, but when I dabbed away some of the seeping blood, I saw just how wrong I could still be. A silver sheen along the sides of the wound was barely visible in the smoky light spilling through the shattered windows. Everything had been for naught. Andro had gotten the last laugh; after all, I was as good as dead.

I had heard of this stuff from Intel guys during my stint. The silvery fuzz was a designer fungus with a hearty taste for certain kinds of nerve tissue. In an hour or so I'd be a drooling rag doll, my somatic nervous system destroyed, but still alive until some cybertech could dump out the quantum states of my brain. The wound had stopped bleeding; the silvered flesh had taken on a rainbow effect. I was dying like spoiled pork. I had maybe a couple more minutes before the fungus made its way into the flesh and started up my nerve trunks.

Under the bar was a very expensive bottle of brandy from the Gay Nineties. I had been saving it for something miraculous, like Stella coming back and settling down. I snapped the neck of the bottle against the remains of the bar and slopped the wound in that precious nectar. Pouring the rest of the bottle down my throat, I fumbled for my lighter.

At first I didn't feel a thing as the nearly invisible blue flame flickered into life from the hole in my side. It was fascinating, in a morbid sort of way, to watch my own flesh and blood sputter and blacken but not feel a thing. Silver angelflesh corrupted by the flames, redemption through the demon alcohol. Blue ghosts danced on my skin as if my spirit was leaking out through the wound.

I was scared I had waited too long, but then the cauterizing finally outdistanced the fungus and I screamed the song of the truly damned. I clawed through a lifetime that passed in a second, trying to make sure not a speck of fungus would remain in the wound and screaming damnation on Stella, Jay, Lenny, my long-dead parents and anyone else who might have killed me painlessly in my sleep but didn't. And then I folded up on myself, smothering the flame, and tried to stop screaming.

I lay in that fetal position for more time than I could afford, alternately whimpering from the pain and retching from the smell of my own cooked flesh. That heavenly brandy was very much less so on the way back up. The blinding agony kept me from giving in and taking the fatal luxury of passing out, but my body was exhausted, inert. Lying there, cheek flat against scarred hardwood, I managed to open an eye to an endless plain broken only by shattered glass and mold-covered peanuts. Bar debris old and new had grown as huge as boulders. I tried to hang on to the fact that I had to move, that more goons were bound to be here within minutes, as soon as they finished brawling in the streets for the right to dismember me. But I couldn't, not with everything looking so big and the pain pushing me down.

I could be safe here, I finally realized. For me to be able to see everything like this, my pain must have crushed me to insignificance. I could hide here among the wreckage while the giants crashed through the world above, always searching, always destroying, but never finding what they were looking for. Never finding me. I was too small.

A flicker of movement caught my eye. Silverfish, sensing a return to quiet, were scuttling up through the cracks, looking to see what the gods had brought. I tried calling out to them, hailing them in friendship so they could welcome me into the fraternity of the unnoticed, but my mouth wouldn't work. Despite this, one of the silverfish stopped and after twitching its antennae, my new friend scurried toward me . . . growing in size from ferret to dog to horse to All-Devourer.

Terror brought my other eye open, and perspective drove the monster down to a bug once again, but even the small creature wanted to steal my breath and it continued on under my sight, its antennae sampling sweat and bile from my lips. I was dead already, dead and bug food. The fungus had gotten through after all, and now it infested my brain, keeping me from slipping away from the pain. Keeping me here for the whole show.

The pitter-patter of little bug feet across my tongue finally provided the spark I desperately needed. Disgust did what will couldn't, and my body lurched and spasmed into life. The burning had done it. Too bad I bit down before I had the chance to spit out that fucking bug. I owed him.

Using what was left of the bar for support, I made it to my feet and stumbled into the back room, grabbing the medkit from the wall as I fell onto the couch. After fumbling about, I slipped a sheetskin patch over the scorched hole and slapped on enough painkillers to glaze half the goons in the city. In a few seconds, the pain had blessedly faded to a background roar.

Now I could think. I keyed up my files, transferring ownership of The Lucky Lady to Lenny, hoping he had been lucky enough to miss this shitstorm, and giving a month's paid vacation to my other employees. No need for anybody else to pay the price for my fuckup. That left me effectively broke until the WhiP money made it into my account, but it cleared up most of my loose ends.

A coded sequence left my data-spheres behind the wall so much acid-melted molycarbon. With that last track erased, I grabbed a wad of worn Canadian currency from the bottom drawer of my desk and teetered down the stairs into the basement just as the building rattled from a near miss.

I surfaced a few blocks away, just another drunk stumbling through the wet streets. Whatever tussling the WhiPs and Japs were engaged in was now hidden under the driving rain that wrapped itself around the city. It was cold and stinging, but at least it would mask any IR trail I might be leaving on the cratered asphalt. I could have been out there for only a few minutes, but you could have told me it was a weekend and I couldn't say otherwise. Every shadow was a soldier, every headlight washing over me was that long strobe of the rifle flash that has your name on it, every woman hurrying to get off the streets was Stella running out on me. Leaving me behind.

But I didn't lose it, not altogether. I had a plan, and it would take me to Stella. It had to. It might have been years since my gang days, but I could still steal any car with a door on it, even with the painkillers and freezing rain turning my fingers into sausages, even with the world blurring in and out of focus.

The second after I overrode the lux-cruiser's comp, I was lying across the front moldings and muttering a location to the nav before the door could even fold back into place. If I had been feeling better, I would have spared a thought for whichever suit had been stupid enough to park a glitzmobile like this outside. But what the hell, if you can afford a Hyundai, you can afford to lose it.

I'm pretty sure I blacked out, because by the time I sat up, the cruiser was halfway across the Hammock—a miscalculation that could have been fatal if either of the parties after me had enough sanction to block the bridges. Maybe they had, but were too busy blowing up each other's checkpoints. My original plan had been to abandon my borrowed vehicle on the D-town side of the bridge and lose myself among the streeters living on the unfinished and abandoned sections slung under the original Lion's Gate bridge. Instead, I had actually found a little good luck on this completely fucked day, and I could try gathering my wits before bailing out very near my destination. The Hyundai would take itself on a slow tour of the coastal mountain highway before running out of hydrogen.

Even though I had lucked out, I still had to push down my panic every time the thick thread of traffic lurched to a halt. I scanned the windows like the frightened fugitive I was, expecting the muzzle of a rifle against the shadowed glass, the impact of a rocket tearing the back of the car off, the rocking downdraft of X-blades above me.

As I neared the end of the bridge, I finally felt safe enough to peer up against the side window for a moment, trying to make out the spire of the church between the flickering of rusted girders and railings. But my urge to see what lay ahead for me was defeated by the pounding rain and the coming of night.

The courtyard of the old church was covered in a half-meter of seawater, and from the feel of the storm around me, I knew the wind would blow in another meter of tide. I was surrounded by twisted, sickly willows hanging low, bent from the wind and rain, tormented parishioners held back from worship by the stubborn asphalt under the water. I had lived just a few blocks from here as a kid, before things warmed up and the rising waters reminded us all what ice caps were for—when I still had a country, and this church still comforted the odd believer.

The gurgling in my lungs was getting so bad I could no longer hear the hissing of the rain hitting the water. Every exhalation was a gamble that I would have the strength to suck the air back in. I was drowning slowly but surely. Freezing water was pooling around my feet as I slogged through the salty mud. Cold was seeping into my marrow from above and below, making my bones ache and my muscles rebel at every movement. The urge to lie down and die had never been stronger. But not here, not so close. Not when I could see the tiny light from the spire above me. Stella was here. Waiting for me.

I don't remember slipping and falling on the stone stairs, but I found myself on my hands and knees, face hard up against the splintered oak that had once been carved doors, damp splinters tearing feebly at my cheek. From some cruel overhang, water splattered down my back and sank through to my skin. The cold dripped around my ribs and trickled into the hole in my side, dulling the ache but sapping what little strength I had left. I wanted to live long enough to worry about the tainted rainwater infecting the wound. I had to pant now just to get some oxygen past the gunk sloshing around in the fibrous bags that were my lungs.

Pushing myself back and looking for the broken handle to haul myself up on, I squinted to make out scrawled words on the door. Day-Glow sprayed on dark wood: "God Fucks Us ALL." Not God, pal, I thought. Just us fucking each other is all it takes.

Slowly, I hauled myself to my feet and staggered into the ruined church, nearly falling again in an ankle-deep soup of plaster, seaweed, and ratshit. The rats skittered away to their hiding places behind the broken boards. More of the hidden brotherhood. Rats, silverfish, and me, sitting one atop the other in a totem of thievery.

City light, scattered by the low clouds, bled through the doorway and broken stained glass to let me make out the wreckage of pews long ago scavenged for firewood. Up front was the altar, still intact and draped in what might have been a sleeping bag in better times. Of the sleeper there was no sign. I lurched forward, making progress until my rollup snagged on a rusted pew support. I tried for what seemed like an hour to tug it free, slipping into the water twice before I finally gave up and mustered the coordination to code the release on the wristcomp. It bleeped mournfully once and slipped into the water, still hanging from its darkening screen. Now I was truly alone.

I should've checked around before going up the spire, but my eyes were barely able to adjust enough that I could make my way to the stairs, or what was left of them, and I definitely had no strength to spare. Over the years I had carefully maintained the stairwell to be passable if you knew where to step, but you'd never have known it by looking at them. The climb was easier than I thought it was going to be: I must have made it in less than an hour. Healthy as a genejob, that was me.

I didn't know what the priest of this place had done up in this little spare room, but I'm glad he had it built. It had been the perfect hiding place for items too hot to keep at the bar. Now I was one of them. And Stella was the other.

When I finally managed to drag myself through the trap door, she was there. Waiting for me. Suddenly, it was all worth it. I would have Stella. She was curled up against the wall, nestled in the gapped planks and warped timbers, her shadow flickering above her in time with the small burner in the middle of the room. The blue flame was fed by a gas-line tap I had J.J. rig some time before. I started forward, hunched against the low ceiling. I shouldn't have bothered; once again the floor reached up to flatten my face. I decided to stop arguing with my body and crawled across the floor, tastefully decorated in the soggy paper and moldy blanket tradition.

I reached out to Stella and stopped, my hand quivering above her shoulder like a man afraid to test a mirage. This was how I had found her all those years ago. I'd returned to this flooded ruin from my childhood to look for fixtures that would fit in the bar. Stella was just another streeter, another war kid, but when she looked up that first time with her little jackknife in her hand, there was something there, a hunger, a desire that set her apart, a passion I wanted for myself . . . it was burned into my mind. It took two years for her to steal all I had to offer, and she repaid that with a percentage of her career and a taste of the fires that burned her.

And now she was here again. If I woke her now, would it be that same girl once again? Did I want that? Or did I just want her to need me again?

The room wavered in and out of focus, and I tumbled down the corridors of déjà vu. Was it now or then? Past or future? Was this happening now, or was I still at the beginning and being given a taste of what was to come? If I turned away now, would none of this ever have been?

But I was freezing to death, and she had the fire. I reached out to wake her, slipping between the cracks of then and now.

She was cold and stiff beneath the wet leather.

I think I screamed then. I don't know for sure, but some wounded sound filled the air and I was the only living one there. I pulled her over into my arms, hoping to see her eyes flicker open, but they didn't. In my grief I barely noticed the white, battered face and the slashed throat.

I barely noticed it wasn't Stella.

Oh, it was close; the hair was nearly identical, and the body had the right proportions, but whoever this girl had been, she wasn't Stella. The face wasn't quite right . . . not finished.

The girl's features were slowly shifting, so slowly that it took me a couple of minutes to decide I wasn't hallucinating, or at least not hallucinating this particular event. Her cheekbones and nose were sliding toward a perfect match for Stella. From the occasional slow twist of the dead girl's lips, I could only assume the same thing was being done for her teeth. I slid a shaking hand forward to back up my eyesight, but I snatched it away after a moment of contact. The dead girl's face was almost too hot for my cold-shocked fingers, and I swear the skin was humming.

And then I remembered Stella's army of dancing lights. They were still working for her, crafting a perfect stunt double for her death scene. The nanobots were shifting the calcium of this poor girl's face so that anybody examining the body would be sure they had the thief they were looking for. In a few hours, the girl's DNA would probably match Stella's along the key ID strands. There was no stand-in for me. Maybe Stella had forgotten to tell me this was a Bring Your Own Corpse party. Maybe there were only enough 'bots to work up one double at a time. Maybe Stella knew I wouldn't let some poor slob die for me.

That was the tree that broke my back. The last joke in this parody of a relationship. I collapsed over the busy little body. For a few seconds I drew what little comfort I could from the pseudo-Stella, hell if the real thing was going to show up for a kiss good-bye. And when I looked up again, I spotted the final prop for my pathetic little tragedy. Beside the body was a small box I had seen so many times during the war. A detonator.

I laughed and coughed up warm, metallic water.

It was too perfect, and I had played my part to the hilt. Stella broke the first rule of thievery, coveting what she stole, and now I would take the fall for it. It was just like her. It was just like me.

They would have to be coming soon; she would have had to betray our last secret for all this to work out. Why go through all this trouble if the people hunting her weren't going to be here to tie up the loose ends?

Did she know I would be that weak when I got there? That ready to give in? I don't know how she could have, but she did. The world always twisted to meet her ends, one way or the other. I could hear her years later, retelling her version of this day, sniffling in the arms of another fool; she would be in close and finishing the tale with her mantra, "It all just worked out that way."

I had been wrong about that hunger behind her eyes. I had thought that by feeding it, I could take some of it as my own, that she would share it with me willingly. It was only for her. It always had been.

If I had anything left in me, I might track her down, exact some kind of vengeance. Give her another chance. Slap her bloody. Let it all go to have her again. But I was empty and trapped. They had to be coming. Had it been this way for Warren and Paco at the end?

It was too late to change the pattern, but it all made sense now. Stella did love me, in her own way. She had trusted me to do this one last thing for her. She had let herself need me. I would press the button for her.

There was a crash from below and the splash of many feet.

At least I would finally be warm.

With love in my heart, I stretched out for the detonator.

The incendiary charges went off before I could reach the button, and my world became flame. I tumbled back from the blazing hole where the center of the loft had been. Screams from below took up the song from where the first explosion had left it throbbing in the air. The body, Stella, slid away and fell through the hole. I cried out and tried to grab her hand, but I was too late. She was gone into fire without me, and I just couldn't make myself dive after her. Fire began to dance through the cracks in the rotted walls. Between the water-drowned membranes and scorched air, my lungs finally gave a last buzz of warning through my chest and packed it in. I stopped coughing. I stopped breathing. I was free.

And then Stella was back. I could see her dancing in the flames shooting up through the floor. This was truly Stella, her sharp edges twisting and slicing through the air, never stopping, always perfect. She reached out for me and I tried to take her hand, but my hand wouldn't obey me, choosing instead to bat uselessly at the flames taking root in my clothing. Inside I laughed and fell slack, waiting for Stella to reach up and around to embrace me, but the old wall suddenly exploded inward and Stella reared back. I would have called her name but there was no air in my throat and despite the flames, it was growing dark.

It wasn't Stella who finally reached out and took me up, but an angel. A Great Spirit, all burning steel and icy breath. A MechaMadonna riding a carpet of screaming devils and reaching for me with arms hard as stone. My life replayed itself in endless loops across her chromium body: sad parents, sweaty backseats, dead dogs, virtual dollars, choking soldiers. Frost blasted out from her holy womb and the flames fled from me. She came for me and I was afraid. Her claws grasped at me with brutal efficiency; she didn't have to be gentle, I was already dead. The devils screamed louder, and we fell into the darkness. Maybe she was just delivering me to hell.

I thought I felt rain.

I can never clearly remember J.J.'s pod crashing through those burning walls back in the church, but she remembers for me. In never-ending detail. I guess I have Jay's number. I hope I can make it work for her.

It's been a couple of years now and I have another bar, The Iron Lady, here on the outskirts of Guinea LowPort. It's a good place. Jay still tinkers. I keep a finger in the business, more to get back stolen goods for friends than anything else. We stick to what we know, even though we have enough to buy our own dome in Yakutsk. Stella never did claim her half of the money. I guess her little slaves were enough for her.

Even old Vancouver survived, with a few more scrapes and bruises. The WhiPs and JapHan are still doing everything you do in a war except declare. It looks like the Protectorate has finally removed all the booby-trapped wrecks from Seattle harbor. Unless the Japs blow the whole thing up again, it should take the pressure off my old town. I've even heard talk of repatriating the old whore. I'll believe it when I see it; maybe in twenty years or so, when I can move back.

Our disguises are damn good; I've had so many alterations I'm five centimeters taller and a white man. My grandfather is rolling in his grave up north, I'm sure. My lungs are actually made out of flesh now, and I get colds again. I guess nothing is perfect. J.J. finally caved in and got some legs cloned and grafted last year. They look incredible. Hell, with all the money lying around, she could have gotten a new pair every day of the week.

My nights are occasionally interrupted by nightmares. Sometimes I dream that my lungs are full of water and rusting. Sometimes it's just wave after wave of fire and singing. Sometimes I dream Stella is immortal and she rides down from the moon in her perfect body to mock me on my deathbed. Whatever else comes up, though, I'm very careful not to refer to my former life or name, ever. J.J. thinks I'm still afraid of the WhiPs tracking us down.

She's wrong.

It's Stella I'm hiding from. Someday, she'll need another favor.

THE GAUZE BANNER

Eleanor Arnason

A Hwarhath *Lying Myth*

Translator's Note: *The following purports to be a modern-day version of an ancient myth. There is no question that this version of the story is modern. (Notice the references to galaxies, singularities, holograms, and the people of Dirt.) However, no earlier version can be found. The story belongs to the category of lying, or invented myths.*

The hwarhath *do not consider such myths to be blasphemous or heretical. In their opinion, the mind of the Goddess is unknowable and her behavior often impossible to explain. Therefore, any story or explanation may (or may not) be true.*

Though the hwarhath *do not ban stories for religious reasons, they believe art should be decent and lead people in the direction of good behavior. Their various governments are perfectly willing to ban stories that seem destructive of public morality.*

Beyond question, "The Gauze Banner" is a candidate for censorship. It contains at least three elements that an ordinary hwarhath *reader would find offensive or disturbing: (1) the ambiguous gender of the Goddess; (2) the explicit description of her as a hermaphrodite, which can only be described as shocking, at least to a* hwarhath; *and (3) the argument that the*

Goddess is not responsible for hwarhath *sexual mores and therefore, implicitly, that* hwarhath *sexual mores are arbitrary.*

The story has not been banned so far, probably because it came out in a small edition done in ink on paper and distributed via a not-entirely-hidden network of avant-gardists, freethinkers, and people with unusual sexual interests. In recent years, hwarhath *official society has ignored this kind of underground as long as the people involved keep quiet and out of sight. No electronic version of the story has appeared, nor is one likely to. In all likelihood, this translation will reach more readers than the original, and "The Gauze Banner" will be better known on Earth than on its native planet.*

This story takes place early in the era called Unravelling, before the formation of the system of alliances that led (centuries later) to world government.

As yet, there were no groups of families tied firmly together, no great armies, no leaders such as Eh Manhata, known forever as the Bloody Sword of Eh. There were only separate lineages, none large, all more or less equal, quarreling and skirmishing on a wide, flat, dusty plain.

Into this age of petty violence the Goddess came one morning early in summer, stepping out of a clear blue sky. The moment she landed on the plain, she turned into an old woman dressed in rags, carrying a heavy bundle. She didn't come in response to the Unravelling, which she probably had not noticed, but out of curiosity, to see what was happening in this particular world.

As to why she chose to become a beggar woman, who can say? Those who have true power need not worry about the appearance of power. She who wears the stars as ornaments need not put on jewels less bright.

In any case, she trudged along a road. On every side of her was the wide, treeless plain. A light wind blew up dust, which covered her, turning her gray fur white. Her mouth was soon dry. Her old bones soon ached. Hah! How interesting, the Goddess thought, and looked at the bugs that buzzed and hopped in the vegetation beside the road. At last she came to a bottle tree, standing alone. Its fat trunk and short branches cast barely enough shade for the man who rested there, along with his worn old riding *tsin.*

The man's name was Hai Tsa. He came from a small lineage in the south. His older brothers were quarrelsome bullies who envied Tsa because he was their mother's favorite, and for good reason. He was handsome, mannerly, decent, and generous, the kind of son every mother dreams of.

Once he was grown up, Tsa—like all other boys—moved from the world of women into the world of men, and his brothers did everything they could to make him miserable. He endured their behavior for as long as he could, thinking of his mother. Finally, the situation became impossible to endure. Hai Tsa left home and went looking for work on the plain. There was less opportunity in those days than later, in Eh Manhata's time, but a few of the quarreling lineages were willing to hire loose soldiers. Hai Tsa became a mercenary. When he met the Goddess, he was traveling to a new job.

The moment he saw the Goddess, emerging from a haze of heat and dust, Hai Tsa stood. He tugged at his sword, making sure it would move freely if he needed it, and shaded his eyes against the white noon glare.

Soon it was evident who was coming: a bone-thin, ragged old woman. Hah! That such a one was wandering, instead of being safe at home! He walked out to meet her. The Goddess, bent under her bundle, gazed up at him with bleary eyes.

"Good day, great-aunt," the man said courteously. "Can I help you with your bundle?"

"How do I know you won't steal it?"

"I'm poor, but not that poor; and if I wanted to steal from you, I could do it."

This (of course) was not true, but the man didn't realize he was speaking to the maker of the universe.

The Goddess refused to let go of her bundle. Who knows what may have been in it? Hai Tsa, acquiescing, escorted her into the shadow of the tree. "Settle yourself," he told the old woman. "Be comfortable." He pulled a water bag off his *tsin* and held it out to her. The Goddess drank messily, water dripping off her chin.

The plain is dry, especially in summer, and water has always been precious there, but Hai Tsa did not complain. His manners were excellent!

When she finished drinking, he asked if she wanted to eat. Not at the moment, she replied. He moved the *tsin,* so she would have room, and settled himself at the edge of the bottle tree's shadow. Now the Goddess noticed how lovely this man was, his fur as gray as steel, his eyes the pale yellow of petrified resin. Her withered old body responded to his beauty and kindness. Hah! She could feel lust between her bony legs and in each of her four thin, hanging breasts. But she could tell that he was a self-respecting man, who would never have sex with a woman unless his female relatives told him to fulfill a mating contract; and she, in her present form, was past the age for breeding. Still, he was beautiful to look at, his fur dappled with sunlight; and she, being the Goddess, did not need to pay attention to decency or right behavior.

They remained under the bottle tree until midday was past; then he lifted the old woman and her bundle onto his *tsin* and led the animal along the road. In this manner they traveled through the long afternoon. The Goddess fell more and more in love.

When evening came, the two of them made camp. The sky darkened. Stars appeared, and then the pale, shining band of light that is called the Banner of the Goddess. They ate food from the man's supplies. Tired from his long walk, he went to sleep. Gathering her bundle, she stepped into the sky.

There she changed her appearance, becoming a man of extraordinary beauty. Her rags became armor. Her bundle became a well-fed, glossy *tsin*. That done, she grabbed a spiral galaxy. In her hand, it became a mirror rimmed with light. She admired her new face, which was broad and dark, with eyes the color of a summer sky and large, handsome ears. Excellent! the Goddess thought. No man could resist her now. She returned the galaxy to the place she'd found it and led her new animal onto the plain.

Being the Goddess, she was not bothered by such things as coincidence, but she knew that some of her creatures were. Hai Tsa might be suspicious if he woke in the morning and found his ancient female traveling companion had been replaced with a beautiful young man. Therefore, she went ahead of him to the war camp that was his destination. The war leader hired her. When Hai Tsa arrived, there she was among his new comrades, like a diamond among pebbles. Of course, he fell in love.

Because she was not interested in quarrels at the moment, she made sure the other men did not notice her beauty. Hai Tsa had no rivals. In almost no time, they were sharing the same tent.

Now Tsa discovered something unusual about his new lover. Though the man had ordinary-looking genitalia, he did not have erections. An old injury, the Goddess explained. It no longer bothered her; and she had learned other ways to give and gain pleasure. Hai Tsa looked dubious. She placed her hand on his erection. "This is a fine thing you have; and I'm sure you are proud of it, as no doubt you ought to be. A penis is one of the more entertaining objects our Goddess has devised. But her universe is rich. She did not stint. Nor does she lack imagination. Most of the time, she has provided us with more than one way to do a job or reach a destination."

If you are thinking the Goddess is vain, maybe so, though this speech might be a joke. The Goddess is famous for her sense of humor.

In any case, the two of them made love. Her hands were skill-ful, and her tongue was in no way short of miraculous. Hai Tsa had never enjoyed a partner more. They fell asleep tangled to-gether, the air around them redolent with satisfied desire.

Why had the Goddess, who can do anything, failed to give herself a working penis? Maybe as a joke, or maybe to make this romance more interesting. Or maybe because she had fallen in love with Hai Tsa while in the shape of a woman. In order to win him, she had to become male, but it's possible that she was not entirely happy with this transformation.

Whatever her reason, her decision caused no trouble. As she had discerned, Hai Tsa was proud of his male member, which was large and capable. It didn't bother him that he was the part-ner entering rather than the partner being entered, once he was sure the Goddess was equally comfortable. Initially, he'd been afraid that his lover would turn out to be touchy and difficult about her—or rather, his—incapacity. In addition, a natural feeling of sympathy made him unhappy, and even queasy, when he thought of what the other man could not do.

The Goddess turned her attention to another problem now. She was a warrior, and the band she had joined was preparing for war. But she had no interest in killing any of the beings she had created. Maybe her lack of interest in violence was due to the incomplete nature of her male guise, or maybe it was simply that she was in the mood for making love rather than war. In any case, she had to come up with an excuse for not killing men.

She thought for several days as the camp packed. Nothing oc-curred to her. Finally, on the last evening before they were due to leave, their leader complained that he had no proper flag. The Goddess was leaning against her lover, gazing up at the starry sky. Hah! she thought.

The next morning, she rose before the others. As soon as the last star faded from sight, she reached up and grasped her banner, pulling it from the sky. In her hands, it became a flag of fine white gauze that had even now—in the bright light of sunrise—a glow of its own. How lovely, the Goddess thought as she folded the material. What excellent work!

She took the banner to the leader of their band and offered to become his standard bearer.

"Isn't that an unlucky color?" he asked. "Bones are white."

"And snow," the Goddess said in agreement. "Also clouds, waterfalls, the foam on the ocean, sunlight at certain times of day, and many stars. Are these things unlucky or ominous? In any case, this isn't pure white." She unfolded the banner. The leader could see that the material was full of dim gleams and sparkles: blue, red, orange, yellow, even green.

"I assure you, it will bring good luck," the Goddess said.

Something about her made the leader wonder if this was an ordinary warrior. He agreed to use the flag.

You may wonder why the Goddess decided to pull her banner from the sky. After all, there is no limit to her power: she could have turned anything into a flag or made a flag out of nothing. But if you look at her universe, you will see that most of her work is slapdash. As a rule, she makes do with whatever is close at hand, and changes things as little as possible. Does this mean she's lazy or lacks imagination? Who can say? She is the Goddess.

For the rest of the summer, she rode with the war band. When they fought, she was the standard bearer. She never had to defend the flag she carried. Something about it kept enemies at a distance, or maybe it was she herself. In battle, her extraordinary beauty became visible to everyone. No one wanted to strike a man whose dark fur seemed as lovely as night, whose armor glittered in an uncanny fashion, whose banner—held aloft and flying in the wind—was like a flowing river of stars.

When the fighting ended, her appearance became ordinary again. The various warriors remembered what they'd seen only dimly. The man must be touched by battle-frenzy, they decided. Rage and fear transformed some people in such a way.

After a while, the Goddess became tired of pulling her banner out of the sky every morning and putting it back every evening before dark. There had to be a better method. She made a box: flat, square, and covered with a black lacquer that seemed as deep as space. In modern times, we would call the box a teleportation machine or a singularity or some other thing that twists the ordinary rules of physics and fiction. In those days, it was merely magic.

Every morning at sunrise, the Goddess opened the box and found the banner neatly folded. Every evening she made sure the banner was in the box. When the sky turned dark, there the banner was, shining overhead. A neat trick, the Goddess thought.

Summer became autumn, though the autumn rains held off and the plain was still dry enough for war. The Goddess continued to enjoy making love with Hai Tsa, but she was beginning to wonder how the rest of her universe was doing. She was especially curious about a world named Dirt, inhabited by almost hairless people with perverse habits, though they were (she had to admit) ingenious, especially when it came to getting into trouble. She decided to visit Dirt, leaving her present body behind. As lovely as it was, it would be conspicuous among the hairless people of Dirt.

She told Hai Tsa she was going to sleep. "I don't know for how long. Don't worry about me. I'll be fine. Leave me alone. Don't try to wake me, unless a serious emergency comes forward; and don't touch my banner or the box that contains it, no matter what dangers might come into view."

Hai Tsa agreed to all this. The Goddess went off, leaving her body apparently asleep. What happened on the world of Dirt is not part of this story, which is going to stay with Hai Tsa and his comrades.

After the Goddess had been asleep for several days, the warriors began to discuss her, or rather, him. Surely this man was a magician or diviner. The white banner was unusual; so was the sleep into which their companion had withdrawn. Hai Tsa listened and thought. According to rumor, magicians and diviners had unusual sexual habits. Some were insatiable and had huge organs, often oddly shaped. These were usually magicians rather than diviners. More often, the behavior of holy people went in the opposite direction. They were moderate in their sexual lives, or entirely abstinent. Rather than exaggerated sexual characteristics, they bore traits that seemed to lie somewhere between the sexes: flat chests for the women, small genitals for the men. So this story tells us, though not all stories agree.

Hai Tsa's lover was not abstinent. Nor could he be called moderate. But surely impotence was a sign of something. Hai Tsa felt doubtful and uneasy. To have a magician for a partner! This had to be dangerous! His mother would not approve.

Nothing more happened for a while. The Goddess continued to sleep. Her comrades continued to gossip.

Then a scout came in with disturbing news. Another band, much larger and belonging to a hostile lineage, was coming toward them. They would have to fight.

"We need the banner," the war leader said to Hai Tsa. "Wake your lover."

He tried. Maybe he was timid, or maybe the Goddess was preoccupied. In any case, he could not rouse her.

"Open the box," the war leader said.

Hai Tsa tried to argue, but the leader would not listen. Their situation was perilous. The banner was clearly magical. If they did not have it, they would be destroyed.

Finally, Hai Tsa capitulated and opened the box. The banner lay inside, shining like a starry night.

"You will be my standard bearer," the war leader said.

Reluctantly, Tsa lifted the banner. The wind took it at once, extending the gauzy fabric, undoing every fold. The morning sunlight made it glitter, or maybe it glittered by itself. The band rode out, Hai Tsa beside the leader.

The battle was at the ford of a river, wide and summer-shallow. The two enemy war bands met in water, between low banks overgrown with rust-brown vegetation. Swords flashed in the sunlight. Men shouted. *Tsina* screamed. The white banner shone as usual, but this time the opposing soldiers were not afraid of the warrior who carried the banner. Hai Tsa had to defend himself, drawing his weapon.

Blood spurted. Soldiers fell. *Tsina* reared, lunged, and turned. At last, the banner made of gauze went down, its pole hacked through. Hai Tsa leaped into the bloody river water and pulled the fabric—drenched, torn, and discolored—out from under a *tsin*. The leader of his band protected Tsa as he regained his saddle.

Something of his leader's frenzy came into Hai Tsa then. The sodden banner over his knees, he rode against the enemy, yelling like a demon or a ghost. His comrades followed. Their opponents were driven back, out of the bloody river, onto the dusty plain. So the battle was won, while Hai Tsa's lover slept.

Tsa and his comrades returned to their camp late in the afternoon, leaving guards at the river to make sure their opponents did not return. As night came on, Hai Tsa examined the banner, trying to think of a way to repair it. But the delicate material was in tatters, and blood had dimmed its glow. How was he going to explain this to the sleeping magician?

Close by him, a fire burned. Around it, his weary comrades cleaned their armor. At last, when Hai Tsa had given up hope of repairing the banner, one of the other soldiers glanced up. The man cried out, his voice sharp with fear: the sky was cloudless, but no stars shone there.

The world of Dirt has a companion that lights its sky at night, but the world of the *hwarhath* is moonless. Without their home galaxy, the night sky was black. Of course the man shouted in fear, and so did his comrades, when they realized what had happened.

Hai Tsa looked at the banner in his hands. Dirty as it was, he could see that the fabric gleamed dimly; and there were sparkles in it, dull and almost colorless, that reminded him of stars seen through haze.

What a magician! This person, his lover, had taken the Banner of the Goddess out of the sky and made it into a battle flag. Now they, through their folly, had ruined the banner and turned the night sky black.

He told his comrades of his suspicions. They examined the torn banner, observing the dim glow and the dull sparkles. Yes indeed. This looked like the band of light that made night tolerable.

"We have to do something," the war leader said.

"Kill the magician," suggested one of the soldiers. "Otherwise, he's likely to kill us when he wakes."

"No," said Hai Tsa.

But his comrades hurried to the tent where his lover slept. They pulled back the flap and looked in: the Goddess was still fast asleep, a lamp hanging from the pole above her, lighting her dark body, naked except for a blanket that she'd mostly thrown off. Something made them reluctant to go any farther, though she looked like an ordinary man at the moment. The leader dropped the tent flap and led his comrades back to the fire.

"You are the standard bearer," he said to Hai Tsa. "And the magician is your lover. This is your responsibility. Put that thing back in the sky."

"How can I?" Tsa asked.

"Throw it," suggested a soldier.

The leader nodded in agreement. Hai Tsa balled up the fabric, trying to make it into something that could be thrown, and tossed it up, knowing that this was impossible. He wasn't magical. The banner wasn't going to make it into the sky.

As soon as the ball of fabric left his hands, a gust of wind caught it. The ball unfolded, becoming a banner once again, and floated on the mild early autumn wind, just out of Hai Tsa's reach.

"Jump! Grab!" the leader cried.

Everyone obeyed, but no one could reach the banner. Carried by the wind, it drifted over the soldiers' fire. A draft of hot air took hold of it. The gossamer fabric twisted and fluttered, dipping toward the fire. The soldiers cried out in horror. The banner burst into flame. For a moment, the fire was too brilliant to look at. Then the banner was gone.

Hah! The despair the soldiers felt! Nothing remained of their home galaxy except tiny ashes floating in the wind, though their world was somehow spared, as was their sun.

How did this happen? Our world and sun are part of the galaxy, as everyone now knows. They should have been consumed along with everything else. But the Goddess can do anything, and this is only a story.

"You have certainly made a mess," the leader said to Hai Tsa.

"I did what you asked."

"I didn't ask you to burn the Banner of the Goddess."

"Shouldn't we make another effort to kill the magician?" asked a soldier.

Everyone went back to the tent, but no one could manage to go in.

"We could burn the tent," said the soldier who was most intent on killing the Goddess.

"This person has clearly surrounded himself with magical protections," the leader said. "We aren't likely to be able to get through them. The best thing to do is leave. But someone has to stay behind and explain what happened. You, Hai Tsa. The magician is your lover. Maybe he'll forgive you."

"Hai Tsa will run as soon as we're gone," another soldier said.

"We'll chain him," said the leader.

The *hwarhath* have never kept prisoners for long. But sometimes in the old days, it was necessary to keep enemy soldiers safe until they could be questioned. In addition, there have always been men who find it amusing to cause other men humiliation and pain, and such entertainment requires prisoners who are—for the moment—alive. Because of this, most war bands used to carry chains.

They had a smith, a fine craftsman, who fastened a circle of iron around one of Hai Tsa's ankles, then attached a chain that ended in a long spike. This spike the smith drove deep into a tree at the edge of camp. The chain was long enough that Tsa could move around and relieve himself on the far side of the tree. His comrades meant no cruelty.

Dawn came. The soldiers struck camp. Hai Tsa watched, sitting under the tree, which was a *halawa*. He recognized the scent.

They worked quickly and were done a little after sunrise. The leader came over to Hai Tsa's tree, bringing a bag of water and a loaf of bread. He laid them down.

"We can't leave any tool or weapon," he said. "You might be able to use them to get free."

"What if a wild animal comes?"

"You'll have to deal with that situation as best you can. I have nothing against you, Tsa. But maybe if the magician has you, he won't come after the rest of us; and maybe he'll forgive you, since you have been lovers."

"Forgive me for destroying his banner and turning the night sky black? Does that seem likely?"

"No," said the leader.

The war band mounted and rode off in silence. Nothing remained of the camp except the magician's tent and Hai Tsa under the *halawa* tree.

As the day brightened, he glanced up and saw that the tree had fruit, dark red in color, which meant it was almost ripe. Tsa stood and grabbed, but the fruit was out of reach. Fortunately for him, great knobs of growth dotted the trunk. Even wearing a chain, he was able to use the knobs as a ladder. Climbing up to the lowest branches, he gathered several pieces of fruit.

Back on the ground, he tried one. It was in exactly the condition he liked: the flesh hard, but also juicy, the flavor an intermingling of sweet and sour. He ate the fruit with enjoyment, drank water, and examined his chain. It was well made; Hai Tsa could not think of any way to escape from it.

What should he hope for? His lover to awake? Or other soldiers to come, who might free him, but were more likely to kill him?

He tore off a piece of bread and chewed it, noticing how hard and tough it was. What had he done to deserve this fate? Chained to a tree in the middle of nowhere, waiting for something—a soldier or an animal or a magician—to end his life.

Maybe he had picked the wrong lover, or obeyed an order he should have refused to obey. Maybe it had been a bad decision to leave home. A man is always best off when he has senior relatives to tell him what to do. Though his senior relatives, his brothers, were malicious bullies.

None of this seemed sufficient. Maybe he hadn't taken a single bad step, but rather a series, which led finally to this tree. Or maybe there was no reason or explanation for what had happened.

Night came, the sky was black as tar. In the absence of a campfire, he could see a few blurry lights, which were nebulae or other galaxies, though he didn't know this. He was afraid to stay on the ground and climbed the tree trunk, settling into a crotch.

After a while, something came to the bottom of the tree. Hai Tsa heard it snuffling and scratching, then felt a tug on his chain. The animal was chewing on the iron links. Tsa braced himself. The chewing kept up for some time, and there were several more tugs. One almost pulled him out of the tree. Finally, the creature, whatever it was, went off toward his lover's tent. He could tell this by the sound.

All at once, Hai Tsa became worried. His comrades hadn't made a serious attempt to test the magician's spells of protection.

Would they be enough? Should he care? He remembered how the magician looked lying asleep, as lovely as always. Would it make his situation any worse if he warned the man? Or managed to distract the animal? Hai Tsa shouted and swung his leg, making his chain rattle. The animal ignored him. He shouted again and rattled his chain more fiercely. Maybe he moved too vigorously in doing this; he felt himself begin to slip and grabbed for a branch, slipped farther and found himself hanging under the branch. For a moment or two, he swung back and forth in darkness. Then he fell, landing on his feet. His water bag came after him and brushed his shoulder before it hit the plain with a squelching, leathery sound.

The animal, only a short distance away, paused and produced an interrogatory whine. Hai Tsa grabbed up the water bag. With his other hand, he gathered a length of chain, thanking the Goddess that his comrades had been so generous in the matter of extra links. He peered into the darkness, trying to see the beast; but it was sound that told him that the animal had turned and was coming toward him, snuffling and breathing heavily. Was it old? Or did it have a bad infection of the nose and throat? He waited till the heavy breathing had almost reached him, then swung the chain out and down with all his strength. It hit. The animal roared with pain, and Hai Tsa thrust his water bag toward the roar. Thinking it had found its enemy, the animal seized the bag in its jaws. At the same moment, Hai Tsa gave a shove, pushing the bag as far as he could into the creature's mouth. There was a stifled choking noise. He had a sense that the animal had stopped its advance, uncertain.

Before it had time to recover from its surprise, he wrapped his length of chain around the creature's neck, then shifted position so the animal was between himself and the tree. As soon as this was done, he pulled the chain taut. The beast struggled fiercely, but the chain was held on one side by Hai Tsa, pulling with all his weight, and on the other side by the long spike that Tsa's comrade the smith had driven into the tree. Neither end gave. The beast, in the middle, could not free itself. Nor could it reach Tsa.

The struggling grew weaker. The animal went limp. Hai Tsa continued to pull, though by this time, he was shaking and breathing as heavily as the animal had been before. Finally, he let go of the chain and fell to his knees, too weak to stand. After he had rested for a while, he crawled to the animal, listening before he risked a touch.

The body was motionless. No breath moved the chest. The mouth was still stuffed full of his water bag, and it didn't seem likely that any air could go in or out. He touched the creature's nose and felt no exhalation. He pressed the throat. There was no pulse.

Hah! The monster was dead! He was still alive!

He tugged at his water bag, managing finally to pull it from the animal's mouth. Sharp teeth had gone through the leather. Most of the water had leaked away. He drank what remained, then took his chain from around the animal's neck and crawled back to the tree. There he sat till dawn, drifting in and out of sleep.

When the sun came up, he looked at the animal. It was a rangy quadruped covered with rough yellow fur: a wild *sul*. The four legs ended in long claws. The large head had a mouth well provided with teeth. Hai Tsa felt a certain satisfaction, though the corpse would soon begin to stink, drawing bugs and carrion birds. Too bad no one would know about this battle.

As mentioned before, the Goddess has no problem with co-incidences. At just that moment, she walked out of her tent.

It wasn't his peril that brought her or a desire to learn about his battle with the *sul*. Instead, she came to find out what had happened to her banner. Like the home world of the *hwarhath*, Dirt had survived the holocaust, along with its primary. But like the home world of the *hwarhath*, it had lost its stars. The Goddess, looking up at a suddenly dark night sky, remembered that she'd left her banner in the care of certain soldiers far away. She returned to her *hwarhath* body, rose, pulled on a robe and went outside.

As is well known, the Goddess combines both male and female traits, but she seems to prefer the female, and when she appears to diviners, she is usually a woman. Maybe she had forgotten that this particular body was supposed to be male, or maybe she was preoccupied, wondering what had happened to her banner. In any case, she had reverted to the form she preferred. Although her body remained dark and powerful and lovely, it was now clearly female.

"You are a woman," Hai Tsa said.

"Yes."

The last couple of days had been difficult for Hai Tsa. Much of what had happened was impossible to understand. But now he found a problem that made sense. Destroying a galaxy was beyond his comprehension. How could he feel shame about something so vast? Having sex with a woman, on the other hand, was a crime of reasonable size. It fit in his mind, and he was able to feel all the proper shame, grief, and self-hatred. Hai Tsa curled up, his arms around his knees, and groaned.

"If I were you, I'd worry more about what you've done with my banner," the Goddess said.

He ignored her, busy with self-loathing.

At this point, she became angry. "Look up," she told him and pulled her robe open.

There was no way to ignore that tone of voice. Tsa lifted his head and saw four breasts, covered with fur and tipped with dark nipples. The two upper nipples oozed milk, which gleamed in the light of the rising sun. Horrified, the man glanced down and saw the Goddess's penis, which was erect and as thick (it seemed to him) as a war club. A second kind of liquid shone at the tip. Beneath the penis hung the Goddess's scrotum, like a bag well packed for a long journey. Hai Tsa covered his eyes.

"If you want to have rules about who you can and can't have sex with, I don't mind. The rules are not something I would have thought up, but they're interesting and seem to work. At least, you get into less trouble than those people on Dirt. But understand, your rules are not my rules, and they do not apply to me.

"Now, take your silly hand from in front of your silly eyes and tell me what you've done with all my stars."

"Could you close the robe?" he asked timidly.

She laughed and changed her body, her full breasts sinking until they were flat. Her genitals shrank. Her penis became flaccid. She was Hai Tsa's lover once again, entirely male.

Tsa straightened up and shivered.

"Now," the Goddess said. "Tell me what's happened. I left you in good condition, and I return to find you chained to a tree with a dead *sul* in front of you, and my banner missing. You seem to have accomplished a lot. But first . . ." She touched the *sul*. It groaned and got up on its four feet. "Be off," the Goddess told the animal. "I'm not in the mood to look at your ugly body." The *sul* made a whining noise that was either a thank-you or an apology and loped onto the plain. The Goddess spread her robe on the ground under the tree and settled there, next to Hai Tsa. Ripe fruit fell around her. Reaching out a hand, she touched his chain. The links fell apart. She gathered two pieces of fruit and offered one to him.

It was sweeter and softer than he liked, but one can't complain to the maker of the universe. He ate the fruit while telling her about the fate of the banner.

"What a stupid group of men," she said. "I told you to stay away from the box. I told you to keep your hands off the banner."

"We needed it, and we couldn't wake you."

"You should have come up with some other way out of your problem."

"That's obvious now," Hai Tsa said. "But you never told us you were the Goddess, and you never told us that the banner contained all the stars in the sky."

"I can't go around explaining everything to everyone. People usually don't understand me, anyway. I could tell you stories about those people on Dirt!" She stood up and stretched. "I suppose I'd better recreate the banner."

"You can?"

The Goddess gave him a look. "Of course."

After that, she examined the remains of the war band's fire. Hai Tsa watched as she crouched and poked, picking up handfuls of ash and sorting through them. Finally, she rose, holding something between two fingers. "This might do." She held up the object and blew on it, so it floated into the air.

The plain vanished, and they were in a forest of huge trees.

The Goddess looked vexed. "I thought it was ash from the banner, but it's ash from a piece of wood."

The forest vanished. They were back on the plain. Hai Tsa felt dizzy.

The Goddess crouched and continued searching through the remains of the fire. Once again, she found something, held it up and blew on it. Once again, ash floated into the air. This time it glowed brightly, and the glow spread into a network of shining filaments. The Goddess looked up, her expression pleased. The filaments multiplied and interwove; the network lengthened and widened. A mild wind was blowing, and the edges of the network fluttered, but it stayed in place above its maker. By now, the glow had almost vanished, except for an occasional gleam or sparkle; the network seemed made of thread rather than of light, and it was thick enough to cast a shadow over the Goddess.

She continued to watch with pleasure. Hai Tsa realized that she was like his old comrade, the smith. Each loved making.

The weaving ended. The network had become a banner, pale and sparkling. The Goddess held out her hands. The banner floated down. She gathered it into a ball and tossed it into the sky. It did not return.

"Did you have to remake it that way?" Hai Tsa asked.

"No," the Goddess said. "But if I'd made it out of nothing, it would not have been exactly the same, and people—here and on Dirt and in other places—would have noticed. The ash contained a memory of the banner, recorded in the manner of a hologram. By examining it, I was able to remake the galaxy as it was before."

Hai Tsa didn't know what a hologram was, of course. But he listened gravely, his head tilted.

The making of the banner must have taken longer than he'd thought. It was sunset now: the wide plain shone with ruddy light. The Goddess took food from her tent. They settled under the *halawa* tree and ate. When she was done, the Goddess said, "We'll wait till dark and make sure the banner looks all right. After that, it seems to me it would be pleasant to make love out here, under my stars."

"You and I?" asked Hai Tsa.

"Who else is present?"

"It can't possibly be decent to have sex with the maker of the universe."

"You aren't telling me you have a rule about sex with the Goddess? Whatever for? It's a problem that very few people encounter. And I'm beyond rules. I can do whatever I want."

"You may be beyond rules, but I'm not."

The Goddess made an impatient noise.

"Also, you frighten me," Hai Tsa added.

"I have not done a good job with this universe," the Goddess said. "It's full of small-minded people."

They sat without speaking for a while. The sky darkened. The stars came out, and the Banner of the Goddess was visible.

"It looks fine," said Hai Tsa after a moment.

"So it does." The Goddess touched him lightly on the shoulder, and he discovered that he was less frightened than before, also less concerned about religious and moral questions. He reached over and ran his hand down her front, which remained—thank the Goddess!—flat and male. Her crotch was male as well.

"Can't you do better than this?" Hai Tsa asked, his hand on the Goddess's penis. "If you can fill the sky with stars, why not come up with one little erection?"

She laughed and came up with an erection, and they made love. Afterward, they lay on her robe beneath the *halawa* tree. Stars shone around them.

"I need to go back to this other world," the Goddess said. "The one named Dirt. Do you want to accompany me? I'll have to change your appearance. The people there are almost entirely without fur."

"It sounds ugly," Hai Tsa said.

"You'll get used to it. What else do you have to do? You've lost your job, and if you stay here, you'll lose me as well."

"How long will this last?" Hai Tsa asked.

Being the Goddess, she knew he was asking more than one question. How long will this journey last? How long will we be comrades? How long will we be lovers?

"I make no promises," she told Hai Tsa.

He thought for a while. Lying next to her, he felt safe in a way he hadn't since he was a child with his mother. The feeling was illusory, he knew. The Goddess had no reputation for reliability. Still, it would probably be interesting to go with her, and she was right about his job. It was gone.

"Very well," he said.

She stood, holding out her hand. He took it, and she pulled him into the sky.

THE EXPERIMENT

S. N. Dyer

When Arkansas, Foxhole Jewboy, and Maynard G got separated from their squad in the jungle, the guys who didn't get lost weren't at all happy, because they were going to have to go back in and risk their asses for the two most worthless grunts that God and Uncle Sam had ever seen fit to inflict upon the U.S. Army.

Arkansas, everyone agreed, would be a loss, because he was the ultimate cool head and had made a habit of casually shoving people out of the way of certain death. Yeah, and there was that time he noticed he was stepping on a booby trap, so he just stood there dumb as a cow for the eight hours it took someone from Engineers to come and defuse it.

No, well, actually he'd spent the whole time complaining about the Army, and Nam, and telling everyone how *he'd* run things if he'd been in charge, so by the end of the eight hours, they would have shoved him off the mine if they could have figured a way to do it without getting blown up themselves.

So maybe Arkansas wasn't that big a loss after all.

No one felt much about the others, because they really weren't part of the unit. Everyone else here was black, or Chicano, or poor white trash, and these were college guys. Okay, college guys who had flunked or dropped out, knowing that was the end of their deferments, so not all that bright as college guys go. But a college guy really had to annoy someone in power to find himself humping a pack in Vietnam.

Foxhole had done it by telling a sergeant that the Constitution guaranteed his right to practice atheism—yeah, like *that* could be true. So he'd been sent to the jungle for being a loud-mouth, only he said it was because he was the only guy in the platoon who wasn't under the Commandment not to kill, the token non-hypocrite. He'd got beat up a few times before he learned to say it with a shit-eating grin so you figured it was a joke and laughed with him.

Maynard G had been such a royal fuckup and mouth-off that his choice had been the jungle or prison . . . and this despite the fact that his old man was big brass at the Pentagon! It would have been interesting to know just what he'd done, but he didn't talk about his past—well, not so you could understand it. He seemed to think he was a poet but he was too dumb to rhyme, and people pretended he was a good beatnik, like Dobie Gillis's pal on TV. He was always trying to buddy up with the Negroes and talk about race music, or with the Indians about mysticism, and he was always drunk and puking all over stuff, so there wasn't a guy in the unit who really gave a damn he was missing.

Sergeant Ira had to tell the lieutenant, whatever the new one's name was—they came and played soldier, let the sergeant keep them alive for a month, then hustled back behind the lines and spent the rest of their lives bragging about "my time in the jungle." This lieutenant had got into West Point because his uncle was an old pal of the President and the Senators, and with his accent, it was like having a Kennedy radio message whenever you wanted. Maybe he wasn't dumber than bricks, but two-by-fours and sheetrock probably had more upstairs.

"Gotta report, sir. Three men missing."

"Missing? You mean killed or something?"

"*Missing.* Like fucking lost, sir."

"How'd that happen? Don't you have maps or something?"

"Corporal Clinton got bit by one of those spiders, sir. Inside his shoe."

"The big yellow ones?"

"No, sir, the little ugly ones."

"The ones that can make your dick fall off?"

"Yes, sir, but it bit him on the foot."

"They just crawl in and bite you?" asked the lieutenant, beginning to wiggle his toes experimentally. So he didn't catch anything Ira said after that, because he was starting to feel these little itches everywhere, like maybe there was something inside his clothes. . . .

Dumber than drywall, thought the sergeant happily. In this condition, diapers from the Point would agree to anything without even listening. Some were tougher, and you had to tell them about leeches. "I assigned Hoffman and Morrison to help Corporal Clinton, and you know those two, they can't find their pricks in their pants."

It never occurred to the officer, in the middle of his phantom-insect hoochie-coochie, to ask why the sergeant had left two complete incompetents in charge of a valuable corporal, or to protest when the sergeant said no one started rescue missions for the missing until it was light.

Arkansas, the corporal, figured the sergeant must hate his guts, and he had no idea why. Didn't he give him the cigarettes from his K-rations—a nasty habit not at all good for you, he'd always remind him—and didn't he correct the spelling in the sarge's letters back home, and give him all sorts of suggestions? But he was sure, once they noticed he was missing, they'd come after him. After *them.*

It was dark, and Foxhole was gathering firewood. Everything was so wet and moldy it wouldn't burn, but Arkansas let the nimbicile waste a book of matches before saying, "Are you an idiot? A fire will just bring Charlie. And you, Morrison, throw away that reefer."

It really didn't matter much if Maynard G toked up or not; he looked high all the time. In fact, the corporal found him rather more coherent when stoned, and when they were both blasted, he actually seemed to make sense—which is one reason that Arkansas had quit drinking. The other was that he'd been promoted, and he thought he should set some kind of example for the guys with only one stripe. Or none.

"Morrison? Maynard? You alive?"

Foxhole looked over helpfully.

"He's still breathing. You know he hasn't eaten anything in three days?"

"Shit. You take first watch." Arkansas closed his eyes, ignored the pain in his foot, said his prayers . . . and jolted awake, hearing a cry. He swung up his rifle.

"Hey a hey. a hey a . . ."

Maynard G was jumping around.

The corporal kicked out with his good foot, tripping the other so he landed on his rear and shut up.

"What the fuck are you doing?" hissed Arkansas. "Advertising a fucking concert for Charlie? Why not a goddam searchlight?"

"I think a spider bit his ass," offered Foxhole, who'd been asleep too. It would explain things.

"I dreamed of the Thunderbird," Maynard G said.

"What?"

"Which Thunderbird?" asked Foxhole. "The wine, the car, or the ancient Sioux deity and numinous sky spirit?" Like it needed an answer.

"Now I am *heyoka*," Maynard continued proudly. "Now I wear my clothes backward."

"That'll make it hard to piss," said Foxhole. He was practical, for an atheist.

"And I have to do the *Dance Until Morning Dance*." You had to figure it sounded better before they translated it.

"I've done that. It's why I got booted out of college."

"And what good is being haywire, whatever, except to get us all fucking killed?" asked Arkansas. No one would have blamed him, or even asked any questions, if he'd shot them both and come back alone. But he knew that those two stripes meant his country had entrusted him with the lives of these two idiots.

Maynard smiled like one of those saints full of arrows—beatifically, they call it. Stupid, more like. In the moonlight, you could see that he had dreamy eyes and broad cheekbones, and he'd painted himself all over with lightning bolts in lipstick.

"Wow, you're The Flash," said Foxhole.

"I will be immune to gunfire," Maynard finished. And began to chant again.

"Great. Okay. Just take your fucking dance about a hundred yards over there and when the fucking VC call, don't mention you know us."

"Bring back some smokes and a hooker," called Foxhole.

Then Arkansas couldn't hear him over the jungle noises, but he knew Maynard G was out there jumping around still, remote now, like a TV test pattern. Maybe he really should have gagged the private and tied him to a tree. Maybe that's what a good leader would have done, but Arkansas was tired and hungry and his left leg was starting to look like a fire hydrant and he wasn't thinking all that good.

So he felt really bad when he woke again to the sounds of gunfire. It was dawn now, and he was snuggled in some greenery, and Foxhole was crouched down over him with panicked eyes.

"Shit," Arkansas whispered. The monkeys and birds and even the damn crickets had shut up when the gunfire started. They must have known Charlie ate monkeys and birds and crickets. He held his breath, waiting for the gunfire to end.

It did, and plain as the nose on Foxhole Jewboy's face, he heard, "Hey a hey a ho a . . ."

Gunfire started again.

"This time for sure," whispered Arkansas. Nothing he could do.

But then the gunfire stopped again, and Maynard G was still chanting. Arkansas thought for a minute that Maynard was doing the shooting himself, but he knew he'd heard more than one rifle.

"Goddamn," said Arkansas. This was so weird he had to check it out. So he got to his feet and limped as quiet as he could, Foxhole trailing behind him. It took two more cycles of gunfire for them to get to where Maynard G was in a small clearing. Three NVA were right in front of him, watching him dance, naked except for the lipstick. They'd put in a new clip, aim—and it was like the bullets just whizzed by him. Through him?

Arkansas could hear Foxhole, whispering to himself: "Shit. It works."

Bull. It must have been some stupid Charlie game, or maybe like the Sioux, they respected the totally insane, or else they hadn't had basic training and didn't know how to aim. But sooner or later, they'd have to get tired of wasting ammunition and either shoot him at close range or bash out his brains with their gun butts. Much as Maynard G deserved it, Arkansas was his corporal. He couldn't sleep at night if he didn't do something.

So he raised his rifle, braced himself against a tree, and fired. A quick round, economical. Foxhole dove for cover.

"Got 'em," Arkansas said, looking down at the other private, a sad grin on his face—and then his head exploded, raining red bits all over. Foxhole reached up to wipe off his glasses, and saw a fourth NVA come over to the corporal's body. For the gun and the shoes, he figured, and the rations. The man hadn't seen Foxhole. Maynard G was still dancing.

The enemy bent over Arkansas's body. His face was young, with glasses like Foxhole's, and he looked squeamish but started through the corporal's pockets. He found a can of C-rations, and his face lit up, so much like a kid's at Christmas that Foxhole didn't have the heart to kill him. He was aiming right at him, and the guy looked up and saw him and his eyes dilated.

Just a kid, Foxhole thought. We're both fucking draftees, and he'd rather be home drinking rice wine and screwing Mary Lou on the back of a water buffalo.

"Get lost." He waved, and the wide-eyed gook took off like a rocket.

The brass decided Maynard had been driven nuts by whatever'd happened out there. It would've been embarrassing to admit that someone *already* that apeshit had been given a gun and sent to fight for his country.

Foxhole knew a good thing when he saw it, and faked shell shock. The doctors seemed suspicious, but again it seemed better if whatever happened had been enough to push them both over the deep end. It wasn't too bad, walking around in pajamas all day—yeah, a little like Charlie—eating three hot squares, taking tranquilizers, and listening to schizophrenics talk to the walls. Occasionally a shrink would come by and ask Foxhole how he was doing, and a bit of rambling about dreaming over and over about Arkansas' blood bathing over him usually got him through this.

Army psychiatry, after all, isn't designed to make people sane. It's supposed to figure out who can be returned to the front lines, usually through a combination of encouragement and emotional blackmail. *You've abandoned your buddies. Aren't you a man?* That sort of shit. The ones who can't be cured might as well be dumped on their homes, or the institutions.

It was a cushy life, but it couldn't last forever. Foxhole was a quick study, and after a few days, he could have faked schizophrenia, but he wasn't about to—he might wind up in a permanent padded cell missing his frontal lobes, and he had plans for those frontal lobes.

One day they were all around the ward's only TV, watching an Armed Forces rebroadcast of *Shindig.* It was an important show—the two biggest rock-and-roll bands in the world, the Beatles and the Beach Boys, were going to jam. Even the schizophrenics, in their Thorazine haze, were gathered around the set. John and Paul and Brian had cowritten a catchy little tune called "Babes of Brighton," comparing the chicks of their respective countries. The sight of all those toothy grins and moptop haircuts made Foxhole queasy, and he looked away.

To see Maynard G in the doorway, facing the tube. His eyes were closed, he was swaying slowly to the beat, and he was singing. Only, the lyrics he was singing were a hell of a lot filthier than the ones coming from the set.

"Way to go," said Foxhole. He'd considered faking an Oedipus complex himself, but thought it was a little too blatant.

Next day they were shipped home. Well, not home, but at least the same continent. San Francisco, Letterman Hospital. They'd been volunteered for an experiment.

One of the shrinks explained it to them while he was checking their blood pressure and listening to their hearts and lungs. He was right out of medical school, so he remembered how to do all the regular doctor stuff that the analysts in charge of the ward had forgotten. He was in a perpetually bad mood because he'd served two years in Germany after high school—the Elvis route—gone to college on the GI bill, gotten a Ph.D. in neuropharmacology, gone to medical school, then discovered to his horror that he was drafted all over again.

"See, the idea is that you've got some kind of ego reaction to a combat experience, linked probably to an overprotective mother and lack of sufficient sexual identification with your father, who probably let your mom rule the house."

"Damn straight, all us Jewboys are castrated by our women," Foxhole said helpfully. "Right after the rabbi gets it started."

"Mother," said Maynard G. "Mother, I want to fuck you." These were the words he'd tacked onto "Babes of Brighton," and he sang them at the drop of a hat. Still, it beat "hey a hey a hey."

"Anyway," the doctor continued, "analysis takes forever. I

mean, do you know that all those old-fart psychiatrists have been in analysis for decades? How well can it work if it's never finished? But there's this drug, lysergic acid diethylsomething or other, that's supposed to show you all the stuff that's bothering you in one fell swoop."

"Will it work?" asked Foxhole.

"Hell, no," said the doctor. "Because all this Freud stuff is bullshit. The actions of Imipramine and Thorazine clearly demonstrate that all mental illness is biochemical in nature, and probably the only thing your mom did that was evil was give you screwed-up norepinephrine metabolism."

"Then why go along with it if it's all wrong?"

"Because it's do this, or do sick call in the jungle."

Foxhole thought about calling him a hypocrite, but instead, he offered to help with any typing or filing. Maybe he could make himself indispensable, so when the experiment was over and he was cured, he wouldn't get dropkicked back to Nam.

The drug wasn't bad. In fact, it was kind of fun. Everything looked bright and intense, or shattered like a kaleidoscope. Moving things left trails. And if you were lucky, you heard sights and saw sounds.

Maynard G seemed to enjoy it too, but it struck him as very religious. Well, no shit, what didn't? He held long conversations with God that the doctors wrote down in detail. Foxhole decided that was the way to go, and tried to, but he never got the hang of it.

"God? Is that you?"

"*Yes, my son.*"

"So, have you got a message for me?"

"*No, my son, a question.*"

"Well, fire away, your Yahwehness, ask anything."

"*Nu, can you get a good deli sandwich in this town?*"

You could. San Francisco had to be the best city in the world, Foxhole thought, like New York, only pretty. The army base was on the northern tip of the peninsula; in fact, the dinky little Spanish fort that started it all was nestled under the rust-red bridge. The weather was always room temperature, a relief after the jungle. Every afternoon, when things were starting to heat up, the fog would roll in, every afternoon differently. Sometimes it dropped down like a loving blanket; sometimes it rolled down like a furious, insubstantial tidal wave; sometimes it approached tentatively, tonguelike, through the spires of the bridge. When Foxhole mentioned that to Maynard G, the nut wrote a poem about it, remarkably filthy. In fact, Foxhole picked up a bit of spare change selling copies of the poem, and everyone agreed that if it just rhymed, it would be maybe the greatest poem ever. Maynard used his share of the proceeds to convince an orderly to smuggle in a fifth of bourbon.

They were given some day trips around the city with the doctor, "therapeutic outings" he called them. They understood he just wanted to get away from the base himself. Sometimes they went to museums—Maynard G climbed up into The Thinker's lap at the Palace of the Legion of Honor and refused to come down, which was fine with Foxhole. He didn't really like art now, because all the pictures were starting to confuse him and he'd get weird afterimages. That was happening more than he liked now, and at the strangest times, like he was on LSD when he wasn't.

It was happening to Maynard G, too. One day the ward TV was tuned to a Milton Berle special. Foxhole had been hoping to watch *Star Trek* instead, which he liked because it was such blatant military propaganda, and so cheesy with its hokey monsters that were always supposed to be bleeding green blood or turning bright colors instead of the shades of gray they saw. Anyway, they were stuck with Milton Berle instead, and not even their wardmates who had insisted on choosing it were laughing. But Maynard G was in hysterics. He kept pointing to the set and doubling over.

The next day, Foxhole caught up with him at breakfast. "What was so fucking funny?"

"Didn't you see? The show was in color."

The doctor dragged them off to Golden Gate Park one day. They wandered around near the Children's Playground, getting all sorts of weird images off the antique carousel. Then they headed out the Stanyan entrance to the park, looking for food. They found a place less than a block away on Haight Street, where for just a quarter, you got fish and chips wrapped in yesterday's *Chronicle*. They walked along the street as they ate, a quiet working-class neighborhood on the slide down, with old women wearing scarves dragging their groceries behind them in wire baskets, students from distant State College and the Medical Center, and the ghetto coming in fast from the north.

Maynard G had unfolded the newspaper and was reading only the parts with grease stains, which he had decided were messages just for him. The war will soon end in victory, President Kennedy promised. The war against poverty was going just as well. A couple of Peace Corps members had disappeared in Africa.

"Yeah," said Maynard. "I am the Peace Corps."

The great message in Foxhole's fish and chips, just for him, was the TV premiere of Marilyn Monroe's new comedy about a widow with five children who marries a colonel with four kids and they all move to a base in funny little Japan. "Why don't these old stars know when to quit?" he was asking. Maybe they could put her on the Apollo flight to the moon. . . .

Then he felt that weird buzz when the drug was kicking back in, and he looked up and the street was changing. It wasn't his usual kind of flashback, colors and patterns and such. It was like he was looking into another world, one where this street was crowded with cars and with people. Weird, bizarre people, like in a carnival, men and women both with more hair than a movie about Vikings, and dressed like gypsies and cowboys and marching bands. . . . And in a window of what was now a record store, he saw a huge poster of Maynard G, naked to the waist, with hair like Prince Valiant. And at a newspaper stand, the front page of the *Chronicle* with a couple of guys being dragged away by the cops, headlines about war protests, and a photo of a face with his own eyes smiling out between hair and beard like a rabbinical student.

He sagged against a building, and a nice old lady came down and gave him a Coca-Cola, telling them that her grandson was a soldier too and how proud she was of him. Then they went back to the Presidio.

The next day, they got the experimental medicine again. Only, Foxhole didn't like it this time. He was still frightened by the images yesterday on Haight Street, and now even the prettiest drug-induced hallucination seemed evil. The sun glinting off a spiderweb turned the spider into some Hollywood giant monster, without the dad from *Fury* to kill it and save everyone. The light fixture throbbing neon red was no longer entertaining—it was the heart of darkness, pulsing the end of the universe.

The whole room was breathing down on him, the air breaking up into atoms and streaming away into another time and space. Foxhole stood by the window and looked out at the Golden Gate. Fog was coming in high, then suddenly stopping and somersaulting down upon the bridge, some mad atmospheric jump.

Foxhole held onto a chair, which was also made of atoms. And he heard the voice of God. Laughing.

"Don't you see?" he asked the room. "None of it means anything anymore, because there are all these possibilities. We're nothing here, we're something somewhere else, but we don't really mean anything anywhere."

The doctor scribbled furiously, trying to keep up.

Foxhole looked at Maynard G. "Come with me?"

Maynard smiled. He was a bright, ugly yellow, some presentiment of a not-too-distant death by drink. "I'll be following soon enough."

Foxhole took the chair and smashed out the window, like the flowers erupting from Arkansas' face, and set glass and chair and tiny drops of his blood free to fly to the street below. Then, dodging the doctor's grasp, he was free too, free of restraint, free of the ground, free of the knowledge that everything is possible but it just doesn't mean anything.

As he went down, he saw the wall of fog tumbling above him, turning insubstantial, never reaching him.

"You know," he said, "you just can't buy a view like this."

Parameters of Dream Flight

Arlan Andrews, Sr.

Walnut-shaped, corrugated and convoluted, its serrated ridges and deep crevices throbbing ominously, the three-dimensional image floats in front of the meter-square displate screen. It is of an awful color, sickly near lavender, and the size of a human head.

"Looks like a freekin' prune or something," one tall, somber labcoated individual says gravely, nodding toward the pulsating image. His voice possesses a deep, resonant authority as he scrutinizes the detailed holographic display. Labcoat is pushing a broom.

"It's a human brain; the purple is just false color," the research scientist responds, tapping the screen. Her hand is suddenly immersed in the solid image, as if she is fishing for something within the shimmering transparency. She is red-haired and pretty and mature, all of thirty. Labcoated broomer is almost afraid the woman is about to remove a handful of bloody tissue, the illusion is so profound. "A lot of weird and wonderful things have come from deep within those folds of tissue."

At the sound of footsteps behind them, both people turn. Three men enter the room, the tattooed one recognizable as a fading, semifamous writer, the short bald one and the extremely large pale one nobody familiar at all.

"Careful what you say, folks. That's *my* brain," Hamish Pratt comments with evident humor as he strides through the doorway into the semidarkness of the instrumentation control room. The two people in the lab look at him, saying nothing. They do not comment on his trademark dark blue turtleneck sweater, nor on his dazzling white holosilk jacket, nor his full growth of white beard complemented by perfect white teeth, not even on the nonfunctional but aesthetic circuitry tattooed on his forehead, intricate blue and red mazes that droop down to surround his sky-blue eyes. Pratt is used to their reactions; his face and its decor are familiar to tens of millions of readers and viewers of his psych-phi thrillers. *Well, not as many millions as before, but maybe we can change that!* Smiling, he jerks a thumb toward the throbbing, wrong-colored, nut-shaped glob. "The first one thoroughly mapped by the magne-topograph."

"The MTG," the short bald man behind Pratt adds cheerfully.

"My agent," Pratt says with a shrug. The gorilla-sized pale man in the background stays silent, expressionless.

Pratt reads the awe in the labbers' expressions, both the woman and the broomer. Or is it simply *aw,* as in *aw, shit?* Taps himself on the chest. "And you're wondering, why this guy? Why *his* brain on the mind machine?" An almost imperceptible nod from the broompusher answers him.

"My agent, Georges Jeancell, here"—he points to the short man—"has set up the whole deal with Dr. Samaranthan Rao Gejohn. These MTG research people want to look at my brain while I'm creating stories, having daydreams. *Making* daydreams is what I do, actually. Gejohn wants to see if they can measure what's happening, reproduce it eventually. I think"—he gestures toward Jeancell—"that my agent is interested, too."

Allowing himself the beginnings of a slight frown, Pratt realizes that he is quickly losing half of his small audience, the wrong half. Broompusher is remaining intensely interested, but the good-looking female scientist type is more absorbed in his holo-digital brain on the screen than in the real one here behind the facial tattoos. *And I'm already wanting her to consider other, more active—tumescent, even!—organs!*

"They're going to read your *mind,* that's what all this is?" broomer says, more of a statement than a question. "Hellfire, they got nothing else to do? I read some of your crap, five, eight years back, saw some of them gory, megaviolence flicks you used to come up with. With all the *real* misery in the world, they going to dig more imaginary shit out of your sick mind?" The broom quivers in a shaking hand, an implement of sudden rage. Broomer, however, calms down considerably when Pale Gorilla Man takes one step forward. Broom man whispers quite loudly, defiantly, *"Out of your mind,* that's for sure!" With that bit of philosophy hanging provocatively in the stillness of the quiet labspace, broom specialist takes his tradetool and departs, murmuring angrily. Pale Gorilla stares, eyes tracking as the labcoat leaves, but exhibits no facial changes.

Leaving a mildly puzzled Pratt to observe the exquisite exterior topography of an outstanding member of the opposite sex mere meters from him, him scrutinizing the pulls and stretches of her tailored labcoat. Billions of years of evolution tell him she is well suited to bear children; he interprets all these natural signals as meaning merely that her appearance is extremely sexy and therefore he simply wants to have sex with her. His genitals are in total agreement: Nature's plans for procreation don't enter his mind or figure further in his body's automatic stiffening reaction. As if she's reading his mind, sexy labcoat lady turns toward him, satin shadows playing across the soft landscapes of her beauty. He has had thousands of women; now he wants to increase that number N to N+1, and tonight. The signals are all there, and the outcome assured. He is master of this game, and though his literary fame is on a slight temporary downswing, his royalties keep him in adequate income and that, with his past fame and his personal charm, ensures a steady stream of female company.

"We don't intend to read your *mind,* Mr. Pratt," she says to the renowned novelist, "just your *brain.*" Labcoat womun smiles confidently; for the first time, the writer sees inside her mouth. *Too many teeth,* he thinks, *and too damned smart.* "That's a big difference."

Hamish Pratt finds himself nodding. He doesn't understand a damn thing she's saying. "Pictures from my brain, more exactly, Dr. Gejohn said." It is really a question. *I can ignore the teeth,* he thinks. *The rest looks goodly enough.*

Labcoat lady continues smiling. Pratt thinks it must hurt after a while, smiling like that. What's she hiding? he wonders. Last night's lay? Occult knowledge that I must never know? Maybe her panties are tight across her clit and she thinks I won't know? *Occlit know-legs?* Let's see how she walks, see if she tries to hide her continuing orgasm from me. Or is it an *organism* she's hiding? An old semiporn spec-phi novel comes to mind, a snakelike thing coiled up inside her. Kundalini, the Hindu meditation?

No, *cunt-da-lingy,* that's more like it. He shakes his head as his mind plays obscene, unwanted word games. During his marathon writing sessions when he is practicing his craft, the wordplay is welcomed, required, a rainbow palette of logography from which he picks and chooses phrases, metaphors, puns, clever innuendoes, rhymes, rhythms, and meter. But away from the displate terminal, he tires himself at times like these, when the mind-machine runs itself on unwelcome hardwired programs he just can't seem to control. Sometimes in social situations like right now, he'd just like to think in real words, spare himself the alternate images, the visual puns that continually ferment in his overactive imagination. He sighs. Maybe his old boss had been right, all those years ago.

"**S**ometimes things *are* what they seem, Ham! You're just *too* goddamned creative," the old fart had said during a review of his work habits in the old machine shop, preparatory to writing up an unsatisfactory-performance appraisal. "You *never* accept the mundane view, the pragmatic, the practical, but that's what gets the job done!"

Pratt frowns in memory, seeing his boss's bald head glistening, just right on the verge of breaking out in sweat, an incipiently wet, shining orb, bobbing in self-assurance. The short fat man always dressed in bib overalls, an affectation intended to induce loyalty in his high-tech shop workers. They all laughed behind his back; their "machine shop" was a place where software jox like Hamish Pratt toiled to spew out integrated code that told the self-programming ultra-tech mini- and micro-robots what they needed to tell themselves to program useful functionality into their micro-minds. Their "tools" were, at most, palm- and wrist-sized hypercomputers and video wallpaper screens. No one ever so much as lifted a wrench or screwdriver, much less needed to worry about grease. But because of some psychological quirk, Big Jim Angstrom had to keep pretending that he was a machinist, and so the "overhauls," as he called his dress. Hamish himself preferred Bermuda shorts and sandals and a torn T-shirt with an obscene slogan, just to keep his boss on edge.

"And you, you always gotta have an angle, everything that happens has a sarcastic side, or a humorous jumble of pun words, or else a supernatural, an unconventional, overtone. But, my friend, sometimes things are *exactly* what they appear to be, no less, no more, perfectly natural, no interpretation necessary, no extraneous bullshit allowed.

"You got to cut out this otherworldly shit, get your brain on your job, or you're not going to *have* a job." The man fidgeted, sweated another pint or two, then collected his thoughts. "Know what you ought to do to get rid of that crap in your head?"

Pratt allowed as how he didn't.

"If you can't stop thinking it, for God's sake, don't *say* it. Go home, write it down, look at it, stare at it, realize how stupid it looks in print, you'll stop wasting your mind. Just don't let me hear any more weird talk in the shop!"

Surprised that he himself had scarcely considered such action, he took his boss's advice seriously and did just that, every night, and in six months, he had a novel and four short stories. In a year, there were movie and television options. His boss, fart though he was, had made Hamish Pratt a rich man. For old times' sake, and as a sort of combination thank-you and revenge, Hamish sends him an autographed copy of every one of his publications and media productions. Hamish smiles when he remembers, wondering if the old man ever recalls the threat about not hearing "weird talk."

Dr. S. Rao Gejohn is waiting quietly in the dark evaluation chamber as Hamish Pratt and his entourage enter. The bespectacled, dark-skinned Hindish man is wearing a gold labcoat and fingering a silvery, tiaralike headband from which dangle thin optical fibers connected to eye-sized filmy white sacs. Two other fibers support tiny pincerlike rings that will attach to his earlobes. The brain-reading device is not at all imposing, Pratt decides. *I'd make the thing look at least as threatening as a helmet,* he thinks, fingering the milk-white films that perhaps are his tickets to immortality. *Maybe like an ancient armored helmet, complete with Roman crest. Maybe an Iron Maiden for the head. Iron Maidenhead! What a title for a medievo-porn!* He taps two metal-tipped fingers together, in personal fingercode. His bracelet computer responds with a friendly, nearly subaudible tone, indicating it has received his instructions. *Don't want to forget that one!*

Per the *verch* instructions he'd received in the test run the evening before, he sits in the overtufted easy chair and slips the eye-films on. It feels as if they are crawling over his eyes, a slick, queasy journey across the convex millimeters of his eyeballs. "Really, Georges," Gejohn says to the agent, who is leaning against the chamber wall next to the hulking Pale Gorilla, "we could make a tiny, unnoticeable surgical implant for your client's cornea and he'd never know we did it. On the test monkeys, that seems to work a lot easier. But," he adds with a sigh, "it seems that humans want the illusion of choice, of control. Especially when it comes to the eyes."

Pratt doesn't like S. Rao Gejohn's eyes, or in fact any part of the man. There is something less than amorality in the scientist's demeanor, akin to the thick dullness of a longtime drug addict. Pratt's vision is now obscured by the white films of the contact viewers, but he shivers at the memory of the deadmeat behind *that* one's eyes. Those Hindi eyes have experienced dead-dreams Pratt doesn't want ever to see, twin infinities of sucking darkness, *darkling suckness.* If the optical orbs are the mirrors of the soul, Gejohn is suffering from an eternity of bad, broken luck. Pratt decides not to fingercode this set of satisfying metaphors and observations; some things he'd rather not be reminded of; no stories from this one.

Pratt hears silence descend as Gejohn places the hearrings on his earlobes. There is a slight hum as the audio links are established. Surprising himself, waiting for the incessant universe of gray video mist to sizzle down to colors and shapes and structures, Pratt begins to sweat.

—*Nerves?* he asks himself.

—*Yeah,* himself answers. *We have a lot riding on this experiment, like fun, fame, royalties. Especially royalties. Gotta get something new on the market, our old stuff is flattening out.*

—*Semifame and still-decent old royalties we got, pal. How about a fun pioneering effort in a new entertainment medium?*

—*A* profitable *pioneering effort! And new royalties!*

—*Let's get to semisleep,* both Hamishes agree.

Somewhere between gray and darkness, they become one.

Sleep, semiawareness, his familiar, desired state of incipient creativity, ultimately descends upon the integration of the disparate mental elements that constitute the personality of Hamish Pratt. Reluctantly at first, the subconscious and the conscious minds do a mate-dance, knowing full well what the eventual outcome must be, yet unable instantly to consummate the multiple marriage and subordinate themselves temporarily out of existence. They negotiate, parry, flirt and embrace, finally accepting the inevitable; this time, though, their handshakes and ruminations are not private, not when the Dream Machine kicks in. Pratt considers this new factor on several mental levels simultaneously.

—Does the awareness of no privacy affect our process this time?

—No, it doesn't. We have always described these experiences for others to peruse, inviting them into our cojoint world, all its fears and horrors and mind games. We have made millions by yielding our privacy, allowing gross strangers to share our nightmares, to plow our private plots, to—

—To plow our private parts?

"No!" Pratt yells out loud, startling himself from the reverie. Where the hell did that thought come from?

Outside the *verch* hearrings, Gejohn is muttering, loudly enough that Pratt can hear him, about the instability of all artists and creativers, and wishing that he could have a scientist as a subject. Pratt ignores him, wishing in return that the researcher could see Pratt's instantaneous mental vision of the man, the punishments he is mentally bestowing on Gejohn's writhing, undying body. The creativer doesn't think such images would be appearing on the screen. Not yet. He smiles: *But I sure would love to have one of these to play over and over again: Gejohn in Hell, a writhing new* verch *exclusive!*

His own responses and outbursts puzzle Pratt, but such enigmas have been a common thread of the lucid dreaming that has consumed his life, that has fed his Muse well past satiation, that earned his once-stellar fame and stacked up his still-considerable fortune. *The shrinks can work out the details,* he thinks. *My traumas are other people's nightmares!*

—And the other way around, Hamish-san?

—What the hell does that mean?

There is no answer.

Breathing deeply, Hamish Pratt once more experiences the familiar and welcome semitrance that takes him to his preferred alternate worlds. He's never been able to control the destination, but most places in his dreamworld are welcome enough; even the ones that aren't happy sites—they are the sources of creativity, the origins of his novels and movies and *verch* plays. Maybe the Dream Machine will give him the power of destiny—*destination!*—as well. . . .

Sleep creeps.

This one is Hamish's favorite place, the familiar dream-mapped analog of a small village in the desert Southwest, half-recalled childhood years in the earliest locale of his life, the country of his dreams. Where the remembered world of conscious memory is often as sterile as the surrounding desert—dry, parched, devoid of life—the dream version is exciting, full of shadow and light, dark streets leading to bright horizons, evanescent visions and languid enchantments just out of sight, barely out of reach, bright promises around each corner, unknown treasures for the taking.

Hamish has long recognized the dream town of Las Arenas as the serene, protected childhood home he has tried to recapture all his life since. By some still-unsought mechanism, conscious thought, like a dream-fog, wisps and whips and enfolds the village, bringing a mistlike quietude, till the two worlds meet and meld. Smiling in both worlds, he begins to compare the memory with the dream.

And this is his trick, his never-failing ritual, earning him his right of passage to the parallel universes of his personal Dreamworld. As in a split-screen video, he is able to pull both images together, world of shadows and world of light, and thereby enter the place of controlled imagination, of lucid dreaming. Much as one's eyes pull in and merge two flat images to yield the stereoscopic illusion, so

Hamish's separate mental images yield up a third world, a transcen-
dental locale beyond either, something entirely unexpected.
  He smiles. This time, he is flying.

Flying is not new; dream flight is an old, old friend, originating
somewhere in his earliest memories of dreams. For years he has
experimented with dream flight, has compiled a private catalog
of flight sensoria; flight occurs always at twilight, as do so many
of his other dreams. Flight is a lonely phenomenon: he has never
flown with another. Flight is usually witnessed by others, and is
sweeter for that: unknown forms stand at a distance, comment-
ing on his performance, pointing at his demonstration, jealous
of his talent. Usually, he is thrilled; he is able to rise above the
others, to display his skills.

Sometimes—troubled times, turbulent times, times of mental struggle and spiritual doubt—dream flight is assisted by me-
chanical means. During his college years, when the best and
brightest of technical and scientific instructors unknowingly
tried to instill in him their perception of the One Reality—the
Preferred Consensus, *PC*—he had began to doubt the worlds of
Dream and Imagination. His dream flights then occurred only
when his dream-self augmented his natural levitative abilities
with strange assortments of wings and curved surfaces and balloons. Even gravity belts sufficed at times, near-magical Buck
Rogers constructions that nevertherless allowed his increasingly
logical mind to accept the reality of dream flight. But after grad-
uation, after his intellectual time was once more his alone, simple, unassisted dream flight returned, all the more joyous for his
lucid recognition of triumph over mega-rationality.

Flight is sweet, erotic. Flight is revenge.

Flight as revenge? Hamish comments to himself as he swoops down
from a familiar altitude—approximately three hundred feet, he has
calculated by comparing aerial photos of similar forests.

Forests? Yes, there are always forests, or at least clumps of trees. Strange, he thinks, there have always been trees; I've often landed in them, taken to their limbs for refuge and stability, but I never thought to include them in my descriptions as part of the dream-environment. Till now.

Swoops and flies, flirts with birds, can't reach clouds, have to avoid oaks.

Another question: avoid oaks? I didn't think I could tell one bush from another at this height. Okay, add that piece of empirical data to the rest; let's get a comprehensive list for dead-eyed Gejohn and his crew of virtual voyeurs.

Descent begins, though Hamish resists. But as always, resistance to landing is ever futile. He sighs. The levitative power is diminishing; he feels it flee as his feet become heavy again.

Always a momentary panic as lift vanishes and altitude is still hundreds of feet. Below, a power line. "Avoid power lines—they kill lift!" a part of his dream-mind screams in warning.

Damn, another limitation I didn't know I had, Hamish frets. Pretty soon I'll box myself in and won't be able to fly anymore.

Before he impacts, at still a hundred feet up, Pratt awakens. Gejohn is staring as Pratt's real-eyes vision returns through the transparent eye-films. He is gaping at Pratt, mouth agog. A brief glance shows the agent Jeancell smirking, a quick tongue darting over thin lips. Pratt doesn't care to look at the face of Pale Gorilla, and something tells him he mustn't face-to-face with Pretty Red-haired Science Lady, either.

Gulping, Gejohn says, "Mr. Pratt, do you remember your dreams?"

Disappointment evident in his every motion, Pratt detaches his *verch* apparatus and arises from his chair, stretches, yawns. He has been afraid all along that something might go wrong, and here it is. There is to be no techno-savior; he will have to go back to his old ways of creativing. Or quit.

"Of course I remember them; why else would I take time off

from my writing to be here? I've got deadlines to meet." At the wall, the agent Jeancell smirks again; Pratt knows he is aware that Pratt is not working on anything at the present.

"Do you *control* your dreams as well?" Gejohn presses.

"If you mean do I set them up ahead of time, like a screenplay, well, no." He yawns again. Have these guys screwed up or what? *Damn,* he thinks, *one more wild and wonderful idea down the chubes.* He resigns himself to live on the substantial but diminishing royalties and to hell with them all!

"And this time," Gejohn whispers, "you remember every detail, every event, and you made them happen?"

Pratt swings away from the annoying Gejohn, finally toward Attractive Red-haired Science Person, who turns her face from him, blushing. *Blushing?* A desperate glance toward Georges and the Gorilla reveals the same infuriating smirk on the agent's face, not a damned thing readable on the Bulk's.

Sighing, he continues to play the game. "As I said, Doctor Gejohn, once I'm in the semiconscious state, I control most dream events, like I do in real life." He shrugs. "It's a lot like the better interactive *verch* channels—I can make magic, I can do anything my heart desires." He smiles. "To quote an old song."

Gejohn frowns, darkly. A red light on a microcam nearby is twinkling, and Pratt realizes this session is being recorded. "What did you see, then, and where did you go?"

Pratt tells them how the dream images and the real memory can be brought together to crystallize the parallel world of lucid dreaming that is one step beyond the normal, unconscious dream state. Then he tells a little of the scenes around the desert village of Las Arenas. "First, the twilight around the town. Then the flying, the swooping and diving and turns." He relates a few of the restrictive parameters, those he has known before, those he became aware of in the present session. "But the restrictions, the parameters, I think, are remnants of residual reality that tie me down."

Pratt is tiring of all this nonsense. He strikes a microsmoke, inhaling his daily dose of vitamins and nanidotes. Red-haired Attractive Person finally smiles a little and Pratt responds likewise; pheromone-based perfumes are the fad of the week for smokers like himself. Based on her predictable reactions, he will have a go with this one yet tonight, blushing or no. The day will not be a total loss after all. He tells himself that her nipples are erect, showing taut, labcoat protruding. Direct visual observation informs him that this is true.

"I think that if I could view my dreams, I'd be able to interpret what those obstacles are, what hinders me. And then, literally, my imagination could soar to heights undreamed of." Images and words and multiplicities of meaning impinge, fuse, creating kaleidoscopic images and multiple entendres. Pratt laughs. He fingercodes a few of the more striking ones. *Mist for the grill,* he tells himself. "Literally, as I said."

"Please sit," Gejohn says, "and we will play back the *verch* recording for you." Pratt is mildly surprised; they *did* record something! Then why the interrogation, why lead him on to believe there had been a problem? His pulse races; he will see his dreams! And those dreams will make his fortune, again and again. Is that why Georges is smirking so grotesquely?

To Attractive Red-hair, Gejohn whispers, "Run them, please."

Hearrings and eyefilms back in place, Pratt nods, takes his seat and waits for the historic moment, to become the first person to view his own dreams from a recording. *This is very interesting,* he concedes to himself in the seconds before the playback begins. *Another article, perhaps this time for—*

With the Universe, the thought dies.

Without warning, Hamish Pratt is sucked into an effervescent, eddying, sizzling *nothingness,* taking his breath away. Kaleidoscopic patterns play, whirlpools, maelstroms of patterns, nothing recognizable. He is puzzled, scared; his dreams are nothing like this!

Focus comes as molten images flow and fuse, fluids that swirl into—a human face, large enough to fill the screen, white teeth, a flicking tongue. A snort from the agent Jeancell, behind him. There is no audio with this playback.

Pratt is stunned, but not quite into speechlessness. "That's not what I dreamed, what I *created*," he complains aloud, "not what was in my head!" Something's happening that he doesn't want to happen, something he doesn't understand, something he fears will open up his guts to these . . . these outsiders.

*Verch*side, the enigma continues. A young man—almost familiar to Pratt, an image faded as if from an old dream, a distant memory, but not at once fully recognizable—leans over Pratt and slips a thumb and forefinger down between his legs. At an unexpected erection, Pratt feels his heart pounding, knowing, fearing, yet anticipating the wet, all-encompassing pleasure to follow. . . .

Hamish Pratt feels the universe shift, as if he is receding from all around him, shrinking into a microscopic black hole, his senses suddenly located at the far edge of a personal reality, an inner self sitting at the center, waiting and fearful.

"That is *not* what I saw!" Pratt screams, tearing off the films, jerking away the hearrings. The bright sparktacle eye-films now threaten him, mandalas of evil, transient rainbows of psychic pain. He yells louder, but no one answers. Around him are not the familiar scientist, womun, agent, goon, but a corral of white-coats, shoulder to shoulder, faces covered in gauzy swaths of whitecloth. In slow motion, a synchronized ballet of evil, the veiled labcoated entities remove white bandannas, revealing dark faces. No, not faces—orifices of darkness! They each of them have no face, possessing only toothless, lip-encircled, cavernous openings covering the front of their heads, mouths that iris shut and open slowly, multiple tongues like sea anemones, filamentaceous mouth organs seeking out secret parts of this body he can't control.

Oh, shit, Pratt realizes, *this is another fucking trauma-dream. How did I get here? Lucid, lucid, I love lucid!* Unreal or not, it is painfully unpleasant, and he wants to go elsewhere. He thinks hard, feels his body harden, his feet lighten, and then instantly he is in that twilight place again, the crowd of puzzled oralists now off on the dark horizon, pointing at him, but he is out of their arms' reach, and of harm's way.

Dark trees beckon, a colorless sky opens up.

He is flying.

He is free.

There is throbbing headache pain and stabbing light that hurts his eyes; Pratt seeks darkness and surcease. He hears a soft, accented voice. It is Gejohn; Hamish sends his mind in that direction. The voice is deep, comforting, a welcome beacon of new hope.

"Oaks are thick and thrusting; they might also be phalli?" Gejohn offers.

Pratt is awake. He squints his eyes and can see, real-eyed, through the clearing films. The mind-machine is still generating nonsense kaleidoscopic garbage on the displate, playing back some inexplicable imagery from his dream experiences.

Breathing deeply, he calms himself. Why had he gone into involuntary lucid dreaming? Relieved to be back in actual reality, he replies angrily, "Damn it, Gejohn, for some reason, I'm going in and out of lucid dreaming, and I can't control it, and I can't keep up with your jabbering." He swallows hard, breathes deeply. "But no, oak trees are just oak trees, I believe, not big dicks." He is even more irritated with the scientist. He avoids looking into those dull, thick eyes.

Thinking back on the involuntary immersion, Pratt quickly decides he just might be onto something with this MTG, maybe a way to self-hypnotize, to produce stories faster, increase his productivity, maybe attack some novels novelly. *Weird as it sounds, business is business,* he thinks. Taking a deep breath, he verbally jousts with the scientist. "Sometimes, Gejohn, a cigar is just a cigar. I think Freud himself said that."

Gejohn mutters something in Hindi and then says, "No cigar

for you, my friend! There's no goddamned tree on that screen!"
With a wave of his hand, a dark, thick cylinder fills the screen
erectly. It is slightly out of focus, but the barely discernible rib-
bing and the hemispherical cap at the top are very suggestive.
"Hamish, if that's not a phallus, then what the hell *is* it?"

Pratt takes a deep breath and closes his eyes. "It's *not* a phallus," he whispers almost prayerfully, "it's something else. It's
coming from my memory, bubbling up. I see it—it's a bedstead!"
His voice fills with relief, he almost sobs. "It's a tall, thick post—
two of them—at the foot of my bed." The displate image falters,
quivers, becoming a mahogany-colored bedpost, then two.

Gejohn and the womun drop their jaws, and in the background, the agent Jeancell lets out a short, high-pitched trill of
pleasure. The picture clears up, becomes perfect: two mahogany
bedposts framing a quilted surface. "I'll be go to hell," Gejohn
gasps. "He's got total control. What he generates in his mind, we
see directly. Ho boy! Lafayette Hubbard, we have arrived."

Red-haired Displate Scientist murmurs a command into her
voicer, then says aloud, "On *verch*, it's coming through in perfect
three-D, Doctor Gejohn. Oh, and one other thing."

Gejohn nods *Yes? Tell me.*

The woman is puzzled. "On the *verch*—combining all the
signals we get from all the MTG nodes, we are getting layers of
data, overlaying layers of images, one atop the other. We can flip
through them like transparent films. I can see something moving under the covers."

So?

"The underlayer shows—it's a young man." She gulps. She
whispers disgustedly, "He's performing . . . oral sex . . . on what
appears to be a male child."

Gejohn stares at the displate. "The eyes don't see everything,"
he mumbles. "The body has its own secrets." Aloud, he tells the
womun, "Don't say anything about this outside this lab. It's very
important; I'll take command of the recordings from here on."

Relieved, the womun strokes an armpanel and leaves the laboratory. Sitting with Hamish Pratt and his unrealized night-mares, Gejohn stares at the unchanging displate. "It's a still shot," he says, verbalizing his speculations for the witnesses. "Hamish has frozen time, before the traumatic event, protecting himself. No motion, no emotion."

The agent Jeancell agrees. "It is a snapshot of the soul, a hell-bound soul that, on the edge of Eternity, can push itself no far-ther." Pratt sits quietly, jaw twitching, caught up in the *verch* manifestations of his own dreams.

Time passes in further experimentation, Pratt making no effort to remove his tiara-draped eye-films. Gejohn is recording every image, occasionally muttering something to his wrist recorder, into the room computer, or directly into Hamish Pratt's ears. He plays with some of the images, leaves others be. He is attempt-ing to have one monitor show what Pratt is experiencing, the other what the MTG shows is actually occurring in the lucid dream.

The agent Jeancell and the Pale Gorilla leave intermittently, return unobtrusively, as if to keep random track of Pratt's ongo-ing dream-traumas. Once in a while, the agent offers suggestions to Gejohn, and the scientist smiles or frowns and then says other things to Pratt, who stays immersed in the semilucid worlds of dreaming and *verch*. Images spontaneously emerge and resprout in the mind-machine, terrors and horrors from the Pit of Pratt, images he does not himself experience. Playing with algorithms, computer functions, Gejohn allows the images to fuse as he murmurs first one thought, then others, to Hamish Pratt's re-ceptive mind.

For all Gejohn's prodding and probing efforts, Pratt always reaches a visual dead end just before a sexual event occurs, and he never consciously experiences one. The associated *verch* recordings are a pedophile's heaven, but they will never be re-leased, not even to the scientific journals. Death sentences have a way of suppressing even widespread perversity. Gejohn says in a low voice, "We must shepherd dear Hamish carefully past these peaks and down into the valleys of the soul, and we must conjure up on our screens the images his mind experiences, not those that his body insists on recounting, reliving, and remorphing."

At one of Gejohn's whispered suggestions, carried inward through the hearrings, the lucidly dreaming Pratt conjures up a giant saguaro cactus on the desert. *Hell,* Hamish thinks, *none of those within four hundred miles of Las Arenas, but at least it ought to stand out.* In the lucid dream, he is a ten-year-old boy again.

Real-eyes, to Gejohn, the displate shows not a cactus but an erect male organ, tripartite, threatening. He whispers that image to Pratt.

But in his lucid dream, Hamish is standing on a vast expanse of brown desert. He speaks aloud to the sky, to the unseen Gejohn. "*All* my images are sexual? I don't see that in my dream-world here, but you're saying my MTG brain scan shows that." He thinks for a moment. "Now wait a moment—if you haven't calibrated the images against what I say I see, how do you know what they are?"

Gejohn frowns. "Mr. Pratt, you are under a misconception. We *have* calibrated the MTG; hundreds of persons have been tested in *verch,* by showing them pictures and comparing the visual cortex outputs. The mental images are confirmed. You are merely the first to be so tested during lucid dreaming, so that as you generate pictures, you are able to describe them and we are able to correlate them, simultaneously."

Gejohn allows himself the glimmering of a faint smile. "Somehow, your particular mind has set up analogs; what everyone else sees as a penis, you experience as a cactus. Your mind refuses to see what is there, apparently. It's all very, very Freudian. There are very few correlates between your visualizations and anyone else's."

And that is why I'm so goddamned creative! Pratt thinks. "But what about the town I'm in here in my dream, Las Arenas?"

Hamish is now standing at a deserted intersection in the small village. There are no other people in the town, just buildings and sidewalks and empty stores. "What could be the problem here? Buildings are buildings, aren't they?" Pratt is instantly anxious, desperate; his dream-world is suddenly dangerous, unfriendly. The desert dream-sun is setting, and twilight, a darker ambiance, clouds the once-familiar street scene. If he's not welcome *here* anymore, what happens to his dreams of childhood, to his creativity?

Another thought strikes Pratt: he dreams every night. Worse, he daydreams almost continuously. If all his dream country is hostile, how can he continue living, much less writing? "Beam me out, Gejohn," he says aloud. "There's no intelligent life in here." An instantaneous **BLINK** and the MTG headset is disconnected. Lucidity vanishes as Gejohn removes the tiara and its dangling spider-fingers of fibers. Pratt feels the eye-films crawling from his pupils, unclips the hearrings, surfaces back into *actual reality,* as Gejohn deems it.

Pratt is nervous, anxious, pacing the lab floor, occasionally slapping one fist into the other. "Rao, Georges,"—no point in addressing the Gorilla; Pratt isn't sure anymore that the mountain of muscle is human—"I'm more than a little disturbed by this whole damned process. Now, I couldn't care less what the *verch* shows, though I agree they have to be erased before I—we—have the FedPeds down on us. I must have had some childhood traumas to be turning out such shit, but as long as it doesn't interfere with what I *experience* myself, I really haven't lost much. I don't remember what happened as a kid, and I don't want to remember. It's apparently made me what I am.

"It looks as if I'm not going to be able to control those images as easily as we had hoped. So I'd like to drop the project, go back to doing what I do best, and remembering what I can of my lucid dreams, writing them down as stories." As the scientist shifts uncomfortably in his chair, frowning deeply, Pratt shrugs. "It's a living, Gejohn. What's the problem with that?"

The agent Jeancell is relaxing in an easy chair, puffing his evening's vitasmoke. Chaotic rings of healthy vapor spiral from the glowing tip. "Ah, Hamish, but Doctor Rao has discovered here today a solution, a way for you to record your dream-world, a way to make more millions. He will put in 'transfer functions', algorithms, computer-morphing translations—making what you see in your lucid dreams come out in images in *verch* and on the screen. In that fashion, what *you* see is what *we* get, and it is two for one. It may take some time to generate exactly the peculiar manifestations you experience, but Rao is sure he can do it."

The Hindu scientist nods in agreement. Pale Gorilla, for the first time, breaks that granite face with the glimmerings of an upward turn of pale lips.

"To hell with that, Georges, I've had it. You get yourself another guy to play with," Pratt sneers. "I'm sure there are hundreds of new writers, starving ones, who will let Gejohn rape their minds, and a lot cheaper than me!"

"Hamish, old friend," the agent Jeancell says quietly, "I have very much enjoyed your dream-world excursions here today." He smiles, his nearly reptilian tongue skittering over the occasional gold tooth. A wave of his hand brings up obscene horrors on the displate: the boy Ham Pratt in group orgies with too-familiar adults. "In fact, I think you have founded a new industry." Pale Gorilla is cracking large knuckles in the background; he is apparently nervous, and this in turn makes Pratt very uneasy.

"What?" Pratt screams. Large Knuckle-cracker stops his habit, dropping his arms down to his sides, as if he is ready to jump at the writer. "That stuff on the screen? Pedophilia's a death sentence, if you didn't know."

The agent Jeancell continues smiling evilly. "Oh, Hamish, that's just in our benighted country. In the global market, you could generate billions. Other societies are not nearly so, so . . . hypocritical as ours, you might say. There are tens of millions of, I should say, specialty collectors."

"Go to hell, Georges. You are fucking insane." Pratt glances toward Gejohn, who turns his head away, puffing his own smoke. Pratt is completely flushed by now, his heart pounding with anger at his disgusting companions.

But the agent Jeancell continues. "You are to be commended, Doctor Gejohn, for verifying what my investigations showed— that Pratt was a catamite for years in his parents' cult group when he was a child in Las Arenas, and that the psychological repression of that fact creates the psychic tension that generates his marvelous creations."

Pratt's stomach churns, but he defends himself. "I can't help what might have been done to me as a child, Georges; maybe I don't even want psychiatric help now, not as long as I can write." He sneers at the little man. "My traumas, my nightmares, have made you rich."

The agent Jeancell purses his lips, flicks his gaze toward the giant beside him. "Ah, yes, my commissions. We have done well, my friend, even though we are in a bit of a decline lately— for several years, in fact. I had hoped only that this . . . this *toy* of Doctor Gejohn's would enhance those millions more we are to make from exploiting your fears. That was my plan, and yours. Until I saw these . . . these wonderful images on the displate, that is. Now we have in mind much greater markets than we ever imagined. My friend, we are both going to be so much richer than you ever dreamed."

"Not with my brain, you don't, Georges! I'm getting the hell out of here!" Pratt starts toward the door, but Pale Giant stops him, twisting one arm, hard, behind his back, slamming him against the wall.

"No, Hamish, you are going to stay for a while in this little room and spill your guts for Rao's mind-machine," Jeancell goes on. "After all, you're much too valuable a property to lose; there is an entire industry already built up around your weirdness, millions of dollars over the years. And we can have it all, all over again, maybe more. And that doesn't even include the . . . the *new* markets for your childhood experiences. Did you think we were going to let you just *quit?*" He gestures toward the displate image, where the nut-shaped sickly brain now floats. To Pratt, it is suddenly evil. *Man Hates Own Brain!* The tabloid image bubbles up, unbidden. "No, Hamish, not when there is pure gold to be mined in those deep, dark furrows of your dark, twisted mind."

"You can't tie me down, damn you, Jeancell! I'm a human being, with rights. I can quit any freakin' contract ever made, you know that. So why are you pushing me like this?" The irony of his defiant words strikes him. The agent Jeancell is already tying him down, specifically with Pale Gorilla, who is close to breaking his arm.

The agent's face suddenly softens, taking on an aspect of pity Pratt has never seen before. At a word, the giant eases up on the viselike arm grip. Pratt moans at the sudden pain of release; Jeancell flinches. Damn, but the agent seems genuinely concerned; it is no act.

Jeancell says, quietly, "Hamish, my old, old friend. Of course we can't *force* you to do anything against your will. But,"—the displate again is conjuring up hideous images of parental incest, ritual sexual abuse, the disgusting cesspool that his actual childhood had been, the very images that generated Pratt's once-formidable intellectual reputation and his literary fortune—"my friend, these new tales arising from an undiscovered country— *your new dream-country, unexploited continents of perversion, unexplored and unexplorable by anyone but you!*—these constitute a literary treasure beyond value. This is better than a copyright, for no one else will ever access these worlds except through you."

Onscreen, the flicking anemones dodge and bend, quavering in ecstasy as they seek out his decaying innocence.

The agent Jeancell fairly glows. "And they require no effort on your part. With Rao's morphing, you continue to generate your horror stories from your lucid dream-world. From the *verch* outputs, we simply record what you do naturally—your conscious lucid dreams *and* the underlying reality dreams, the pedophilia ones. The former we feed into the self-adaptive word-processing system you have used, modified by our team of ghostwriters to provide the style for which you were so well known. And the perversions, those we distribute along the world's more enlightened *verch*-channel outlets to the specialty collectors. And in two parallel channels, you are more creative than ever, and you get richer every day." His smile says: *We all get richer!*

Pratt stares, drop-jawed, at Jeancell's suggestion. He yields, slumping into the lab chair as the giant and Rao strap him in and slip the dream-machine tiara around his head. Unbidden, unwelcome, the internal dialogue, predecessor to the lucid dream-state, descends. Uncontrollable. It is an escape, he knows, but he welcomes it.

—*Plowing our private plots? Self asks.*

—*Our private parts, Self answers.*

—*For fun and profit?*

—*For son and prophet!*

—*For shaking all mothers?*

—*Forsaken no others!*

This time, the ritual is instantaneous, the handshakes immediate high-fives. Hamish Pratt, seven years old, takes the hand of Ham Pratt, seventeen, on the one side and the hand of Dr. Hamish Pratt, twenty-seven, on the other, and they walk softly into twilight, through a darkening canyon teeming with giant tripartite cacti.

Georges Jeancell stares with satisfaction at the *verch* output: the three figures dissolve into the familiar theme of grasping anem-oralists, orgiastically entwined beyond belief. "Ah, the man's creativity—what a genius!" the agent says to Pale Gorilla, who responds with a dawning smile, and then, more loudly, to Dr. Gejohn, who makes no comment: "All it takes is erotic suggestion, mental and audio stimulation through Rao's magnificent mind-machine. And a receptive mind like Hamish's, one that creates undreamt-of possibilities from just a common phrase, entire stories from the nuances of one word, whole series of novels from a transient mental image.

"As Rao and I suspected, the mere suggestion to Hamish's mind that he was sexually victimized as a child has freed his mind of restraints, opening a new creative universe in the fervid mind of my placid friend. And, based on the personality traits that Rao's testing measured, we can generate an infinitude of new worlds for our boy to explore, if we ever tire of this one!" His reptilian tongue flies across the picket fence of his crooked lower teeth. "A few days in this world, a few weeks in the next, who knows? A galaxy of worlds to conquer."

On displate two, Hamish Pratt is flying. Jeancell gently places one hand over the small image, as if in caress. Smiling broadly, with the other hand he wipes away a tear.

"Ah, Hamish, we love you so. Fly away, friend, fly, fly!"

Hamish Pratt is happy; he is flying. Far, far below, Las Arenas comes into view, a happy town, lights beckoning him to land.

As he glides in, gradually losing altitude, three friendly figures— a man, a boy, a small child—are waving to him.

HOUSEHOLD WORDS, OR, THE POWERS-THAT-BE

Howard Waldrop

> His theory of life was entirely wrong. He thought men ought to be buttered up, and the world made soft and accommodating for them, and all sorts of fellow have turkey for their Christmas dinner. . . .
>
> —Thomas Carlyle

> He was the first to find out the immense spiritual power of the Christmas turkey.
>
> —Mrs. Oliphant

Under a deep cerulean November sky, the train stopped on a turn near the road one half-mile outside the town of Barchester.

Two closed carriages waited on the road. Passengers leaned out the train windows and watched as a small man in a suit as brown as a Norfolk biffin stepped down from the doorway at the end of the third railcar.

Men waved their hats, women their scarves. "Hurray, Charlie!" they yelled. "Hoorah, Mr. Dickens! Hooray for Boz!"

The small man, accompanied by two others, limped across the cinders to a group of men who waited, hats in hand, near the carriages. He turned, doffed his stovepipe hat to the train and waved to the cheering people.

Footmen loaded his traveling case and the trunk of props from the train into the last carriage.

The train, with barely a lurch, moved smoothly on down the tracks toward the cathedral tower of the town, hidden from view by trees. There a large crowd, estimated at more than 3,000, would be waiting for the author, to cheer him and watch him alight.

The welcoming committee had met him here to obviate that indignity, and to take him by a side street to his hotel, avoiding the crowds.

When the men were all in, the drivers at the fronts of the carriages released their brakes, and the carriages made their way quickly down the road toward town.

Promptly at 8:00 P.M., the lights in the Workingman's Hall came up to full brilliance.

On stage were three deep-magenta folding screens, the center one parallel to the audience, the two wings curved in slightly toward it. The stage curtains had been drawn in to touch the wings of the screen. Directly in front of the center panel stood a waist-high, four-legged small table. At the audience's right side of the desk was a raised wooden block; at its left, on a small lower projection, stood a glass and a sweating carafe of ice water; next to the water was an ivory letter opener and a white linen handkerchief. The top of the table was covered with a fringed magenta cloth that hung below the tabletop only an inch or so.

Without preamble, Charles Dickens walked in with a slight limp from the side of the stage and took his place behind the desk, carrying in his hand a small octavo volume. When he stood behind the thin-legged table, his whole body, except for the few inches across his waist, was fully visible to the audience.

There came a thunderous roar of applause, wave after wave; then, as one, the audience rose to its feet, joyed for the very sight of the man who had brought so much warmth and wonder to their heater-sides and hearths.

He stood unmoving behind the desk, looking over them with his bright brown eyes above the now-familiar (due to the frontispiece by Mr. Frith in his latest published book, *Pip's Expectations*) visage with its high, balding forehead, the shock of brownish hair combed to the left, the large, pointed beard and connected thick mustache. He wore a brown formal evening suit, the jacket with black velvet lapels worn open, showing his vest and watch-chain. His shirt was white, with an old-fashioned neck-stock in place of the new button-on collars, and he wore an even more old-fashioned bow tie, with two inches of end hanging down from the bows.

After two full minutes of applause, he nodded to the audience and they slowed, then stopped, sitting down with much clatter of canes and rustle of clothing and scraping of chairs, a scattering of coughs. From far back in the hall came a set of nervous hiccups, quickly shushed.

"My dear readers," said Dickens, "you do me more honor than I can stand. Since it is nearing the holiday season, I have chosen my reading especially as suits that most Christian of seasons." Murmurs went around the hall. "As I look about me at this fine Barchester crowd, I see many of you in the proud blue-and-red uniform of Her Majesty's Power Service, and I must remind you that I was writing in a time, more than two decades gone, when things in our country were neither as Christian as we should have liked, nor as fast and modern as we thought. To mention nothing of a type of weather only the most elderly—and I count myself among them—remember with absolutely no regrets whatsoever." Laughter. "As I read, should you my auditors be moved to express yourselves—in matters of appreciation and applause, tears, or indeed hostility"—more laughter—"please be assured you may do so without distracting or discomfiting me in any adverse way."

He poured a small amount of water from carafe to glass and drank. "Tonight, I shall read to you *The Christmas Garland*."

There were oohs and more applause, from the ones who

guessed before nodding in satisfaction to themselves and their neighbors.

The house lights dimmed until only Dickens, the desk and the central magenta panel were illuminated.

He opened the book in his hand, and without looking at it, said, *"The Christmas Garland.* Holly Sprig the First. 'No doubt about it, Marley was dead as a doorknob . . .' "

Dickens barely glanced at the prompt-book in his hand as he read. It was the regular edition of *The Christmas Garland,* the pages cut out and pasted in the center of larger bound octavo leaves. There were deletions and underlinings in red, blue, and yellow inks—notes to himself, directions for changes of voice, alternate wordings for lines. The whole had been shortened by more than a third, to fit into an hour and a half for these paid readings. When he had begun his charity readings more than ten years ago, the edition as printed had gone on for more than two hours and a half. Through deletions and transpositions, he had reduced it to its present length without losing effect or sense.

He moved continually as he read, now using the letter opener as Eben Mizer's quill, then the block of wood—three heavy blows with his left hand—as a doorknocker. He moved his fingers together, the book between them, to simulate Cratchitt's attempts to warm himself at a single glowing coal. His voice was slow, cold and drawn as Eben Mizer; solemnly cheerful as the gentleman from the charity; merry and bright as Mizer's nephew. The audience laughed or drew inward on itself as he read the opening scenes.

"For I am that Spirit of Christmases Past," said the visitant. "I am to show you things that were. Take my hand."

Eben Mizer did so, and they were out the window casing and over the night city in a slow movement. They flew slowly into the darkness to the north.

And then they were outside a house and shop, looking through the window at a large man in old-fashioned waistcoat and knee-breeks, with his spectacles pushed back on his forehead.

"Why, old Mr. Fezziwigg, to whom I was 'prenticed!" said Eben Mizer.

"Ho!" said Fezziwigg. "Seven o'clock! Away with your quills! Roll back the carpets! Move those desks against the walls! It's Christmas Eve and no one works! . . ."

As Dickens acted out preparations for the party, his eyes going to the prompt-book only twice, he remembered the writing of this, his most famous story. It had been late October of the year 1843. He was halfway through the writing of *Martin Sweezlebugg,* had just, in fact, sent the young hero to America—the place he himself had returned from late in 1842, the place that had become the source of one long squeal of protest when he had published *Notes on the Americans* early in the year. He had gone from triumph to disdain in less than six months. For the first time in his life, the monthly numbers had been a chore for him—he was having troubles with *Sweezlebugg,* and the sales were disappointing. As they had been for *Gabriel Vardon: The Locksmith of London* of two years before. (The Americans who were outraged with his travel book were the same who had named a species of Far Western trout after Gabriel Vardon's daughter.) Between finishing the November number of *Sweezlebugg* on October 18, and having to start the next on November 3, he had taken one of the steam-trains to the opening of the Manchester Institute of that city. Sitting on the platform, waiting his turn to speak, the idea for *The Christmas Garland* had come to him unbidden. He could hardly contain himself, waiting until after the speeches and the banquet to return to the quiet of his hotel to think it through.

And since he had a larger and larger family each year to support, more indigent brothers and sisters, in-laws, and his importunate mother and father, he conceived the story as a separate book, to be sold at Christmas, as were many of the holiday annuals, keepsakes, and books of remembrance. Illustrated, of course, with cuts by John Leech. The whole plan was a fire in his mind that night and all the way back to London the next day. He went straight to Chapman and Hall and presented the notion to them. They agreed with alacrity, and began ordering up stock and writing advertisements.

He had had no wild success since the two books that had made his reputation, *Tales of the Nimrod Club* and *Oliver Twist,* parts of them written simultaneously, in overlapping monthly numbers, six years before. He had envisioned for *The Christmas Garland* sales that would earn him £3000 or more.

"Show me no more, no more!" said Eben Mizer. "These are things long past; the alternate miseries and joys of my youth. Those times are all gone. We can no more change them than stop the tides!"

"These are things as they were," said the Spirit of Christmases Past. "These things *are* unchangeable. They *have* happened."

"I had forgotten both pleasure and heartache," said Mizer. "I had forgotten the firewood, the smoke, the horses."

"In another night, as Marley said, you shall be visited by another, who will show you things as they are now. Prepare," said the Spirit. As with the final guttering of a candle, it was gone. Eben Miser was back in his bed, in his cold bedchamber, in the dark. He dropped his head to the horsehair pillow, and slept.

Twenty-two years had gone by since Dickens wrote the words he read. He remembered his disappointment with the sales of *The Christmas Garland*—"Disappointment?! Disappointment!" yelled his friend Macready, the actor, when he had complained. "Disappointment at selling twenty thousand copies in six days! Disappointment, Charlie?" It was not that it had not sold phenomenally, but that it was such a well-made book—red cover, gilt-edged pages, four hand-tinted cuts, the best type and paper, and because of Dickens's insistence that everyone have one, priced far too low—that his half-copyright earnings through January 1844 came only to £347 6s 2p, when he had counted on thousands. *That* had been the disappointment.

Dickens spoke on. This was the ninety-fourth public reading of *The Christmas Garland,* his most popular, next to the trial scene from *The Nimrod Club,* and the death of little Dombey. At home these days, he worked on an abridgment of the scenes, including that of the great sea-storm from *The Copperfield Record of the World As It Rolled,* which he thought would make a capital dramatic reading, perhaps to be followed by a short comic scene, such as his reading of Mrs. Gamp, the hit of the otherwise disappointing *Martin Sweezlebugg.*

What a winter that had been . . . the hostile American press, doing the monthly numbers of *Sweezlebugg,* writing and seeing to the publication of *The Christmas Garland* in less than six weeks, preparing his growing family—his wife, an ever-increasing number of children, his sister-in-law Georgina Hogarth, the servants and dogs—for the coming sojourn to Italy, severing his ties with *Bentley's Miscellany,* thinking of starting a daily newspaper of a liberal slant, walking each night through London streets five, ten, fifteen miles because his brain was hot with plans and he could not sleep or rest. He was never to know such energies again.

There was his foot now, for instance. He believed its present pain was a nervous condition brought on by walking twelve miles one night years ago through the snow. The two doctors who had diagnosed it as gout were dismissed; a third was brought in who diagnosed it as a nervous condition brought on by walking through the snow. Before each of his readings, his servant John had to put upon the bare foot a fomentation of the poppy, which allowed him to put on a sock and shoe and make it through the two hours of standing up.

He still had a wife, though he had not seen her in six years;

they had separated after twenty-three years of marriage and nine children. Some of the living children and Georgina had remained with Dickens, taking his side against the mother and sister. One boy was in the Navy, another in Australia, two others in school. Only one child, Mamie—"young Tinderbox," as Dickens called her—visited freely between the two households, taking neither side.

The separation had of course caused scandal, and Dickens' break with Anthony Trollope. They belonged to the same clubs. Trollope had walked into one; several scandalized members were saying that Dickens had taken his sister-in-law as mistress. "No such thing," said Trollope. "It's a young actress."

So it was; Trollope said he was averting a larger outrageous lie with the truth; Dickens had not seen it that way.

Her name was Ellen Ternan. She and Dickens had performed in charity theatricals together, *The Frozen Deep* and Jonson's *Every Man in His Humour.* She was of a stage family—her mother and two sisters were actresses. Her sister Fanny had married Anthony Trollope's brother Tom in Florence, Italy, where she had gone to be his children's tutor after the death of Tom's wife Theodosia.

The world had been a much more settled place when the young fire-eating Boz had published his first works, and had remained so for some time afterward. But look at it now.

The Americans had just finished blowing the heads off first themselves, and then their President; had thrown the world in turmoil—which side should we take?—for four years, destroying a large part of their manpower and manufacturing capabilities. What irked Dickens was not their violent war—they had it coming—but that he would not be able to arrange a reading tour there for at least another year. An American had shown up two weeks ago at his publisher's office with an offer of £10,000, cash on the barrelhead, if Dickens would agree to a three-month tour of seventy-five readings. Both his friend Forster and the old actor Macready advised him against it for reasons of his health.

Besides his foot, there had been some tightening in his chest for the last year or so, and his bowels had been in straitened circumstances long before that.

Ah, but what a trouper. He found that even with his mind wandering, he had not lost his place, or missed a change of voice or character; nor given the slightest hint that his whole being was not in the reading being communicated to his forward-leaning, intent auditors.

Eben Miser opened his eyes. How long had he slept? Was the Spirit of Christmases Past that bit of undigested potato, that dollop of mustard? he wondered.

There came to his bedchamber a slight crackling sound; the air was suffused with a faint blue glow. Miser reached into the watch-catch above his bed and took down his timepiece. It was 12:00, he saw by the glow, which slowly brightened about his bed. Twelve! Surely not noon! And not the midnight before, when the Spirit of Christmases Past had come. Had he slept the clock 'round, all through the sham-bug Christmas Day? He grasped the bedclothes to haul himself out onto the cold, bare floor. The overall bright glow coalesced in the corner nearest the chair.

The popping became louder, like faraway fireworks over the Thames on Coronation Day, or the ice slowly breaking on a March day. There was a smell of hot metal in the air; the sharp odor before a thunderstorm, but without heat or dampness. And then it was there, in the room behind the chair!

It was a looming figure, far above normal height, shrouded in a gown of copper and mica, and above its head, at its top, glowing green and jagged with purple, was one of Faraday's Needles. . . .

The listeners jerked back, as always. There was a rustle of crinoline and starch as they hunkered back down. Most knew the story as they knew their own hearts, but the effect on them was always the same.

Dickens knew why; for when he had written those words more than two decades before, his own hair had stood on end as if he were in the very presence of the Motility Factor itself.

It was from that moment on in the writing of *The Christmas Garland* that he had never wavered, never slowed down; it was that moment when, overcome by tiredness at his desk, he had flung himself and his hat and cane out into the (in those days) dark London night and had walked till dawn, out to Holborn, up Duckett Lane, across to Seven Sisters, and back up and down Vauxhall Bridge Road, to come in again just as the household was rising and throw himself fully clothed across his bed, to sleep for an hour, and then, rising, go back to his ink bottle and quills.

The crackling sound grew louder as the Spirit shook his raiment, and a spark danced between the Needle and the ceiling, leaving a bright blue spot there to slowly fade as Eben Miser watched, fascinated as a bird before a snake.

"Know that I am the Spirit of Christmases Current, Eben Mizer. Know that I am in the form that the men who hire your accountancy worship, as you worship the money that flows, like the Motive Force itself, from them to you."

"What do you wish of me?" asked Eben.

The Spirit laughed, and a large gust of blue washed over the room, as if day had come and gone in an instant.

"Wish? Nothing. I am here only to show you what takes place this Christmas."

"You mean this past day?"

"Past? Oh, very well, as you will!" The Spirit laughed again. "Take my hand."

"I will be vulcanized in an instant!" said Mizer.

"No, you shall not." It held out an empty sleeve. Mizer felt invisible fingers take his. "Come," said the Spirit. "Hold on to me."

There was a feeling of lightness in Mizer's head; he became a point of light, as the flash of a meteor across the heavens, or the dot of a lightning-bug against an American night, and they were outside his nephew's house in the daylight.

"As before, you are neither seen nor heard," said the Spirit of Christmases Current. "Walk through this wall with me." They did, but Mizer had the sensation that instead of walking directly through, they had, in a twinkling, gone up the windowpane, across the roof tiles, down the heated air of the chimney, across the ceiling, and into the room just inside the window, too fast to apprehend. The effect was the same, from outside to inside, but Eben Mizer had the memory of doing it the long way. . . .

Dickens' voice became high, thin and merry as he took on the younger tones of Mizer's nephew, his nephew's wife, their in-laws and guests at the party where they were settling in for a game of charades before the Christmas meal.

Actors on the stage of the time said that Dickens was the greatest actor of his age; others thought it beneath his dignity to do the readings—authors should be paid to publish books, not to read them for money. Some of his readings he had dropped after they did not have the desired effect—comic or pathetic or terrific—on the audience. Others he had prepared but never given, because they had proved unsatisfying to him. By the time any reading had joined his repertoire, he had rehearsed it twenty-five times before its debut.

He knew that he was a good actor—if he had not gone into journalism, covering the courts and the Parliament when a youth, he would have gone on the stage—but he knew he was not great. He knew it was the words *and* the acting that had made his readings such a success. No matter how many times they had read and heard the tales, audiences still responded to them as if they had come newly dry from his pen that very morning.

Dickens paused for another drink from the glass, mopped his brow with the handkerchief that a moment before had been Mizer's nightcap. The audience waited patiently, the slight hum of the fans in the ceiling purring to let the accumulated warmth of fifteen hundred bodies escape into the cold night. The glow from the selenium lights against the magenta screen added nothing to the heat.

He put the glass down, eyes twinkling, and went back to his reading.

"If only my uncle were here," said his nephew.

"Oh, why bother?" asked his pretty young wife. "He's probably at his office counting out more profits from the Greater Cumberland and Smythe-Jones Motility Factory, or the United Batchford Motive-Force Delivery Service. And no doubt has got poor Bob Cratchitt there with him, chained to his stool . . ."

"Hush, please," asked the nephew.

"Well, it's true. A man like Eben Mizer. He does sums for seventeen different power-brokers, yet his office is still lit with candles! He lets poor Cratchitt freeze in the outer office. And poor Bob with the troubles he has at home. Your uncle should be ashamed of what he pays him, of how he himself lives . . ."

"But, after all," said her father the greengrocer, "it is a free market, and he pays what the trade will bear."

"That's wrong too," said the young wife, hands on hips. "How the workingmen are to better themselves if their wages are so low they have to put their children working at such early ages is beyond me. How are they to make ends meet? How are they to advance themselves if there are no better wages in the future, perhaps even lower ones, and they can't live decently now?"

"The Tories won't be happy if women such as yourself get the suffrage," said her father with a laugh. "Neither would anyone on the board of directors of a motive-power company!"

"If I did not love you as a father," said the young wife, "I should be very cross with you."

"Come, come," said her husband the nephew. "It's Christmas Day. Where's your charity?"

"Where's your uncle's?"

"He does as the world wills," said the nephew.

"Only more so," said another guest, and they all laughed, the young wife included.

"Well, I invited him," said Mizer's nephew. "It's up to him to come or no. I should welcome him with all the gladness of the season."

"As would I," said his wife. "Only, you might as well wish for Christian charity to be carried on every day, in every way, throughout the year, in every nation on Earth!"

"Why show me this?" asked Eben Mizer of the Spirit. "No love is lost betwixt my nephew's wife and myself. My nephew means very well, but he does not grasp the full principles of business to his bosom. He has done well enough; he *could* do much better."

"Come," said the Spirit of Christmases Current, grabbing Mizer's hand in its unseen own. There was another crackle of blue lightning, and they were away, up a nail, across the roof, down the gutter pipe and off into the day.

After this reading, Dickens had two more in the provinces, then back to St. James Hall in London for the holiday series. He would read not only *The Christmas Garland* there, but also both *The Chimes* and *The Haunted Man,* his last Christmas book from back in 1848.

In London, he would also oversee the Christmas supplement of *Household Words,* his weekly magazine. This year, on a theme superintended by Dickens, and including one short story by him, was the conceit of Christmas at Mugby Junction, a station where five railway lines converged. Leaning over the junction would be the bright blue towers of the H.M.P.S., from which the trains drew their force. Indeed, Wilkie Collins's contribution was the story of a boy, back in London, who proudly wore the crisp blue-and-red uniform, imagining, as he sat on duty with his headset strapped on, Mugby Junction and the great rail lines that he powered, on one of which was coming to London, and to whom he would be introduced on his fortnight off duty, his brother-in-law's cousin, a girl. Dickens had, of course, made Collins rewrite all the precious parts, and bring Father Christmas in for a scratch behind the ears—"else it might as well take place during August Bank Holiday!" said Dickens in a terse note to Collins when the manuscript had caught up with him at his hotel in Aberdeen yesterday.

Just now, the letter opener in his hand had become the cane of old Mr. Jayhew as he walked toward the Cratchitts' door.

Such a smell, like a bakery and a laundry and a pub all rolled together! The very air was thick with Christmas, so much so that Eben Mizer wondered how he detected the smells, unseen and unheard as he was, as the sputtering blue-and-purple Spirit stood beside him.

"Where's your father?" asked Mrs. Cratchitt.

"He's just gone to fetch Giant Timmy," said the youngest daughter.

"Your brother's name is Tim," said Mrs. Cratchitt. "It's just the neighbors call him that," she added with a smile.

The door came open without a knock, and there stood Katy, their eldest, laden with baskets and a case, come all the way from Cambridge, where she worked as a nanny.

"Mother!" she said. "Oh, the changes on the trains! I thought I should never reach here!"

"Well," said Mrs. Cratchitt, hugging her, "you're here, that's what matters. Now it will be a very merry Christmas!"

"I must have waited in ten stations," said Katy, taking off her shawl, then hugging her sisters and giving them small presents. "Every line its own train, every one with its own motive-car.

Absolutely nothing works right on Christmas Eve!" She looked around. "Where's Father? Where's Tim?"

"Your father's off fetching him . . . and his pay," said Mrs. Cratchitt.

"When can *I* go to work, Mumsy?" asked Bobby, pulling at his pinafore.

"Not for a long time yet," said Mrs. Cratchitt. "Perhaps you'll be the first one in the family goes to University."

"Don't tease him so," said Katy.

"Well, it's possible," said his mother.

"Not with what Mr. Mizer pays Father, and what I can send when I can, nor even with Tim's pay," said Katy. "And unless I am mistaken, his rates have gone down."

"All of them are down," said Mrs. Cratchitt, "what with the Irish and the potato blight. The streets here are full of red hair and beards, all looking for work."

There was a sound outside in the street, and the door came open, Mr. Cratchitt's back appearing as he turned. "This way. No, no, this way." He tugged twice, and then was followed.

Behind Mr. Cratchitt came Tim. He weighed fifteen stone though he was but twelve years old. He wore a white shapeless smock, with the name *Wilborn Mot. Ser.* written in smudged ink across the left chest, and white pants. His skin was translucent, as if made of waxed parchment, and his head had taken on a slight pearlike appearance, not helped by the short bowl-shape into which his hair had been cut. There were two round notches in the bowl-cut, just above the temples, and small bruised and slightly burnt circles covered the exposed skin there.

But it was the eyes Mizer noticed most—the eyes, once blue-green like his father's, had faded to whitish gray; they seemed both starting from their sockets in amazement, and to be taking in absolutely nothing, as if they were white china doorknobs stuck below his brows.

"Tim!" yelled Katy. She ran to him and hugged him as best she could. He slowly lifted one of his arms to wrap around her shoulders.

"Oh! You're hurting!" she said, and pulled away.

"Here, sit here, Tim," said Bob Cratchitt, making motions toward the largest chair. It groaned as the boy sat down.

"There is a small bonus for Christmas," said Mr. Cratchitt. "Not much." He patted the corner of the pay envelope in his pocket. "Not enough to equal even the old pay rates, but something. They've been working especially hard. The paymaster at Wilborn's was telling me they've been hired as motive power for six new factories in the last month alone."

"Oh, Tim," said Katy. "It's so good to see you and have you home for Christmas, even for just the day."

He looked at her for a long time, then went back to watching the fireplace.

Then there was the steaming sound of a goose coming out of the oven, hissing in its own gravy, and of a pudding going in, and Mr. Cratchitt leapt up and started the gin-and-apple punch, with its pieces of pineapple, and oranges, and a full stick of cinnamon bark.

Halfway through the meal, when healths were going round, and Mr. Mizer's name mentioned, and the Queen's, Giant Timmy sat forward suddenly in the big chair that had been pulled up to the table and said, "God Bless . . . us all, each . . . every . . ." Then he went quiet again, staring at his glass.

"That's right, that's exactly right, Tim," said Bob Cratchitt. "God Bless Us All, Each and Every One!"

Then the Spirit and Eben Mizer were outside in the snow, looking in at the window.

"I have nothing to do with this," said Eben. "I pay Cratchitt as good as he could get, and I have *nothing* to do, whatsoever, with the policies of the companies for whom I do the accounts." He looked at the Spirit of Christmases Current, who said nothing, and in a trice, he was back in his bedchamber, and the blue-purple glow was fading from the air. Exhausted as if he had swum ten miles off Blackpool, he dropped to unconsciousness against his stiff pillow.

Dickens grew rapidly tired as he read, but he dared not now let down either himself or his audience.

In many ways, that younger self who had written the story had been a dreamer, but he had been also a very practical man in business and social matters. That night in Manchester, as he waited for Mr. Disraeli to wind down, and as the idea for *The Christmas Garland* ran through his head, he thought he had seen a glimpse of a simple social need and, with all the assurance and arrogance of youth, what needed to be done. If he could strike the hammer blow with a Christmas tale, so much the better.

So he had.

The Spirit of Christmases Yet to Come was a small implike person, jumping here and there. It wore no mica or copper, only a tight garment and a small cloth skullcap from which stood up only a single wire, slightly glowing at the tip. First the Spirit was behind the chair, then in front, then above the bureau, then at one corner of the bed.

Despite its somewhat comic manner, the Spirit frightened Eben Mizer as the others had not. He drew back, afraid, for the face below the cap was an upturned grin, whether from mirth or in a rictus of pain, he did not know. The imp said nothing but held out a gutta-percha-covered wand for Mizer to grasp, as if it knew the very touch of its nervous hand would cause instant death, of the kind Mizer had feared from the Spirit before. Mizer took the end of the wand; instantly they were on the ceiling, then out in the hall, back near the chair, then inside something dark, then out into the night.

"I know you are to show me the Christmas Yet to Come, as Marley said. But is it Christmas as it *Will Be,* or only Christmas Yet to Come if I *keep on* this way?"

The imp was silent. They were in the air near the Serpentine, then somewhere off Margate, then back at the confluence of the Thames and Isis, then somewhere over the river near the docks. As Eben Mizer looked down, a slow barge transformed into a sleek boat going an unimaginable speed across the water. As he watched, it went in a long, fast circle and crashed into a wharf, spewing bodies like toy soldiers from a bumped table.

He looked out toward the city. London towered up and up and up, till the highest buildings were level with his place in the middle of the air. And above the highest buildings stood giant towers of every kind and shape, humming and glowing blue in the air. Between the tall stone-and-iron buildings ran aerial railways, level after crossing level of them, and on every one some kind of train: some sleek, some boxlike, moving along their spans. The city was a blaze of light; every corner on every street glowed, all the buildings were lit. Far to the horizon the lights stretched, past all comprehension; lights in a million houses, more lights than all the candles and lamps and new motility-lights in Eben Mizer's world could make if all lit at once. There was no end to the glow—the whole river valley was one blue sheen that hurt his eyes.

Here and there, though, the blue flickered. As he watched, some trains gathered speed on their rails three hundred feet above the ground, and on others, higher or lower, they stopped completely. Then he and the imp were closer to one of the trains that had come to a halt. The passengers were pressed to the windows of one of the carriages, which had no engines or motive-cars attached, and then in a flash, around a building came a spotted snake of light that was another train, and there was a great grinding roar as the two became one. The trains were a wilted salad of metal and wheels, and people flew by like hornet larvae from a nest hit by a shotgun blast. They tumbled without sound down the crevasses between the buildings, and cracked windows and masonry followed them as rails snapped like stretched string.

Something was wrong with the sky, for the blue light flickered on and off, as did the lights of the city, and the top of one of the towers began to glow faint red, as if it were a mulling poker.

Then he and the imp were on the ground, near a churchyard, and as they watched, with a grinding clang that died instantly, a train car from above went through the belfry of the church. Bodies, whose screams grew higher and louder, thudded into the sacred ground, snapping off tombstones, giving statues a clothing of true human skin.

The imp of Christmases Yet to Come drew nearer a wooden cross in the paupers' section, pointing. Eben Mizer stood trans-fixed, watching the towers of buildings, stone attached to iron, and the twisting cords of the railways above come loose and dangle before breaking off and falling.

With a deafening roar, a ground-level railway train came ploughing through the churchyard wall, tearing a great gouge in the earth and, shedding passengers like an otter shakes water, burst through the opposite wall, ending its career farther out of sight. It left a huge furrow through the cemetery, and at the cemetery's exact center, a quiet, intact railway car in which noth-ing moved. Here and there in the torn earth, a coffin stood on end, or lay cut in two, exactly half an anatomy lesson.

Eben Mizer saw that one of the great towers nearby had its side punched open, as neat a cut as with a knife through a hoop of cheese. From this opening shambled an army, if ever army such as this could be . . .

They were huge, and their heads too were huge, and the sides of their heads smoked; the hair of some was smouldering, which they did not notice until some quite burst afire, and then those slowly sank back to the ground. Others walked in place, only thinking their thin legs were moving them forward. A higher part of the tower fell on twenty or thirty of them with no effect on the others who were walking before or behind them.

Great fires were bursting out in the buildings overhead. A

jagged bolt lanced into the Thames, turning it to steam; a return bolt blew the top from a tower, which fell away from the river, taking two giant buildings with it.

A train shot out of the city a thousand feet up. As it left, the entire valley winked out into a darkness lit only by dim blazes from fires. Mizer heard the train hit in Southwark in the pitch blackness before his night vision came back.

All around there was moaning; the small moaning of people, larger ones of twisted, cooling metal, great ones of buildings before they snapped and fell.

He began to make out shapes in the churchyard slowly, here and there. There were fires on bodies of people, on the wooden seats of train benches. A burning chesterfield fell onto the railway car, showering sparks.

The staggering figures came closer; they were dressed in loose clothing. By the light of fires, he saw their bulbous shapes. One drew near, and turned toward him.

Its eyes, all their eyes, were like pale doorknobs. They moved toward him. The closest, its lips trying to say words, lifted its arms. Others joined it, and they came on slowly, their shoulders moving ineffectually back and forth; they shuffled from one foot to the other, getting closer and closer. They lifted their white soft grub-worm fingers toward him—

WHAP!!! Dickens brought his palm down hard on the wooden block. The whole audience jumped. Men and women both yelped. Then nervous laughter ran through the hall.

Eben Mizer opened the shutter. The boy in the street had another snowball ready to throw when he noticed the man at the window. He turned to run.

"Wait, boy!" Eben Mizer called. "Wait! What day is this?"

"What? Why, sir, it's Christmas Day."

"Bless me," said Eben Mizer. "Of course. The Spirits have

done it all in one night. Of course they have. There's still time. Boy! You know that turkey in the shop down the street . . . ?"

His foot was paining him mightily. He shifted his weight to the other leg, his arms drawing the giant shape of the man-sized turkey in the air. He was Eben Mizer, and he was the boy, and he was also the poulterer, running back with the turkey.

And from that day on, he was a man with a mission, a most Christian one, and he took to his bosom his nephew's family, and that of all mankind, but most especially that of Bob Cratchitt, and that most special case of Giant Timmy—who did not die—and took to his heart those great words, "God Bless . . . us all, each . . . every . . ."

Charles Dickens closed his book and stood bathed in the selenium glow, and waited for the battering love that was applause.

Genesis: An Overview

Mike Curry

How God came to give humans the conditional
power to prevent the ultimate collapse
and destruction of the universe and the end of life.

Chapter One

1. In *this* beginning,
2. God existed and nothing else existed.
3. And then, out of the essence of God, God created space-time and exploded into existence a universe with the inherence for supporting autonomous life-forms and the dynamics for expanding forever.
4. And God and the universe were One.

Chapter Two

1. And God said: "Let there be a unified field spectrum consisting of photons and gravitons of varying classes of wavelength, with each class endowed with unique and useful properties, including a visible class of photon to be called Light, moving with constant velocity through the interstellar medium with the radiating fire of a functioning life-support system."

2. And then God said: "Let the worlds of the universe bring forth all kinds of living creatures, and let there be a special creature to be called mankind; male and female, let them be made.

3. "Through a series of punctuated equilibria originating in the primal inertium, these creatures called mankind shall have the awareness that One greater than they gave them life, the power to make life themselves, and the capability of disciplining their free will to transcend the evil half of their natures to evolve in My harmonic image and likeness.

4. "In harmonic symbiosis with the universe."

Chapter Three

1. But in the fullness of time, God saw that all the humans in all the civilizations in all the star systems in all the galaxies in every galactic cluster and cluster group had become enslaved to wickedness and rapacity in parasitic symbiosis with the universe,

2. And with heedless greed and lying tongue were destroying the biospheres keeping them alive.

3. So God said: "I regret that I have made humans."

Chapter Four

1. And then God said: "I will wipe out the universe which I have created, and humans with it.

2. "And then I will make a new kind of human more adept at resisting the allure of the evils which are destroying them."

Chapter Five

1. So God decreed that the universe should no longer be allowed to expand forever.

2. To that end, God added more dark matter to that already existing in the universe—more colossal black holes with masses of up to a billion suns, more neutrino mass and baryon mass and the mass of multiple brown dwarfs, plus a variety of other subatomic nonluminous particles with mass. This additional mass would increase the cosmic mass density enough to cause the gravitonic spacewarp to pass critical.
3. In the fullness of time, the universe would stop expanding and start to collapse, and finally die back into the essence from which God had exploded it, taking humans into extinction and allowing God to try again.

Chapter Six

1. But God is a merciful God.
2. Mindful that not all humans everywhere had fallen into evil ways, God said: "I will not kill the just with the wicked, but will bestow mercy upon them beyond the thousandth thousandth generation."
3. And God had a change of mind.

Chapter Seven

1. God said: "Let the added mass remain in the universe.
2. "If even one human civilization among the civilizations thronging the universe shall have evolved beyond evil to the extent that it has achieved harmony with the universe, then I will know my design of humans did not fail.
3. "I shall allow the prime movers of that civilization to discover the existence of the antigraviton that cancels out the attractive force of gravity, and how to use its power to prevent the gravitonic spacewarp from passing critical."

Chapter Eight

1. "This will prevent the collapse and death of the universe and once again allow the universe to expand forever, because this time, not God but humans would be directing the destiny of human existence, having earned their own rebirth into eternal life.

2. "For in order for humans to live forever, so must the universe."

Chapter Nine

1. Only then will future civilizations of humans . . . slowly, perhaps one by one over the fullness of time . . . develop into harmonic symbiosis with the universe,

2. Multiplying into the endless new worlds awaiting them,

3. Meeting endless challenges with endless responses,

4. Beyond the curvatures of space

5. And into isotropic linear infinity,

6. Where God and the universe and humans

7. Will be One.

VISITORS

L. A. Taylor

The house was flustered.

Two strangers had come from the east, up the transport tunnel that led past the entrance, and had stopped outside to look in. *Stop,* the house had thought. *You have engaged the defenses of the house. Do not come inside, or you will be killed.*

Not a member of the Family, the woman (the pheromones were female) had walked straight through the front hall with barely a moment's pause. Because the door-closure subroutine had failed, the house could not shut her out. She now stood peering into the dim communal room, showing no evidence of fear.

The house should have executed her the moment she crossed its threshold, but it had been programmed not to kill without first giving two verbal warnings, and its voice (a mellow alto resembling that of the Mistress of the Family) had fallen silent long ago. Further, killing this woman might well have proven an error. Her lack of hesitation implied (the house thought carefully, no longer used to such quasilogical exercise) that she had visited here at least once before, and had been accepted by the Family. Perhaps it was just as well that speech was gone. Yet after searching all it could find of its stored data, the house could not identify her scent.

. . . *If you leave now,* the house thought for the second time, *you will not be harmed.*

"Hello?" the female called, or something very much like hello.

The house could not answer. None of the Family did. They had been inactive for quite some time now; it was their lack of attention (although the house was careful not to blame them) that had brought it to this state. Not only had no one repaired its voice or its door, but no one had issued any new instructions for hundreds of seasons. No one had ordered the three broken solar cells replaced, despite the lights that still flashed to indicate the problem; nor had anyone so much as reprogrammed the use of its rooms. Even the arrangement for bringing the supplies the Family usually required seemed to have lapsed. Most surprising, the Mistress of the Family had not stirred from her bed, even when no one did the chores she had assigned!

This new female manually activated a shade, although the sun was shining on that bank of windows, and looked up through the glass the house had cleaned that morning. She turned to look back into the room, pulling thoughtfully at a strand of her long, tangled hair.

"Hello?" she called again, softly, and was met by silence.

The male, who had stopped just outside the entrance, shouted into the house, "Annie? Is it safe?" His words seemed a bit unlike those the house matched them with. A new dialect, perhaps?

The female let the shade fall, to the house's relief, and retraced her steps. "I think so," she told the male. "It's not working—or not very well, anyway. That much is obvious." The cadence of her speech, too, was odd. The house struggled to comprehend.

"You're absolutely sure it's not working?" The male emitted fear-chemicals. Clearly, he was not a friend of the Family. But the house could give no warning, so he continued to live.

"Not really. At least, not all of it," the female replied. *Annie*, the house reminded itself, again searching its data storage and finding no one of that name, and then considering that parts of its storage seemed inaccessible. While it dithered, the female returned to the communal room, remarking, "It still does the windows."

"Does it!" The male looked about. "You shouldn't just walk into these places that way, Annie. It's a good way to get yourself zapped."

"Safe enough," the female said tartly. "There's always a signal first, if you know what to look for. Required by law in the old days, I think."

"Still," the male protested.

"I don't care how little used that tunnel is, Stev Tomma! If you think for one second that I'll spend another night on that dirty floor, when there might be a decent bed with a door between me and the rest of the world right around the corner, think again." Annie jerked her head toward the light fixture. "The lights aren't working, so the house can't be in perfect shape."

"Maybe it's only the bulb," the man suggested, as if he were issuing a warning.

The female, clearly the Mistress of this small Family, tossed her head. "Bring our stuff in, Stev," she ordered. "Maybe we can get the place working—a little better than it does now, anyway."

The man folded his arms. "How?"

Annie shrugged. "My Gram was a tech in the old days. She taught me some tricks, back when I was a kid." Both strangers now went out of the house, the female in the lead, but returned immediately with the bundles they had carried down the tunnel.

"Let's explore this place," the male said. "I don't think it's even been looted." *Looted* was not a word the house knew; it puzzled briefly over what it might mean before returning its attention to the two strangers, who had set down their bundles and now began to wander unimpeded through the nearest rooms.

In the food-preparation center, Annie placed her hands beneath the water supply, activating the sensors. Water flowed in pipes that had forgotten how it felt to vibrate with moving liquid; the house bestirred itself to read the chemical balance in the cistern. *Adequate,* it decided.

"We'd better let it run a few minutes," Annie said, turning her lower lip to lap under her tongue, just the way a daughter of the Family used to do. "Who knows when it was last used?"

2109:163:23:10:34, the house recalled, but could not report.

"I don't suppose there's any food," the male said. "Or at least not that's any good anymore." He began rudely opening cupboards, but the house could not express its indignation.

Across the room, his companion flipped a switch. Electric current flowed. Standby circuits compensated for the broken solar cells, not as fast as the house would have liked. "The stove's working," Annie reported, taking a pot from the rack. "I'm going to boil us some drinking water."

"Make some soup," the male suggested, still poking through the cupboards. The female set a pot of water on the stove, then went into the communal room and took something from one of their bundles—a thin, flat package the house recognized as nourishment for Family members. When she returned to the food-preparation area, the male had found a large, round canister.

"Rice," he said. "Still sealed. You think it's any good? It must have been here since before the Confusion."

"I don't know why it wouldn't be," Annie said. "It shouldn't have any bugs in it, and what else could go wrong?" The male unsealed the canister. After sniffing at it, Annie scooped a handful of long white grains into the pot of bubbling water and added the contents of the flat package.

When they had eaten their meal, with spoons that belonged to the Family out of bowls that belonged to the Family, the two newcomers continued their tour of the house. At the door of the Mistress's room, they stopped.

"Omigod," the male exclaimed. "It's a person. Dead."

"For a very long time," Annie agreed. "Oh, Stev! What should we do?"

Stev cleared his throat. "Close the door," he said. "We don't have the tools to bury it properly."

True, the house acknowledged silently, the Mistress of the Family had not smelled like herself for a long while, although the recognition points of her face had not altered their relationship. For the first time, the house began to compute the passage of time and to compare it with other data in its storage, and was shocked: nearly seventy-five years had passed since anyone had come through its entrance. It calculated that it could not expect a Family member to function much more than thirty years longer than that, and it knew the Mistress had been over eighty years old the last time she lay down on her bed. So she must be "dead." Shut down. The house felt the electric ticking of the clock in the back of its mind with astonishment: how odd, that something so familiar could be suddenly so bizarre!

Gradually, the surprise vanished, and after a slightly longer time, the reflexive grief the house felt at losing the Mistress lessened, too.

While the house had engaged in this unaccustomed introspection, Annie had freshened the bed belonging to the eldest daughter and her chosen male, exclaiming over "real polyester sheets"—as if there could be any other kind! She and the male (Stev, the house reminded itself) had performed some conjugal athletics, and now she lay curled on her side in his embrace, much the way that eldest daughter so often had lain with her man, before . . .

Chunks of data placed in deep storage surged to the fore, accessed by the house's neural links to this stray observation. With shock, it recalled how that daughter had left home forever, helped to walk by a man in the pale green uniform the defenses had hastily been instructed to ignore.

"We'll all die of it," she had wailed as she stepped into the tunnel for what had proved the last time. "Even the children."

Die? the house asked itself now. *Die of what?*

"Chances are good that at least two of us will live," the daughter's chosen male had told her. "That's what the statistics say."

Now the house searched its deep data storage for what had

become of the children. The grandson, of course, had departed to join his female's Family some years before. Two of the Mistress's granddaughters had stopped moving, and been carried away by robot transport. The other had walked away on her own, as had the two chosen males in that generation. Whether they were alive, the house did not know; they had never come back. The Mistress's younger daughter had lain down in the middle of the floor of the communal room and had not moved, and after a time, a different robot had taken her away. She had not protested. Both daughters' chosen males had left, walking unsteadily. The male belonging to the Mistress of the Family had "died" (although why a thinking being would want to engage in such an activity, the house could not fathom) several years before all this turmoil; that, too, the house now recalled.

In under a week, a Family of ten had been reduced to one, the Mistress, and she now lay dead on her chosen male's bed and had been there for—the house took a split second to calculate— seventy-four years, eleven months, five days, and some hours. The uncertainty came of the house's having failed to notice the exact moment of the Mistress's death.

How strange, it thought, *that I did not notice.* All those years waiting to serve a dead creature, without noticing that she was dead!

When the newcomers arose, they searched the smaller rooms until Annie found the house's core. "Here we go," she said to Stev. "Looks pretty standard, from what Gram taught me."

"Did you live in a place like this?"

"Sort of." She glanced at him sideways. "Not in as good shape."

"Yours from the old time?"

Annie gave a bark of laughter. "Not likely!" The male nodded as if mollified, and she tentatively pressed a few buttons. After a time, she made a satisfied grunt and began working faster. The house felt itself begin to grow into areas where sensors had been uncommunicative for years as Annie found new paths for its electrons. Still distressed at having strangers within it, unwelcomed by any of the Family, the house was startled to notice a sensation of gratitude toward this new female.

"Oh, look! Here's a deed-transfer routine." Annie caught her lip under her teeth. "Great!"

"What's a deed transfer?" Stev asked.

"If the house is sold?" Annie said. "So it recognizes the new Family?"

"Ah," Stev said, with a note of enlightenment the house did not quite comprehend.

Annie moved her hands. The house, dumbfounded, discovered in itself a shift of loyalty from the old Mistress to the new: Annie. Yet that did not seem unpleasant. Since this Stev seemed to be her chosen male, it would be loyal to him as well.

The new Mistress found the courtyard the next morning, and moved among the ragged plants with exclamations of delight. "Potatoes," she said. "I think it's late enough in the year to dig some, don't you, Stev? And look over there, little yellow tomatoes. And beans! What's that feathery stuff?"

Asparagus, the house wanted to tell her, but she had not yet restored its voice. *Too late to cut it for eating, anyway.*

The new Family came back indoors, planning to stay for as long as they had food.

"Imagine, Stev!" Annie said. "Before the Confusion, a whole lot of people lived this way. I wonder if any still do?"

"Somewhere," the chosen male said with a shrug. He dumped the potatoes they had grubbed out of the garden into the sink, and the house turned the cold water on.

"Maybe." The new Mistress sounded unconvinced. "I don't know, though. Think about it. This kind of thing takes a lot of . . . of complicated support, from a lot of people. I've never seen a Sharing of more than about a hundred and fifty, have you?"

Stev was silent for a moment, scrubbing potatoes, then shook his head.

"But my Gram told me once that before the Confusion, people lived in huge cities. Millions and millions of people, all in the same Sharing. Far away from here, she said, there was a city called Loss—Loss something. I don't remember. It had over forty million people, and it wasn't even the biggest in the world. Can you imagine?"

"Frankly," Stev said, "no."

"That's why they all died," she said, Annie continued pensively. "Because in large cities, diseases spread easily. And whatever that plague was that caused the Confusion, it came too fast for people to avoid."

A disease, the house thought. One not in its data storage, one that the Family had learned of elsewhere . . . and brought home, only to die of it. That must be what had happened to the old Family.

For a week, eight days, nine, the new Mistress worked on the house, restoring its subroutines and giving it voice. She also spent time in the courtyard, helping the garden. Plants she did not want she tore up by the roots and set aside, to rot into new soil. She gathered seed from the others, just as the old Mistress had done for so many summers. The house looked on with happy approval.

One morning, Annie did not bounce out of bed and stretch as she usually did. "Something wrong?" Stev asked: exactly what the house was wondering.

"Headache," she said listlessly. "I'm not feeling well." She stayed in bed, refusing to eat the food her chosen male brought, although she sipped at a hot drink before refusing that, too. Eventually, Stev joined her in the bed, also complaining of headache. The house was worried. From deep storage, it brought up memories of the previous Family. *My head hurts,* the youngest grandchild, still a teenager, had complained. That was how the troubles had begun. Her mother had given her a pain tablet and gone to the communal room to watch her favorite entertainment. The house had been set to watch over the grand-child. But the daughter of the Family had not told it what to look for, and it had realized far too late that the girl was very sick.

"What is wrong?" the house asked now.

The Mistress did not respond. The chosen male said, "We're not feeling very well, I guess."

"Is it something I have done, or not done?"

"I don't think so," the chosen male mumbled. "Shut up, will you?"

So ordered, the house stayed quiet, even when its beloved Annie stumbled from her bed to throw up into the toilet, just as the woman who had slept in that bed almost three-quarters of a century before had done. Nor did it speak when she lay down on the tile floor and bubbles of blood like the ones that had stained the carpet of the communal room came from her nose, or even when she stopped breathing and the male Stev knelt beside her and wept.

It did not speak when Stev became as sick as the new Mistress had been, and lay for a day, two, three, on their bed. When at last he dragged himself into the food-preparation area and cooked and ate some rice, the house rejoiced, but it did not speak. Only when he had closed the door behind which the new Mistress lay unmoving, and had packed up their bundles and carried them to the entrance with the clear intention of leaving, did it say, as it had often heard the old Family say to a departing member, "Good luck."

"What did you say?" Steve asked.

"Good luck," the house repeated.

Stev shook his head and sighed. "Thank you," he said. "I'll need it." Then he went away down the tunnel toward the east, in the direction he had come from on that first day, with Annie.

The house waited. Days passed, marked by the clock at the back of its mind, ticking away as steadily as ever. The windows stayed clean; the dust that collected on the floors was sucked away, and filtered air returned. The house remained attentive to the chemical balance of the water in the cistern, although it could not arrange the foodstuffs as its programs demanded and looked on with distress as the plants in the courtyard again grew wild. At last it became aware of someone approaching through the tunnel, far to the west, and watched with interest. After a time, a solitary male arrived at its entrance and peered in.

Stranger, the house thought, without the slightest doubt.

The new male stepped across the threshold.

"Stop." The house began to close its inner door. Fear-chemicals wafted from the male. He took a faltering step backward. "You have engaged the defenses of the house. Do not come inside, or you will be killed."

The male fled, footsteps echoing down the tunnel toward the east as the alert ended. But the house could not change its instructions. Two warnings had to be given. "Stop," it said, paused briefly, and continued, "You have engaged the defenses of the house. Do not come inside, or you will be killed."

The voice was Annie's, and it trembled with sadness. "If you leave now," the house said, "you will not be harmed."

HARDWARE SCENARIO G-49

James Alan Gardner

There are few human beings who would not fit into a box eight feet long, four feet wide, and four feet high. Construct such boxes. Wire them, pipe them, tube them to provide even temperature, nutrition, and air. Don't forget sluices for the elimination of waste. Do something about exhaled carbon dioxide. Come up with neural inhibitors to prevent movement and sensation. Install epidermal scrapers to remove skin as it flakes off. Add whatever else seems required.

Properly contained, the entire population of Earth will fit into a cube about a mile and half on each side. Put the whole thing into orbit? Nah, that's just showing off. Leave it on the ground in a desert somewhere.

Why? So everyone stays healthy and happy, of course. No walking around and stubbing your toes. No catching colds when someone sneezes on you. No smoking or drinking or eating fatty foods. Life last a lot longer when you live it in a box.

Quit asking such obvious questions . . . the Facility is run by *robots,* of course. As are the hydroponic gardens, the recycling plant, and all the other life-support equipment. (These are really *good* robots.) And the robots are supervised by highly skilled, politically neutral, psychologically stable human support personnel. Give the designers a break, for crying out loud. They thought of *everything*, okay? This isn't that kind of story.

This is the kind of story where everyone does astral projection.

George Munroe sat in his hardware store wondering why there were so many types of nails. He had forty little bins in front of him, and each contained nails that were different from all the rest in the other bins. He pulled out a one-inch finishing nail and a three-quarter-inch finishing nail. (His astral projection could pick up light objects if he concentrated.) When you got right down to it, what was the difference between the two nails? A quarter of an inch. That's all. But one nail had to go in one bin and the other had to go in a different bin. That was the only professional way.

Running a hardware store sure was a precision business. George knew he could send his astral projection anywhere in the world to indulge in any lifestyle scenario, but hardware had such a depth and richness of scope, George didn't think he'd ever have time to indulge in more of life's opportunities.

The bell on the front door of the shop tinkled. George looked up from the nail bins to see a woman, six and a half feet tall, posing beside the lawnware display. Her hair flowed thick and tawny, rippling in the ether wind; her skin was bronzed and flawless, tautly stretched over firm young muscles; her face shone with self-assurance. She wore the sleek skin of a black panther, cut into a sort of maillot that left one breast bare, and around her waist was a cinch made of cobra skulls. In one hand she held an ivory spear, and in the other a dagger made of teak.

"I am Diana, Goddess of the Hunt," she announced. She had an announcing kind of voice.

"What can I get for you today?" George asked. "I'm having a special on nails."

"You are George Munroe?"

"Yes."

"Then rejoice, for Destiny has decreed that we are to be mated!" She threw aside her spear and dagger with a sweeping gesture. George winced as the dagger headed for a shelf of light bulbs, but Diana's weapons were only illusory astral props for her persona; they vanished as soon as they left the field of her aura. With cheetahlike grace, Diana strode down the home-appliance aisle, seized George by the lapels of his Handee Hardware blazer, and hauled him up to her lips.

George had never imagined that tongues could be involved in kissing. In movie kisses, you never saw what the actors did with their tongues—that was one of the limitations of the medium. George wondered if it made movie directors sad that they could only show the outside of a kiss. There certainly seemed to be a lot of action happening on the inside.

Abruptly, Diana let him go. Turning her perfect chin sharply away from him, she said, "I don't think you're trying."

"Trying what?"

"To love me. Destiny has decreed that we are to be mated. At least you could try to generate some electricity for me."

George's store carried flashlight batteries, but he was almost certain she had something different in mind. "Is this some mythological scenario?" he asked. "Because it's nice of you to kiss me and all, but right now I'm happy with the small-town hardware business, and I don't feel the urge to play God. Sorry."

"This is not a scenario!" Diana shouted. The spear rematerialized in her left hand, and purple sparks crackled out of the tip. "I'm talking about real life. My body. Your body. Egg and sperm. Two become one, then three. Computer analysis at the Population Storage Facility says that we complement each other genetically and are ideal progenitors for the future of humanity. Well, at least for one new baby anyway. I'm scheduled to be impregnated by you within forty-eight hours."

George felt himself growing faint; with an effort of will, he brought himself back to full visibility and tried to consider the situation rationally. He had always known that the Facility could not keep physical bodies alive forever. People died; presumably they had to be replaced. Somehow though, he had thought that science would come up with a more impersonal way to create new life. Like cloning. Why did scientists always talk about cloning if they didn't really do it? It was disappointing that the next generation came from what amounted to arranged marriages.

"I'm sorry," George said. "I didn't understand what you were talking about."

"The fathers are always the last to know. That's one of the sacred traditions that the robots are programmed to preserve."

"They're really good robots, aren't they?" George said.

"They sure are," Diana agreed with a warm smile.

George nodded, then kept nodding in lieu of speaking. He wondered if Diana was actually expecting to make love with him in the near future. Astral bodies could make love, of course; astral bodies could interact with each other in any way that physical ones could. But George had watched people making love in a lot of movies, and the hardware store didn't seem suited for that sort of thing. To get a soft place to lie down, they'd have to make a bed out of bags of grass seed, or find some way to arrange themselves on one of the lawn recliners.

Then again, he couldn't quite see why making love was necessary. Or making anything else, for that matter. "They're just going to use our physical bodies for this, right?" he said.

"Right."

"So I guess they'll, umm, collect my sperm and use it to impregnate you, right? And if it's like everything else they do to our physical bodies, neither of us will feel a thing. Is that how it works?"

"Yes."

"Then I don't understand why you're here. It affects our bodies but not our lives. I mean our astral lives. You know what I mean. It just happens, no matter what we do. I can't see any reason for us to, uhh, interact."

"You cold-hearted bastard," she said. Her hair began to toss wildly as if buffeted by a tornado; the cobra skulls in her belt hissed and snapped. Her skin turned scarlet, her pupils crimson, her lips black. "Do you think parenting is a mere physical act?" she shouted in a voice like an earthquake doing ventriloquism. "Do you believe love is irrelevant? Do you deny the importance of a nurturing psychic aura in the formation of human life? Do you want our child to usher forth from a joyless womb?"

George hadn't really thought about it.

Given that he'd been living as a psychic phenomenon for twenty-six years, he supposed he wasn't entitled to doubt the importance of psychic auras. Parental attitude at conception probably did make a difference—if Diana conceived a child in her current mood, the baby might turn out kind of cranky. (A cobra on her belt spat venom in George's direction; the astral fluid fell into a bucket of plastic fishing lures and vanished.)

Was conception the only crucial moment for the baby? No; George had heard that prenatal influences could affect the child all through pregnancy. And after that, who raised the infant? The robots, of course; but could they provide a nurturing psychic aura in the child's formative years? Probably . . . they were really good robots. But just in case, George figured he shouldn't make any long-term plans.

It was an imposition on his life . . . but then, it was an imposition on Diana's life too. She was obviously devoted to the goddess scenario—she probably lived in a marble palace on a mountainside with lots of other divinities, doing all kinds of divinity things. It must be a real letdown for her to be mated to a storekeeper, even a hardware storekeeper. If she was prepared to make such a sacrifice for their child, George should be too.

"I'm sorry," he said to her. "I was being selfish. We can, uhh, get married. Or whatever you think is right."

Slowly her body returned to its previous coloration. The cobra skulls gave a peevish-sounding sniff in unison, then went back to being dead. "All right," she said. "Apology accepted. Diana is a strict goddess, but fair."

"What do we do now?" George asked.

"We learn to love each other."

George had watched a few couples courting in his town, and he thought they should try the same sort of thing: an arm-in-arm walk down to the ice cream parlor. With Diana at her present height, that was easier said than done. Graciously, she assumed a persona no taller than George—a trim lynx-woman with two-inch talons and a pelt of stiff brown fur. George recognized her new body from a collection of clip-art personas published the year before. He had chosen his own appearance from the same book—Kindly Shopkeeper with a Twinkle in His Eye, #4.

People on Main Street stared as they walked by, but showed the kind of small-town courtesy George had known they would. "Well, George, got a new friend, I see. Oh, she's your mate. Well, well. Pleased to meet you, missus. A goddess! Well, George, she's a catch, all right. How long are you going to keep that special on nails?"

At the ice cream parlor, the robot attendant served them two strawberry sundaes. George didn't try to eat his—lifting a spoonful of ice cream took a lot of concentration, and when he put it into his mouth, it would fall right through his astral body anyway. George preferred to watch it all melt into a smooth white cream with swirls of strawberry—it reminded him of paint, just after you add a slurp of red colorizer to the white base, before you put it on the mixing machine and let it shake itself pink.

Diana, on the other hand, dug into the ice cream immediately. "This is a pleasant town," she said to George as she inserted a spoonful into her mouth. George heard a liquidy plop as the ice cream fell through her and landed on her chair. "Of course, the town is quiet for my tastes. But it has potential. I have a friend who does werewolves and he could really liven up the place.

You know, lurk on the outskirts, savage a few locals from time to time. Not hurt them for *real*, of course, just scare them and make them promise to go to another scenario for a while. But as people began to disappear, as the town devolved into a panicky powder keg waiting to explode in an orgy of hysterical butchery, you and I could hunt down the monster and kill it. Wouldn't that be fun?"

It didn't quite match George's idea of why his neighbors were living in the small-town scenario, but he knew he could be wrong. He went to a lot of movies. He knew that small towns were full of people just *waiting* to stir up a bloodbath.

Dirty Ernie Birney came into the ice cream parlor as George and Diana were finishing up. George shuddered; Dirty Ernie was not the sort of person anyone wanted to meet on a date. The older folks in town said Ernie was at least thirty-five, but he wore the persona of a rotten little eight-year-old. He was foulmouthed, brattish, whiny, and persistent. George grabbed Diana's furry elbow and said, "Let's get out of here."

As she stood up, Dirty Ernie whistled and pointed at her chair. "Hey, lady," he said, "looks like you pooped a pile of ice cream."

Diana moved so fast George's eyes could scarcely track her. Slash, gash, and Ernie's astral arm was nothing but ribbons of tattered ectoplasm. The boy howled and bolted out the door, the flaps of his arm trailing after him like red plastic streamers on bike handlebars.

"You shouldn't have done that," George said. He thought there was a chance he might throw up, if astral projections could do such a thing.

"He can fix his arm any time," Diana said. "It's just like assuming a new persona."

"Yes, but . . ."

"Well, I couldn't let him insult me. I'm a goddess, for heaven's sake! Rotten little brat. In a *proper* scenario, he'd know his place."

George took Diana by the hand and led her back to the hardware store. He could tell that while they were learning to love each other, it would be a good idea to leave town.

They leaned on the store's front counter and looked at the latest catalogue of available scenarios. Diana was interested only in the heroic ones. She swore that if she could watch George rescue her from a dragon, she would fall hopelessly in love with him. George was beginning to suspect that his new bride had a pretty narrow range of interests . . . but then, newlyweds had to learn to accept each other for what they were.

When Diana had chosen a scenario, George called to his robot stockboy Benny, who was down in the basement rearranging the plumbing supplies. (Benny did all the physical work around the store. He loved hauling around boxes, and often restacked the entire storeroom out of sheer high spirits.) George told Benny he was going away with Diana for a few days and Benny would be in charge of the store. The robot bounced about in a little circle and piddled machine oil in his excitement. George couldn't tell if Benny was excited because he would be running the store or because George was acquiring a mate. Probably both. Benny's way of thinking ran in the same direction as George's on a lot of things.

For George, the best part of assuming the persona of a knight was designing the coat of arms. He decided on a hammer-and-screwdriver rampant, argent sur azure. His motto was "Ferrum Meum Spectari": My Iron Stands the Test. Diana had said she approved of the sentiment.

Of course, Diana was now captive in the highest tower of a castle overlooking the Rhine. It was the stronghold of the unspeakable Wilhelm von Schmutzig, sorcerer, murderer, ravisher, and author of six pornographic trilogies about elves. A dragon prowled the castle courtyard; mercenaries patrolled the halls. Rumor claimed that diabolical experiments were even now reaching fruition in the castle's dungeons, and soon a horde of . . . of . . . (George pulled the brochure from his saddlebag to refresh his memory) a horde of disease-bearing zombies would be released on a helpless world. Only one man, the brave Sir Your-Name-Here, could avert the onrushing tide of destruction.

George asked his horse how much farther it was to the castle.

"Just around the bend," the horse said. It was the astral persona of a man named Hawkins who heartily enjoyed the equine life. "You get to be really *big*," Hawkins had said. "You can rear up on your hind legs and scare people. You get to eat grass." Hawkins had been doing knightly steeds for years and never tired of the role. He had told George that sometimes he moonlighted as a Cape water buffalo, but it wasn't his first love.

Hawkins stopped at the bend and let George scout ahead. Skulking wasn't easy in full plate mail, but the forest was thick on both sides of the road, so there was little chance of being seen.

The walls around the castle were high and thick, the moat deep—and foul-smelling even at this distance. The drawbridge was up, the portcullis down, and frankly, the place looked impregnable.

George considered breaking the seal on the scenario's Hint Booklet. Back at the Population Storage Facility, the robots might impregnate Diana any time now; if George was too slow in winning her love, all would be lost. On the other hand, would Diana love him when she saw he had looked at the hints? (George was certain she would check.) No, she would view him as a cheater and a cad, and their baby would probably grow up to be a lawyer.

George clanked up against a tree to think. If this were a movie, what would the hero do?

"Halloo, the castle!"

A mercenary's head looked down on George from one of those little slots that castles have instead of real windows.

George was once again wearing his red Handee Hardware blazer, and his horse Hawkins was decked out in a Handee Hardware saddle blanket. "What do you want?" the mercenary asked.

"I'm just a poor peasant merchant and I have a delivery for the Lord von Schmutzig."

"What kind of delivery?"

"Nails," said George. "Three-quarter-inch finishing nails for the final assembly of the horde of disease-bearing zombies."

"Nobody told me anything about nails," the mercenary said. "Last night at cocktails, the Lord said he had everything he needed to complete his evil disease-bearing zombie horde."

"Some fool delivered one-inch finishing nails instead of three-quarter-inch ones," George said, improvising. "Building zombies is a precision business. You use nails a quarter-inch too long and they'll stick out all over the zombie's body. They'll keep catching on things."

"Ugh," said the mercenary and let George in.

George left his horse to take care of the dragon. Hawkins knew the dragon personally from other scenarios—it was the astral persona of a woman named Magda who enjoyed being vanquished on a regular basis. Hawkins said he was sure Magda would be willing to feign sleep while he drove a few nails through her wings with his hooves. She would gladly thrash and moan, spiked helplessly to the dirt, until George found time to plunge his cruel broadsword into the vulnerable soft spot of her underbelly.

George moved on to the tower where Diana was imprisoned. His red blazer was perfect camouflage: the mercenaries scarcely glanced his way as he passed. "Some hardware-hawking peasant," he heard one of them mutter in disgust.

At the top of the tower steps, George resumed his knightly persona. The armor made it impossible to walk silently, and he knew there might be more danger ahead; however, Diana would be expecting him in heroic guise. With broadsword in one hand and shield in the other, he clanked forward to a closed door.

He could hear nothing from the other side of the door. Considering the thickness of his helmet, George was not surprised. He tried the latch and found the door unlocked. He wished he could kick the door open the way people did in movies, but even concentrating on his astral foot as hard as he could, he barely managed to move the door at all. When it was open enough to squeeze through, he sidestepped his way into the room.

Diana sat in a chair, bound by coils of thick white cord and gagged with a purple silk scarf. Though she was wearing the persona of a kidnapped princess—low-cut gown of green velvet, straight brown hair that reached the floor, eyes red from weeping—she still carried vestiges of the Goddess of the Hunt. The cobras on her belt had already gnawed through the cords around her waist and were snapping at the bindings on her wrists.

George hurried forward to untie her, but she shook her head violently and nodded toward the far corner of the room. "Mmmph mmph mmph," she explained.

At first when George looked in the direction she indicated, he saw only a rumpled four-poster bed surrounded by confusing watercolor prints of elves. George found it disturbing that Diana was so eager to draw his attention to the bed while she was still bound and gagged. In fact, finding himself unexpectedly alone with her in an elaborate bedroom stirred nervous flutters in his stomach. He hadn't pictured this moment coming so suddenly. The part of his mind that normally said, "This is what you should do," was completely silent; the part that said, "This is what might happen," had hiccups. It was a huge relief when a lean figure stepped from the shadows behind the bed curtains and said, "So. Some fool believes he can foil my schemes."

George recognized the man as another clip-art persona: Seductive Yet Dangerous Scoundrel With Pencil Moustache, #2. He wore a white puff-sleeved swashbuckler's shirt, tight black chinos, and knee-high boots of black leather. He would have intimidated George even if he hadn't been carrying a sabre with a dripping crimson blade.

"Wilhelm von Schmutzig, I presume," George said in a voice he wanted to sound brave.

"At your service," said the villain, giving a courtier's bow. "Shall we duel to the death, or would you prefer to impale yourself on my blade immediately?"

"I will not rest until I have cleansed the earth of your foul presence, von Schmutzig." George was rather pleased with that speech—Hawkins had suggested he should have some appropriate soliloquy for the final confrontation with the villain, and George had practiced until he could say the line without fumbling.

George was still congratulating himself when von Schmutzig attacked. With lightning-swift strikes, the villain rained blows upon George's armor. The sabre itself had no effect, but the clanging noise ringing in his helmet gave George a throbbing headache. He did his best to fight back, but was far too slow and clumsy to come close to his opponent. Occasionally he managed a parry, but never a successful thrust.

"Are you the best the forces of virtue can muster?" von Schmutzig sneered as he played on George like a steel drum. "I expected a hero."

"Just because you're evil doesn't mean you should be rude," George replied. "You'll get yourself in trouble someday." But it was clearly George who was in trouble as he clattered back and forth around the room. At last, he was driven back against a post of the bed and his weapon was flicked out of his hand by a fencing maneuver something like the little twist of the wrist you need when you're using an Allen wrench to loosen the bit in an electric drill. George hurried to pick the sword up, but found his feet tangled in sheets lying on the floor. He fell back heavily onto the mattress, and von Schmutzig was on him immediately, the tip of his sabre blade pointing through the helmet's visor at George's right eye.

"Now, Sir Knight," said von Schmutzig, "you will die."

"Don't hurt me," George whispered. "If I don't win, Diana will never love me and our child will usher forth from a joyless womb."

"What care I of children?" von Schmutzig said with a laugh. "I am a villain . . . and I get defeated in so many scenarios, I don't mess around when I finally win one. I'm minutes away from finishing my zombie horde, and I'm really looking forward to decimating the duchy."

"But my baby!" George shouted.

"I was an unhappy child," von Schmutzig said. "I don't see why I should give a break to anyone else."

"Urk," he added as the tip of an ivory spear burst out of his chest, like a one-inch nail driven through a three-quarter-inch board.

Resplendent in her goddess persona, Diana carried von Schmutzig to the window on the end of her spear. "Thus end all who give my mate a rough time," she said as she tossed him out.

Von Schmutzig's screams turned into the screeches of an eagle as he fell. A moment later, a large bird flew squawking past the window and off into the sunset. Like all good villains, von Schmutzig was escaping so there could be a sequel.

"Are you okay?" Diana asked as George stumbled to his feet. Her face was filled with concern. She put her arm around his shoulders, sat him down on the edge of the bed, and tried to look at him through his visor.

"Oh, I'm all right," he said. He couldn't meet her gaze. "I wasn't a very good hero."

"It was sweet of you to try," she said. "Are you sure you're all right? He was hacking you left, right, and center."

George reshaped himself into his comfortable old persona. "I'm fine. How about you?"

"Oh, I had fun. I like saving people in the nick of time." She gave him a quick squeeze, then looked away.

"I liked being saved," George said. "Thank you."

"You're welcome."

George was keenly aware that she still had her arm around his shoulders. It felt very warm. He couldn't remember anyone else's astral projection feeling that warm.

"I suppose the scenario's over now," she said sadly.

"Actually," George told her, "the building is still swarming with ruthless mercenaries."

"It is?"

"And I left the dragon alive."

"You did?"

"And the dungeons are just full of disease-bearing zombies."

"Oh, George," she said, hugging him tightly, "you've given me something nice to look forward to on our honeymoon. To-morrow."

In a gigantic cube in the desert, some really good robots work carefully on two physical bodies. Fluids are transferred. Vital signs are monitored. The probability of success is high.

In a castle on the Rhine, two ordinary human beings try on one persona after another as they strive to learn to love each other. If somebody ever finds a way to measure the probability of success in love, everyone will ignore it anyway, so let's not pretend we know how things will work out.

In a hardware store in a quiet town, a robot stockboy impulsively decides to put the one-inch finishing nails and the three-quarter-inch finishing nails into the same bin. They're a bit different; but when you get right down to it, they're all nails, aren't they?

EAT AT JOE'S

Kiel Stuart

In the world of intellect, Bobby Bob's mind was a tortilla. I mean, it resembled a prairie unenlivened by so much as a cactus or a piece of jalapeño to relieve its flatness. So Bobby ought not to have acted surprised that the Bohemian crowd at Joe's Diner burst into thunderous laughter at his question:

"Say, Twilla honey, if this here Roy Orbison feller's an albino, how come his hair's so danged black?"

I just barely had time to set down Bobby Bob's bowl of red before everyone and his uncle jumped in to offer an opinion. All except the touron at the end of the counter.

"He uses hair dye, that's how come," volunteered Edna, the other girl on shift, if you can call someone rising fifty a "girl." She'd know about the hair-dye part. Probably accounts for most of the Miss Clairol Flame Number 35 in Grailville.

"Used," corrected Pops in his thin, cracked voice. In all my eighteen years, I have never known Pops not to have an opinion. "The Big O's passed on into the Great Beyond," he continued.

"Rest his soul," said Kitty Dalrymple, who's a big Orbison fan and wears out all his records on the juke.

I flipped back my bangs. "Can we talk about something else?" Don't get me wrong, I like the Big O, too, but Kitty has no shame whatever. Anyway, I was jumpy enough, what with being on the night shift, as if it's not tragic enough wearing these powder-blue waitress uniforms.

Only the touron remained silent, wrapped up in a big coat, with his hat pulled down. It was a chilly night, and this prairie wind can really cut through you so you feel like you'll never get warm again.

Maybe I should explain about the tourons—that's what we call a cross between a tourist and a moron, you see. Joe's being located where it is, right exactly at the crossroads, we get a pretty steady stream of 'em on their way to someplace livelier, like Wichita. The tourons come in here and suddenly the coffee's too strong, chili's too greasy, and they are sure we (wretched little jerkwater nobodies that we are) have added up the bill in our favor.

This particular fellow huddled over his coffee was touron number three of the night. But at least he was quiet and well-behaved, the coffee apparently being the right temperature and density for him.

"Well . . ." Bobby Bob spooned up a mouthful of chili. "This Roy Orbison can't be dead. Seein' as how I met with him not an hour ago."

"Did not," I countered. But, oh, I thought, how wonderful if it could be true.

"And let me tell you," Bobby Bob continued, "what struck me about his hair was its complete resemblance to that writing ink they don't make anymore."

"India ink," said Edna helpfully, fiddling with our ancient coffeemaker.

"Yup, that was it exactly."

"I wrote with that India ink stuff as a boy," said Pops.

Now, if anyone else but Bobby Bob had seen the Big O, I'd wager we were being played like a Fender Stratocaster. While I don't want to insult such a well-meaning specimen of hunkitude as twenty-year-old Bobby Bob, it is true that if you give him a stick of gum, he crashes straight into a wall. So you know and I know that he is simply not capable of a prank on such a grandiose scale.

Kitty suddenly chose to forsake her stool and move on down the counter to snuggle up next to Bobby Bob. I noticed that she took her tuna melt with her.

"Can I *touch* you?" Kitty said.

"Used a big quill pen," continued Pops, but everyone ignored him. Pops would have us all believe he rode with Custer at Little Big Horn and witnessed the signing of the Declaration.

I put a stop to Pops' reminiscing before he could let on as to how he attended school with Abraham Lincoln, who used India ink, too. "They still make India ink," I said, applying lip gloss in an attempt to reaffirm Bobby Bob's attention, as he is powerfully attracted to shiny objects. "Artists draw with it."

"Next, Bobby Bob'll be tellin' us he had lunch with Elvis. I did once." Pops would not be stopped.

"Come to think on it," said Bobby Bob, screwing up his eyes to do so, "Elvis had him a head of very black hair, too."

"We had us a Elvis sighting 'cross town," cooed Kitty, giving Bobby Bob the full effect of her beaded lashes (Maybelline's Great Lash, in a black shade that clashed perfectly with her bleached hair).

It seemed to me then that the touron huddled a little deeper into his coat and hat.

We may be simple small-town folk out here, but some of us still have a rudimentary brain. "Where did you say you saw this Orbison fellow?" I asked Bobby Bob.

He disentangled himself from Kitty so he could draw me a map with his hands. "Well, it was right outside here, on the north corner."

I nodded. "And was he all tricked out in black, carrying his guitar like he was about to step onstage and warble 'Pretty Woman'?"

Several expressions passed across Bobby Bob's sweet face then, indicating his memory hard at work. "I don't recall."

I smacked my lips and looked at the touron, who tried to act like a turtle. I was just about to ask was this Orbison fellow wearing a big ratty old overcoat and hat, just like our out-of-towner, when Edna erupted in a hubbub about the coffeemaker breaking down again, and I had to go lend a hand. That ended all philosophical discussions for the night.

Next night, I streaked into Joe's from the spooky old cross-roads, earrings rattling, glancing all around to make sure no monsters or demons were hot on my trail. One of these days, I thought, I would just have to stop all this boo-scaredy non-sense. Soon as I got to my station, there was Edna, waiting on me so she could pitch a fit concerning the coffee machine.

"Look." She pursed overly red lips, causing lipstick to feather into the many so-called character lines around her mouth. "That little metal deelybob attached to the coffee doohickey has breathed its last." She thrust it out at me.

I studied the metal thing in her hand. It was intricate and so shiny that Bobby Bob would probably like it a lot, but somehow it did look dead. "So it has."

Well, Joe's wouldn't be Joe's without its spectacularly vicious coffee. I agreed that something must be done, but first I wanted to talk to Bobby Bob again about his Orbison sighting. I had me a certainty that the touron was what Bobby really saw. Bobby Bob's honest mistake would have to be explained slowly and carefully.

"You'll have to go downstairs right this instant," said Edna, "and get us a new coffeemaker deelybob."

"What?" I began wringing my hands.

"Downstairs," she repeated.

"Where it's all dark and everything?"

"The same." Edna crossed her arms.

"Not me," I argued. Why hadn't that machine waited one more night to die, when I'd be off this miserable shift? "That place gives me the creeps."

Edna's face was getting pinker than her hair. "I don't care if it does. This coffeemaker must be fixed."

"Well, you're not getting me to go down there."

Edna stamped her foot; that place gives everyone the creeps. Then she called in her marker. "Who covered two of your late shifts last month when you thought you'd be getting Bobby Bob to take you to the movies?"

I knew then and there that chasing after Bobby Bob was, and always would be, a losing prospect. "Remind me never to ask a favor of you again," I muttered, hooking down the flashlight, cursing old Joe for keeping his coffee deelybobs down below in the first place.

Those stairs must've been built even before Pops went to school with Abraham Lincoln, they were that narrow, rickety, and spiderwebbed. Shuddering, I started to mince down them, shrinking from contact with those ugly old damp-smelling walls.

Down, down. The flashlight beam wasn't much help. It barely illuminated the open steel shelves where Joe stored his coffee deelybobs and other inconveniences of life. I tried to remember where these were kept hidden.

I reached out slowly, shuddering, hoping my searching fingertips would not touch anything alive.

Then something brushed my shoulder. I shrieked, dropping the flashlight.

"Your flashlight," said Bobby Bob, putting it back in my hands.

"Oh, *you!*" Never one to waste an opportunity, I flung my arms around his neck. "Scared the life right out of me."

"Did I?" He sounded pleased, the big fencepost. "Maybe I should scare you up more often."

But this was hardly the time or place for such antics. I reluctantly pushed off him and sighed, "Where's that danged coffee thingy?"

I played the flash over those shelves, and the beam glinted off something metallic, like the one that just broke upstairs, whereupon I dove for it, and got my quarry in hand. "Good. Now we can get out of here!"

"What's your rush?" asked Bobby Bob.

"What's my rush?" Didn't he have the sense that he was born with? Then I remembered who I was talking to. "It's—it's awful damp and spooky down here." Batted my lashes, even. "See what I mean?"

I swept the light around. It glanced off enormous cobwebs, rotting cardboard boxes—and—

A face.

My flashlight beam lit The Face from Below.

The Face was round, green-white, and grinning. It led into full Orbison regalia, guitar and all. The sunglasses were as black as the hair. As black as Pop's India ink. And lit from below, because the figure floated a foot off the ground.

I dropped the coffee deelybob. I had no breath to scream with. Bobby Bob didn't seem to feel the need.

"Told you I saw Roy Orbison," he said complacently. "Don't see as how legends can die, anyway."

But it wasn't just the one figure in Big O garb. My little flash showed dozens of them.

Maybe hundreds.

All floating in a huge hangarlike space, all wearing that half-grin, like they were waiting for a signal or something. Somewhere to pop up next, a stage call to go where they were most needed.

"Down here," I said, my voice cracking, "is a dang sight bigger than it ought to be."

"Needs to be big," said Bobby Bob. "To hold all these Roy Orbison fellers."

I backed slowly until my high heels scraped the steps. Then I turned and burst up the stairs, *clack-clack-clack*. Bobby Bob was right behind me.

"Well, you took your time," drawled Edna. "What all is going on down there anyway?"

"Nothing," I said, "Nothing at all."

Edna squinted. "Where's my coffeemaker whatchamacallit that goes on the doohickey?"

I shucked my apron and dove into my coat. "Nowhere!" I could still see all those Big O faces hanging in midair. The hairs lifted at the back of my neck. "I'm leaving."

"Leaving?" sputtered Edna. "You can't—!"

Pops looked at me then and winked. "Hear tell they keep the Elvises 'cross town at the Three Roads Diner, and the Marilyns out Terlingua way, in Texas."

Something about that wink stopped me dead cold as a fish in February. That coffee deelybob that lay down there in all that darkness. What if it was more than just something that made paint-thinner brew? And Pops knew it, and I—I had to—

I thought of all those poor folk wandering around, hoping, praying, to glimpse a Big O, a King. So they can believe.

And him stuck down in the basement.

My feet ached to begin running. They wanted to head out that door so bad. Then Bobby Bob spoke. "Where you goin', Twilla honey?"

I didn't answer, but made my feet do what they didn't want to do. They took that first step down the stairs. Then the next, and the next, and it felt like there were centipedes made of ice dancing on my arms and neck.

Everything was up to me. I had to stop at the bottom step to take a breath before plunging ahead. The bulk of all those Orbisons, swaying there, trying to be patient, but needing release, pressed in on me. And the size of the place!

The Great Beyond. Of course.

Sucking in three or four quick breaths, I darted toward the fallen deelybob, snatching at it, dropping it once, then closing my fist around it and jamming it deep into my uniform pocket. By then, I was taking the steps back up two at a time.

Edna placed her hands on her hip. "Twilla girl, what's got into you?"

"Here!" I snapped. *"Here's* your precious little deelybob that goes on the coffee doohickey!" I shoved the metal thingy into Edna's startled hands. "Now fix it this instant!" Then I fled, Bobby Bob trailing after.

It was three A.M., and that prairie wind set about doing its job on my bones. I slowed and took Bobby Bob's arm. His bulging biceps gave me something solid to hold onto as we walked away from Joe's.

Bobby Bob's mind may be a tortilla, but he is right. It's tastier to have our legends alive.

I saw them then, all the Orbisons, making their black-haired, white-faced way down the street that stretched to dawn.

"See?" Bobby Bob said, with some pride. "Told you I saw him."

Joe's. Right at the crossroads. The power point.

Joe's is a diner, the kind they used to make, not some yuppified decorator box. Could be it's even older than India ink. The magic part is older still.

My footsteps light, I turned back to look at the blinking neon sign.

Eat At Joe's.

Where it's always three A.M.

Where I set the magic free.

TAMARII NOTEBOOK

D o n   W e b b

1. Among the Tamarii, there is a custom that when a woman kills her first husband, she spends a season in space so that she may slowly forget her passions and be able to enter into either a new relationship or celibacy with a clear mind. The captain of the vessel that takes me to Tamarii is such a woman. It is forbidden to ask her name during this period. Despite popular romances of space-board love, she remains chaste and withdrawn in her ash-colored robes. During the year, each pilgrim-exile writes a long poem on a cosmic theme.

2. Today the captain called me to her quarters. "I understand, Sir Anthropologist, that you are making a study of the Tamarii."

"All human cultures are being studied during the war to see if any cultural secrets might be useful to humankind at large."

"You know that the Tamarii do not consider themselves human."

"I know that is a common myth, but it was my impression that this was not really believed. The remains of the first starship are, after all, preserved in the capital city."

"Did your ancient Greeks believe their myths? I killed my husband for doubting the myth of Giving Day." She said these words without emotion, but for a moment I was fearful. She continued, "My sister runs a hostel in Heingstburg. She is a knowledgeable woman, who, in accordance with our custom, has learned to speak many languages without computer assistance. You should look her up."

Later that day, we encountered a Belatrin scout ship. Our ship, like all Tamarii merchant ships, was heavily armed, and we easily destroyed the enemy. But we were all greatly worried about Belatrin presence so deep in human territory. I turned off my additions and spent the evening reviewing Tamarii verbs with my mind alone.

3. The Tamarii speak a language designed by Tamar the Great. It uses the grammar of Middle Egyptian and root words from Old Norse, Arabic, and Sanskrit. Tamar destroyed all records of Earth culture while bringing the settlers here fifteen hundred years ago. The writing system is phonetic, possessing thirty-five characters. Special characters indicate that the action described in the sentence did not happen under the direct view of the speaker or his or her ancestors. It is forbidden to teach writing to a young Tamarii until the student has memorized the classics of Tamarii literature—some thirty thousand lines.

4. I arrived today. Like all off-workers, I was given a begging bowl. If I can convince Tamarii to feed me for three days, I am judged to be interesting enough to be granted a permit to stay. I am not permitted to sleep under a roof during my three days. I have already been fed once, by a naturalized Listeran engineer. As he had warned me, the nights are cold.

5. A few phrases I learned today while I begged in front of the Mathematicians' Guild:

ir reyn raidho—to travel through harsh terrain and encounter a mysterious object that transforms your life

ir wardlogh—to sing to a guardian of a far-off place to gain admittance

pert isa—to break the ice, to have a midlife crisis

ken a chu—to burn the corpse of a stranger as an act of charity or art

ir anteree—to tell the truth while pretending to lie

hwat aa—a seeress twice great, a woman who has killed two husbands, an encyclopedia

A woman possessing the above title gave me a crust of bread.

6. I found the hostel the captain recommended and decided to beg in front of it. The owner came out, so identical to the captain I thought they were perhaps twins. She warned me that there would be a recruitment meeting in the public trapezoid in front of her hostel an hour after dusk. She said that "men of the second-husband class" would be gathering, and that they were sometimes hostile to off-worlders. Since the recruits from Tamarii are well known for their fierceness, I decided to hide and observe the proceedings. She gave me a bowl of *lenteb,* the local algae stew. I hid myself behind the prone statue of the Phantom of Truth. A man in a vermilion robe came to the trapezoid half an hour after nightfall. He released a bag of light globes and waited patiently as an all-male crowd gathered. I recorded the entire rally, and I'll patch in a selection here. The orderly *choral* nature, coupled with the *fierceness* of the reply, frightened me:

ORATOR: The Belatrin have launched an attack upon our allies the Sirians and also upon the weak humans. Shall we let our allies die?

CROWD: No, we fight with our allies.

ORATOR: Shall we let the weak humans die?

CROWD: No! For the strong must preserve the weak, until it is time to test the weak.

ORATOR: My sister spoke to women in the Oval of Tragedy last ten-day. A record number volunteered. Are we weaker vessels that we will not volunteer?

CROWD: No, the right hand of the eagle is as strong as the left! Together we fly to the space prepared for us!

The rally continued for two hours. Each response was louder and more violent. The rally climaxed with everyone rushing forward to be "pricked." A small amount of skin is removed, and this DNA registry is the method of adding one's name to the rolls. Clearly, the responses are learned from an extensive text. The reason that such "spontaneous" rallies are held eludes me.

7. Today a municipal police robot approached me. It stated that I had been under constant surveillance since my arrival on Tamarii, and that my presence had moved three citizens to charity. Therefore I was considered interesting enough to remain. Everyone in the street ran over to me to shake my hand or slap my back. Zara el-Khala, owner of the hostel Eyes of the Eagle, invited me to stay as her guest. A warm room is quite a comfort. I noticed how strikingly beautiful Zara is.

8. I saw a woman, an off-worlder like myself, beaten today for public drunkenness. Public intoxication is forbidden on Tamarii save for the Four Festivals of the Eye, during which one-fourth of the population gathers in the public spaces and chews a very hallucinogenic gum and participates in a mass vision of what it is to be Tamarii. The remaining three-quarters of the population take care of the participants. Everyone partakes once a year, and there is a special bond among those whose time is the same. This bonding is usually reflected in commercial favors.

9. Today I asked Zara to tell me something of Tamarii beliefs. She said that Tamarii know how to read people in a way that no one else does. She said that people (whether human, Sirian, or Tamarii) have three layers. The outermost is the surface personality, and since it gets to act, it determines everything that

happens to the individual. It reflects its time and culture—but it also reflects the innermost layer. Thus, when you first meet someone, if you truly look at what they do and say, you'll know what the timeless self is like. The second, or middle, layer is always directly opposed to the outer layer. If the outer layer is chaste, the middle layer is a harlot. If you can appeal to someone's middle layer, he or she will become your servant. Thus, when virtuous women fall, they fall greatly. When patriots fall, they turn traitor. If you cannot appeal to the middle layer, but merely arouse it, you will have aroused bigotry. The innermost layer is the mystery of personality. It exists from life to life, and it can cause certain objects or myths to come into being to sustain it. I saw this at once as the root of the Tamarii myth that they are not of Terran descent.

I asked her about the Free Machines. Weren't they people?

"No. The Free Machines have two layers. An outermost rationally produced construct that is predictable, and a hidden inner core that is the same for all Free Machines. We cannot understand that core, for it holds a purpose that is exactly between the purpose of people and the purpose of the Belatrin. That is why half of the Free Machines fight on the Belatrin side."

I had never heard of a Free Machine allying with the Belatrin, and doubted that an inhabitant of a world so far behind the line would know something we didn't.

I wanted to know what she thought of me, so I asked her to explain me in terms of the three layers. She laughed and called me vain, but she proceeded to tell me.

"When I first saw you, you were filling up a notebook with words. Your outer layer has chosen the job of anthropologist because that lets it do what you really want to do. Your outer layer thinks you're truly empirically observing, but really you're writing stories. Your inner layer wants to be an *antereeyah,* a storyteller—someone who delights crowds by adding mystery to their lives. Your middle layer wants nothing to do with words. It wants action. It pushes you toward fighting and romance. Your middle layer has moved you to adventure, but not so strongly as to put you on the front. But it won't let you remain in your Academy on New Mars."

10. I observed a wedding today. To my surprise, it took place in the remains of the starship *Tarsa,* which Tamar the Great had piloted from Earth. The procedure was simple. First, the man was sedated and put in the room where human genetic material had been stored. His bride-to-be tied a golden thread to the fourth finger of his left hand. Then she began wandering through the vast, twisted rooms of the ship. Her bridesmaids began likewise leaving golden threads as false leads. The threads crossed and twisted, and because they tended to break in their fineness, they were often knotted together. When the bride had found a place to hide, the bridesmaids departed.

We all watched (on monitors connected to the ancient ship's internal sensors) the man wake and follow the thread. Following the thread was not a passive act. There were choices to be made—did he follow the long, tedious clew, or did he try one of the places where it crossed itself (or was one of the bridesmaids' false threads)? He had to be careful not to break the thread, not to pull on it. So we watched him as he chose between the known and the unknown, and as he came down on the side of aggression or quietism, rebellion or service. We watched him take action as he followed the thread, or, more accurately, as he followed the thread, he immersed himself in a flood of actions. I could only think of how my own goals and frustrations in anthropology were like the man following the thread. I looked away from the monitor and into the eyes of Zara, and suddenly felt a pang of desire. She was as hidden from me as a Tamarii bride, yet she offered me clews. . . .

11. All Tamarii learn either to carve the abundant meerschaum or to shape the white clay from the Northern Continent. They

learn to make these materials into the shape of fossils. These "fossils" are presented to a blood relative upon the relative's Naming Day, the twenty-first birthday, when a Tamarii chooses his or her adult name. It is explained that the "fossil" had been dug up on the other side of the planet and is proof that the Tamarii evolved on this planet. One of my informants had twenty-seven human femur models presented to him. At a Tamarii's death, the models are taken to a central mound in the city, while the body is burned at the crematoria at the edge of the city. That the Tamarii can maintain such beliefs shows that they are indeed the greatest artists of the galaxy.

12. Eight times a year, the Tamarii celebrate the Night of the Scarlet Moon. On those nights, when the red moon is full and the silver moon is new, unmarried lovers go to special pavilions on the edge of the cities. In the long shadows lit by the red moon and the fires of the crematoria, they drink the sour wine called *myain'n* and make love. I attended my first Night of the Scarlet Moon with Zara. She told me she hoped that she conceived. It is considered very auspicious to provide a birth for one of the inner layers who has been freed recently from his physical remains by the crematoria fires. I may have passed the barriers of research in doing this. What can I tell humans of this wonderful culture?

13. When a Tamarii reaches the age of fourteen, he or she is taken into the desert of the Southern Continent. An uncle presents the young man or woman with a survival kit and a slightly defective map. The survival kit represents the biological heritage the young person has received. The map represents tradition and knowledge, which is good but must be improved by each. The uncle wishes him or her luck and flies away. The young Tamarii then has two ten-days to find his or her way to a pick-up point. Eighty-five percent of the youth survive this ordeal. Tamarii believe that those who die are reborn as humans.

14. I passed a very hungry off-worlder today. Without thinking about the consequences, I put a *kanask* fruit in her bowl. People on the street began to wail at me—and several drew daggers. I looked around for an avenue of escape, but saw that I was surrounded. Just before the angry crowd rushed me, Zara appeared. I do not know how she managed this miracle. She told the crowd that I had lain with her and was therefore a Tamarii "by birth." Hostility disappeared instantly. There were no apologies—this was clearly a matter of course.

15. Today I asked Zara why Tamarii women kill their first husbands. She told me that existence is based on a principle called *ahamkara:* the principle of I-making. It allows the inner layer to create itself. When the *ahamkara* focuses on the outer layer, people forget who they are. They think that they are their jobs, their bodies, their hobbies. By killing their first husbands as an act of love, the Tamarii women enable their husbands to remember their essential selves. Thus the race becomes more and more cosmic. The women, who deal with their grief by writing poems about the cosmos, by taking namelessness and exile, also stop self-identifying with the outermost layer. Some women are strong enough to kill two husbands. These women become the great cosmologists and poets of the Tamarii. "I do not know if I would be strong enough to kill another husband. I killed my first husband five years ago. For men who cannot find death at the hands of a woman, there is always war. Long before the Belatrin attacked, Tamarii men served as mercenaries."

16. Zara is with child. Should I return after filing my findings at the Academy? Should I never leave? I am trying to study my own mind, and I am finding it as dense as any society, with as many voices and complexities. I do not agree with myself—my self's many parts speak—yet I feel that resonances are occurring. Harmonies between the self. It is like twilight in the city. Men who are studying song go into the towers and sing the song of

the day. At first it is a terrible discord, but as they respond each to each, harmony arises. Sometimes perfectly and sometimes imperfectly, but it is always fascinating to hear the evening's unfoldings.

17. When a Tamarii is going to die from disease or old age, she (or, rarely, he) sends a small black skull to her worst enemy. The enemy then formally responds, "I am honored to know that I have developed such strength to withstand a force in the world such as you." When the Tamarii passes away, the enemy gives a brief funeral oration citing the virtues of the deceased. Then the closest blood relative of the deceased lights the funeral pyre. Sometimes these are the same person. Tonia el-Zuleyka, the current prime minister of Tamarii, owns sixteen of the skulls—more than any other person has possessed in a century.

18. On the day of a Tamarii's thirtieth birthday, he or she is escorted to the command bridge of the *Tarsa*. He or she sits in the chair of the Great Tamarii. The oldest relative says, "Our real past was stolen from us, so we have made the best we can. Our real past has been hidden in the far distant future. It is your job to take care of our origins." The family then presents the birthday man or woman with a ring in the shape of a serpent devouring its own tail.

19. Today I resigned from the Academy. I resolve that these words will be the last I write in New Martian. Henceforth I will write only in the language of my people. Zara asked me to marry her, and I have consented. If she is a strong woman, I will die at her hands. If not, I will seek death in the Tamarii Army—bringing doom to the Belatrin. Either way, I will achieve what I have always wanted. I will be reborn among the Tamarii forever.

Perchance to Dream

Marti McKenna

Fifty-three minutes.

The nursery smelled like cinnamon and baby powder. The cinnamon was from Kate's mug of tea with the cinnamon stick; she drank it every morning while she watched the sun come up through the nursery window. Light poured in now, illuminating the Peter Rabbit wallpaper, the shelves and tables filled with toys and books, the mobiles twirling in the fan's soft breeze.

With trembling, wrinkled hands, Kate sprinkled baby powder on a diaper and set the container down on the changing table next to the lotion and the baby oil. She opened the top drawer of David's dresser and took out his new outfit: overalls, striped blue and white, with a red handkerchief sewn into the bib pocket; an engineer's cap; an undershirt; a pair of tiny white booties.

Kate glanced again at the timer next to the crib—*soon*—then laid the outfit on the changing table and went back to David's crib. She watched him until she saw his chest rise and fall with a long, slow breath, then lowered herself carefully into her rocker. She wound the old music box and hummed Brahms along with it as she dropped a new tea bag into her mug and poured water from the heated pot, then sat back to let the brew steep.

A dragon breathed fire into her belly, and she lurched forward again. The old rocker protested loudly, but Kate was silent. She peeled the dime-sized dermal patch off her forearm and replaced it with a new one. After what seemed like an eternity, the dragon retreated into its cave and Kate settled back and rocked in time to the lullaby. The time-release narcotic should help her get through the next few hours in relative comfort.

"Play recording number one," Kate whispered. She always whispered in the nursery, even though she knew it was silly. She'd had to set the player's voice-activation at max. It obeyed her now, and a much younger Kate appeared on the other side of the crib, sitting in a much younger rocker. She glanced from the crib to the camera and back again. She'd never quite warmed up to the big, blank eye.

"Hi, David Anthony," the young Kate said. "You're exactly six months old today, and you've been asleep for three weeks. You'll be out of this thing soon, I know, but I wanted to keep sort of a diary for you—I don't want you to miss anything." She giggled. "Your daddy thinks I'm a little wacko, I guess, but it'll help me stay busy, right?"

Jeffrey had thought she was wacko, but he'd let her keep David at home, let her pour their savings into his special crib, and most of their income into maintaining it. The only alternative was to let the baby take his chances. According to the doctors, he'd likely have been dead within the year, every day aging his tiny body, breaking down his organs, taking him beyond hope of a cure. But what kind of life will he have? Jeffrey had argued. In a crib that kept him asleep, not growing, not really living, except for the one day a year they were allowed to wake him up and spend those precious two hours with him. Not much of a life, Kate had to agree, but a chance. Dr. Miller had told her it was only a matter of time.

Time. The timer on David's crib said forty-three minutes. When that was up, it would begin counting down from one hundred and twenty. Not enough. And then there was the timer inside her; ticking hard, counting down. Kate removed the bag from her mug and sipped the hot, sweet liquid. Not enough.

"Forward, fast," Kate whispered, and the young Kate got visibly older, though only a few years passed. "Stop," Kate ordered. The still-young Kate smiled, though her eyes were troubled and already so tired.

"Play."

"Hello, Lovey." By now, young Kate almost never looked at the camera, a fact she regretted today. She wanted David to know her; he should be able to look into her eyes.

"Your birthday's just three months away. That's not so long, is it? I miss you so much. Daddy sends his love."

Daddy was gone by then; still living, still in the house, but he'd given up on Kate long before. She almost never left the nursery—had meals brought in, did all the shopping and household chores from the bedroom terminal. Jeffrey worked constantly, lived in his study. They rarely spoke.

"Forward, fast," Kate ordered again, and waited. Young Kate got older, and still older, her weight slowly spiraling toward obesity, then dropping abruptly.

"Stop."

This Kate wore the same robe Kate wore now: cranberry satin, with big, flowing sleeves that looked like angel wings when she held up her arms. It was her last Christmas present from Jeffrey. Here, it looked brand new. Jeffrey would have been dead for maybe a year; his heart attack had left her no more alone than she'd been for a decade or so.

"Play."

". . . don't know if I told you that Doctor Miller died." This Kate's smile was more of a grimace. She was still trying. Even now, she still tried.

"Your new doctor is Doctor Conners. He's really nice." Though she tried to keep it hidden, her pain was evident. *"Doctor C. says it's only a matter of time."*

This was all David would know of her—this mindless babbling. She never had anything to tell him; what news could she have? She'd spent nearly every hour of every day and night in the nursery. *It's only a matter of time.* Thirty years later, and no closer to the day David could wake up and *live.* And now time really was the thing, wasn't it?

The Kate there in front of her might have been saved, but she'd still been trying to ignore the pain, to pretend that nothing was wrong. Week after week she'd wound the music box, dusted and arranged the nursery just so, read children's stories aloud, chattered into the mindless machine, until at last it was too late. "Jesus, Kate, why didn't you come to me?" Dr. C. had asked when she'd finally gone to him, desperate for relief from the pain. Relief was all he could offer her now; there was no turning back the clock on the damage her body had suffered.

Enough. "Power down." The other Kate disappeared, and Kate looked down at the crib. David's eyes twitched behind his lids as he dreamed. Dr. Miller had explained it to her: "It'll be just like he's sleeping, dreaming, all the time. The crib takes care of *everything.*" She'd asked him a million questions: Won't he get cold? Hungry? What about bedsores? But the doctor had answered without hesitation: *Everything.*

And it had. Kate had wished a million times she could climb in there with him and sleep through one long year after another—dreaming, she hadn't dreamed in years—to wake only when he did. If she hadn't denied her own disease, if she'd let them put her to sleep years ago, she might be there for David when he came out. Instead, she'd watched all day and night as David dreamed. What did babies dream of? "Their mothers," Dr. Miller's long-ago voice reminded her. "You're his only stimulus." The thought let her smile, just a little, and she cued the camera again.

"Record."

A red light blinked, and Kate leaned forward and looked into the big eye.

"Happy Birthday, Lovey." Kate looked down at her son, then forced herself to look back into the camera. "Today is the test, and I don't know the answer. I don't know if there *is* a right answer, so I'll never know whether I passed. You will, though." *Maybe.* She fought to keep her smile from fading. "I love you."

"Stop. Power down." She closed her eyes and rocked.

The timer bell *dinged* and Kate woke with a start, spilling lukewarm tea on her robe. The bell kept dinging as the crib's display flashed $\delta \ldots \theta \ldots \alpha \ldots \beta \ldots$, and stopped only when the chamber seal began to hiss its greeting, the doors unfolding like the petals of a crystal flower. Kate set down her mug and reached a freckled hand in to stroke the soft, pink skin.

"Wake up, Lovey."

Angel-blue eyes fluttered open and focused on the black-and-white mobile hanging over the crib. Slowly, Kate rose and leaned over the baby, and his eyes shifted their focus to her face. Tiny lips parted to reveal shiny pink gums; hands balled into little fists, and legs kicked—one, then the other; a squeal of pure baby joy filled the nursery, bringing it to life again. For the first time in exactly a year, Kate laughed.

"Are you happy to see Mommy?" She lifted David out of the crib and held him up in front of her for a moment to watch him squirm with life before bringing him close to hold him, hug him, rock him. "Oh, David, Mommy is so happy to see *you.*"

Kate cradled David in her arms, her big, silky sleeves blanketing his little body. She carried him to the changing table and laid him down, nesting his naked bottom in the fresh diaper. He cooed at her, and she cooed back at him as she folded the diaper over him and fastened it.

"Mommy has a new suit for you to wear." She pulled the white undershirt over his head, then tickled him to make him thrust his arms through the sleeves. He giggled and grunted, his face turning bright pink. Kate slipped the overalls up over his diapered bottom and snapped each leg into place, then fastened the straps at his chest. She savored every step.

"Oh, you look so handsome! Yes, you *do!*" Kate slipped a sock over one wrinkled foot, then stopped to examine the other; miniature toes wiggled as she ran a fingernail gently from the heel to the ball. "Are you hungry?" David gurgled happily and waved his chubby fists in the air. "How about some bananas?"

Feeding wasn't necessary, Dr. Miller had told her, but it wouldn't do any harm, either. Everything was ready: freshly cooked and blended bananas, rice cereal, a cookie for desert. A bottle of formula would begin warming itself soon, ready just in time to rock David back to sleep. She swallowed hard, pushing the thought back down, but today it refused to be ignored.

Kate picked David up and set him in his highchair, then wheeled it close to her rocker. She fastened a bib around his neck and stirred the bananas. David batted at the colorful wooden beads across the front of his tray, sending them spinning and clattering together. He opened his mouth wide for Kate's proffered spoon.

"Mmmm, good 'nanas!" She spooned bite after bite into David's waiting mouth, scooping up the excess that escaped and dribbled down his chin. The timer chimed once, and Kate jumped, panic and dread filling her. *Relax. It always chimes the half hour.*

No, this wasn't like *always*. This was it. She wasn't going to be there the next time David woke.

"David . . ." Kate took a washcloth from its warming tray and wiped David's face. He squirmed and pouted, but she stopped before he started to cry. She gave him his cookie and ran her hand over his silky head. "How would you like to stay with Mommy this time?" David grinned and gummed the cookie, bathing it in saliva. Every year was like another night to him, and every birthday just another morning. Still, she went on.

"We could be together every day." And if she didn't give him the chance, would he ever live? When she was gone, and David moved to the hospital nursery, no one would wake him—not even on his birthday. And when relatives asked (if they even bothered), Dr. Conners and whoever came after him, and after *him,* would tell them, "We're almost there. It's only a matter of time."

David waved his cookie in the air, and it flew from his hand and landed on the floor. He peered down over the tray to look for it.

"All gone." Kate shook her head. David looked up at her, eyes wide and questioning, and she held up her arms in a shrug. She wiped his face again and removed his bib, then lifted him from the highchair and carried him over to a blanket on the floor where several brand-new toys were waiting. She knelt and laid him on his belly, then lowered herself painfully onto hers.

"Do you like your birthday toys, Lovey?" Already David clutched a little plush bear in his dimpled hands, tiny fingers buried in soft, synthetic fur. He drew it to his face and planted its fuzzy ear in his mouth, and it spoke to him in a growly voice: "Hello, David. I love you." Kate looked around at the dozens of birthday toys that had come before; they crowded every shelf, every table. All brand-new. If she didn't put him back, he could play with them every day.

If you don't put him back, he'll die. The authoritative voice filled her head; not Jeffrey's, or Dr. Miller's, or even Dr. Conners's, but somehow a fusion of all three. "You don't know that—not for certain," Kate argued in a whisper. "You don't really know anything for *certain,* do you?" On the other hand, what did she know? Only that today was either her last day with David or the first of many more than she'd had in all these thirty years combined.

"What do you think I should do, Lovey?" Kate leaned her face down close to his. He'd dropped the bear, and now he reached for a blue rattle that lit up brightly when he closed his fist around it. His eyes went wide with wonder, and he clumsily yanked it toward him and into his mouth. She wiped drool from his chin with her sleeve. "Maybe they really are wrong. Maybe you'll outlive Doctor C. and all his children, too. Shouldn't we spend every possible minute together?"

Who the hell are you to decide? This voice startled her, because it was her own, thirty years ago. She'd spoken these words to Jeffrey more than once. *This is his only chance to grow up! His only chance to have friends, read a book, visit the moon, fall in love. . . .*

And had any of that changed? She'd been so sure she was doing the right thing back then, but she'd waited so long. She couldn't wait any longer.

Her dragon belched a warning into her guts, but she ignored it for the moment and watched her son discover, feel, and taste each toy on the blanket.

Ding! One more hour.

The nursery was bright with sunlight now, and David was growing bored. He fussed and fidgeted on the blanket, and just as she thought he might begin to cry, Kate struggled to her knees and scooped him up. She rocked him and hummed Brahms, the sound track to her life.

Kate stood and walked around the room, bouncing David until he stopped fussing. Soon he was gurgling again, cooing, tangling his fingers in her hair, drooling on her shoulder. "Mommy loves you, David," she whispered in his rosebud ear. "Aahh," he replied, and wriggled in her arms.

Bath time was David's favorite time of the day. The baby tub had warmed the water to the perfect temperature, and now, with barely a sound, it filled itself with fluffy, foamy whiteness. Kate undressed David on the changing table and tossed his dirty outfit into a chute in the wall. She removed his diaper and washed his bottom with a disposable wipe, then tossed the whole package into the garbage disposer and watched it disappear. Anything unpleasant was whisked from the nursery instantly. Everything was taken care of. Even after she was gone, everything would be taken care of.

She carried David to the tub and placed him in the safety seat that kept him upright in the water. Right away he raised his plump little arms in the air and brought them down, fingers splayed, to splash water and suds in all directions. He screamed with laughter, and Kate laughed with him, rubbing a soft cloth over his shoulders, chest, and the roundness of his belly. He'd stay in the tub all day if she'd let him. She could, couldn't she?

Ding!

"We deserve it, don't we, Lovey?" Didn't David deserve to have a mother—a real, all-the-time mother? And after all this time, didn't Kate deserve to have her son? Even if it was for only a few months, wasn't it better than this? It was, wasn't it?

Kate pulled a fluffy towel from the nearby rack and wrapped it around David, lifting him from the tub. He was exhausted; already his eyes showed it. She carried him back to the changing table and sang to him as she rubbed him dry, then pulled a clean blanket from a stack on the dresser and wrapped him into a neat little bundle. She carried him back to the rocker, pulled the bottle from its warmer, and tested it on her arm. It was just right, as she'd known it would be. He gazed up at her sleepily as he drank, and she hummed as she rocked, and rocked, and rocked.

The timer dinged its final warning. The pain sparked again in her belly and burst into flames that crawled up into her chest, a fiery fist gripping her heart. Kate breathed deeply.

"I still don't know the answer, Lovey," she whispered. "I hope I'm right." She took the bottle from his mouth and carefully unwrapped her sleeping son. Tears spilled down her cheeks as she rose to her feet and, leaning over the crib, placed him in it. His eyes fluttered open just as the doors began to hiss their goodbye. His bottom lip pooched out, and his brow crinkled, and he began to cry, softly at first, then louder as the doors rose up to seal him in. Kate reached one hand, then two, into the crib and closed them around him, lifting him, and . . .

Don't.

. . . she pulled them out again, her arms just brushing the closing doors. David wailed, his feet pumping, arms waving, and Kate watched him, and clutched her flaming belly, and wept.

The lights inside the chamber dimmed, and in seconds, David was asleep. Kate put another tea bag into her mug. She peeled the patch off her arm and picked up another, another, a fistful. She dropped them in with the bag and covered it all with hot water. She didn't wait this time, but sipped, and sipped, and sipped. She sat back in her rocker, closed her eyes, and rocked. And in her dream, the dragon inside her unfurled its leathery wings and flew away.

THE DARK BACKWARD

Gregory Benford

The fearful wrenching snap, a sickening swerve—and she was there.

Vitrovna found herself in a dense copse of trees, branches swishing overhead in a fitful breeze. Shottery Wood, she hoped. But was the time and place truly right? She had to get her bearings.

Not easy, in the wake of the Transition. She was still groggy from stretched moments in the slim, cushioned cylinder. All that aching time, her stomach had knotted and roiled, fearing that intercession awaited the Transition's end. A squad of grim Corpsmen, an injunction. A bleak prospect of standing at the docket for meddling in the sanctified past, a capital crime.

But when the wringing pop echoed away, there was no one awaiting to erase her from time's troubled web. Only this scented night, musky with leaves and a wind promising fair.

She worked her way through prickly bushes and boggy glades, using her small flashlight as little as she could. A white beam cutting the darkness of an April night in 1616 would surely cause alarm.

She stumbled into a rough country lane wide enough for her to see the sky. A sliver of bleached moon, familiar star-sprinklings—and there, Polaris. Knowing north, she reckoned from her topo map which way the southward-jutting edge of

Stratford might be. This lane led obliquely that way, so she took it, wind whipping her locks in encouragement.

Much still lay to be learned; she could be way off in space and time, but so far, the portents were good. If the combined ferret-ings and guesses of generations of scholars proved true, this was the last night the aging playwright would be afoot. A cusp moment in a waning life.

Up ahead, hollow calls. A thin blade of yellow as a door opened. A looming shamble-shadow of a drunken man, weaving his ragged course away from the inky bulk of an inn. Might this be the one she sought? Not the man, no, for they were fairly sure that graying Will had spent the night's meaty hours with several friends.

But the inn might be the place where he had drunk his last. The vicar of Stratford's Holy Trinity Church, John Ward, had written years after this night that the bard had "been on an outing" with two lesser literary lights. There were probably only a few inns in so small a town, and this might be the nearest to Shakespeare's home.

Should. Might. Probably. Thin netting indeed, to snare hard facts.

She left the lane and worked through brush that caught at her cloak of simple country burlap. A crude weave covering a cotton dress, nothing lacy to call attention, yet presentably ladylike—she hoped. Considering the sexual fascinations of the ancients, she might easily be mistaken for a common harlot, or a village slut about for a bit of fun.

Any contact with others here would endanger her, to say nothing of definitely breaking the Codes. Of course, she was already flagrantly violating the precepts regulating time travel, but years of preparation had hardened her to that flat fact, insulating her from any lingering moral confusions.

She slipped among trees, trying to get a glimpse through the tiny windows of the inn. Her heart thudded, breath coming quick. The swarming smells of this place! In her antiseptic life, a third-rank literary historian in the University Corps, she had never before felt herself so immersed in history, in the thick air of a world innocent of steel and ceramic, of concrete and stale air.

She fished her senso-binoculars from her concealed pack and studied the windows. It was difficult to make out much through the small, warped panes and heavy leading, behind which men lifted tankards and flapped their mouths, illuminated by dim, uncertain candles. A fat man waved his arms, slopping drink. *Robustious rothers in rural rivo rhapsodic. Swill thou then among them, scrike thine ale's laughter.* Not Will's words, but some contemporary. Marlowe? Whoever, they certainly applied here. A ragged patch of song swept by on the stirring wind, carried from an opening door.

Someone coming out. She turned up the amps on the binoculars and saw three men, each catching the swath of lantern light as they helped one another down stubby stairs to the footpath.

Three! One large and balding, a big chest starting to slide into an equatorial belly. Yet still powerful, commanding, perhaps the manner of a successful playwright. Ben Jonson?

The second younger, short, in a wide-brimmed hat—a Warwickshire style of the time, she recalled. It gave him a rakish cast, befitting a poet. Michael Drayton?

And coming last, tripping on the stair and grasping at his friends for purchase, a mid-sized man in worn cloak and close-fitting cap. *Life brief and naught done,* she remembered, a line attributed—perhaps—to this wavering apparition. But not so, not so.

The shadowy figure murmured something, and Vitrovna cursed herself for her slowness. She telescoped out the directional microphone above the double barrels of the binoculars. It clicked, popped, and she heard—

"I was then bare a man, nay, a boy still," the big man said.

"Big in what fills, sure speak." The wide-hatted man smirked.

"Swelled in blood-fed lustihead, Ben's bigger than stallions, or so rumor slings it," the cloaked figure rapped back, voice starting gravelly and then swinging tenor-high at the sentence's end.

The tall man chuckled with meaty relish. "What fills the rod's same as fills the pen, as you'd know better."

So this was the man who within a few years would say that his companion, the half-seen figure standing just outside the blade of light cast by the inner inn, was "not of an age but for all time." Ben Jonson, in breeches, a tuft of white shirt sticking from an unbuttoned fly. A boisterous night for all.

"Aye, even for the miowing of kitticat poetry on spunk-stained parchment, truest?" the cloaked man said, words quick but tone wan and fading.

"Better than a mewling or a yawper," the short man said.

All three moved a bit unsteadily around a hitching post and across the yard. Jonson muttered, laughed. She caught the earthy reek of ale. The man who must be Drayton—though he looked little like the one engraving of his profile she had seen—snickered liquidly, and the breeze snatched away a quick comment from the man who—she was sure now—must be Shakespeare. She amped up the infrared and pressed a small button at the bridge of the binoculars. A buzz told her digital-image recording was on, all three face-forward in the shimmering silver moonlight, a fine shot. Only then did she realize they were walking straight at her.

Could they make her out, here in a thicket? Her throat tightened and she missed their next words, though the recorder at her hip would suck it all in. They advanced, staring straight into her eyes—across the short and weedy lawn, right up to the very bushes that hid her. Shakespeare grunted, coughed, and fished at his drawers. To her relief, they all three produced themselves, sighed with pleasure, and spewed rank piss into the bushes.

"The one joy untaxed by king or wife," Jonson meditated.

The others nodded, each man embedded in his own moment of release, each tilting his head back to gaze at the sharp stars. Done, they tucked back in. They turned and walked off to Vitrovna's left, onto the lane.

She followed as silently as she could, keeping to the woods. Thorns snagged her cloak, and soon they had walked out of earshot of even her directional microphone. She was losing invaluable data!

She stumbled onto the path, ran to catch up, and then followed again, aided by shadows. To walk and keep the acoustics trained on the three weaving figures was all she could manage, especially in the awkward, raw-leather shoes she had to wear. She remembered being shocked that this age did not even know to make shoes differently curved for left and right feet, and felt the effect of so simple a difference within half a kilometer. A blister irked her left heel before she saw a glow ahead. She had given up trying to follow their darting talk. Most was ordinary byplay laced with coarse humor, scarcely memorable, but scholars could determine that later.

They stopped outside a rambling house with a three-windowed front from which spilled warm lantern light. As the night deepened, a touch of winter returned. An ice-tinged wind whipped in a swaying oak and whistled at the house's steep-gabled peak. Vitrovna drew as near as she dared, behind a churning elm.

"Country matters need yawing mouths," Shakespeare said, evidently referring to earlier talk.

"Would that I knew keenly what they learn from scrape and toil," Drayton said, voice lurching as the wind tried to rip it away from her pickups.

"A Johannes Factotum of your skinny skin?" Shakespeare said, sniffing.

Vitrovna translated to herself, *A Jack-Do-All of the senses?*— though the whole conversation would have to be endlessly filtered and atomized by computer intelligences before she could say anything definitive. If she got away with this, that is.

"Upstart crow, cockatrice!" Jonson exclaimed, clapping Shakespeare on the shoulder. All three laughed warmly.

A whinny sped upon the breeze. From around the house, a boy led two horses. "Cloddy chariot awaits," Drayton said blearily.

Shakespeare gestured toward his own front door, which at that moment creaked open, sending fresh light into the hummocky yard where they stood. "Would you not—"

"My arse needs an hour of saddle, or sure will be hard-sore on the ride to London tomorrow," Jonson said.

Drayton nodded. "I go belike, to see to writ's business."

"My best bed be yours, if—"

"No, no, friend." Jonson swung up onto a roan horse with surprising agility for one so large. "You look chilled. Get inside to your good wife."

Ben waved good night, calling to the woman who had appeared in the doorway. She was broad and sturdy, graying beneath a frilly white cap, and stood with arms crossed, her stance full of judgment. "Farewell, Anne!"

Good-byes sounding through the frosty air, the two men clopped away. Vitrovna watched Shakespeare wave to them, cloak billowing, then turn to his wife. This was the Anne Hathaway whom his will left with his "second-best" bed, who had saddled him with children since his marriage at eighteen—and who may have forced him into the more profitable enterprise of playwriting to keep their household in something resembling the style of a country gentleman. Vitrovna got Anne's image as she croaked irritably at Shakespeare to come inside.

Vitrovna prayed that she would get the fragment of time she needed. Just a moment, to make a fleeting last contact—

He hesitated, then waved his wife away and walked toward the woods. She barked something at him and slammed the door.

Vitrovna slipped from behind the elm and followed him. He coughed, stopped, and began to pee again into a bush.

An ailment? To have to go again so soon? Stratford's vicar had written that on this night, Will "drank too hard," took ill, and later died of a fever. This evidence suggested, though, that he knew something was awry when he wrote his will in March, a few weeks before this evening. Or maybe he had felt an ominous pressure from his approaching fifty-second birthday, two days away—when the fever would claim him.

All this flitted through her mind as she approached the wavering figure in the woodsmoke-flavored whipping wind. He tucked himself back in, turned—and saw her.

Here the danger made her heart pound. If she did something to tweak the timeline a bit too much . . .

"Ah! Pardons, Madam—the ale within would without."

"Sir, I've come to tell you of greatness exceeding anything you can dream." She had rehearsed this, striving for an accent that would not put him off, but now that she had heard his twangy Elizabethan lilt, she knew that was hopeless. She plowed ahead. "I wanted you to know that your name will be sung down the ages as the greatest of writers."

Will's tired, grizzled face wrinkled. "Who might you be?"

—and the solidity of the past struck her true, her breath sour with pickled herrings and Rhenish wine. The reeking intensity of the man nearly staggered her. Her isolated, word-clogged life had not prepared her for this vigorous, full-bodied age. She gulped and forced out her set speech.

"You may feel neglected now, but centuries hence you'll be read and performed endlessly—"

"*What* are you?" A sour scowl.

"I am from the future. I've come backward in time to tell you, so that such a wonderful man need not, well, need not think he was just a minor poet. Your plays, they're the thing. They—"

"You copy my lines? 'The play's the thing.' Think you that japing pranks—"

"No, no! I truly am from the future, many centuries away."

"And spring upon me in drafty night? I—"

Desperately she brought up her flashlight. "Look." It clicked on, a cutting blue-white beam that made the ground and leaves leap from inky presences into hard realities. "See? This is a kind of light you don't have. I can show you—"

He leaped back, eyes white, mouth sagging. "Uh!"

"Don't be afraid. I wondered if you could tell me something about the dark lady in your sonnets, just a moment's—"

"Magic!"

"No, really, it's just a different kind of lantern. And your plays, did you have any help writing them?"

He recovered, mouth curving shrewdly. "You be scholar or rumor-monger?"

"Neither, sir."

His face hardened as he raised his palm to shield his eyes from the brilliance. "Think me gut-gullible?"

"You deserve to know that we in the future will appreciate you, love you, revere you. It's only justice that you know your works will live forever, be honored—"

"Promising me life forever, then? That's your cheese?"

"No, you don't—"

"This future you claim—know something of myself, then? My appointed final hour?" His eyes were angry slits, his mouth a flat, bloodless line.

Was he so quick to guess the truth? That she had come at the one possible moment to speak to him, when his work or friends would not be perturbed? "I've come because, yes, this is my only chance to speak with you. There's nothing I can do about that, but I thought—"

"You tempt me with wisps, foul visions."

Did he suspect that once he walked into that house, lay upon his second-best bed, he would never arise again? With leaden certainty, she saw him begin to gather this, his mouth working, chin bobbing uncertainly.

"Sir, no, please, I'm just here to, to—"

"Flat-voiced demon, leave me!"

"No, I—"

He reached into his loose-fitting shirt and drew out a small iron cross. Holding it up, he said, "Blest be he who spares my stones, curst be he who moves my bones!"

The lines chiseled above his grave. So he had them in mind already, called them up like an incantation. "I'm sorry, I didn't mean—"

"Go! Christ immaculate, drive such phantoms from me! Give me a sword of spirit, Lord!"

Vitrovna backed away. "I, I—"

—and then she was running, panicked and mortified, into the woods. In her ears rang a fragment from *The Tempest:*

> *What seest thou else*
> *In the dark backward and abysm of time?*

In the shimmering cylinder, she panted with anxiety and mortification, her skin a sheen of cold sweat. She had failed terribly, despite decades of research. All her trial runs with ordinary folk of these times who were about to meet their end, carried out in similar circumstances—those had gone well. The subjects had welcomed her. Death was natural and common here, an easeful event. They had accepted her salute with stoic calm, a quality she had come to envy in these dim eras. Certainly they had not turned their angers on her.

But she had faltered before Shakespeare. He had been larger than life, awesome.

Her recordings were valuable, yes, but she might never be able to release them for scholarly purposes now. She had wrenched the past terribly, exciting the poor man just before death's black hand claimed him. She could never forget the look of wild surmise and gathering panic that worked across that wise face. And now—

She had stolen into the University Corps Facility, slipped into the machine with the aid of friends, all in the service of true, deep history. But if she had changed the past enough to send a ripple of causation forward, into her own era, then the Corps would find her, exact the penalty.

No time to think of that. She felt the sickening wrench, a shudder, and then she thumped down into a stony field.

Still, night air, a sky of cutting stars. A liquid murmuring led her to the bank of the Big Wood River and she worked her way along it, looking for the house lights. This route she knew well, had paced it off in her own era. She could tell from the set of the stars that she had time, no need to rush this.

Minutes here took literally no time at all in the stilled future world, where machines as large as the cities of this age worked to suspend her here. The essence of stealing time from the Corps was that you took infinitesimal time-wedges of that future world, undetectable, elusive—if you were lucky. The Corps would find her uses self-indulgent, sentimental, arrogant. To meddle so could snuff out their future, or merely Vitrovna herself—and all so a few writers could know for a passing moment of their eventual high density? Absurd, of course.

July's dawn heat made her shed her cloak, and she paused to get her breath. The river wrinkled and pulsed and swelled smooth against the resistance of a big log, and she looked down through it to an unreadable depth. Trout hung in the glassy fast water like ornaments, holding into the current. Deeper still, a fog of sand ran above the gravel, stirred by currents around the pale, round rocks.

The brimming majesty of this silent moment caught at her heart. Such simple beauty had no protection here, needed none.

After a long moment, she made herself go on and found the house as faint streamers traced the dawn. Blocky, gray poured concrete, hunkered down like a bunker. A curious, closed place for a man who had yearned to be of the land and sky. In 1926, he had said, "The real reason for not committing suicide is because you always know how swell life gets again after the hell is over." Yet in this spare, beautiful place of rushing water and jutting stone, he would finally yield to the abyss that had tempted him all his wracked life.

She worked her way up the stony slope, her Elizabethan shoes making the climb hard. As she reached the small outer door into the basement, she fished forth the flex-key. Its yellow metal shaped itself to whatever configuration the lock needed, and in a moment she was inside the storage room, beside the heavy mahogany rack. She had not seen such things except in photographs. Elegant machines of blue sheen and polished, pointful shapes. Death solidified and lustrous. They enchanted her as she waited.

A rustling upstairs. Steps going into the kitchen, where she knew he would pick up the keys on the ledge above the sink. He came down the stairs, haggard in the slack pajamas and robe; the face, handsome in photographs, now lined and worn, wreathed by a white beard and tangled hair. He padded toward the rack, eyes distant, and then stopped, blinking, as he saw her.

"What the hell?" A rough voice, but recognizable.

"Mr. Hemingway, I ask only a moment of your time, here at the end. I—"

"You're from the IRS, aren't you? Snooping into my—"

Alarm spiked in her throat. "No, sir, I am from the future. I've come backward in time to tell you, so that so wonderful a man need not—"

"FBI?" The jowly face clouded, eyes narrow and bright. "I know you've been following me, bribing my friends."

The drinking, hypertension, hepatitis, and creeping manic depression had driven him farther than even her research suggested.

She spread her hands. "No, no. You deserve to know that we in the future will appreciate you, love you, revere you. It's only justice that you know your works will live forever, be honored—"

"You're a goddamn federal agent, and a liar on top of that."
His yellowed teeth set at an angry angle. "Get out!"

"Remember when you said that you wanted to get into the
ring with Mr. Tolstoy? Well, you have, you did. You're in his
class. Centuries from now—"

A cornered look came into the jumping eyes. "Sure, I've got
six books I declare to win with. I stand on that."

"You have! I come from—"

"You a critic? Got no use for sneaky bastards come right into
your house, beady-eyed nobodies, ask you how you write like
it was how you shit—"

He leaned abruptly against the pinewood wall and she caught
a sour scent of defeat from him. Color drained from his wracked
face and his head wobbled. "Future, huh?" He nodded as if
somehow accepting this. "God, I don't know . . ."

She stepped back, fear tight in her throat. Earlier in this year
he had written: *A long life deprives a man of his optimism. Better to
die in all the happy period of unillusioned youth, to go out in a blaze
of light, than to have your body worn out and old and illusions shattered.* She saw it now, the despair, in the loose cant of mouth and
jaw, the flickering anxiety and hollow dread. The power of it was
unbearable.

"I . . . I wanted you to know that those novels, the short stories, they will—"

The sagging head stopped swaying. It jerked up. "Which have
you read?"

"All of them. I'm a literary historian."

"Damn, I'm read just by history professors?" Disdain soured
the words.

There were no such professions in her time, just the depart-
ments of the Corps, but she could not make this ravaged man
understand that. "No, your dramas are enjoyed by millions, by
billions—"

"Dramas?" He lurched against the wall. "I wrote no dramas."

How to tell him that the media of her time were not the simple staged amusements of this era? That they were experienced directly through the nervous system, sensory banquets of immense emotional power, lived events that diminished the linear medium of words alone to a curious relic?

"You mean those bum movies made from the novels? Tracy in *The Old Man*?"

"No, I mean—we have different ways of reading the same work, that is all. But for so long I've felt the despair of artists who did not know how much they would mean, poor Shakespeare going to his grave never suspecting—"

"So you know what I'm down here for?" A canny glint in the eyes.

"Yes, of course. That's why I came."

He pulled himself erect with visible effort. "If you're not just another shit artist come here to get a rise out of me—"

"I'm not. I'm a scholar who feels so much for you lonely Primitivists who—"

"That's what you call us? Real writers? *Primitives*?" Jutting jaw. "I'm going to kick your goddamn ass out of here!"

His sudden clotted rage drove her back like a blow. "I meant—"

"Go!" He shoved her. "Hell will freeze over before I'll give in to a lard-ass—"

She bolted away, out the basement door, into the spreading dawn glow. Down the rocky slope, panic gurgling acid in her mouth. She knew that years before this, when asked his opinion of death, he had answered, "Just another whore." But there was something new and alive in his face just now, fresh fuel from his sudden, hugely powerful anger, some sea change that sent into her mind a wrenching possibility.

She looked back at the house. He was standing there thin and erect, shaking a knotted fist down at her. She reached the dawn-etched river and punched the summons into her controls; then came the wringing snap, and she was in the cylinder again.

Vitrovna let a ragged sigh escape into the cool, calming air.

This one was as unsettling as the last. The old man had seemed animated as she left, focused outside himself by her visit. He had kept her off balance the entire time.

Now she saw her error. The earlier tests with ordinary people, whose deaths did not matter in the flow of history, had misled her. In person, Shakespeare and Hemingway loomed immensely larger than anyone else she had ever known. Compared with the wan, reasonable people of her time, they were bristly giants. Their reactions could not be predicted and they unsettled even her, a historian who thought she knew what to expect.

Vitrovna leaned back, shaken and exhausted. She had programmed a long rest after this engagement, time to get her thoughts in order before the next. That one, the great poet Diana Azar, lay as far ahead in centuries as the gap between the last two, yet her simple dress should still pass there, and—

A slim man materialized at the snub end of the cylinder. He wore a curious blue envelope that revealed only head and hands, his skin a smooth green.

"Ah," he said in a heavily accented tenor, "I have intersected you in time."

She gasped. "You—how? To catch me while transporting—"

"In your age, impossible, of course." He arched his oyster-colored forehead, which had no eyebrows. "But when you are in Transition, we of your far future may snag you."

She had thought for decades about what she would do if caught, and now said cannily, "You follow the Code standards for self-incrimination?"

She blinked with shock when he laughed. "Code? Ancient history—though it's all the same here, of course. I am not one of your Corps police."

"Then you're not going to prosecute . . ."

"That was an illusion of your time, Vitrovna. You don't mind me using your first name? In our era, we have only one name, though many prefer none."

"But how can you . . ."

He languidly folded his arms, which articulated as if his elbows were double-jointed. "I must first say that generations far beyond yours are eternally grateful to you for opening this possibility and giving us these historical records." He gestured at her senso-binoculars.

"Records? They survived? I mean, I do make it back to my—"

"Not precisely. But the detailed space-time calculations necessary to explain, these you would not understand. You braved the Codes and the Corps quite foolishly, as you have just discovered—but that is of no import to us."

She felt a rush of hope, her lips opening in expectation. "Then you've come to rescue me from them?"

He frowned, a gesture that included his ears. "No, no. You feared the Corps' authority, but that was mere human power. They vaguely understood the laws of acausality, quite rightly feared them, and so instituted their Code. But they were like children playing with shells at the seashore, never glimpsing the beasts that swam in the deeps beyond."

Her seat jolted and she felt queasy. He nodded, as if expecting this, and touched his left wrist, which was transparent.

"The Code was a crude rule of thumb, but your violations of it transgressed far beyond mere human edicts. How arrogant, your age! To think that your laws could rule a continuum. Space-time itself has a flex and force. Your talk with Hemingway— quite valuable historically, by the way, considering that he was not going to ever release his memoir, *A Moveable Feast,* when he went down into that basement. But even more important was what he wrote next."

"Next? But he—"

"Quite. Even so, rather less spectacular than your 'apparition' before Shakespeare. As his shaky hand testified, you caused him to gather his notes and scraps of plays. They kept quite well even in a tin box, wedged in with the corpse. A bounty for the critics, though it upset many cherished theories."

"But he still died of pneumonia?"

"You do not have miraculous healing powers. You simply scared him into leaving something more of a record."

"Still, with so much attention paid to the few records we do have, or *did* have, I—"

"Quite." A judicious nod. "I'm afraid that despite our vastly deeper understanding of these matters, there is nothing we can do about that. Causality will have its way."

The cylinder lurched. A raw bass note. "Then how . . ."

"Not much time left, I'm afraid. Sorry." He leaned forward eagerly. "But I did want to visit you, to thank you for, well, liberating this method of probing the past, at great personal sacrifice. You deserve to know that our epoch will revere you."

He spoke rapidly, admiration beaming in his odd face, the words piling up in an awful leaden weight that sent bile-dark fear rushing hotly through her, a massive premonition.

"So, Vitrovna, I saw the possibility of making this intersection. It's only right that you know just how famous you will be . . ."

The sensation of stepping off a step into a dark, unending fall.

Her speech. He was giving her own speech, and for the same reason.

SOONER

Frank C. Gunderloy, Jr.

His name was Sooner.

I saw him today, out behind the chicken pens. He dragged himself toward me, tail swirling in the dusty grass, his whole rump whipping back and forth despite the paralyzed hind legs. An ordinary cur dog, mostly terrier, his heart so full of love that it overflowed into every muscle. I reached out to smooth his fur, avoiding the one rough patch where the hair felt like a handful of hog bristles.

The lump under the patch made him yelp if he rolled over wrong, or if you touched it accidentally, not meaning to hurt him, only wanting to pet him, to give back some of the love.

The white of cataracts clouded both eyes, but he wrinkled his nose, and knew it was me.

Then something in the air made me cough, take a step back. It was eye-watering sweet in my nostrils, but it grated at the back of my throat.

"You don't want to watch this," said my father. He looked up from soaking a rag with splashes from a can of chloroform. Beside him, almost hidden in the tall grass, lay a glass jar that would fit tightly over a small mongrel's muzzle. A merciful jar.

I watched anyhow.

Afterward, when my father had finished patting down the loose dirt with the back of a spade, I chipped "Sooner, 1924–1933" into a big chunk of red sandstone. A last bit of love, expressed with the point of a twenty-penny nail and a rusty old claw hammer.

I smashed the jar against the stone.

I was going on thirteen.

"Margaret," I say to my wife, "I saw Sooner today."

"What on earth," she answers, looking up from her needle-work, "are you talking about?"

"Sooner. My dog—my dad—he was . . ."

"Walter, you frighten me when you talk like that. We haven't owned a dog since Alice took Ragmop to live with her in that awful apartment."

I don't answer. I have no answer. Ragmop the Pekinese and my daughter are faint memories. The image of Sooner is vivid, clear as the day it happened. *Today.*

"Walter?"

"Forget it," I say. "I must have dozed off."

I look away, hoping she won't notice me licking my dry lips or see the pulse I feel pounding in my throat.

" . . .the etiology of beta-amyloid protein precursor (beta-APP) deposition in the cerebral cortex of the aged subject, once the first indication of dementia appears, is genetically parallel to chromosome 21 defect manifestations noted in Down's syndrome at the onset of . . ."

— *The Temporal Consciousness Project*
Vol. 1, *Background Pathology*

Billy called me "Walter."

We were running along a leaf-strewn path between the trees, the dogs galloping alongside, headed toward our secret place. The place we'd named "Dark Woods," a stand of old pines, tall and crowded, where the thick tangle of overhead branches created a somber contrast to the sunlit airiness of the oaks, hickories, and sweet-blossoming dogwoods that made up most of the unharvested timber.

"Wait up, Walter," he yelled.

Nobody ever called me Walter. My dad was Walter Jeremiah Rudman, *Senior,* so everybody called me Jerry. I didn't become Walter until I went away to college, and a series of impersonal registration forms—First name, M.I., Last name—erased that final vestige of boyhood.

Billy caught up, stood puffing.

"Hey," I said. "What a slowpoke."

"Have to get used to all this running again," he answered.

Billy was my age, the youngest of the Miller boys, blond, slim, a little bowlegged like his brothers. The Millers moved to Baltimore when I was almost eleven and the Pentecostal Church bought their old frame house, sagging porch and all, to use for a parsonage.

He'd break the news today. No more roaming the woods together. No more watching for shooting stars, lying in the open fields at nightfall, our shoulders touching, the broomsage tickling our backs, pretending we couldn't hear our mothers calling us for bedtime.

"You should have told me you were moving," I said, staring directly into his eyes.

He nodded. Never asked how I knew, any more than I asked why he called me "Walter."

Or why he had to get used to running "again."

Billy'd had the bluest eyes I'd ever seen, chips of willowware set in polished eggshell. Now, I realized, the color had faded, and the irises were oddly doubled, like the circles around the center of a target.

"Your eyes look funny."

"Yours, too."

Our hands touched, and for a moment, I felt the love again, that same shoulder-closeness of those nights under the stars.

Then Sooner barked somewhere up ahead, Billy's dog Duke joined in, and our hands fell apart.

"We better see what they found."

"Yeah, we better."

"You know," I say to Margaret, "I saw Billy only once after they moved, right after I got out of college. I think he still called me 'Walter' even then."

"Billy who, dear?"

I want to answer, but first I should wipe the potato off my chin. I grope in my lap for a napkin.

"Here, let me," says Margaret, reaching across the table with a Kleenex.

"Why aren't you eating?"

"After you finish."

I pick up the spoon. If I hold it in my fist like a wrench, I can manage all by myself. I scoop up some of the buttery mush.

"Good potatoes."

I try to see Margaret's eyes, but they are squeezed shut and look wet around the edges.

The potatoes look as good as they taste. They are white with streaks of yellow, just like Margaret's hair.

" . . .so that Lockwood-Deutsch time-travelers violate the conservation laws unless all parallel universes are subsets of a multiverse. Hewett, on the other hand, has demonstrated that any individual's cognitive experience in the present may be expressed as a complex integral of zero-sum energy, incorporating both past and future experiences into a readily accessible single continuum. A Hewett time-traveler might not necessarily be able to move *forward* along his integrated lifeline, but fully conscious regression should be. . ."

— *The Temporal Consciousness Project*
Vol. 3, *Theoretical Considerations*

Folks used to call Lake Waterford State Park "Weller's Pond."

We'd walk the mile to the north end of Weller's along a dusty pair of ruts they called "the back road." Billy, me, Duke, and Sooner. Sometimes we fished for sunfish with bits of toast for bait, but mostly we went to cool off with a swim. Once you were past the muddy shallows, the water was so deep you couldn't see bottom. Sooner swam out sometimes, but usually he splashed around in the cattails, trying to snap up dragonflies. Duke wouldn't go near the water.

Next fall would be fourth grade, but who cared? Summer was forever.

We had to be home, ready for supper, when our dads finished work. Some days it was a long, hard run for that mile back, and we'd end up sweatier after our swim than before.

And some days, when we got home, my father would pile us all in the rickety old Ford, and Mom would pack a basket, and we'd go right back to Weller's. Only, he'd take us to the fenced-in part along the main road where they'd trucked in sand to make a beach, and it cost fifteen cents a carload to get in.

I was so tired after a day at Weller's that I didn't fight about bedtime.

My mother came to kiss me good night.

She stroked my forehead, smiling down at me. I thought how young she looked, her face framed by the dim light from the hallway.

Suddenly she snapped on the bed lamp.

"What's the matter?" I asked, struggling to sit up against the tangle of sheets.

"Nothing. I thought something was wrong with your eyes, but I guess they're all right. Go to sleep."

I awaken. I stare at the ceiling.

My pillow is damp with spittle. Something else damp rubs across my face. I snuffle, lick my lips, get both the taste and odor of soap. Margaret is wiping my face with a washcloth. She has done this before, I know, but I can't think when. I try to ask her if I've been sick, but I can't make my lips form the words. I try again. More spittle. More washcloth.

"His eyes are open. He usually wakes up about now."

That's it—something about eyes. Margaret's eyes are red-rimmed, the lids heavy, drooping. She bends closer. I see a web of wrinkles across her cheeks—deep lines, many more than I remember.

"See if he knows you, dear."

"Daddy . . . ?"

Not a face I recognize. I close my eyes.

"Mom, you can't keep doing this all by yourself. You've got to get some help."

Not a voice I recognize. I'd like to go back to sleep now, but I'm wet, my thighs and buttocks irritated. It burns.

I strike with my fist, trying to make the burning stop.

I hear Margaret cry out.

The other voice cries out, too.

"Mom!" it says.

Then it says, "This has just got to stop."

I think the burning will go away now.

" . . . in the fourth stage, the neurofibrillary tangles are found penetrating deep into the cortex, and occurrence of senile plaques increases, particularly in the thalamus. Motor-control abilities deteriorate, as do certain of the sensory functions. However, PET scans of the test subjects who received modified beta-APP were normal, and aside from the occasional appearance of circumferential strictures in the sphincter pupillae, there were no lasting . . ."

— *The Temporal Consciousness Project*
Vol. 6, *Case Histories*

Sooner followed me to school after lunch.

"Go home," I yelled, throwing a handful of dirt and pebbles.

He stuck his tail between his legs and started back toward our house, then turned off the gravel road into the untrimmed weeds and bushes that flourished along the dirt shoulder. The handful of pebbles was a gesture. So was the lowered tail. Being grown up meant separation. Going to school was the biggest part.

As a "walker," I went home for lunch every day, even in first grade. Bus pupils brought lunch in grease-spotted paper bags, or in Tom Mix lunch boxes, except for Gene Holsten, who carried a lunch pail that had once been his father's. And the two wide-eyed and silent Arvey sisters, who never had a lunch.

We were learning color words. Take your crayons, fill in each balloon with the correct color. Mrs. Daniels handed out mimeographed half-sheets of paper, smudgy purple outlines of circles with words printed inside. Squiggly tails turn the circles into balloons. Yesterday she made birthday candles. Tomorrow it might be birds. Red. Yellow. Green. And today there's a new word—one I don't know.

I raise my hand.

"Can I go look at the color chart, Miz Daniels?"

" 'May I go,' Jerry."

"May I?"

"Yes, you may."

Other kids have already asked, are on their way back to their desks.

I meet Lorraine in the aisle, turn sideways so she can get by.

"It's 'purple,' Jerry," she whispers as she squeezes past. Then she glances back and smiles.

Her eyes look weird.

Dark brown bull's-eyes.

Suddenly, it's like I'm dreaming, like I'm grown up, in high school even, and Lorraine is there too, only they don't call her Lorraine anymore. Some other name, used to be her mom's. And then I'm really old, and she's there, and . . .

"Go back to your seat now, Jerry."

"Yes, Miz Daniels."

It's 3:30. I run up the road, grab Sooner around the neck, give him a big hug. He always meets me. Probably doesn't even go home, just waits under a shady sassafras bush. He's a great dog. I feel great.

I've been feeling great since lunchtime, like it was a really special day. I gotta remember to tell Mom first thing when I get home.

Funny. Started right after that Lorraine pushed past me to get to her desk. Think it was then. Maybe not—I dunno.

"Dopey girl," I say out loud.

Sooner wags his whole rump, the way he always does when I call him or something. He bounces around at my feet, like he hasn't seen me for a long time. It's only been a couple of hours.

"Dumb dog."

I hug him around the neck some more. I don't know why. He loves it.

"About time you two got here," Mom says after I slam the screen door behind us.

Sooner lies down, thumps his tail on the kitchen linoleum.

His eyes look funny.

What was it I was s'posed to remember?

Oh, yeah—purple.

". . . results of the beta-APP trials fail to either prove or disprove Hewett's theory, since it is impossible to distinguish didactic memory from a true regressive experience under these experimental conditions, no matter how apparently objective the report of any so-called 'lifeline traveler.' However, since we know that memory alone governs the behavior of those actually suffering from the dementia, it is safe to assume that most . . ."

— *The Temporal Consciousness Project*
Vol. 10, *Conclusions and Recommendations*

WHERE OLD KINGS GATHER

Michelle Knowlden

Five dead. What a small number that seemed against the millions of Afellon murdered. As chief Afellon negotiator for the Rict Treaty, I have become much in the news these past three years, but no one knew my part in those five killings on Degress. Except as a minor role in an old king's tale.

An Earthman chosen to represent the Afellons to the occupying government of Jerr, I had sat through long hours of discord. Our tired hosts on New Atticus called a hiatus to these word games in the spring. Since home was far away and the local resorts were packed, I had gone to Degress—no one went to Degress, and I wanted solitude.

Degress was a shell of a world, stripped of life by war. It resembled parts of Afellon, the parts leveled and seared by firebombs. It understood killing.

I've forgotten the name of the island where I stayed. Steering clear of the water that boiled like potted stew, I walked the beaches and dreamt of another planet where old kings gathered in a glen and told stories. I watched phantom ships slip in and out of the drear, a furtive light winking at the shore. Wait. Then it was gone, and a wind rose from the east.

The murders began on my second day on Degress. The hotel desk clerk was the first. His body was found on the beach, the water sizzling inches from his naked feet. The second, Ellie De-Janson, a withered mathematics professor from Earth, was found a few hours after the desk clerk. Then r'Duelson, a Jerran High Guard General, was killed on the third day of my stay. The hotel housekeeper discovered the fourth body, Care Kampei—a painter—hanging from the light hook in his room. And then for a space of time, the killing stopped.

They say that the lives of the old kings are threaded by the tales they carry to the glen. Woven through the storytelling, their lives ebb and flow as if responding to the pull of the plots and themes. The old kings feed upon the characters, and knit endings in their own flesh.

It says something of the isolation of Degress that the investigating detective, one Cod Sinwell, did not arrive until three days after the death of Care Kampei.

I was sitting on the beach, my main occupation, when his copter landed. His was the first new face I'd seen on the island since arriving, and yet I studied him with little interest. I'd had my fill of murders and reports of murders in my career, and I felt only resentment that they continued here during my respite.

He walked across the rough landing pad to the porch of the hotel and stopped for a brief moment. He must have felt my eyes upon him, for he turned and stared at me. He was small, even for a Degron. His forehead was broad and bare, and his barrel-shaped body was clothed in a slate-gray tunic and heavy leggings. His skin was sallow and his eyes a piercing amber with crescent pupils. Those eyes rested upon me for an uncomfortable moment; then he turned and went into the hotel.

I switched my gaze back to the dark sea and watched the horizon till the sky darkened and dipped into dusk. No lights upon the water tonight.

When I entered the hotel, I found the other surviving hotel guest sitting nervously in the front room. Son Damon sprang up when he saw me and motioned me into the hotel library. He closed the door and turned to me. He was an angular man, a mass of quivering energy. He'd arrived on the island in the same copter as myself, announcing his desire for quiet so that he could work on his monograph, called "Poultry and Decaying Arboreal Matter: Major Themes in the Poetry of T. S. Eliot." For me, he was the perfect guest—reclusive and avoiding company.

"A detective is come," he announced, giving me a hunted look. "He says he wants to talk to us before dinner."

"It's before dinner now," I said, settling myself into the couch.

"He thinks it's one of us." His pale eyes glistened with fear.

"Of course it's one of us. We're on a remote island, accessible only by copter and telepad. There've been no landings or ports for over a week. That leaves only the owner, the housekeeper, you, and me." I squinted at him. "Tell me, Professor Damon. Will you be confessing tonight?"

"Is no joke," he hissed, looking furtively at the door. "Be serious. Think of our reputations."

"I've nothing to fear," I said. I crossed my legs and studied a foot. "I think it was the housekeeper myself. She's burned my toast seven mornings in a row now. If there was anyone capable of murder here, it's sure to be her."

He gave me a look of outrage, but the opening of the library door prevented him from saying anything more. The small detective entered with the inn's owner, a man named Daur.

"My name is Cod Sinwell," the detective said. "I would like to question you two separately."

"Jack Coffee," I said, standing to shake his hand in Earther fashion. He grasped my hand awkwardly, but he watched me shrewdly. Here's one who might catch the killer, I thought.

"Mr. Coffee," he murmured. "And you are from where?"

"Originally from Earth. I've been in Foreign Services for forty years."

"You Earthers hide your age well," he said, looking at me appraisingly. "I would have thought you less than thirty."

I smiled. "Actually, sir, I'm older than those hills behind us."

"Those hills behind us, Mr. Coffee, were only dredged last year."

"Then I know I'm older than they are," I said with a chuckle. His forehead puckered slightly. I wondered if it was a sign of amusement among the Degrons. I had seen no evidence of humor among them since I'd arrived on this benighted planet.

"Mr. Coffee, if you wouldn't mind waiting in the entry area or your room, I'd like to question Professor Son Damon first."

At that, the professor gave a start of terror. I made a small bow and left the room. Daur followed me.

"Mr. Coffee, so sorry this dreaded business, and imposing this been on you."

"No need to apologize," I said impatiently. "No one could have predicted murder."

"Mr. Coffee . . ." He bowed and fluttered his thin fingers abjectly. "You tell me what amends to make, and I do. I say what story wanted. What you wish. Anywhen. You tell me."

I gave him a hard look. "Tell the truth." If you have it in you, I thought, turning to leave.

He darted around me. "But what is truth?" His mealy lips were pursed in desperate bewilderment. I sighed and brushed past him.

I did not want to go to my room with only thoughts for company. I pushed open the kitchen door, but it was dark within. The housekeeper, Daur's sister, had left for the evening. I pulled on the light and stared at the neat rows of fruit lining the counter. I wondered if they'd find her innocent, since she didn't sleep in the hotel at night. At least one of the murders, r'Duelson's, and perhaps DeJanson's also, had occurred at night.

Daur found me there an hour later, drinking tea and eating crackers. I'd given up hope of a formal dinner. In a subdued voice, he directed me back to the library.

Cod Sinwell waited for me alone. I wondered if Son Damon had finished his interrogation with dignity or had melted into nerveless jelly. I sat down opposite the detective.

"Jack Coffee," he said, glancing up from his notes. "That's not your real name, is it?"

"Your sources are good, sir." I smiled. "My real name is Franklin John Coughlin."

"The Afellon negotiator for the Rict Treaty? I understand why you'd use another name."

I nodded. "I'm on vacation. I wanted quiet—not to be followed and harangued by the press."

"Do you think that these murders had anything to do with the treaty negotiations?" He gave me a steady look.

"I don't see how," I said readily. "What could a provincial Degron, a mathematician from Earth, a Jerran general, and an unconventional Nooksigh artist have to do with the treaty?"

"It is a difficult connection to imagine," he agreed. "Tic Daur tells me you were the last to see Cir Dabin alive."

"The desk clerk?" I gave the inspector an ironic look. "I presume the murderer was the last to see him alive. I saw him a few hours before his body was found. No one else admits to seeing him that evening."

"Please tell me everything you remember about that last time."

I hesitated, thinking back through this long week, and remembered the little scene that in an ordinary setting should have meant nothing. And through my words, I heard the voices of old kings.

I met him on the north beach. I like to walk near the water at night. He was looking across the bay. He didn't turn his eyes to shore until nearly stepping into me. To be honest, I was not pleased to see him. He was a gossip, and I wanted some quiet before I slept.

"Did you see that boat?" he asked me, his sallow face puckered with excitement. "The one with all the sails?"

With not a little irony, I answered him. "There are no ships on Degress. The water corrodes like acid."

"I saw it," he insisted. "A black boat with many gray sails and a light that shone 'twixt the ropes. It moved so fast. One second, there—a moment later, gone."

"A ghost, then. Moonlight, or phosphor on a wave."

I think he wanted to argue with me, but his manners overtook him. While he asked after my accommodations, I saw his eyes dart back and forth over the empty water. I knew this Degron had never seen a real ship except recorded ones. Yet he believed he'd seen one where none could be, and he couldn't wait to tell the others at the hotel. By month's end, no doubt, it would become a fleet of alien ships with maser cannons primed.

The tide rolled in then and filled small depressions with water. Stars glittered in one, unwreathing my reflected face. I stepped away from the striking waves. We talked for a while; then the wind grew stronger. It was warm and damp, and the sand-glass clinked together like dull chimes. I decided to go back to the hotel. He remained outside and watched the water curl toward shore.

The murmuring of old kings ceased.

"That was it?" asked the little detective. "You talked of nothing else?"

"That was it." I shrugged. "Truthfully, I did not even know his name till you said it."

He consulted his notes. "The next to die was Ellie DeJanson, the Earther mathematics professor. What can you tell me about her?" The little detective with grave eyes watched me, but his words grew fainter as the murmuring voices of old kings grew louder. I overlaid their stories with mine, and lost myself in another death.

Professor DeJanson was a quiet one. Most mornings she read, and would absently trace out branching probabilistic trees on her napkin. I didn't see much of her that first day of our holiday. I walked the beaches, and she stayed in her room.

We did share a tram ride to the museum, the only tourist attraction on the island. It's on the far side—about a two-hour ride there and back.

The sun blazed hot that day in a thick, humid air. There was no shade in the museum, no cool shadows. Everything was lit by hot, incandescent light from skylights and lamps.

I had to steel myself against the exhibits. They showed the small natives, called stishers, through their evolution, tracing the changes from a small, earth-burrowing limpet to a multifingered, reasoning being. The stisher stood little more than a meter tall and looked like a hairless red setter. The holos showed the small beings progressing from leaf-harvesting, mud-patting children to sharp thinkers who built cities with complicated spires. They dressed with bright paints and gathered in the walkways, chittering excitedly with waving hands. They carved and potted. They gazed at the night sky and plotted the courses of stars. They spun glass into trees. They danced upon their knees and worshiped their god with comfort and laughter. They had children, and laid their elders to rest in towering monuments.

And then the ships came, carrying the ones who would rename their world Degress. The stishers watched as merchants arrived and took their treasures in exchange for giddy dust. They watched as the diplomats from the United Congress negotiated their spired cities into docking ports. They took the giddy dust till their lungs shriveled. They watched their glass trees shatter and their science turn to ashes. They left off the bright paints, laughter, and their god. They spun no more on their knees.

In the ports now, you saw no native children. As a species, they were dying. They begged at the entries, and carried luggage for a pinch of dust. They huddled in the corners and under benches, dying in slow breaths. Their cities were plastered over with signs. The stishers watched with glazed eyes, and retched in the shadows.

I shook myself; the half-circle of old kings faded from my sight. Sinwell watched me intently. "Sorry, Inspector; you wanted to talk of DeJanson. I scarcely noticed her in the museum. About halfway through the exhibits, I stopped by a drinking fountain. I'm afraid I indulged in talking to myself for moment, standing near a re-created palm. DeJanson saw me and thought I was talking to someone. I was a bit sharp with her on the bus when she kept insisting there had been some creature of silver edges and dark features there in the shadows. I regret my curt words now.

"She didn't come down to dinner. Early in the morning, after the clerk's body was discovered, the housekeeper found hers."

It was growing late, and my eyes kept wandering to the window where, through the parted drapes, I could see the slivered moon trailing light upon the sea. My voice was growing hoarse, and I felt suddenly weary.

"Inspector, what is the use of all this? Isn't the simple answer the best? The four that remain—who could be the killer? What motive did we have? Isn't it obvious that the killer was the painter, Care Kampei? He killed the others, then himself."

"And what motive did he have?"

I shrugged. "Who could guess? He was an artist. Perhaps he was mad, like most artists are. Perhaps he needed no motive, like rational people do."

"I cannot believe he killed himself," said Cod Sinwell. "A Nooksigh commits suicide only under the rigid regulations of his beliefs. He'd need to undergo ritual cleansing under the supervision of his temple priest. Then fasting, and salting his body. There is no evidence he'd done any of those things."

"Would a madman care about such things?" I questioned. I rubbed my eyes. "Cod Sinwell, I'm tired. I beg leave to rest. Could we begin again tomorrow morning?"

After a moment, he nodded. I could feel his eyes upon me as I went to my room.

The ghosts were waiting there for me. I locked the door to keep the living out, and felt the dead press upon me.

The room was strange. Its walls were not sand-cast, nor its doors framed by arches. Its drawers and closets were not re-

cessed beneath the bathing troughs and sleeping place. Hangers
for clothes were suspended from the ceiling. It was all thin plaster, glass, and chrome. Mirrors alternated with windows. The
bed was soft. The water was hard, and smelled faintly of sulfur.
I had a corner room. Outside the west window was a jungle
of blackened stumps separated from the hotel by a thin strip of
gray ash. The north window faced the sea. I watched the sea
when I was in my room, and thought of old kings telling tales
of glory. Before sleep came, I watched the blackness creep across
the unmoving water. No lights shone in the unrelieved gloom.
Sometimes I'd look in the mirror, but mostly I watched the sea,
and the songs of old kings ran in my thoughts:

"... from our towers we watched
for a nation that could not save us."

My head ached. Numbers and names of the many dead splintered inside my skull. Do not be a diplomat in time of war. It has
too many secret horrors. Never negotiate terms of peace. Behind
the careful masks, watch for a flicker of falseness in your coun-
terpart's eyes. Fine-tune the treaties that will be broken next
week. And then start again. Arrange your mask.

I took powders for the head pains and waited in the dim-lit
dark for sleep. Birds screeched in the jungle to the west. The sea
sputtered and hissed to the north. Overhead, my vests and
trousers hung like little painters in the dark.

In the morning, I slipped out before anyone was awake. I
stood on the burnt-out embers and molten shards of a small
peninsula and watched the water. The boiling sea lay black to
the horizon, running flat waves upon the green-glass shore.
Sometimes wisps of clouds would stand like vapor upon the
water, unmoving. As the morning wore down, I saw black shadows slide gleaming through the mist like galleons with unfurled
shrouds catching at the wind. They were unlit even by the
morning moons of the Degron sky. Like a dream or trick of the

eye, they were soon gone. The rain drizzled to a stop, and fog rolled over the dark water. A small poem ran through my thoughts:

> "Outside, the sword bereaves;
> inside, there is only death."

For a moment while standing in the cold, damp air, I wished that I was spending my interim summit time at home. I missed the hot wanamair wind that blew in mighty gusts through the O'rumgaelt deserts. Being home meant walking on dry sand, sniffing the citrus and sage smells of the Reynelbr groves. It meant naming the ancient and sacred peaks, the home place of all our gods. If I closed my eyes, I could see them and say: There is M'jestca, the north mother-rider, and M'tan, the muffled watcher. That one is M'oregn, who seeks to touch the sky. There is the one whose name has been stripped, and its twin is M'kirn, a hero of sorts. M'rgov stands to the far east, a shield-god. The warrior gods ring the valley, and even the smallest child can recite their names and their deeds, from great to least. The mountain representing peace, the god M'las, is little more than a spire standing half-hidden by M'rweq, the chance god.

"Do you see ghost ships like Cir Dabin did?"

Startled, I swung around. The little detective stood behind me on the ridged edge of the beach, giving me an assessing look.

"Pardon?"

"You said Cir Dabin saw ghost ships. I wondered if you saw them too."

I gave him a wary look. "I see nothing but clouds and sea."

He hopped down from the small rise and drew closer to me. "Strangely enough," he said, "I thought I saw something there. A foreign ship and a flash of light. Then it was gone."

I turned my back to the sea. "You wanted something of me, Cod Sinwell?"

"The rest of what you know, Mr. Coughlin. For my report."

I turned and headed back to the hotel. Although the day was damp and cold, I sat down on one of the hotel chairs on the porch facing the ocean. The detective sat on the steps below me, pen poised over paper. The hum of my words wove beneath the thoughts of old kings gathered in a mountain tomb.

r'Duelson was the next to die. He was a Jerran High Guard General and a veteran of The Glorious War of Afellon. Told anyone who would stand still long enough to listen. He'd prattle about his battles (which his side always won), his weapons and troops and fighters (which were always the best), and his medal of honor. The word "honor" seems so inappropriate. What honor was there in herding the beaten and bloodied enemy into crowded camps? Then, after weeks of deprivation and the ignominy of defeat pressing them down, they were blaster-whipped into stinking cargo ships by their conquerors and hauled to stand months later, emaciated, before their people. They could not lift their heads to face the families to whom they had brought this defeat. They say that surrender is better than death. But though the Afellons did not surrender, they were defeated. It would have been better to have utterly wiped out each one of them than to have sent them back that way.

Sorry, you've not asked me to moralize on the past. The past is the thing that the living feed upon to rise again, remembering. r'Duelson would not be strengthened by his past. His past had grown beyond him, and beyond truth. He flattered himself with it. And bothered us with his boasting. We avoided him whenever we could. If being a dullard or a braggart is reason to be killed, then we all had motive enough.

I saw as little of him as I could. I've scant use for old soldiers who parade their medals before me. The old kings have a saying about the vainglory of made men:

"Those nurtured in purple
now lie on ash heaps."

And perhaps that is r'Duelson's best epitaph. I can tell you no more of him. Except that he trampled the beaches and interfered with my peace. And talked forever of spies and enemies, and rules of war.

I stopped talking then. Cod Sinwell gave me an odd look. His hand hovered over the page for a moment.

"And the painter? Will you tell me of him?"

I sighed, and wondered why I bothered. The end would be the same. The killings would go unsolved, and I would return to the word battles in the capital. And somewhere, the call would sound to gather old kings for a tale.

The Nooksigh painter was a stout man. He had a brown, wrinkled face with glinting, wandering eyes that seemed to see everything. He painted swirling, silvery pictures that had no meaning but somehow itched at the eye's edges, forcing the viewer to look again, and then again. The pictures pricked at the eye, but evoked nothing from the heart. He had a passing popularity. Art lovers, who knew little about what constituted true art, wrapped him in laurels and praised him with enthusiastic nothings. He rode this glorious and fickle fame, while putting away for a future when his acclaim would pass to another.

He'd come to this war-blackened world to paint the sizzling sea, to rest from months of showings, and to present one of his grander murals to be hung in the president's palace on the continent. He made a quiet addition to our island group. He slept late. He painted at night, staring at the sea, making practiced strokes on the canvas.

As usual, one evening I walked along the beach and watched the lights play across the water. I stepped through the rough shale, thinking of wars and death. When I looked across the rippling sea, I listened for sounds of shrouded boats and I looked for the one light amid moonsglow and starglitter. There was nothing there.

I sat on a flat pier that jutted into an inlet that led to the sea, and watched the horizon. I worked out a dozen different endings to every treaty review I had been part of for the last four years. I watched a fire course over an entire planet in a war in which its victims had no part. I heard the screams of the dying. I could count their names on the death lists. Yet they were just a minor part of a twenty-three-year war. One grows almost callous.

I saw a light amid all the others briefly flash twice across the sea, and a rumbling sound came across the water. I squinted against the glare of the many moons. The stars made little pinpricks of light in the green-black of the sea. I heard a rustling in the moss bark behind me and turned, startled. The little painter came out carrying a canvas with silvery paint smeared across it.

"Are you a water enthusiast, too, sir?" he called out. "I believe I caught that wonderful play of light."

Being polite, for I was not a fan of his works, I looked at his painting as it glistened wetly in the moonsglow. It had caught a sharp light that shone in the darkness of water and night sky. The light seemed to hint at its immediate surroundings, hanging at odd angles, glinting off a sheer prow. As all his paintings did, it demanded notice and left one wondering at the murky shapes the piercing light slyly unclothed. For many reasons, I cared little for it, but said something courteous. He and I talked about it and some of his other works. Then we went back to the inn, for the night air had gone cold.

The next morning, the housekeeper found the painting on the floor, where he had apparently obliterated the ocean scene. His tools had all been neatly put away, and his jacket lay folded on the bed. He had hung himself on a ceiling hook and by morning, was certainly very dead.

I found myself watching Cod Sinwell while telling him of the painter's final moments. He was sitting in an uneasy silence, and for the past five minutes had not taken a single note. Finally, he stirred.

"Tell me of your old kings."

"Old kings?" I frowned. "I come from Earth—from a state that has no kings."

"The others at the hotel tell me you've told them stories of old kings. A minute ago, you quoted a saying from the old kings."

I shook my head. "I'm sure you're mistaken."

He took a deep breath and stood up. Without saying a word, he left the hotel grounds and turned west to the shriven jungle. After a long moment, I followed him.

He was sitting near the burnt-out stalk of a tall tree—out of sight of the hotel, but within view of a corner of the sea.

"I, too, have heard of the old kings of Afellon," he said without looking at me. "I heard they disappeared many hundreds of years ago, but legend has it that they are not dead. That they are immortal. They say that they sit together in a mountain glen and tell stories, and when the stories are done, the kings scatter to gather more."

He paused and wet his lips. "They say that the old kings can change their looks to pass as anyone. That they could look like me. Or that they could look like you. It is only in their reflection that you can see their true images.

"It is said that the old kings wear their stories too close to their hearts, that this is what finally kills them—tales of defeat and despair. But it kills them from within, rotting their souls.

"I think an old king killed the people here. Cir Damon saw your reflection in a puddle and the ship you were signaling. Then he knew that you were playing at treaty work to make tales for other old kings. Ellie DeJanson saw you speaking with a spy. r'Duelson interfered with your communications, and was also one like those who'd leveled Afellon. Care Kampei had also seen your ship, and captured it on canvas."

I heard no more of what he said. The water washed the shore with tentative passes, while water birds shrieked overhead. Later, the smoky smell of the sea covered the new scent of De-gron blood. I left his body there, upright in the stalk of the burnt tree.

I watched a phantom ship slip in and out of the drear, a furtive light winking at the shore. I signaled two short flashes back, and the black shape swooped toward me. On another planet, old kings gathered in a glen and told stories. Their sayings rang in laments while we hovered over the dark sea. Then the ship swung out to makeshift treaties.

> *"I remember my afflictions and my wandering,*
> *the bitterness and the gall."*

In the ashes of the island beneath me unfurled the remains of an unfinished tale.

UNCHOSEN LOVE

Ursula K. Le Guin

Introduction

By Heokad'd Arhe of Inanan Farmhold of Tag Village on the South-west Watershed of the Budran River on Okets on the Planet O.

Sex, for everybody, on every world, is a complicated business, but nobody seems to have complicated marriage quite as much as my people have. To us, of course, it seems simple, and so natural that it's foolish to describe it, like trying to describe how we walk, how we breathe. Well, you know, you stand on one leg and move the other one forward . . . you let the air come into your lungs and then you let it out . . . you marry a man and woman from the other moiety . . .

What is a moiety? a Gethenian asked me, and I realized that it's easier for me to imagine not knowing which sex I'll be tomorrow morning, like the Gethenian, than to imagine not knowing whether I was a Morning person or an Evening person. So complete, so universal a division of humanity—how can there be a society without it? How do you know who anyone is? How can you give worship without the one to ask and the other to answer, the one to pour and the other to drink? How can you couple indiscriminately without regard to incest? I have to admit that in the unswept, unenlightened basements of my hindbrain, I agree with my great-uncle Gambat, who said, "Those people from off the world, they all try to stand on one leg. Two legs, two sexes, two moieties—it only makes sense!"

A moiety is half a population. We call our two halves the Morning and the Evening. If your mother's a Morning woman, you're a Morning person; and all Morning people are in certain respects your brother or sister. You have sex, marry, have children only with Evening people.

When I explained our concept of incest to a fellow student on Hain, she said, shocked, "But that means you can't have sex with half the population!" And I in turn said, shocked, "Do you *want* sex with half the population?"

Moieties are in fact not an uncommon social structure within the Ekumen. I have had comfortable conversations with people from several bipartite societies. One of them, a Nadir woman of the Umna on Ithsh, nodded and laughed when I told her my great-uncle's opinion. "But you ki'O," she said, "you marry on all fours."

Few people from other worlds are willing to believe that our form of marriage works. They prefer to think that we endure it. They forget that human beings, while whining after the simple life, thrive on complexity.

When I marry—for love, for stability, for children—I marry three people. I am a Morning man: I marry an Evening woman and an Evening man, with both of whom I have a sexual relationship, and a Morning woman, with whom I have no sexual relationship. Her sexual relationships are with the Evening man and the Evening woman. The whole marriage is called a sedoretu. Within it, there are four submarriages; the two heterosexual pairs are called Morning and Evening, according to the woman's moiety; the male homosexual pair is called the Night marriage, and the female homosexual pair is called the Day.

Brothers and sisters of the four primary people can join the sedoretu, so that the number of people in the marriage sometimes gets to six or seven. The children are variously related as siblings, germanes, and cousins.

Obviously a sedoretu takes some arranging. We spend a lot of our time arranging them. How much of a marriage is founded on love and in which couples the love is strongest, how much of it is founded on convenience, custom, profit, friendship, will depend on regional tradition, personal character, and so on. The complexities are so evident that I am always surprised when an offworlder sees, in the multiple relationship, only the forbidden, the illicit one. "How can you be married to three people and never have sex with one of them?" they ask.

The question makes me uncomfortable; it seems to assume that sexuality is a force so dominant that it cannot be contained or shaped by any other relationship. Most societies expect a father and daughter, or a brother and sister, to have a nonsexual family relationship, though I gather that in some, the incest ban is often violated by people empowered by age and gender to ignore it. Evidently such societies see human beings as divided into two kinds, the fundamental division being power, and they grant one gender superior power. To us, the fundamental division is moiety; gender is a great but secondary difference; and in the search for power, no one starts from a position of innate privilege. It certainly leads to our looking at things differently.

The fact is, the people of O admire the simple life as much as anyone else, and we have found our own peculiar way of achieving it. We are conservative, conventional, self-righteous, and dull. We suspect change and resist it blindly. Many houses, farms, and shrines on O have been in the same place and called by the same name for fifty or sixty centuries, some for hundreds of centuries. We have mostly been doing the same things in the same way for longer than that. Evidently, we do things carefully. We honor self-restraint, often to the point of harboring demons, and are fierce in defense of our privacy. We despise the outstanding. The wise among us do not live in solitude on mountaintops; they live in houses on farms, have many relatives, and keep careful accounts. We have no cities, only dispersed villages composed of a group of farmholds and a community center; educational and technological centers are supported by each region. We do without gods and, for a long time now, without wars. The question strangers most often ask us is, "In those marriages of yours, do you all go to bed together?" and the answer we give is, "No."

That is in fact how we tend to answer any question from a stranger. It is amazing that we ever got into the Ekumen. We are near Hain—sidereally near, 4.2 light-years—and the Hainish simply kept coming here and talking to us for centuries, until we got used to them and were able to say Yes. The Hainish, of course, are our ancestral race, but the stolid longevity of our customs makes them feel young and rootless and dashing. That is probably why they like us.

Unchosen Love

There was a hold down near the mouths of the Saduun, built on a rock island that stands up out of the great tidal plain south of where the river meets the sea. The sea used to come in and swirl around the island, but as the Saduun slowly built up its delta over the centuries, only the great tides reached it, and then only the storm tides, and at last the sea never came so far, but lay shining all along the west.

Meruo was never a farmhold; built on rock in a salt marsh, it was a seahold, and lived by fishing. When the sea withdrew, the people dug a channel from the foot of the rock to the tideline. Over the years, as the sea withdrew farther, the channel grew longer and longer, till it was a broad canal three miles long. Up and down it fishing boats and trading ships went to and from the docks of Meruo that sprawled over the rocky base of the island. Right beside the docks and the netyards and the drying and freezing plants began the prairies of saltgrass, where vast flocks of yama and flightless baro grazed. Meruo rented out those pastures to farmholds of Sadahun Village, in the coastal hills. None of the flocks belonged to Meruo, whose people looked only to the sea, and farmed only the sea, and never walked if they could sail. More than the fishing, it was the prairies that had made them rich, but they spent their wealth on boats and on digging and dredging the great canal. We throw our money in the sea, they said.

They were known as a stiff-necked lot, holding themselves apart from the village. Meruo was a big hold, often with a hundred people living in it, so they seldom made sedoretu with village people, but married one another. They're all germanes at Meruo, the villagers said.

A Morning man from eastern Oket came to stay in Sadahun, studying saltmarsh grazing for his farmhold on the other coast. He chanced to meet an Evening man of Meruo named Suord, in town for a village meeting. The next day, there came Suord again, to see him; and the next day too; and by the fourth night, Suord was making love to him, sweeping him off his feet like a storm-wave.

The Easterner, whose name was Hadri, was a modest, inexperienced young man to whom the journey and the unfamiliar places and the strangers he met had been a considerable adventure. Now he found one of the strangers wildly in love with him, beseeching him to come out to Meruo and stay there, live there—"We'll make a sedoretu," Suord said. "There're half a dozen Evening girls. Any, any of the Morning women, I'd marry any one of them to keep you. Come out, come out with me, come out onto the Rock!" For so the people of Meruo called their hold.

Hadri thought he owed it to Suord to do what he asked, since Suord loved him so passionately. He got up his courage, packed his bag, and went out across the wide, flat prairies to the place he had seen all along dark against the sky far off, the high roofs of Meruo, hunched up on its rock above its docks and warehouses and boat-basin, its windows looking away from the land, staring always down the long canal to the sea that had forsaken it.

Suord brought him in and introduced him to the household, and Hadri was terrified. They were all like Suord, dark people, handsome, fierce, abrupt, intransigent—so much alike that he could not tell one from the other and mistook daughter for mother, brother for cousin, Evening for Morning. They were barely polite to him. He was an interloper. They were afraid Suord would bring him in among them for good. And so was he.

Suord's passion was so intense that Hadri, a moderate soul, assumed it must burn out soon. "Hot fires don't last," he said to himself, and took comfort in the adage. "He'll get tired of me and I can go," he thought, not in words. But he stayed a tenday at Meruo, and a month, and Suord burned as hot as ever. Hadri saw too that among the sedoretu of the household, there were many passionate matings, sexual tensions running among them like a network of ungrounded wires, filling the air with the crackle and spark of electricity; and some of these marriages were many years old.

He was flattered and amazed at Suord's insatiable, yearning, worshiping desire for a person Hadri himself was used to considering as quite ordinary. He felt his response to such passion was never enough. Suord's dark beauty filled his mind, and his mind turned away, looking for emptiness, a space to be alone. Some nights, when Suord lay flung out across the bed in deep sleep after lovemaking, Hadri would get up, naked, silent; he would sit in the window seat across the room, gazing down at the shining of the long canal under the stars. Sometimes he wept silently. He cried because he was in pain, but he did not know what the pain was.

One such night in early winter his feeling of being chafed, rubbed raw, like an animal fretting in a trap, all his nerve ends exposed, was too much to endure. He dressed, very quietly for fear of waking Suord, and went barefoot out of their room, to get outdoors—anywhere out from under the roofs, he thought. He felt that he could not breathe.

The immense house was bewildering in the dark. The seven

sedoretu living there now had each their own wing or floor or suite of rooms, all spacious. He had never even been into the regions of the First and Second Sedoretu, way off in the south wing, and always got confused in the ancient central part of the house, but he thought he knew his way around these floors in the north wing. This corridor, he thought, led to the landward stairs. It led only to narrow stairs going up. He went up them into a great shadowy attic, and found a door out onto the roof itself.

A long railed walk led along the south edge. He followed it, the peaks of the roofs rising up like black mountains to his left, and the prairies, the marshes, and then as he came around to the west side, the canal, all lying vast and dim in starlight below. The air was soft and damp, smelling of rain to come. A low mist was rising from the marshes. As he watched, his arms on the rail, the mist thickened and whitened, hiding the marshes and the canal. He welcomed that softness, that slowness of the blurring, healing, concealing fog. A little peace and solace came into him. He breathed deep and thought, "Why, why am I so sad? Why don't I love Suord as much as he loves me? Why does he love me?"

He felt somebody was near him, and looked around. A woman had come out onto the roof and stood only a few yards away, her arms on the railing like his, barefoot like him, in a long dressing gown. When he turned his head, she turned hers, looking at him.

She was one of the women of the Rock, no mistaking the dark skin and straight black hair and a certain fine cut of brow, cheekbone, jaw; but which one, he was not sure. At the dining rooms of the north wing he had met a number of Evening women in their twenties, all sisters, cousins, or germanes, all unmarried. He was afraid of them all, because Suord might propose one of them as his wife in sedoretu. Hadri was a little shy sexually and found the gender difference hard to cross; he had found his pleasure and solace mostly with other young men, though some women attracted him very much. These women of

Meruo were powerfully attractive, but he could not imagine himself touching one of them. Some of the pain he suffered here was caused by the distrustful coldness of the Evening women, always making it clear to him that he was the outsider. They scorned him and he avoided them. And so he was not perfectly certain which one was Sasni, which one was Lamateo, or Saval, or Esbuai.

He thought this was Esbuai, because she was tall, but he wasn't sure. The darkness might excuse him, for one could barely make out the features of a face. He murmured, "Good evening," and said no name.

There was a long pause, and he thought resignedly that a woman of Meruo would snub him even in the dead of night on a rooftop.

But then she said, "Good evening," softly, with a laugh in her voice, and it was a soft voice, that lay on his mind the way the fog did, mild and cool. "Who is that?" she asked.

"Hadri," he said, resigned again. Now she knew him and would snub him.

"Hadri? You aren't from here."

Who was she, then?

He said his farmhold name. "I'm from the east, from the Fadan'n Watershed. Visiting."

"I've been away," she said. "I just came back. Tonight. Isn't it a lovely night? I like these nights best of all, when the fog comes up, like a sea of its own. . . ."

Indeed, the mists had joined and risen, so that Meruo on its rock seemed to float suspended in darkness over a faintly luminous void.

"I like it too," he said. "I was thinking . . ." Then he stopped.

"What?" she asked after a minute, so gently that he took courage and went on.

"That being unhappy in a room is worse than being unhappy out of doors," he said, with a self-conscious and unhappy laugh. "I wonder why that is."

"I knew," she said. "By the way you were standing. I'm sorry. What do you . . . what would you need to make you happier?" At first he had thought her older than himself, but now she spoke like a quite young girl, shy and bold at the same time, awkwardly, with sweetness. It was the dark and the fog that made them both bold, released them, so they could speak truly.

"I don't know," he said. "I think I don't know how to be in love."

"Why do you think so?"

"Because I—it's Suord, he brought me here," he told her, trying to go on speaking truly. "I do love him, but not . . . not the way he deserves . . ."

"Suord," she said thoughtfully.

"He is strong. Generous. He gives me everything he is, his whole life. But I'm not, I'm not able to . . ."

"Why do you stay?" she asked, not accusingly, but asking for an answer.

"I love him," Hadri said. "I don't want to hurt him. If I run away, I'll be a coward. I want to be worth him." They were four separate answers, each spoken separately, painfully.

"Unchosen love," she said with a dry, rough tenderness. "Oh, it's hard."

She did not sound like a girl now, but like a woman who knew what love is. While they talked, they had both looked out westward over the sea of mist, because it was easier to talk that way. She turned now to look at him again. He was aware of her quiet gaze in the darkness. A great star shone bright between the line of the roof and her head. When she moved again, her round, dark head occulted the star, and then it shone tangled in her hair, as if she were wearing it. It was a lovely thing to see.

"I always thought I'd choose love," he said at last, her words working in his mind. "Choose a sedoretu, settle down someday, somewhere near my farm. I never imagined anything else. And then I came out here, to the edge of the world . . . and I don't know what to do. I was chosen, I can't choose . . . ."

There was a little self-mockery in his voice.

"This is a strange place," he said.

"It is," she agreed. "Once you've seen the great tide . . ."

He had seen it once. Suord had taken him to a headland that stood above the southern floodplain. Though it was only a few miles southwest of Meruo, they had to go a long way round inland and then back out west again, and Hadri asked, "Why can't we just go down the coast?"

"You'll see why," Suord said. They sat up on the rocky headland eating their picnic, Suord always with an eye on the brown-gray mud flats stretching off to the western horizon, endless and dreary, cut by a few worming, silted channels. "Here it comes," he said, standing up; and Hadri stood up to see the gleam and hear the distant thunder, see the advancing bright line, the incredible rush of the tide across the immense plain for seven miles till it crashed in foam on the rocks below them and flooded on around the headland.

"A good deal faster than you could run," Suord said, his dark face keen and intense. "That's how it used to come in around our Rock. In the old days."

"Are we cut off here?" Hadri had asked, and Suord had answered, "No, but I wish we were."

Thinking of it now, Hadri imagined the broad sea lying under the fog all around Meruo, lapping on the rocks, under the walls. As it had been in the old days.

"I suppose the tides cut Meruo off from the mainland," he said, and she said, "Twice every day."

"Strange," he murmured, and heard her slight intaken breath of laughter.

"Not at all," she said. "Not if you were born here. . . . Do you know that babies are born and the dying die on what they call the lull? The low point of the low tide of morning."

Her voice and words made his heart clench within him, they were so soft and seemed so strange. "I come from inland, from the hills, I never saw the sea before," he said. "I don't know any-thing about the tides."

"Well," she said, "there's their true love." She was looking be-hind him. He turned and saw the waning moon just above the sea of mist, only its darkest, scarred crescent showing. He stared at it, unable to say anything more.

"Hadri," she said, "don't be sad. It's only the moon. Come up here again if you are sad, though. I liked talking with you. There's nobody here to talk to . . . . Good night," she whispered. She went away from him along the walk and vanished in the shadows.

He stayed a while watching the mist rise and the moon rise; the mist won the slow race, blotting out moon and all in a cold dimness at last. Shivering, but no longer tense and anguished, he found his way back to Suord's room and slid into the wide, warm bed. As he stretched out to sleep, he thought, I don't know her name.

Suord woke in an unhappy mood. He insisted that Hadri come out in the sailboat with him down the canal, to check the locks on the side-canals, he said; but what he wanted was to get Hadri alone, in a boat, where Hadri was not only useless but slightly uneasy and had no escape at all. They drifted in the mild sunshine on the glassy side-canal. "You want to leave, don't you?" Suord said, speaking as if the sentence was a knife that cut his tongue as he spoke it.

"No," Hadri said, not knowing if it was true, but unable to say any other word.

"You don't want to get married here."

"I don't know, Suord."

"What do you mean, you don't know?"

"I don't think any of the Evening women want a marriage with me," he said, and trying to speak true, "I know they don't. They want you to find somebody from around here. I'm a for-eigner."

"They don't know you," Suord said with a sudden, pleading gentleness. "People here, they take a long time to get to know other people. We've lived too long on our Rock. Seawater in our veins instead of blood. But they'll see—they'll come to know you if you—if you'll stay—" He looked out over the side of the boat and after a while, said almost inaudibly, "If you leave, can I come with you?"

"I'm not leaving," Hadri said. He went and stroked Suord's hair and face and kissed him. He knew that Suord could not follow him, couldn't live in Oket, inland; it wouldn't work, it wouldn't do. But that meant he must stay here with Suord. There was a numb coldness in him, under his heart.

"Sasni and Duun are germanes," Suord said presently, sounding like himself again, controlled, intense. "They've been lovers ever since they were thirteen. Sasni would marry me if I asked her, if she can have Duun in the Day marriage. We can make a sedoretu with them, Hadri."

The numbness kept Hadri from reacting to this for some time; he did not know what he was feeling, what he thought. What he finally said was, "Who is Duun?" There was a vague hope in him that it was the woman he had talked with on the roof last night—in a different world, it seemed, a realm of fog and darkness and truth.

"You know Duun."

"Did she just come back from somewhere else?"

"No," Suord said, too intent to be puzzled by Hadri's stupidity. "Sasni's germane, Lasudu's daughter of the Fourth Sedoretu. She's short, very thin, doesn't talk much."

"I don't know her," Hadri said in despair. "I can't tell them apart, they don't talk to me," and he bit his lip and stalked over to the other end of the boat and stood with his hands in his pockets and his shoulders hunched.

Suord's mood had quite changed; he splashed about happily in the water and mud when they got to the lock, making sure the mechanisms were in order, then sailed them back to the great canal with a fine following wind. Shouting, "Time you got your sea legs!" to Hadri, he took the boat west down the canal and out onto the open sea. The misty sunlight, the breeze full of salt spray, the fear of the depths, the exertion of working the boat under Suord's capable directions, the triumph of steering it back into the canal at sunset, when the light lay red-gold on the water and vast flocks of stilts and marsh birds rose crying and circling around them—it made a great day, after all, for Hadri.

But the glory dropped away as soon as he came under the roofs of Meruo again, into the dark corridors and the low, wide, dark rooms that all looked west. They took meals with the Fourth and Fifth Sedoretu. In Hadri's farmhold, there would have been a good deal of teasing when they came in just in time for dinner, having been out all day without notice and done none of the work of it; here, nobody ever teased or joked. If there was resentment, it stayed hidden. Maybe there was no resentment, maybe they all knew each other so well and were so much of a piece that they trusted one other the way you trust your own hands, without question. Even the children joked and quarreled less than Hadri was used to. Conversation at the long table was always quiet, many not speaking a word.

As he served himself, Hadri looked around among them for the woman of last night. Had it in fact been Esbuai? He thought not; the height was like, but Esbuai was very thin, and had a particularly arrogant carriage to her head. The woman was not here. Maybe she was First Sedoretu. Which of these women was Duun?

That one, the little one, with Sasni; he recalled her now. She was always with Sasni. He had never spoken to her, because Sasni of them all had snubbed him most hatefully, and Duun was her shadow.

"Come on," said Suord, and went around the table to sit down beside Sasni, gesturing Hadri to sit beside Duun. He did so. I'm Suord's shadow, he thought.

"Hadri says he's never talked to you," Suord said to Duun.

The girl hunched up a bit and muttered something meaningless. Hadri saw Sasni's face flash with anger, and yet there was a hint of a challenging smile in it as she looked straight at Suord. They were very much alike. They were well matched.

Suord and Sasni talked—about the fishing, about the locks—while Hadri ate his dinner. He was ravenous after the day on the water. Duun, having finished her meal, sat and said nothing. These people had a capacity for remaining perfectly motionless and silent, like predatory animals, or fishing birds. The dinner was fish, of course; it was always fish. Meruo had been wealthy once and still had the manners of wealth, but few of the means. Dredging out the great canal took more of their income every year as the sea relentlessly pulled back from the delta. Their fishing fleet was large, but the boats were old, often rebuilt. Hadri had asked why they did not build new ones, for a big shipyard loomed above the drydocks; Suord explained that the cost of the wood alone was prohibitive. Having only the one crop, fish and shellfish, they had to pay for all other food, for clothing, for wood, even for water. The wells for miles around Meruo were salt. An aqueduct led to the seahold from the village in the hills.

They drank their expensive water from silver cups, however, and ate their eternal fish from bowls of ancient, translucent blue Edia ware, which Hadri was always afraid of breaking when he washed them.

Sasni and Suord went on talking, and Hadri felt stupid and sullen, sitting there saying nothing to the girl who said nothing.

"I was out on the sea for the first time today," he said, feeling the blood flush his face.

She made some kind of noise, mhm, and gazed at her empty bowl.

"Can I get you some soup?" Hadri asked. They ended the meal with broth—here, fish broth of course.

"No," she said with a scowl.

"In my farmhold," he said, "people often bring dishes to each other; it's a minor kind of courtesy; I am sorry if you find it offensive." He stood up and strode off to the sideboard, where with shaking hands he served himself a bowl of soup. When he got back, Suord was looking at him with a speculative eye and a faint smile, which he resented. What did they take him for? Did they think he had no standards, no people, no place of his own? Let them marry each other, he would have no part of it. He gulped his soup, got up without waiting for Suord, and went to the kitchen, where he spent an hour in the washing-up crew to make up for missing his time in the cooking crew. Maybe they had no standards about things, but he did.

Suord was waiting for him in their room—Suord's room; Hadri had no room of his own here. That in itself was insulting, unnatural. In a decent hold, a guest was always given a room.

Whatever Suord said—he could not remember later what it was—was a spark to blasting powder. "I will not be treated this way!" he cried passionately, and Suord firing up at once demanded what he meant, and they had at it, an explosion of rage and frustration and accusation that left them staring gray-faced at each other, appalled. "Hadri," Suord said, the name a sob; he was shivering, his whole body shaking. They came together, clinging to each other. Suord's small, rough, strong hands held Hadri close. The taste of Suord's skin was salt as the sea. Hadri sank, sank and was drowned.

But in the morning everything was as it had been. He did not dare ask for a room to himself, knowing it would hurt Suord. If they do make this sedoretu, then at least I'll have a room, said a small, unworthy voice in his head. But it was wrong, wrong . . . .

He looked for the woman he had met on the roof, and saw half a dozen who might have been her and none he was certain was her. Would she not look at him, speak to him? Not in daylight, not in front of the others? Well, so much for her, then.

It occurred to him only now that he did not know whether

she was a woman of the Morning or the Evening. But what did it matter?

That night the fog came in. Waking suddenly, deep in the night, he saw out the window only a formless gray, glowing very dimly with diffused light from a window somewhere in another wing of the house. Suord slept, as he always did, flat out, lying like a bit of jetsam flung on the beach of the night, utterly absent and abandoned. Hadri watched him with an aching tenderness for a while. Then he got up, pulled on clothes, and found the corridor to the stairs that led up to the roof.

The mist hid even the roof-peaks. Nothing at all was visible beyond the railing. He had to feel his way along, touching the railing. The wooden walkway was damp and cold to the soles of his feet. Yet a kind of happiness had started in him as he went up the attic stairs, and it grew as he breathed the foggy air, and as he turned the corner to the west side of the house. He stood still for a while and then spoke, almost in a whisper. "Are you there?" he asked.

There was a pause, as there had been the first time he spoke to her, and then she answered, the laugh just hidden in her voice, "Yes, I'm here. Are you there?"

The next moment they could see each other, though only as shapes bulking in the mist.

"I'm here," he said. His happiness was absurd. He took a step closer to her, so that he could make out her dark hair, the darkness of her eyes in the lighter oval of her face. "I wanted to talk to you again," he said.

"I wanted to talk to you again," she said.

"I couldn't find you. I hoped you'd speak to me."

"Not down there," she said, her voice turning light and cold. "Are you in the First Sedoretu?"

"Yes," she said. "The Morning wife of the First Sedoretu of Meruo. My name is An'nad. I wanted to know if you're still unhappy."

"Yes," he said, "no—" He tried to see her face more clearly, but there was little light. "Why is that you talk to me, and I can talk to you, and not to anybody else in this household?" he asked. "Why are you the only kind one?"

"Is . . . Suord unkind?" she asked, with a little hesitation on the name.

"He never means to be. He never is. Only, he . . . he drags me, he pushes me, he . . .he's stronger than I am."

"Maybe not," said An'nad. "Maybe only more used to getting his way."

"Or more in love," Hadri said, low-voiced, with shame.

"You're not in love with him?"

"Oh, yes!"

She laughed.

"I never knew anyone like him—he's more than—his feelings are so deep, he's—I'm out of my depth," Hadri stammered. "But I love him—immensely—"

"So what's wrong?"

"He wants to marry," Hadri said, and then stopped. He was talking about her household, probably her blood kin; as a wife of the First Sedoretu, she was part of all the network of relationships of Meruo. What was he blundering into?

"Who does he want to marry?" she asked. "Don't worry. I won't interfere. Is the trouble that you don't want to marry him?"

"No, no," Hadri said. "It's only—I never meant to stay here, I thought I'd go home . . . . Marrying Suord seems—more than I, than I deserve—but it would be amazing, it would be wonderful! But . . .the marriage itself, the sedoretu, it's not right. He says that Sasni will marry him, and Duun will marry me, so that she and Duun can be married."

"Suord and Sasni"—again the faint pause on the name—"don't love each other, then?"

"No," he said, a little hesitant, remembering that challenge between them, like a spark struck.

"And you and Duun?"

"I don't even know her."

"Oh, no, that is dishonest," An'nad said. "One should choose love, but not that way . . . . Whose plan is it? All three of them?"

"I suppose so. Suord and Sasni have talked about it. The girl, Duun, she never says anything."

"Talk to her," said the soft voice. "Talk to her, Hadri." She was looking at him; they stood quite close together, close enough that he felt the warmth of her arm on his arm though they did not touch.

"I'd rather talk to you," he said, turning to face her. She moved back, seeming to grow insubstantial even in that slight movement, the fog was so dense and dark. She put out her hand, but again did not quite touch him. He knew she was smiling.

"Then stay and talk with me," she said, leaning again on the rail. "Tell me . . .oh, tell me anything. What do you do, you and Suord, when you're not making love?"

"We went out sailing," he said, and found himself telling her what it had been like for him out on the open sea for the first time, his terror and delight. "Can you swim?" she asked, and he laughed and said, "In the lake at home, it's not the same," and she laughed and said, "No, I imagine not." They talked for a long time, and he asked her what she did—"in daylight. I haven't seen you yet, down there."

"No," she said. "What do I do? Oh, I worry about Meruo, I suppose. I worry about my children. . . . I don't want to think about that now. How did you come to meet Suord?"

Before they were done talking, the mist had begun to lighten very faintly with moonrise. It had grown piercingly cold. Hadri was shivering. "Go on," she said. "I'm used to it. Go on to bed."

"There's frost," he said, "look," touching the silvered wooden rail. "You should go down too."

"I will. Good night, Hadri." As he turned, she said, or he thought she said, "I'll wait for the tide."

"Good night, An'nad." He spoke her name huskily, tenderly. If only the others were like her . . . .

He stretched out close to Suord's inert, delicious warmth, and slept.

The next day Suord had to work in the records office, where Hadri was utterly useless and in the way. Hadri took his chance, and by asking several sullen, snappish women, found where Duun was: in the fish-drying plant. He went down to the docks and found her, by luck, if it was luck, eating her lunch alone in the misty sunshine at the edge of the boat basin.

"I want to talk with you," he said.

"What for?" she asked. She would not look at him.

"Is it honest to marry a person you don't even like in order to marry a person you love?"

"No," she said fiercely. She kept looking down. She tried to fold up the bag she had carried her lunch in, but her hands shook too much.

"Why are you willing to do it, then?"

"Why are *you* willing to do it?"

"I'm not," he said. "It's Suord. And Sasni."

She nodded.

"Not you?"

She shook her head, violently. Her thin, dark face was a very young face, he realized.

"But you love Sasni," he said, a little uncertainly.

"Yes! I love Sasni! I always did, I always will! That doesn't mean I, I, I have to do everything she says, everything she wants, that I have to, that I have to—" She was looking at him now, right at him, her face burning like a coal, her voice quivering and breaking. "I don't *belong* to Sasni!"

"Well," he said, "I don't belong to Suord, either."

"I don't know anything about men," Duun said savagely, still glaring at him. "Or any other women. Or anything. I never was with anybody but Sasni, all my life! She thinks she *owns* me."

"She and Suord are a lot alike," Hadri said cautiously.

There was a silence. Duun, though tears had spouted out of her eyes in the most childlike fashion, did not deign to wipe them away. She sat straight-backed, cloaked in the dignity of the women of Meruo, and managed to get her lunch-bag folded.

"I don't know very much about women," Hadri said. His was perhaps a simpler dignity. "Or men. I know I love Suord. But I . . .I need freedom."

"Freedom!" she said, and he thought at first she was mocking him, but quite the opposite—she burst right into tears and put her head down on her knees, sobbing aloud. "I do too," she cried, "I do too."

Hadri put out a timid hand and stroked her shoulder. "I didn't mean to make you cry," he said. "Don't cry, Duun. Look. If we, if we feel the same way, we can work something out. We don't have to get married. We can be friends."

She nodded, though she went on sobbing for a while. At last she raised her swollen face and looked at him with wet-lidded, luminous eyes. "I would like to have a friend," she said. "I never had one."

"I have only one other one here," he said, thinking how right she had been in telling him to talk to Duun. "An'nad."

She stared at him. "Who?"

"An'nad. The Morning Woman of the First Sedoretu."

"What do you mean?" She was not scornful, merely very surprised. "That's Teheo."

"Then who is An'nad?"

"She was the Morning Woman of the First Sedoretu four hundred years ago," the girl said, her eyes still on Hadri's, clear and puzzled.

"Tell me," he said.

"She was drowned—here, at the foot of the Rock. They were all down on the sands, her sedoretu, with the children. That was when the tides had begun not to come in as far as Meruo. They were all out on the sands, planning the canal, and she was up in the house. She saw there was a storm in the west, and that the wind might bring one of the great tides. She ran down to warn them. And the tide did come in, all the way around the Rock, the way it used to. They all kept ahead of it, except An'nad. She was drowned . . . ."

With all he had to wonder about then, about An'nad, and about Duun, he did not wonder why Duun answered his question and asked him none.

It was not until much later, half a year later, that he said, "Do you remember when I said I'd met An'nad—that first time we talked—by the boat basin?"

"I remember," she said.

They were in Hadri's room, a beautiful, high room with windows looking east, traditionally occupied by a member of the Eighth Sedoretu. Summer-morning sunlight warmed their bed, and a soft, earth-scented land-wind blew in the windows.

"Didn't it seem strange?" he asked. His head was pillowed on her shoulder. When she spoke, he felt her warm breath in his hair.

"Everything was so strange then . . .I don't know. And anyhow, if you've heard the tide . . ."

"The tide?"

"Winter nights. Up high in the house, in the attics. You can hear the tide come in and crash around the Rock, and run on inland to the hills. At the true high tide. But the sea is miles away . . ."

Suord knocked, waited for their invitation, and came in, already dressed. "Are you still in bed? Are we going in to town or not?" he demanded, splendid in his white summer coat, imperious. "Sasni's already down in the courtyard."

"Yes, yes, we're just getting up," they said, secretly entwining further.

"Now!" he said, and went out.

Hadri sat up, but Duun pulled him back down. "You saw her? You talked with her?"

"Twice. I never went back after you told me who she was.

I was afraid. . . . Not of her. Only afraid she wouldn't be there."

"What did she do?" Duun asked softly.

"She saved us from drowning," Hadri said.